TRIPLE EXPOSURE

Black, Jewish and Red in the 1950s

DEXTER JEFFRIES

KENSINGTON PUBLISHING CORP.

http://www.kensingtonbooks.com

Names and identities of many people as well as units of the United States Army were changed to protect their privacy.

DAFINA BOOKS are published by

Kensington Publishing Corp.
850 Third Avenue
New York, NY 10022

All Kensington titles, imprints and distributed lines are available at special quantity discounts for bulk purchases for sales promotion, premiums, fundraising, educational or institutional use.

Special book excerpts or customized printings can also be created to fit specific needs. For details, write or phone the office of the Kensington Special Sales Manager: Kensington Publishing Corp., 850 Third Avenue, New York, NY 10022. Attn. Special Sales Department. Phone: 1-800-221-2647.

Dafina Books and the Dafina logo Reg. U.S. Pat. & TM Off.

ISBN 0-7582-0114-1

Designed by Leonard Telesca

First Hardcover Printing: April 2003
First Trade Paperback Printing: April 2004
10   9   8   7   6   5   4   3   2   1

Printed in the United States of America

To Marian "Margaret" Hession, for
being the great Irishwoman behind
this writer

Acknowledgments

I am more than proud to mention the following people who made this book possible, and I apologize to anyone carelessly forgotten. This is my fault and my fault alone.

First and foremost, to Ewa Maraszkiewicz for persuading Douglas Mendini of Kensington that this story was special and needed to be told.

To Douglas Mendini for keeping this project alive and ultimately transforming it into a success.

Special thanks to Karen Thomas, my editor, Ebony Alston, editorial assistant, and Janice Rossi, art director.

To my favorite City College professor, Lennie Kriegel, for getting *Present Tense* to publish the article, "Who I Am," which is the foundation of this book.

For being a reader and photographer, Frank Favia.

To Bob Lapides for encouraging me to write my story for his stalwart literary journal, *Hudson River.*

My dissertation adviser Neal Tolchin mentioned "Who I Am" to Ann Raimes; in turn, Ann Raimes published it in her wonderful anthology *Identities;* both of Hunter College, I thank you.

To an army of readers who not only read but also wrote and made me write some more:

The Monday Night Pratt Institute Group which consisted of Steve Doloff, Liza Williams, "Chip" Benjamin, Helen Anne Easterly, and Suzanne Verderber.

Tricia Lin, Paul Narkunas, and again, Suzanne Verderber for her proofreading.

Alan Carr, Phil Vitale, Stephanie Smolinsky, and Bill Steffens, lifelong friends who always encouraged me to write.

To Barney Pace for his insight and literary craft.

To George Held of Queens College who believes in the power of the written word and passed that message on to me thirty years ago.

To Springfield Gardens High School and an English teacher who taught there in the late 1960s named Fred Cohen.

Lastly, Lenore Hildebrand of Queens College, who told me, as a young man in her freshman composition class, "You have to tell this story someday."

TRIPLE
EXPOSURE

Prologue

First things first, this isn't even my real name. I mean, Dexter Jeffries is not the name I was born with. My real name is Dexter Diaz, but I had to change it due to, due to, well, due to a lot of things. But you can already figure out it must have been pretty goddamned important for me to change my name, right. Racism? Maybe.

Yeah, something like that and a thousand other things. Ralph Ellison wrote about the invisible man which is a start. If you want an idea of what I'm talking about, you would also have to consult Kafka to understand. Then you would have to talk to Dostoyevsky and finally Camus. Confused, uplifting confusion is what I call it.

My real name is Dexter Jeffries Diaz. That name and that identity worked for eighteen years, not a bad run for a name and an identity that I wasn't. How many people are misidentified from day one? Sure, I know you have trouble later or when you're a teenager, but I was having identity problems when I was five. Yes, five. Most people go through some major travail when they're fourteen, fifteen, and then dispose of theirs when they're about sixteen. I got two extra years out of mine. It had its benefits, can't deny that. But it kept me too invisible, and you want to give the general public some hints about who you are; they deserve it don't they? If not, things start to get complicated pretty fast. It's one thing to keep people in the blind, in the dark, but to confuse, well, that's against the rules. Having the name Dexter Jeffries Diaz confused people and made their inquiries into who the real Dexter Jeffries Diaz was all the more complicated. It added time to the game, and it was a good baseball game until those extra innings became a source of horror and torture. That's what I was doing, forcing people to play a few extra innings in the "race game," and nobody wanted to do that. Not really.

So, how did I get that name and why did it work for a certain number of years? For my old man, that name, Stanley Diaz, was good for the duration. He reaped the maximum reward from it. Yeah, good for him. It was one of the few positive things he had going for him when he was playing his extra innings back in the 1930s because he figured out that in the race game, circa 1932, it is way better to be perceived as a Cuban than as a Negro. You might even get to that interview after answering the classified ad that asked for a "Lithographer, must be able to operate a Miehle 4-color press." Lithographer, a printer who can match colors, mix, replicate with exactness, that was what my father did. It's a trade dead and gone now, but it was a terrific profession during its hey day, and the name Diaz as his last name did nothing but improve and ameliorate his position. He loved it. But that's not his real name either. No sir. Because he had figured that it was better to be a Cuban than a Negro, he switched from Negro to Cuban at a very propitious moment when his black mother remarried, to Antonio Diaz from Havana. And if you think about it, all I really did was switch from Cuban to Negro when I was at another auspicious juncture in American history. Switching identities and names is as old as American pie, huckleberry pie, not apple. You're not going to see too many stories with apple pies in them, but you're definitely going to run across some huckleberry. Yeah, it's good too.

Here's a huckleberry story for you if you've never heard one before. I was teaching a class one evening, freshman composition, and this woman asks if she can speak to the "professor" after class; I say sure, no problem. Raina Baez dutifully came up after class and I could see that this was a situation having to do with reality, her life, not a two page essay with the topic "write about a time that you were scared." She related a quick anecdote about applying for a job and while filling out the application being told that she was black. She wanted to know what did that mean. I looked at her and thought, "Are you in the long line of fictitious characters that I've known who feign ignorance about their identity?" But her English was so halting and there was this innocence that suggested she was not a candidate for living a bogus and fraudulent existence. She was just from Panama, a Panamanian and wanted to know what did it mean, that the box Black was checked. Why wasn't there a box for people from Panama or a category for those who hailed from Latin America? I smiled. I thought to myself, "Man, you've got a lot coming to ya."

I shook my head appearing as thoughtful and reflective as possible and informed her that she wasn't Panamanian anymore. Her mouth dropped open as if struck by a Number 4 Lexington Avenue express. I said it again. "You're not Panamanian. You're black from now on. I know it sounds funny. But that's the way Americans are going to look at you. You're dark. They don't care about your native country." As I informed her that she was no longer who she thought she had been for the last twenty years, the open mouth turned into a pained and twisted grimace.

"I'm proud to be a Panamanian; that is my home. My parents live there, now, still," she said to me. I nodded my head, but I made sure to dash any last minute illusions she may have had. A simulated person like myself, even though my active sham existence concluded a few years ago, is still familiar with the process of holding on to those dreams and the pain of seeing them broken later rather than earlier, with no one being the wiser, except you. "Raina, you'll understand after you live here for a few more years. It's a strange country," were the words I left her with. A huckleberry story if there ever was one.

So the old switcheroo, confidence game, you're not what you think, I ain't what you want, one hand behind the back with fingers crossed, the same man that pats you on the back with one hand can pick your pocket with the other, yeah, that's what I'm talking about. And the white folks never knew. Neither did the Cubans. Nor the Puerto Ricans. Nor the Negroes. In the history of America my father and I conceived and manufactured the greatest forgery of human beings ever known, and no one knew about it unless we told them, and there was no reason to tell because a good three card Monte man doesn't tell you where the queen of hearts is; a competent con man does not reveal which shell has the pea beneath it. That's half the fun. The only difference though would be that those street sham-men were trying to make a buck, and my father and I were trying to survive and not die. Big difference I guess. The things people have to do just to live a little bit. Jesus Christ on a mountain. Whew! I can still remember the day I permanently altered my identity by approximately thirty-three percent. It was a courthouse scene, early in the morning:

"NOW, on motion of Bernard Lebell, Esq., attorney for the petitioner it is

ORDERED that the said DEXTER JEFFRIES DIAZ be and he hereby is authorized to assume the name of DEXTER DIAZ JEFFRIES in place and stead of his present name on the 22nd day of January 1971 and it is further . . ." Yes, a great day in my life. A day of liberation. I never wondered about how my father felt about losing his favorite son, but I was too stupid to think about someone else's feelings at the time. Intellectually I would have understood but inside I knew that after being Black, Jewish and Red for so long and suffering, I had to lessen the load. For people to look at me and assume that I was Puerto Rican and then confirm their suspicions by looking at the last name "Diaz," that just wasn't fair and gave the world an upper hand in deciding who I was to be. When I would inform people that I wasn't Puerto Rican (New York in the 1950s did not possess the variety of Hispanic culture that it was to have later), they would say. "Of course, you have a Puerto Rican name." To that I would say nothing because I could not have told them if they were right or wrong. What is a Puerto Rican name? You live in the United States of America and you have a house, a Ford in the garage, two people who work, a backyard with a little vegetable garden, train table in the basement with American Flyer trains whirling around it, you are an American. What is a Puerto Rican? When people were told that I could not speak Spanish, they were very kind and said, gratuitously, "Don't be ashamed of your heritage. Speak a little Spanish."

Puerto Rican, come to think of it, I had heard that word used in my home or was it somewhere else? Yes, it was on the subway and of all people it was my father complaining about how "only a Puerto Rican would sit with his feet up on a seat." So, how is it possible that I am something that my father would complain about?

Another memory revolving around my father is built around a jazz concert uptown in Harlem, City College, Lewisohn Stadium to be exact. It had been a grand evening. There was an outdoor picnic, great jazz musicians blowing away up on a stage that looked like the movie set of *Spartacus* or one of those many Hercules movies, straight out of Athens, Greece. As we walked to our car, parked a few blocks away on Convent Avenue, there were some people sitting on my father's beautiful red Ford. I heard him say something like, "Where do you think you are? San Juan?" The young people with their six pack of cerveza started saying something like "Take it easy," and the next thing I knew they were flying into those ubiquitous garbage cans that supers always keep outside of buildings, beat-up cans without lids or the lids are hanging on chains so kids won't steal them. A lot of noise and then we were in the car. From that point on I knew that no matter what anyone said, I might have not known what I was, but I wasn't a Puerto Rican. That might not have seemed like much, but it eliminated one more potential element for making me mad, truly mad.

Source of Comfort

———⊷«◉»⊶———

IF I HAD only known that people did not want me to be black or white, my life would have been a lot simpler. Or, the converse, if I had known that people wanted me to be black or white, still, my life would have been a lot simpler. That's what it came down to. And what they were asking me to do really wasn't so outrageous. I used to brood and cry about the demands put upon me and think they were extraordinarily unfair because the world would not let me be me. Does it ever let anyone be who they are? The only difference in my case is that there were racial connotations intertwined with their demands.

Later in life, after being tortured and self-tortured, I did realize something that was unfair. When you are something that someone does not desire, all you are doing is making them uncomfortable, nothing more, nothing less. But I've come to realize that the word *uncomfortable* possesses a great deal of import. "I really don't feel *comfortable* with that." Yes, that means that you are not going to participate in that person's reality. You are going to avoid, deny, and reject it. Now you're making someone else really feel *uncomfortable*. Do you have a right to do that?

Professor, we've been trying to figure out something all semester.
Professor, we were wondering about something.
Professor, we have a bet about something.
Professor, we had a big discussion about you.
Professor, could you tell us one thing?
Professor, I've been meaning to ask you this since the first day.
Professor, you have to tell us something about yourself.

7

Professor, we're going crazy trying to figure out something about you.

Yes, most college professors are prepared and enthusiastic about a class that would put so much energy into a series of questions. To see that sort of eagerness in a college classroom is a teacher's dream come true. And I can always tell, now, that it's not going to be a question about literature, James Joyce's life in Dublin, what's the connection between James Baldwin and Richard Wright, or why didn't the Anglo Saxons learn a little Latin during the Roman occupation.

Professor, you see, Doreen and I were wondering if you're Spanish. That's the question you've been waving your hand about?

Professor Jeffries, aren't you mixed?

A difficult question; I would rather have you ask me about the rhyme scheme of Shakespeare's sonnets than that.

We're positive that you're black but very light.

How can Achilles be a hero if he's down in his tent, crying over losing his girlfriend to Agamemnon; that's a better and more reasonable question.

You're Greek and Puerto Rican, aren't you?

McMurphy, if he's racist, how can he still be the hero of the novel? No problem, I can explain contradictions like that. That's my job.

Professor, it's your hair. That's what threw us off. If it were a little kinkier, we would have positively known that you were . . .

Those are my questions, the ones I can't answer. For the first half of my teaching career or maybe more, I always worried about those questions.

Students, always wondering and thinking about me and not my lectures and investing time and energy. Here I am teaching one of the best Hemingway classes that you'll ever get, and all you can think of is whether I am black, white, Puerto Rican, Greek, Dominican, or *mixed* (I hated that word since it sounded like some sort of breed of dog). I am standing in front of you, presenting you with detailed information about a writer's style and tone, and the only thought occupying your mind is whether I am Russian, Iranian, or from Brazil. And what I didn't realize at the time and only recently have come across this very privileged revelation was that, you're not really asking me about my national origin or race. You're asking me whether I will make you feel *comfortable* by informing you that I am like you. You wanted me to be like you and I was there foolishly trying to look for so many other answers, exploring and sweating as I went through so many different places and all you wanted to hear was that I was like you.

LETTERS

September 1, 1977

Dear Pop,

I just found out that you're dead. Kind of tough to hear it the way I did, a few thousand miles away from home. But I think you could imagine the backdrop because you served during World War II in the Pacific, and you would have no problem envisioning this scene. We were up on the Czechoslovakian border, putting in mine fields. They're all over the place between West Germany, East Germany, and Czechoslovakia. It was a cold morning. Sergeant Walters had told me that Lieutenant Collins wanted to see me.

You know those tents, for the C.O.? We got the same ones you had thirty years ago, shaped like a pentagon with dome for a stovepipe to come out of the top. You open the flap and the light always assaults your eyes. You're blind if you're entering because it's pretty dark, and you're blind if you're leaving because of the light. Funny, you also know how you're always a little dirty because of the soot that comes out of the space heater? It's just a common condition that exists when you're in an infantry or engineer unit: dirty, unshaven, always a little unkempt.

Lt. Collins: Jeffries, you better sit down.
Me: Yes sir.
Lt. Collins: I've got some bad news for you.
Me: Oh, am I in trouble about something?
Lt. Collins: No, nothing like that. I just got a telegram from the Red Cross. It took a little time to come up here; your father died.
Me: Oh.
Lt. Collins: I'm sorry. It's a hell of a thing to be way out here in the woods like this . . .
Me: Yeah . . .

Lt. Collins: Was he ill?

Me: Yeah, he was kinda sick for the last few years; heart.

Lt. Collins: Oh, I guess it was related to that.

Me: Yeah, he was sick; that's for sure.

Lt. Collins: According to regulations, you're eligible for an emergency leave. We can put you in a jeep, send you right over to Frankfurt and you'll be back in the world pretty quick.

Me: Nah, that's OK.

Lt. Collins: Jeffries, wait a second. Take it easy. Maybe you want to think about this.

Me: No, look Lieutenant, I know what I'm doing. I'll stay right here.

I know that's difficult to hear from your favorite son, but that was what happened. Just like that. I was in the hazy place of being happy that the suffering was over and terribly sad that you wouldn't live to see how things turned out with me. That's what gets to you. I knew you were ill and being handicapped wasn't for you, no, not the rational man who wanted to figure out everything. But for the black side of you, I was happy that the other type of suffering was ended. You would never have to think, feel or dream about it, the thing that made you mad, the thing that tore your soul to shreds. The "color thing" was over. No more battles, past or present. No more thinking, wondering, second-guessing, undermining yourself because you were an intelligent black man, Negro, a proud Negro, who had been reduced to fodder and folly.

You had fought that fight and lost. Not completely. But you lost because you ended up despising Negroes yourself. That was the ultimate proof of that absurd world's power and control over you. You hated them, and I don't know when it started, 1931 or 1946. I suppose it's arbitrary. Maybe "hate" is just not the best way of putting it. White people can't understand. Even I can't understand and I've thought about it long and hard.

Sorry for rambling. Back to the main point. You're dead. That's what I have to deal with. There are some guys in the platoon trying to convince me to go home. I just walked away from the little group sitting on the forest floor in Germany. I've got a lot to think about.

So, my father passed away when I was stationed overseas. He was pretty important to me. Even when he died, he wasn't dead. Not really. I was in for a terrible shock, or reincarnation, or a raising of the dead. About two weeks after my father died, I got the first letter. I thought it was a bad joke played by someone in the U.S. Army Postal Service. But it wasn't. My father was a decent letter writer, and unknowingly he had written me right up until he died. Therefore, I was slated by fate or whatever you might call it, to receive letters from the dead.

You hold a dead man's letter in a far different way from that of the living. It is indeed special. You feel the electricity. It's as though some miracle has been performed on your behalf and as undeserving as you may be, and I was certainly in that category, a waiver has been signed, and the dead are now the living. That first letter was in my hand, and I walked around in a daze.

Because I was so far away, I had to conduct my own funeral oration or memorial service. I didn't cry about specific memories. If anything, I smiled over and over again. All the things that this Negro, black man, had done. He was a graduate of Brooklyn Technical High School in 1931, with a specialty in drafting. A few years later, in the midst of the Depression, he was an active member of the Communist Party, participating in many rallies, demonstrations, organizing the fledgling labor movement in New York City. When he is stationed overseas during World War II, and is on the island of Tinian, the same little Pacific island that the *Enola Gay* carrying the first atomic bomb took off from, he publishes his own newspaper, *This Small World*. Responsible for the writing, editing, copying, and distribution, the paper, his own version of *Stars and Stripes* with very subtle nuances of left-wing counterpoint. Post-World War II America finds him on the inside cover of *Jet* magazine. He's touted as an up-and-coming Negro businessman with his own automotive dealership and service, catering to a most exclusive clientele because he only accommodates people who own Cords, a fine car built by the Auburn Company. The final segment of my oration was an acknowledgment of his years as a true craftsman, a lithographer whose proudest moment was creating the color plates for the 1960 edition of the *Encyclopedia Britannica*. He was beaming that night when he came home from the lithography plant in lower Manhattan, down near Canal Street, and showed me his copy of Thomas Gainsborough's "Blue Boy."

That made me cry. "The Blue Boy" with that tender face, and my old man holding that poster-size print, before my mom put dinner on the table. That got to me.

Other things got to me also. One time I was riding on the C train to Brooklyn, the last local train from Manhattan. I heard someone on the train ranting a bit and shut him out. Then as I listened closer, I noticed that he was mad but there was a pattern to his rambling and put the *Times* down for a second and shut my eyes:

> Ha, ha, ha . . . young black man, yes, you. Stop killing each other. You must stop. You want to fight someone? Fight someone your size. Put on the boxing gloves, man. Yes, you go in right with one who is your weight. You don't fight someone who is not your weight. Ha, ha, ha. . . . you are mad at the white people. Good. But would you kill the black people? Why do you kill black people? I am not sayin' to kill the white people. Oh no. I am a Christian and we are all white when we are in heaven and we are all black when we go to heaven. Yes, ha, ha, ha . . . I have some of you fooled. You thought I was talking about white and black race. No, no, no, ha, ha, ha . . . no, man, I was talking about your spirit. Young black man, stop killing each other. If the man steps on your sneaker, say OK when he says he's sorry. That's all man, that's all man. You don't shoot the man because he stepped on your sneaker. Think about it. The white man got you so mad that you kill a black man. Ha, ha, ha, ha. That's mad.

My father was mad, unfortunately. Unfortunately, he was mad. Either way the country that he had worked for and fought for drove him mad. It was the same country that his family, his grandparents had slaved for. To be made insane by the United States of America happens every day and it's subtle enough that one is not necessarily aware of its insidious power. Race and race consciousness; Kafka himself could not have envisioned a more flawlessly intricate method or scheme for driving a protagonist insane.

What is unique and so special about this landscape? We are race conscious for sure, but it is our guileful manner of using race and its particular parameters that damages so many human beings. It's maddening to the point of producing paranoia, delusions of grandeur, and schizophrenia. Rational men, strong men and women and intelligent people are broken by this disease, by this illness. Khalid Mohammad, Michael Jackson, Lani Guinier, all pushed to breaking points by race, racism, questions that no human beings should ever have to confront. I never realized how maddening and ludicrous it was until I was enlightened that someone with the same last name as I had was ruining my academic career. Man, did I curse the day I changed my name. Irrational things started to happen and there was no way of asserting the truth, any truth. The first time I heard about Dr. Leonard Jeffries I defended him. I had to. A class of students had the mistaken impression that I was him.

It was September 1990, and I had just been hired by Hunter College to teach a course, "The Harlem Renaissance." I was very happy and honored since Hunter College is one of the best schools in the City University of New York. The summer had been an academic one. Preparing, reading, studying, making notes on yellow legal pads, all these activities bring joy to a teacher's heart, and I had boned up for this course just like a prizefighter getting prepared for a major bout in his career. I went to the classroom enthusiastic and buoyant.

I set my books and papers on the desk and looked out at the thirty-five faces, and I was scared and exhilarated. I took the roll and asked if there were any bureaucratic questions that had to be dealt with before commencing the class. About ten students came up to the desk and formed a line on the left. I was baffled, since in the age of computers there are usually only one or two students who have fallen victim to some glitch down in the registrar's office. Ten, something was amiss.

All of the students were requesting to drop out of the class. I was taken aback and was a bit astounded. Without letting the rest of the class discern that a mutiny was occurring within earshot, I whispered to each student. I asked the third student on line why was she dropping the class. There was a sense of ache in my voice as I asked, "Why are you dropping a class before the first lecture?" She said that it did not fit into her schedule. I asked two more students and they replied in the same demurring manner about scheduling conflicts. The sixth student was bold enough to feel sorry for me and said, "They're dropping the class because you're that guy, the racist. The racist from City College."

The reproaches rolled off my tongue with that swift annoyance of a person who has been wrongfully accused of some immoral turpitude of which he knows with conviction he is completely blameless. It was an incredibly awkward situation, with the class delayed now by about five minutes, students whispering at my desk, and a steady murmur and rustling papers and notebooks in the rest of the classroom. I was now standing.

"What guy, who's this guy?" I uttered.

"This guy Jeffries said that the black race is superior to all other races, white, Hispanic, Asian. The black race is first, superior to all others."

With confidence and anger I informed them that no professor of my alma mater would ever pronounce such racist thoughts and if he did, it was within a certain context or possibly he was being incredibly sarcastic and facetious.

My Hunter College students were just as confident. They gave me small details regarding storm trooper guards that surrounded the professor, his habitual lateness to class, and the muffling of academic dialogue. Details such as these made me uncomfortable since they lent credulity to their case. I apologized to the class about the disruption and concluded this little scene with a two-part plea. First, I was not that "guy" even though my last name was Jeffries and second, this Dr. Jeffries had been quoted out of context and was not racist. I reiterated that professors from City College, the place where I earned my MA in English, were not capable of that sort of virulent racism. It was beyond my comprehension.

Later the entire faculty of the City University and I were to learn that Dr. Leonard Jeffries was indeed racist and mad. Something had pushed this scholar over a line of rationality and irrationality, and he was no longer sane. Ice people, anti-Semitism, Sun people, adorned in African regalia, hauptepping his way through class, speaking triumphantly of melanin and other ersatz science. I wrote him a letter informing him of his disservice to the faculty of City University. He never replied. I was to suffer low enrollments due to his notoriety and our similar names. Mad. Madness.

I think my father, had he witnessed this tragi-comic vignette, would have said, "Looks like you should have stayed Puerto Rican." Maybe he was right.

Spelling Bee

"M-o-r-n-i-n-g t-e-l-e-g-r-a-p-h. Hey, Pop, is that right?" A voice comes through a closed door and tries to filter down a flight of steps to a living room oddly decorated with contemporary furniture and some very avant-garde chairs and tables that have been handmade.

"Say it one more time, Dexter. I couldn't hear you that last time." I walked to the steps of the first landing knowing that there was an echo effect in this staircase, and my voice would be a lot louder by the time it reached the second floor this time.

"M-O-R-N-I-N-G T-E-L-E-G-R-A-P-H. How's that, Pop? Is it right? Is that the right spelling?" This time a gleeful and proud affirmation comes barreling down the stairs. My old man shouts from his bedroom, "That's great. Your first word. That's really great. Do you hear that Pops, Marilyn? Dexter just spelled his first word. I mean, words. *Morning Telegraph.*" My mother says nothing; I didn't know why she did not wish to share in this triumphant moment. I was not spelling the classic rudimentary words, *yes,* and *no,* and *cat.* I was spelling two polysyllabic words. I reveled in the moment. Literacy had just come to me. It was a Saturday morning, and I had gone downstairs to see what sort of day it was going to be. My brother was sleeping. The day, or this part of it, early morning, possessed no particular charm for him. The longer he slept, the longer he avoided reality. Reality was my father. My sister was in her room, door closed, quiet, thinking, reading.

My sister, Vivian, had taught me the letters of the alphabet on pieces of construction paper. I had been asking her and my brother Paul non-stop to tell me what I would learn at school some day. They told me stories that caught and stimulated my imagination to no end. Reading books, adding long columns of figures, playing sports. For a four-year-old in his last year at home, I could hardly be contained. I flipped through, with permission, their school textbooks fascinated by the covers and the places to put one's name and the space for the year to be filled in. "Paul Jeffries—Class 303—1958." My sister's books were even more mysterious since they had fewer pictures and illustrations, and sometimes one had to flip perhaps fifty or so pages before coming across an illustration with a caption that said, *Miss Havisham's Wedding Cake*, or *Huck and Jim relaxed each evening*. With all this enthusiasm I could not be denied. My brother had agreed to teach me the song about the alphabet, and my sister was going to make these beautifully crafted letters, drawn and painted on construction paper. Each letter would have a word that started with that particular letter. Instead of *A* is for apple, it was *A* is for Africa, and *B* is for Bravo, and *C* is for Ciao. And she illustrated these letters with drawings of her own design and imagination.

M-O-R-N-I-N-G T-E-L-E-G-R-A-P-H. This was the culmination of weeks of work and study. Letters, songs, drawings, and me, me trying desperately to belong to that world that my sister and brother had already crossed into. Everyone was proud except my mother. It was the word, the actual words that I was spelling. Even though they were impressive in length, as those letters emanated from my mouth, my mom was just not in a celebratory mood. Spelling the word *hello* would have gotten the desired result. Those two words did not.

Books and records, records and books. In every room of the house, including the dining room, there were vast racks, cases, shelves of books and records. You could not miss them. When you have two thousand 78 rpm records staring at you all catalogued, listed in a highly detailed discography, a permanent space in your head makes way for them and they never leave. You feel their power, and they enter your consciousness. The record label, the artist, the date, accompanying musicians and a brief critique of the record's place in jazz history, all of this data was recorded. I knew already that some records were made in different years. The labels, being colorful, definitely caught my Crayola eye for detail. Even though I could not make out the individual names of the companies, I could definitely see that there was a pattern. Columbia had a little microphone and the letter *C* dominated the word. Decca used large block letters. OK was complicated because it had the letters, *Okeh*, written in italics. I started to realize that a word does not always mean what it says or how it is pronounced.

Our house was like a library with a separate music room where records were stored and housed. It seemed like there was a book on every conceivable subject, and any time we had assignments for school, it was rare that it was ever necessary to go to the local branch of the public library. When my mother purchased the *World Book Encyclopedia,* we were really set. My father, in his emphatic and self-assured manner, beamed proudly. My father, a brown-skinned Negro of medium height, but robust because of his barrel chest, receding hairline and glasses for reading, would say, "Everything you'll ever have to know is right there in those books, from A to Z. Everything. All of man's knowledge from Homer to Einstein is right there at your fingertips. You're lucky. I would have given anything to have this when I was a kid." Of course, we took this as an opportunity to find out what it was like when he was a kid. "Dad," my sister would start off cautiously, "How was it when you were a kid?"

That question and hundreds like it, whether they were initiated by my brother, sister or me, always prompted the same answer. Nothing. No stories about school, home or life before the age of forty. Based on my father's consistent reluctant disposition, we found out nothing. If his inclination was to dissuade us from further interrogation, it worked. If his purpose was to create the sensation that he came to earth when he was forty or more, this was accomplished. Whatever experiences we presented to him, there existed no parallel universe for him. Education, recreation, hobbies, my father either never participated in these activities or they were not an option. It wasn't that he rejected them; they were not available. We couldn't tell since his monosyllabic answers left no room for further queries or investigation. The simple and deadening *yeses* or *nos* left us defeated every time. We longed to hear what we would never hear for he was unassailable in regard to his life before the present. There was now. There was today. There was no yesterday, yesteryear. Everything began and stopped now.

There was a code in the house, I now realize. The silent or the unspoken code was multilayered and viscous. When pushed and cornered with the impossibility that he had been born at age forty, he would reply, "I always had to work." That was a start, but it ended there. "I've been working all my life and there's not too much to tell about that," would come out with a half laugh and smile. The records represented an important time in his life, his history, but we didn't realize that at the time because a record, to us kids, was a toy, something connected with fun and enjoyment. The vast array of books was regarded in the same manner. Whatever potential information they may have revealed about him, this would be impossible to discern as a child. They were just books. Therefore, the two most obvious artifacts in the house of which there was an abundance, were clues that retained no greater dimension until we were much older.

Then there was his special newspaper, the one I had just learned to spell the name of, that never revealed its secrets about him to us. Even as a little kid, I already knew that this wasn't a regular newspaper. For one, this newspaper could not be purchased at the regular grocery store around the corner run by a German-American family called the Braces. I went there to buy fresh rolls on Sunday mornings before the store closed for the day at eleven. Two, I never saw any other adult read this newspaper. It was never in the barbershop. It was never in any other house. I never saw people on the subway or bus reading this newspaper. It was a mystery. Down in the basement, behind a closed door, in a cold corner of an unfinished cellar, there he would sit, looking at his special newspaper. There were piles of them, yellowing with age. We knew he cared about them but as with the records and the books, they withheld truths from us. Only our mother hinted at their reality, and that was with an intermittent aside. More codes, more secrets, more language being employed to cover up something. The *something* was not inherently dark and evil because we could tell from the way our mom cast aspersions at his special newspaper and whatever activity revolved around it, that it was not to be taken seriously. She's upset, every Saturday. Not just an occasional Saturday. Every Saturday she is upset, and this becomes predictable.

Something occurs on Saturday with my father that invariably makes her angry, angry enough to fight with him about that special newspaper. The sporadic quips and excerpts we overhear and listen for are unintelligible. Horses, ponies, odds, three to one, nine to two, thirty to one, a sixteen dollar horse, a forty-eight dollar horse, Belmont, Monmouth, Garden State, Al the Wolf, "handicapping is a science; these charts are going to prove it," all of these things with an atmosphere of incredulity and utmost scientific inquiry, leave us baffled beyond comprehension.

Every family has its secrets, but this one seems beyond even the capacity of Sherlock Holmes. We got the idea about detectives and detecting strongly planted in our heads when we saw our father come home one day with a package. Inside the brown paper package was a beautiful leather pouch, oddly shaped, long and thin on one end, round, and circular on the other. Inside that black leather case was a magnifying glass. Highly polished steel, a piercing piece of glass brilliantly polished, on the whole, an object that radiated the feeling that systematic investigations were going to be conducted with it. My father smiled as he looked at it and told us we could look but not touch. We marveled at it and quickly conjured up who would be the first one to play Dr. Watson and help Holmes hold his very special instrument. We were told and warned that, "This isn't a toy," and that we were not to touch the magnifying glass. The glass itself never appeared upstairs again. It was relegated to that special place in the basement, his corner.

There's always a tension in the house surrounding the basement and the inordinate amount of time that my father spends down there. All I see is a pattern. My father descends into the basement after the morning fight about descending into the basement. Once the fight between him and my mother is concluded he goes to the cellar. If I look down the basement stairs, there he is in a sweater vest, writing down numbers and little figures. My sister has told me these are not just regular numbers but fractions. He writes these little numbers next to the names of other things that are in a straight line. Using the tools of a draftsman, he has a T-square and two triangles to aid him in keeping everything perfect and clear. Fine and delicate writing is seen. He spends hours in the basement in total silence. He smokes one cigarette after another and leans forward to write on papers that he has attached to the wall with tape. He'll lick his fingers on occasion to leaf through a little black book that he has told me is worth one million dollars. I've been amazed ever since hearing that. One million dollars! I'm so happy that we have one million dollars in our basement that I run upstairs to tell my mom. She says nothing. As I run back down, I spell *Morning Telegraph* again and my father says, "That's my boy." One time I make the mistake of telling a neighbor in front of my mother that my father has a book that you can make one million dollars from, and she slaps me right across the face. I never talk about the little black book again or spell the words *Morning Telegraph* in her presence again.

Sometime in the afternoon he comes up, makes a few telephone calls and that's it. He goes down one more time to shut off his fluorescent lights and straighten his drafting table. Once he reappears he informs my mom that he's ready to go shopping or they've made a plan where he'll pick her up in his faithful Ford. Once they are logistically reunified, the house is filled with music as my father puts on a jazz album. Now that it's the late 1950s, he takes to playing 33-rpm records on his hi-fi, the one he built down in the basement. The stereo cabinet has been given an immaculate finish, and the audio tubes bought from Lafayette Electronics up on Liberty Avenue in Jamaica glow warmly, and I think this is another great invention. The same tubes that make music can warm your hands. My parents speak in more code as the records play, one after another. But this is happy code. The names are funny: Duke, Satch, Count, Rex, Bird, Billie, Prez, and every now and then a normal name like Ben Webster. As the song comes on, they talk and laugh and at an appointed time, my mom takes out two tall glasses that are skinny on the bottom and wide at the top and pours them full with a golden liquid. I peer at the golden liquid and watch the bubbles rise to the top of the glass for a long time. I know this is beer, and I love to watch them drink it and eat potato chips from a bowl. The sounds of chips being eaten fill my head and when I'm given my separate little bowl that never breaks, no matter how many times I drop it, I'm really happy.

Sometimes my parents stay home on these Saturday nights, and other times they go out to parties and meetings. Vivian has already indicated that it must be boring to have to go to a meeting on a Saturday night, but Stanley and Marilyn are more than happy. Vivian is told how many of her friends can come over while they're gone. Her best friend is Irene Kelly. She has dirty blond hair, has a large set of 45-rpm records that she carries in a little box. When she comes over, there is a different type of music in the house, and I like it too, because I watch my sister and Irene dance together. They wear white-and-black shoes and white socks and spin all around the living room. Paul is under the same instructions. He too can have one friend come over, and I like Tommy Kapeck because he can fix anything and has already talked my brother into thinking about going half on a lawn mower engine that can be attached to an ordinary bicycle. This will make it into what they've called a *motor-bike*.

I have plenty of friends also and I can be seen riding a large red tricycle up and down the block. As I ride down Westgate Street, I wave hello to all of the people and I'm not aware that they are black, white, or purple. I just know that they wave back, and I'm happy to see them on my little trips. I imagine that I am a bus driver on the Q5A route, from Jamaica to Rosedale, and there are many, many stops that have to be made. There are many people that must be picked up too, and I tap the right rubber cover of my handlebar to let the change drop down into the coin box. The left rubber cover on my handlebar operates the doors, and if I want the rear door to open, I bring the pedal of the bike to its highest point, and tap that. Most important of all, if people wish to tell me that their stop is coming up, I ring my silver bell and pull over and slow down and stop. I'm a good bus driver.

I keep a steady eye on all the comings and goings on the block, and know that there are many more trucks. These trucks always open from the side and are empty. They pull up and a group of men get out, stretch, and have uniforms, sometimes even caps. Soon they walk up to the house they have parked in front of and ring the bell. I always notice that the door of the house is left open. It never shuts. As Joey and Suzy Walsh come out to talk to me, I ask them what is happening. They use the words, *We're moving.* My first question is why, and they always say they don't know and they seem sad. As we talk about being scared and sad, the men start to bring pieces of furniture out of the door that stays open. One item after another is in the hands of those uniformed men. My little friends are silent except for an occasional outburst of, "That man's carrying my toys." The Walshes are there too and are pretty quiet. They say hello to me but nothing else. I am innocent and ask the same question, "Why do you have to move, Mr. Walsh? Can Joey stay or does he have to go too?" Their answers are routine, and they always mention something about a better job. My return trip to the bus depot is slower and a little sadder. As I make my way up to the other end of the block, my mom or dad can see that something is wrong. They make a query. I inform them without getting off my big red tricycle that Mr. and Mrs. Walsh are moving and Joey and Suzy have to go with them. They nod their heads, and my mom comforts me with, "Don't worry. New kids will move into their house; you'll have some new friends."

This is repeated again and again, and I watch every one of my friends disappear within a period of two years. The trucks with the open side doors keep on coming, and I watch boxes of toys that I played with, ushered out by a man who doesn't care how I feel. The phone conversations at night become more frequent, and I hear my mom use more words and expressions that sound interesting, but I can only guess at their colorful meanings. My favorite is *Redlining* because red is my favorite color, but she is never happy when she uses it. Every phone call has tension in it. Frequently she makes the call. Sometimes she gets them. I can see that she is at work on some project, and there are other people are who interested in this topic of *Redlining*. I start to make the connections with the meetings that they are having on Saturday evenings or Sunday afternoons. There are sheaves of paper and clipboards and yellow legal pads that she has taken from her job as an executive secretary. There is writing on these legal pads, page after page, back and front. I have never seen so much handwriting. My mom is happy anytime Alva calls and whoever this is, she always smiles after that phone call ends and says, "There's still hope; we might stop them." I'm happy because she is smiling and starts to write on another page of yellow paper with energy and confidence. There is a counter next to the black wall phone, and both my parents lean against this and take notes whenever they talk about Alva, Dave, and Betty.

The worst thing that I ever heard when I was listening to them while they were leaning on the corner made me cry. I found out that if you are going to listen to big people talk in secret, you are not supposed to let them know that you are listening. I had ensconced myself right around the corner while my mom was talking. I listened for a long time and lost interest until I heard, "I never thought I would say this, but maybe we should move too." My heart moved, and my throat started to hurt. I slipped away from my spot on the wall near the doorway to the kitchen and walked to the living room. *Move* went through my head, men carrying boxes of my toys down the steps through an open door to another open door. I started to cry. I was inconsolable. I loved my house, driveway, backyard with the Long Island Railroad that went by with noisy regularity. Who would help Jonesy put down the gates at the railway crossing on Higby Avenue? I started to wail. I heard my mother call my name, "Dex? Dex? Is everything OK?" Her soft and concerned voice only made me cry more. My crying went up an octave, and I started to gasp. I heard my mother walk out of the kitchen and come to me. I was sitting on the couch crying and crying. She knelt down and started to rub my shoulders. I had planted my hands like posts of iron into the couch and could not be moved.

"Dex, what's wrong? Did you fall down? Are you hurt?"

I kept crying and shaking my head that I hadn't fallen and wasn't hurt.

"Mom, mommy, who, who, who is . . . ?"

"Dex, who what? What are you trying to tell me? What's wrong?"

My cries had alerted my sister, Vivian, who was up in her room. She loved me a lot and wanted to help. She came down, and I saw her white-and-black shoes first as she descended the stairs. She knelt down like my mom and said, "Honeybunch, what's wrong? Tell Mom what's wrong." I kept on crying and although it did not seem possible, I started to become even more hysterical. I gasped and gasped. My mom consulted my sister and I was discussed like a patient in a hospital.

"Vivian, what do you think is wrong?"

"Mom, I don't know. What happened right before he started to cry?"

"I don't know. I was on the phone, talking to Betty and he just started to wail."

They had stood up to talk to each other and went back to the kneeling position. My mom asked again what was wrong. My response was the same, "Who, who is, going to . . . ?"

Standing again my mother said, "Vivian, that's all he can say. Something about 'who.' "

Vivian decided to take a different approach and said, "Honeybunch, do you want a glass of water?" I nodded my head *yes* and she quickly walked to the kitchen. My mother kept on holding my hand. I kept on weeping. Vivian returned with a glass of water.

"Dex, look, a glass of water and a surprise."

She had placed her hands behind her back. She was hiding something.

"Look Dex, a straw, a straw that bends in the middle."

It worked. I stopped crying and held out my hand as she gave me the glass of water. I started to sip the water and drinking the water helped me catch my breath. My mom looked down at me and said Vivian was a good big sister. I nodded affirmatively with the straw in my mouth. She brushed my hair back with her hand. Finally she spoke.

"Dex, why were you crying? Did something happen?"

I put the glass down and my sister caught it right before it fell off the couch. I started to cry again.

"Who, who, who, who will take care . . . of who will . . . help . . . ?"

My mom was patient and said, "Dex, take a breath after each word. If you do that, you'll be able to tell us what is wrong." I listened and tried it the next time I talked.

"Mom, if we move, who will take care of the people on my bus route? Who will pick them up when it is raining or snowing?"

There was a twisted look of pain on my mother's face. My sister looked at her with no expression. They were both quiet. I went back to my straw with the bend in it and sucked up the rest of the water. My sister asked me if I wanted another and I just shook my head. She turned and went back upstairs.

"Dex, you know you shouldn't listen to big people when they are on the phone. Sometimes they want that conversation to be heard only by them. Do you understand? We're not moving."

"Why did you say that? I heard you say that."

"Dex, I was talking about a situation that will never happen."

"But I heard you say the word *move*."

"Dex, I was talking about something else that has nothing to do with moving. Isn't that possible? A person can talk about one thing and it really doesn't mean what you think it does? That is possible? Right? OK?"

"So, I'll still be able to pick up the people on the Q5A?"

"Yes, you can even do it right now. Why don't you get your red tricycle and make one trip to Jamaica right now? People have to get to work now and they're waiting for you. You don't want them to be late, right?"

I blew my nose into a tissue that she held for me. I got up and put on my little jacket. My tricycle was outside in the backyard.

"Dex, don't forget your oil can."

I looked around the pantry that was the last stop before going out into the backyard. My father had given me my own oil can for keeping my "bus" maintained. I picked it up. When I got outside, I bent down and squirted a bit on the big front wheel, and some more on the two back ones. She was ready. I got on and started to make my rounds.

Sleigh Morning

A BRIGHT MORNING in 1959 with a red shingled roof shining, glistening with snow meant only one thing; we were happy. From our second floor bedroom on Westgate Street we were able to see the most precise predictor of weather, the roof of P.S. 161, an ancient wood-framed school that was built in 1890. It had a dome on the front of it and a peaked roof. When the roof was covered with snow, we knew that sleighs would be taken out and instantly reconditioned after a year's disuse. Our dad would help in the process, saying, "Go down into the basement and get some coarse sandpaper; Paul, it'll have the number 100 on the back. Dexter, go into the garage, way in the back on the right side, get some rope. We'll restring these sleds." After that avalanche of activity, we're ready to go sleighing. The rust has been removed and there's some 3-in-1 oil on runners and the primitive steering bar. Our handles have new rope and new knots are tied. We get our sleds out through the cellar door and tug them over to "The Mountain." The Mountain was just a hill but to a six-year-old, it had that alpine appearance. By the time my brother and I get there, it's a scene out of *It's a Wonderful Life*. Red and blue scarves, woolen hats of all designs, some with strings and little balls hanging off the ends. Other hats look like long socks, some recently distributed at Christmas. Galoshes, boots, slip-on yellow boots better suited for an October rainstorm, all blurring together as we make our way to the top of the hill.

There was a line of kids—you couldn't just take off at will. We got to the end of the line and waited, breathing into the air what we called *fog*.

I was small enough and still found the world a fascinating place and *breathing fog* was one of those fascinating things to do.

"Hey, you can't sleigh here."

"Why? We just waited like everyone else."

"Colored kids can't sleigh here, that's why."

Pushing, shoving, you can never really fight or wrestle well with boots, gloves, scarves, and winter coats. It didn't matter. It always seemed like there were ten of them and the number of us was predetermined at two, always two, never more than two, only two: my brother Paul and I. Two against ten, two against twelve, it was already a slaughter. The only thing we could hope for in those days was that some parent who had come to drop off his kid or pick some other kid up would see the mass of tangled arms and legs, hands clasped around a windpipe, bloody noses, and hoods ripped from the jackets and know that something was wrong.

A car door slams; the crunching of adult weight in boots which is different from kid weight. "What's going on here?" is yelled and the punches slow. The little screams and whimpers become silent. You raise your head up and aren't hit. Someone pushes you away with a last disdainful shove. You look right into the blinding light of a brilliantly clear day in 1959, and there are tears not because of the light but because it is just so unfair to always lose and never win. You're grateful for the intervention of the older person, but there is a part of you that would rather die and be pummeled some more than have to be rescued all the time. You feel yourself yanked to your feet by this anonymous adult, and you're placed vertical with the world and in that daze you see a combination of faces, some sympathetic, some glaring, and some triumphant with that "We told you so" look in their eyes. It all concludes with that older voice, saying in a cautionary tone, "You boys better head home."

My brother starts to protest and talk about "being fair" and I caution him just by raising my arm a bit. "Let's go" comes out of my mouth enveloped in a cloud of fog and mist. I'm still out of breath and start to look around for our scattered belongings. I see my mittens in one spot, my hat in another. Our sleds with their new ropes are turned askew. When the crowd of kids sees me start to pick up my things, they're satisfied that the battle is over and that they are victorious. My brother talked to the man. I couldn't hear what they were saying. I knew if I picked up his scarf, and tried to give it to him, that would stop the talking. It worked. I waited while he said a few more words to the man and he had to acknowledge my presence and turn. "Thanks," he said.

We walked over to our sleds and turned away from The Mountain. There was a woman with a green jacket and brown boots with fur at the top of them. Her hair was brown and matched her boots. With a plaid scarf wrapped around her head, she looked like so many other women in the community. As we passed her, she spoke and asked us where we were from. Paul said, "Westgate Street." An extra puff of exasperated fog came hurling out of her mouth. "I didn't mean that," she said in a sour tone. "Where are you from? What are you?" The question was puzzling and mysterious. In November, only about a month ago, I had learned about the Pilgrims and Thanksgiving. Before Paul could say a word, I proudly said, "I'm an Englishman." I was never going to answer that question as quickly and resolutely for another thirty-five years. This Irishwoman in plaid with a face that was a yardstick for contempt quickly replied, "Oh no. You're a little Spanish, or maybe colored." I had waited for a compliment on my understanding of history, America, and the importance of Thanksgiving. She said nothing pleasant or nice in response. I thought she might say, "Right, correct, very good. You really know your history." No, she had nothing but ugly words and feelings for me. I withdrew and gave my sled a tug as we moved away from her and her scarf.

The long walk, pulling your American Flyer that was all ready for action. You can still smell the 3-in-1 oil on the runners. Little rainbow colors follow your sled where the oil is fighting to blend with the snow. The silence. The breathing. The fog. The little pleasure that can still be gained from that is resumed. Then the promise, mutual of course between my brother and me, not to ever, under any circumstances, tell anyone of the battle and ensuing defeat. We prepare our stories for coming home so soon. All you have to do is say that, "There wasn't enough snow." No one will ever check. Other little oaths are sworn to get even, *even* meaning given the opportunity to meet one of those kids in a match where it is five to two, instead of ten to two. Getting even, fantasies, oaths and promises are our only consolation.

"Paul, what do they mean?"

"What do they mean about what?"

"Colored kids can't go sleighing. That. What does that mean?"

"Dex, they're talking about us. We're 'colored kids.' "

"Oh. But colored means dark, like Walter. He's colored."

"Come on. We'll take the long way home; that way we won't get home too fast."

We walk along residential streets with brick and wood-frame houses. Each house has a driveway and a garage. Pulling our sleds with ropes, we drag them lethargically. My rope is too short, and the sleigh keeps banging into my leg.

"Dex, stop for a second. That banging is going to hurt your leg."

"It's all right. Really, it's just a little whomp."

"Look, we have extra rope that Dad gave us. Just stop and it'll take a second."

I'm impatient and a bit lazy, but my brother has already integrated some of my father's positive traits. Attention to detail and maintaining one's gear has been instilled in him. It's been instilled in me, but I'm just too indolent. Taking the time to stop and retie a rope is trivial and a waste of time.

"I told you to stop pulling the damn sleigh."

"Paul, I don't care. It doesn't hurt."

My brother grabs me roughly by the throat and shoves me down in the snow. That hurts. I start to cry; being in the snow on my back is reminiscent of what just occurred not less than an hour ago. I start to bawl and prop myself up on my elbows. Making a good target my brother kicks me in the leg as hard as he can. Now it's one to one. I jump up and grab him around the throat too, and we start to swing each other around. He's tougher and stronger, but I'm faster. By getting around him from behind, I pull his hood as hard as I can toward the ground. This throws off his balance, and he falls to the snow and grabs his neck in pain. I run over and kick him as hard as I can and get scared when I see him start to cry. He jumps up, and I start to run away. I skip over the abandoned sleighs and feel to leave them is immoral. I look behind me and the sleighs are lonely and sad. That one look back allows Paul to catch up. He punches me in the middle of my back with all his fury. With the wind knocked out of me, I collapse into the snow, finished. My brother turns me over on my back and begins to beat me with both fists. Punch after punch lands on my chest, stomach and head. He's doesn't hit me in the face, but everywhere else.

"You're killin' me. Please, I give up. I give up."

No matter what words of contrition or supplication I offer, the punches keep coming into my body. My snowsuit offers some protection; it softens the blows, but it's still a terrific beating, and he only stops when he gets tired. I lie in the snow and cry and my chest heaves up and down in the snowsuit. Salty tears stream down my neck past my scarf and I wonder how he could do this to me. The racial incident is long gone. I think of now, only now. I look at the sky and am amazed that this offers some relief. Large clouds against a blue sky let me drift. I crank my head and notice that something special happens when you look at the fast-moving clouds through dark and bare branches of trees. I can't tell what it is or how it's happening, but it's just like the visual effect that occurs in the subway tunnels that I'm aware of anytime we travel from Queens to Manhattan. If you train your eye on an object and things are moving, either you or the object, it is an extraordinary event. After rushing to the first car despite my parents' fervent pleas not to, Paul and I look out the front of the E or F train with our hands tightly clasped to the sides of our head. It's one of the many tricks that my brother has taught me. If you look at the lightbulbs at a particular angle, they flash by like hurtling stars in outer space. We're entranced.

That's what happened with me on the ground. Paul has walked over to the sled and is tying the new lead rope to mine so it won't slam into the back of my foot. "Come on," he says while still making the appropriate knots. I lie still, think about clouds, the faces on them and the blue sky, and notice that there is another batch of clouds, very thin ones. They are closer to my eyes than the big ones, and they are moving incredibly fast. "Come on, get up; it's ready." I turn my head toward his voice and don't know whether to cry some more or apologize. The anger is gone, but the shame is there in full force. I slowly get up and brush the snow off where it's caked into little hard balls on my woolen mittens. "Dex, Dad's gonna be mad if we come back separate. Then we'll both be in big trouble. Wanna go to the basement?" I keep walking in silence toward him and don't have to answer. Soon I'm right next to him and he test tugs the new rope and its length. We barely look at each other. I finally talk, "Well, at least the fight has a good part to it."

He's baffled and says, "What do you mean, a good part? Don't start."

I smile that he doesn't understand where my mind is going and that he doesn't understand my little secretive ways of looking at our world. I've already been to places that he can't imagine and the pain has gone away enough that I'm not even mad enough to tell on him or worry about "if we come back separate."

"Paul, the fight has a good part to it. It made us take a longer time to get home. Now we don't have to slow down. We can even take the shortcut." My brother doesn't say anything, but I can see that he agrees that there is some good fortune in what's happened. We start pulling our sleds, and mine doesn't hit me in the back of my leg.

Walking to School

———❖———

WALKING TO SCHOOL, autumn days as always, since school commences at that time of year. One composition notebook in my hand with a little plastic case for pencils and maybe a crayon or two. In the other hand, a paper bag, a medium-size shopping bag. Pretty big and disproportionately incongruous since I'm only five and a big bag like that almost hits the ground, even if I keep my hand up to my waist. Awkward, a little clumsy. What's in the bag or what's the bag for? Tissues. Yes, tissues, new and used. You see, my mother did not know that I had allergies and anyone who has them knows that every fall means a savaging time for allergy sufferers. That's now. Then, I guess people didn't know that much. So, I would sneeze and sneeze and sneeze, and my mother thought that I should have a bag for my tissues, new and used. It was practical, that's for sure. But it still made for a certain sort of awkwardness.

That's one type of awkwardness that one knows when he first approaches an institution like school. Then there are other types that no bag, no matter how big or strong, can explain, remediate. Because I was from an interracial relationship, I was always in the middle of things so to speak. I was light enough to be taken for being white and yet dark enough to be taken for a Negro. Diaz being my last name at the time just made things more complicated since I then became Spanish. So bag or no bag, my problem was that I made people uncomfortable, and that's not a good place to be when you're young. I was, just with my presence, not by word or gesture, a source of unpleasantness. Besides my white tissues being pulled out of a paper bag, awkward since I was sometimes confusing the old with the new, there was just me. Teachers,

31

students, parents, just by looking at me made them stop, think, and think again. What were they thinking? I didn't think they were examining me for either offense, the tissues or my color. I was to later learn that it was the latter that was arousing the curiosity and the pain. I was, at least for some years, thankfully oblivious of both. I thought it was great that I had my tissues and my shopping bag, and it was great to have something to carry, and no one could take it away from me. My mother had already contacted the teacher to inform her of the bag's purpose, and the teacher had sanctioned it. It was my special privilege.

School in the 1950s in Queens, New York, is a pretty somber place. Rigor, rote learning, white shirts and red ties are worn on Thursdays for assembly. Before the Supreme Court ruling on prayer in public schools, it is still permissible to read from the Bible during the first minutes of assembly and Mr. MacNamara, dressed impeccably in his suit scares us, and that is the desired effect he wishes to achieve. His body is just as massive as his name: Mack-New-Mara. Three-piece suits and wing-tip shoes are his uniform; gray shirts and black shoes and six feet of him keep us in our place. When Thursdays come around, and that means assembly, I'm in dread of the whole affair. My parents, being atheists, never sent any of us to church for even one service, and we nonbelievers were always addressed with some sort of scorn or contempt. It wasn't overt hostility, and we didn't take it to heart because my sister, my brother, and I were taught that the people who attended the many churches in our neighborhood did that out of weakness. "They need gods because they don't believe in themselves and their ability to change or control their lives," my mother would say with resoluteness. She never hesitated in her presentations of these platitudes. They were said with a certain flourish that came from years of defending and explaining why Marxism was the answer to not most, but all, of the world's problems. I heard the rhetoric, and because she was my mom, she never had to move through the process of making her explanation any more tangible, any more concrete. What could I have said anyway? Who would have the fortitude to craft a reply worthy of her assertion?

Being cut off from the experience of going to church meant that those assemblies on Thursdays, with Mr. Mack-New-Mara up front at the lectern with a Bible that looked as thick as a milk crate, was another instance of me being in a situation where my inability to respond stimulated withdrawal, drifting, dreaming. The walls of the auditorium were adorned with somber paintings, no bright colors, all dark oil portraits of famous scenes from world and biographical history in which individuals sacrificed themselves for some cause higher than themselves. I can't read the plaques but have asked older kids on occasion about the descriptions: "Joan of Arc, asking for inspiration before battle," was one that always caught my attention and made me mournful. There she was, a beautiful and serious woman, suited in armor, kneeling, head bowed in assent, flag in one hand, sword in the other. The forest that she was in was as dark as the one that the prince in Walt Disney's *Sleeping Beauty* had to hack his way through. *Joan, Joan of Arc, you look like no one that I've ever seen before in my life. I can't come up with words other than "sad" to describe you. You don't look scared. You don't look happy. Even though you have the sword and the flag, they're not enough.*

"Our father who art in heaven . . ." this usually left me behind because, again, I had the indescribable impression that Mr. MacNamara was referring to someone who had passed away, was dead and therefore it was easier to drift to the next painting in my section of the auditorium. "Four Navy Chaplains' Heroic Sacrifice." This large oil painting, reminiscent of Joan of Arc, was dark, greenish, and scary. It showed four navy chaplains on a vessel during World War I. They were locked together with their arms intertwined; the decks of the ship are already awash with water from the North Atlantic. They had given their life jackets to others who had already abandoned ship. The chaplains looked forlorn and doomed, but their arms looked firm and strong. *I don't want you men to die or give up your life vests. Why does anybody have to die? How come they didn't have enough life vests to go around?*

"Thy kingdom come . . ." Whenever I hear that line I would give anything to be back in the classroom. The classrooms are dark on rainy days, and lights with giant bulbs hang from the ceilings on long chains. I count the links in the chains and find counting useful. If I count carefully, which I do, I've figured out that some chains have thirty links and some have thirty-one and one has twenty-nine. The rooms are paneled with large pieces of grainy wood. Patterns always run up and down, and I keep track of the smallest detail. I know the windows also have a certain number of panes, and these panes don't vary like the links in the chain. Three, six, nine in the bottom, three, six, nine in the top, nine and nine is eighteen. There are eighteen panes, and these large wooden windows must be raised with a large pole. The luckiest class monitor in the world gets to take care of the windows. You take the pole from its hook and get to move these large windows up and down, as Mrs. Roth requests. At the top of each window there is a rolled shade, yellow, tan, and Mrs. Roth pulls them down in the afternoon but never in the morning. There's a pattern. For some reason, the sun is always on the same side in the afternoon, and it hits her desk and any kids in rows five and six. As soon as she sees the first kid raise his hand to his head to protect his eyes, Mrs. Roth unrolls these large shades, and they creak. I like the sound. I can see that the extra pulleys and wheels keep the cord from breaking loose. She gives it a certain sharp tug to the left and it's tight; it won't fly up. The time it did; it was one of the biggest events of the year. The sixteen-foot shade was pulled down. She tugged the cord to the left. As she walked to her desk, *boom*, it flew up to the top and spun out of control for a few seconds. "Silly old shade," she says and it's a wonderful moment. Walking from her large oak desk that is always covered with construction paper, white paste that has the consistency of cottage cheese, and a ruler and scissors, she continues to talk. "Come on down, silly old shade" as if she's talking to an acquaintance, and the whole class is enchanted, and she has the same voice that she uses when she reads us stories in the afternoon. "That's it; you can't stay up there in the afternoon when Mr. Sun is out. Your job is to protect us from Mr. Sun in the afternoon." The blind obeys her and as if by magic slowly returns to its customary resting place, and this time it stays.

I have several favorite places in the room. In the back are the blocks, and they are always smooth and cool if you touch them or place them on your face or forehead. I licked them once because they looked so clean and beautiful and delicious. Caroline Gilbert told on me. I became the butt of a joke, but I had to laugh. When Mrs. Roth asks me if I was really that hungry, all the children laugh and so do I. The blocks are wonderful. Subways and buildings, those are my specialties. I build tunnels and buildings any chance I get. The blocks fit perfectly and are well balanced. On the other side of the room are the closets. My favorite hook in the clothes closet is seven because that is my favorite number. When I hang up my jacket or raincoat, if I look to the left, I can see Mrs. Roth when she opens her private closet, just for her. It has a mirror and even though she is old, she brushes her hair. One time I even saw her putting lipstick on and mumming her lips together, so they were equally covered with red, top and bottom.

Once my things are hung up I sit down happily on any day other than assembly day. I fold my hands when told and proudly say the pledge of allegiance and sing *My Country 'Tis of Thee*. The *under God* part of the pledge is mumbled because my parents have told me that there is no such thing as God. My dad has coupled my mother's words with his own, like a boxer following an uppercut with a right cross, "Men create gods; gods do not create men." That stays in my mind because of the rhythm of it: *de dedah dah, dah dah dedah dah*. However, every other word of the pledge is sounded with pride. The loudspeaker pauses; there's a pause because the radio station is located in Manhattan, and I know that it takes time for the music to travel from Manhattan to Queens, about five seconds. Five seconds pass, and then there is the sound of music, orchestral, and we sing. I have already figured out that these old words have interesting meanings. *Of thee I sing,* means that I sing about you. There is no question about who I am. When I hear the lines *land of the pilgrim's pride* I know that I am proud to be one and that my ancestors have come to a place called Plymouth, made friends with the Indians, and wear black clothes. They wear white collars and the women wear some sort of white bow around their necks. They walk slowly and even when they attend church, the men walk with rifles crossed in their arms. Why would a man carry a rifle to church? I thought, then, that these people did not trust each other. I thought about how I would feel about sharing a drumstick or a piece of pumpkin pie with a man who doesn't wear a shirt to the dinner table and has feathers in his hair. Just something to wonder about; it does not mean that much because when it's November and Mrs. Roth starts to tape cardboard turkeys to the windowpanes, I'm thrilled. Pilgrim women and men are also taped to the windows. On the bulletin board in the front of the room, there are prints that dramatically capture the history of the Plymouth Colony from the day of the *Mayflower*'s landing to the first Thanksgiving. When I view the paintings up close, I'm reminded of Joan of Arc down in the auditorium because people are kneeling and praying next to a large rock.

I wake up as I realize that I am still in the dark auditorium, and they've wheeled out a full-size television set on a makeshift dolly. Everyone starts to whisper, and the remonstrations are instantaneous. "Everyone put their hands on their heads. You know better than that, to talk during assembly just because a television has been brought out." Dead silence. Four hundred kids from kindergarten to the sixth grade stare straight ahead in absolute silence. You can't hear anything. As your hands start to slip from the top of your head because they are drained of every ounce of energy from your five- or eight-year-old hands, people are selected for further punishment. "You there, six rows from the back, three seats in from the aisle, on the right, yes, my right. Get up. Get up right now and move to the back. Stand there with your hands on your head until I tell you to sit. Face away from the television set. Now, has everyone learned their lesson? Four hundred voices minus the eight in the back respond in unison, "Yes, Mr. Mack-New-Mara."

Satisfied that we've been properly disciplined, we're informed that we are going to watch a miracle, the launch of an American rocket ship into space. It's not the first one, but it's a very important one. For months the word *Sputnik* has been tossed around on radio and TV. The Soviet Union put something called *Sputnik* into space and whatever that is, it has plenty of Americans worried. Yet my parents are happy. Anything to do with Mr. or Mrs. Sputnik brings cheer to the dinner table, and there is a general celebration in the evening and sometimes even in the morning. The radio is on a great deal especially because my parents don't believe in television and any time ours breaks, we are without one for months and sometimes even years. They're happy and we're happy since this is a legitimate excuse to get out of the house to watch television in other kids' homes. Whether it's my Negro grandmother's house or our friends, we have a ticket out on many a Friday and Saturday night.

The celebration continues, and it seems like I'm growing up in a house where everything is the opposite of what I hear, not just in school but what I see and hear on the radio and television. Everyone is afraid of the Russians. My parents love and cherish them. Everyone hates the Reds. My parents shake their heads and say emphatically, "If it wasn't for the Red Army, we'd be speaking German right now." My mother saddens as she thinks of her Jewish relatives in Russia who were killed during the war, adds, "or worse." Nothing makes sense. The imagery is there too. Magazines, books, pictures, calendars, art, all of these tangible things that stay in a kid's head abound in my home and say one thing. The Soviet Union is right, and the United States should show some humility. That's all Marilyn and Stanley Diaz want, a little humility. They can prove their more salient points at the drop of a hat. And when it comes to the most important question of all that is discussed in my house from morning coffeepots to evening coffeepots, what should Negroes do, where should they be, what should they do, another hero of theirs has already answered that question loudly and affirmatively. Big Paul Robeson said that it's the only country where a Negro has a fair chance. Since I am so aware of how unfair things are for Negroes here (I don't think of myself as one and feel sorry for them the way I feel sympathy for the little cosmonaut canine), the Soviet Union sounds like a paradise. In the USSR everyone is equal. Everyone is paid equally according to his or her needs. If you work in a factory and have two children, you are paid more than the man next to you who does the same job and has no children.

They are building a new world, I'm told happily, and the United States could be even better because we are smarter and have more natural resources and we're just sitting on them. Whenever we play that board game about traveling across the United States with little pieces of corn to help you remember Nebraska and a piece of coal to help you think of Pennsylvania, my old man points out, "We've got coal, oil, and the technology to make all the steel that we'll ever need."

On my own, without the game and them, I have figured out that we have a lot in common with the Russian people; in the USSR, there are many different ethnic groups, different colors. I know it because anytime I hear Paul Robeson sing, *Native Land,* I shiver; in this place things having to do with being a Negro just don't matter. His booming voice states, "side by side, the white, the dark, the yellow, build in peace a richer, better life . . ." These records play in the house and that voice tells a truth. When you hear Big Paul sing, you have to feel good about the Soviet Union:

> *Oh rolling, green open fields, rolling plain wide open prairies,*
> *Heroes go riding cross the prairies,*
> *Yes, with the Red Army go the heroes . . .*

I'm struck and stuck. Paul echoes throughout my house, and I am aware of how complicated a black person's life can be when I hear a kid in school say that Paul is a traitor. I listen very closely. The fourth grader in the lunchroom said that he heard his father say that Paul Robeson said, "If there is a war, I won't fight against the USSR." When I pledge allegiance in the morning it's to the United States of America, and he's pledging his allegiance to the USSR. I want to say USA, but I know it's true. That kid in the lunchroom talked like he knew what he was saying. My Paul, for some reason, is connected to a place that is strange, far off, farther than Africa. Why?

My father mentions long expressions like USSR and how they have been able to perform a miracle in such a short amount of time. "Dad, what kind of miracle?" My dad takes a deep breath, his chest comes out with pride, and he says, "Always remember that no matter what you hear, it's the Red Army that stopped the Nazis, ran them back from Moscow to Berlin." I only understand one word, and it's *run* and I ask him how can a man run that far, and he takes the time to explain that when he says *run* he means the word *retreat*. I like the word *retreat* because it has parts and reminds me of *trick or treat* and that reminds me of how the real miracle is the words themselves because they have little secrets threaded throughout them. Just the fact that one word with one sound can mean more than one thing; that is a miracle.

"Pop, why is that a miracle?" I've followed my father upstairs to the bathroom because he always washes when he comes home from his lithography job. Not that he has to worry about being unkempt because at the lithography plant he has already washed and changed from his blue work pants and shirt that says *Stan* on it. No, he just wants to wash his face and neck before dinner. He fills the basin with water and starts to wash. I love the sound that his soaped hands make against his one-day growth. It crunches, and I look up and smile every time I hear the crunchy-crunch sound. His tie and white shirt are hung over the towel rack. He shuts his eyes when he washes his face and bends down into the basin. I'm fascinated that he can wash his neck so carefully that no water splashes where it shouldn't. I sit on the side of the tub and continue, "Pop, why else is it a miracle, I mean, the Reds chasing the Nazis back to where they came from?" He pulls the plug out of the bottom of the basin, so the water will drain. He starts to turn the HOT and COLD knobs, and I ask him why doesn't he ever use the secret handle. He turns to look at me sitting on the tub and is curious as to why I think there is a secret handle on the basin. With the water running and splashing, he inquires as to my theory. "Pop, don't you know? There's a special handle for extra water to come out. It's there in the middle."

With two arms outstretched so he can lean against the basin and take a breather from his wash, he points to the middle porcelain handle. I jump up from the tub and say, "Yeah, that one, that one, right in the middle. That's the one with the extra power. It's spelled with a word longer than hot or cold. You see? W-A-S-T-E! That's the word "W-A-S-H." With his undershirt back on, he buttons his white shirt that still has some starched crispness in it. His face crunches, and his shirt crinkles. My father is just one big source of sounds, even when he eats. He makes his blue knit tie into a knot and puts the tiepin at the collar. He's now ready for dinner and answers. After informing me that W-A-S-T-E is not *wash* and that that knob does not have extra power, we start to walk downstairs. As we descend the staircase, the books begin because my father has made bookcases that are all over the house. Books are to your left and right and in other places.

"Pop, tell me about the miracle before dinner?" My father pauses at the couch and swings me up, and in one motion I'm sitting on it. The couch is against the wall that separates the living room from the dining room. He pokes his head a little around the corner and yells "Pops," and I always wonder why my mother's name is so close to his and he asks, "How much longer before dinner?" She yells back something, and he tells me that we have time for the miracle. I cross my legs in anticipation and smile.

"June 22, 1941. Always remember this date. It's more important than December 7, 1941. It's on this day that the German army invades the Soviet Union and tries to do what Napoléon couldn't do. A hundred thirty-three divisions, one million men, stretched on a thousand-mile front. They try to conquer the greatest and largest country in the world. When Hitler does this, Churchill gets a reprieve. The pressure is now off the British. Little does Hitler know that the Red Army will never surrender. After Stalingrad, the Germans never stop running. They run all the way back to Berlin." I don't know what all this means, but I can see that my father feels as though he is telling me some epic tale worthy of Homer and the Trojan horse. I know about the Trojan horse and can hear the same excitement in this voice. He must be getting close to the miracle.

"So, the miracle is, that within ten years of what the Germans did to the Soviet Union, not only are they back on their feet, but they are putting satellites in space. And soon they will put a man in space and that's after having the Nazis burn almost everything down to the ground. Did you ever hear of the scorched earth plan . . . ?" I haven't been listening as soon as he said *put a man in space* because I know that this is the country that killed the little dog that went up in space. I prayed for the dog that he would live as he was sent into orbit around the earth and envisioned a little dog like mine, a cocker spaniel, with a space suit on and oxygen tank on his back. I think he didn't have enough air. ". . . And that is the miracle. It's time to eat."

During dinner I think of Mr. MacNamara and how he talks about miracles, and I'm starting to get a sense that there are different types and *miracle* is now in that special word category that lets me know that adults sometimes use words the way they want to and it doesn't matter if the definition used in the morning during an assembly is not the same one used that evening in my house. I drift back to dinner and when it's my turn to present a review of what I did in school, my high point is that we watched the "blastoff of a spaceship," and no one died, and it was a miracle.

Barbershop Quartet

———◈———

IT WAS A small barbershop with the ubiquitous striped carousel pole, but that had stopped spinning after Mr. Vitale left. We never knew whether the broken pole was a paltry part of Mr. Vitale's plot to get even with the new black barber who bought his business at a steal, or was it the general perception that black people seemed to degrade anything left to them, whether it was houses, streets, schools, stores or any other aspect of Springfield Gardens that we watched fall into decline. The barbershop held the line though—maybe because it had such an intimate connection to the community. It could fall into pretty extreme disrepair before going completely out of business.

There were four chairs, and you wondered why they never used the last one on the right. The leather straps made that great *whupping* sound when a razor was being sharpened on them, and the aroma from the strap was powerful. Tuesday (barbershops were always closed on Monday) through Friday there was one barber, Mr. Welles, the owner and not-so-sage entrepreneur. Friday things sped up a bit and his second in command, a lanky fellow named Ellis, helped with the evening rush of young men getting pretty for their dances and dates. However, Saturday, that was when Mr. Welles marshaled all his forces and had Ellis on hand as well as his last corporal, his cavalry to the rescue, Pete.

Negro barbershops were supposed to be a Norman Rockwell meeting place, a town hall gathering of men with wisdom, humor, and philosophy. This one never lived up to those expectations. If humor meant making fun of another human being, until they were broken in mind and spirit, there was a river of it. The only thing I ever heard with any certainty was a barely audible murmuring and whispering. People would duck into the shop, Mr. Welles would lean away from whatever head he was cutting or neck that he was shaving, listen to the whisperer, and then stretch over to the cash register where he kept a little pad. With his left arm still holding on to the clippers or the razor, his right hand would write or scribble down something on that small pad. By the time that you looked up, the messenger was gone, and you weren't quite sure as to why there was an interruption. Mr. Welles was one of the many neighborhood number runners, and this was rather incredible to us. Even though we lived in a middle-class neighborhood that was on the decline, even though we had houses with separate garages and driveways, even though we possessed all of the trappings of a *Father Knows Best* environment, many of the recent black arrivals obviously were not aware of this. And wherever they hailed from, they had transported their small lives of petty crime, hustling, and survival with them. Therefore, numbers and the numbers racket came to us from Harlem, Bedford-Stuyvesant, Brownsville, or Jerome Avenue in the Bronx.

Mr. Welles, the number runner. Well, I have to admit it was the black "suburban" version of running numbers and street gambling. You bet your few cents on the number that was supposed to come out by the end of the day, the number being the last three digits of the total pari-mutuel receipts of some local racetrack: 3 5 2, 5 8 9, 6 1 2, it didn't matter. These digits made someone happy for a few moments and led others to follow, believe and hope that their day was coming too; it was just a matter of time. Black people dream, and the numbers racket was part of that wistfulness.

But none of this bothered me. I had no moral scruples at my tender age of eight and between the whispering and the writing and the murmuring, the ballet of men coming and going, I just took this for granted. Yet I hated the Negro barbershop.

I was a hero and mascot to them and knew that every time I entered that place, I was going to suffer and suffer in silence. My suffering reached exponential proportions if it were a Saturday since all three of my enemies would be there, forming an alliance against me. I took my pummeling in silence since, just like the numbers racket which was proceeding right under my nose without any comprehension, I never could have fathomed why I was a hero to these three strange Negro men.

Ellis: *Hey, looky here. Damn, it's you. We've been waitin' for you.*

Pete: *Oh man, yes, yes, yes, yes. Here he is. A number one customer. Yes sir.*

Mr. Welles: *Good morning, sir, and what can we do for the young man from Westgate Street today?*

Me: *A trim, Mr. Welles.*

Mr. Welles: *Right you are, young man.*

Pete: *Whoa, whoa, let's slow things down a bit. James, what about the procedure? We've been following that for a long time.*

Ellis: *Yes sir, the procedure. Let's get that coin out. We've got to flip to see who's going to cut this boy's good hair. Goddamn, look at it. Man, you're so damn lucky.*

Mr. Welles: *You don't know how lucky you are.*

Me:

Ellis: *More than luck—you're blessed. That's more like it.*

Pete: *Shoot, it's a miracle, not to have nigger hair. Damn, that's what I call it. A miracle. You got hair just like a white man, and you don't even have to do anything to it. No conk, no grease, no hot comb, no nothing. Hair, just as silky smooth like a white man's. There will be no busting combing teeth today on some no-good nappy nigger hair. Damn, that's beautiful.*

Me:

Mr. Welles: *You certainly are fortunate. It does feel nice.*

Ellis: *A quarter will do.*

Mr. Welles: *OK, two rounds of heads and tails. You do the flipping young man. You are going to certify, that means pick out, who gets their chance to cut and groom that hair on the top of your head. You ready?*

Me:

Ellis: *OK, Jim, that takes care of you. I see you coming my way. One more flip, OK?*

Me:

Ellis: *There you go, just like the man in the coffin, dead in there. You two guys, stick with your naps and Brillo. This is going to be like cutting Miss Clairol's hair compared to what we usually get. You ready?*

Me:
Ellis: Pete, come here, you have to feel it before I cut it. Goddamn,
Sweet screaming Jesus, a Negro with hair like that. People would do a
lot to have what you have natural.

This was a performance. It never varied. There was the mathematical certainty that the honor of cutting my hair would be divided by chance among Pete, Ellis, and Mr. Welles. I never realized the painful machinations that were being inflicted there, by them, on me, on themselves. The self-loathing. It bothered me since I didn't really know what they were saying half the time.

One time they were making fun of an old man. I can't remember why. He was a character who they felt was ripe for a flailing, Apollo style. He was returning their arrows with an elder statesman's wisdom and language. He relied on his oratory skills more than his capacity to move, twirl, and whirl. He was an old man. I watched in the mirror since my back was to all of the customers. I watched the entire scene in that big wall of mirrors that stretched the full length of the barbershop.

The argument reached some sort of crescendo. Despite the rising voices, yells and shouts, there was a sense of decorum that was maintained. No real swearing, just classic boasting, and bragging. It finally happened. He had won. The old man, through his knowledge of old stories, language, puns, and other linguistic barbs had won. I do not know what he said, but it quieted Jim, Ellis, and Pete. He had a satisfied look on his face. Three against one in a real playing of the dozens, and still he had triumphed.

My eyes were no longer on the reflection since the play was over. The drama had run its course. I went back to my mundane eight-year-old thoughts. But at that point, Ellis, in a dramatic gesture so adroitly executed that it seemed practiced, made a move to the floor of the barbershop. He gathered as much of my shorn hair into a dustpan as possible. He shoved the dustpan right into the old man's face. He shouted, "That might be true, nigger, but you'll never have hair like this."

At that word, the hurtful word, I looked up quickly into that mirror. The old man's face was no longer triumphant. That had all been erased. He looked up at the ceiling. No tears came, but I think they would have if he hadn't had the tin ceiling to look into. All those zigzag tin patterns comforted him since they let him bypass what was directly in front of him.

Pete added his rejoinder, "That's right, nigger—never in a million years will you have hair like this. No matter what you do, you will never have that hair. Don't ever forget that. *You will never, ever, have hair like that. That's one thing that we know.*"

Me:

Home Alone

I HEARD MY father cry once and that was enough. I'm still haunted by the piercing shrieks that went through the bowels of our semiattached home with a driveway and a garage in the back. He howled on this weekday. I know it was a weekday because I was home from school, and he was home from work, a chronic condition for him. He was home so much that I was accustomed to spending a great deal of time with his presence. If I were sick or if there was a school holiday, whatever plans I had to play, fantasize, going to faraway places, those plans were torn asunder with my discovery of someone being in the house after my mother had left for work. Yeah, there was someone downstairs. My brother had taken off for some nefarious activity with his comrades. My mother was taking the Q5A from Springfield Gardens to Hillside Avenue to catch the E or F train to Manhattan, or New York, as we residents of Queens defined our relationship to the greatest metropolis in the world.

So the house was empty except for him. It's hard to describe his movement. I think because he was more intellectual than physical. What I mean is that some people exist in your head by the way they walk, how they hold themselves so erectly that they possess more than who they are; their carriage is who they are. My old man, it was all in his head. When you looked at him, you knew that you were in the presence of someone who was thinking and dwelling in some abstract world far off, distant and remote. The glasses: that was it too. Any time he had those black-framed glasses on I knew he was there in the world of thought, thinking, reading, thinking, digesting, wondering.

That day, that weekday, he was human, more human than I ever knew him to be. He scared me. There's nothing that will scare a kid more than hearing his parents cry. That's how simple it is. The person who is responsible for your well-being, your protection, your nurturing and welfare, has a mission. To be there always, no matter what the circumstances. My father violated that principle one time and one time only and it haunts me now. It has echoed in my mind for forty years. That shriek. That cry. That howl. That humanity. That need. That pain.

There I was, upstairs in the room with two windows that I shared with my brother, reading. No other activity would have been permitted with my father in the house since we were prohibited from watching television on weekdays. You could listen to music and the radio as much as you desired. But no television, the one thing I longed to do. Reading and listening to the phone ring. For years you had to listen for the phone downstairs since that was the only one in the house. You would listen and run downstairs "like a herd of elephants" as my mom would say and try to catch it before the caller gave up. I heard it ring, way down there. My father picked it up, and I heard nothing audible, just human sounds of back and forth. I went back to my book.

I heard him laugh and the sounds of more bantering with the anonymous caller and everything seemed normal or all right. The joking stopped. The bantering slowed down. The call was over. I could go back to my book completely. Then a word that I could decipher, *please*. It was loud enough to hear it in my room. A *please* with a plea to it, not the way an adult should talk to anyone. Adults never have to say *please* like that. Only kids talk that way when they really need something or are afraid of something that seems to be one and the same.

Stanley: Please, Jack, look I'll do anything, anything, I swear. What do you want me to do?
Jack:
Stanley: Jack, please, I swear I'll do anything.
Jack:
Stanley: Jack, please, for God's sake, what do you want out of me? I'll do anything. You name it; I'll do it. Please, I'll beg. I am begging you.
Jack:
Stanley: Jack, that was twenty years ago. Jack, you're talking about

things from before World War II. That's how long ago that was. Jack, it's 1961.

Jack:

Stanley: *Jack, PLEASE, I'M BEGGING YOU. PLEASE LET ME WORK. I'LL DO ANYTHING. PLEASE, OH GOD, THIS IS THE WORST THING THAT HAS EVER HAPPENED TO ME. PLEASE, OH GOD, JACK, LET ME WORK. I HAVE TO FEED MY FAMILY. PLEASE, THAT'S ALL I'M ASKING TO DO. LET ME WORK. LET ME WORK AGAIN. PLEASE, JUST LET ME WORK.*

Jack:

Then this howl began, this long wailing shriek that just sounded like one word with tears and a bellowing enunciation to it. It was a long *ah* that just went on and on, up and up, louder and louder, like a Louis Armstrong glissando on one of his famous histrionic trumpet solos. I got scared and sat upright on the side of the bed. My beat-up Keds were planted squarely on the floor with fear and my hands gripped the edge of the bed with fear and terror. Something was wrong. Why was my Dad asking this man to work? Why was he begging a man to work? What magical and mysterious things were going on that I could not understand? Why was he crying? And finally that howl of pain. Was he hurt physically? That is what it sounded like. Like someone was putting him in pure physical pain and there was something excruciatingly long and tortuous about it.

The call was over but the wailing continued. No words, no, just wailing. I was perfectly frozen and now realized that the most difficult part of this morning was coming down on my head in a few seconds. What was I going to do? Did he know I was home? I had automatically assumed that there was no way he would have done that if he had known that someone else was in the house. Maybe he forgot that kids didn't have to go to school on this particular holiday (he always assumed that school should never be closed except for Thanksgiving or Christmas and he had objections about the extra days attached to those holidays—one day was enough). How the heck could I hide myself? I was good at hiding but this was going to be a masterful feat of deception. My specialty of silence was going to be drawn upon and exercised.

I was so frightened that he would find out that there was a witness to his failure. Even if I didn't know what it meant (*Just let me work*) I had heard the other stuff. This man was scared of something. There was something going on that was bigger and tougher than he was. I did not know what that was either but it was gigantic. I was there. I was present for some special event in his life and I had heard the words *the worst thing that has ever happened to me*. Silence. Quiet. Stillness.

I quickly constructed a plan of action, or better said, inaction. Without getting up I knew I had to close the door of my room that opened to the hallway at the top of the stairs. He would come up. He could not stay downstairs forever. The only bathroom was next to my room. He would be here on this floor. It was just a matter of time. I raised myself on my hands that were planted alongside my hips. I picked myself up and moved down the bed, taking care that when I let myself down each time I did not allow the bedsprings to creak. Now the door seemed a thousand miles away because of this slow and laborious manner of movement. The bed was elongated. I moved in this lateral fashion, very slowly and methodically, like an athlete, a gymnast who has to use the rings in the sitting position and just hold himself perfectly still. Rise up, swing legs to the left, the same motion that a wheelchair-bound person employs when getting from the bed into the chair. Rise up, swing legs to the left, making sure never to let my sneakers hit the floor.

After about six repetitions of this exercise, I was at the end of the bed and leaned over and pushed the door closed, not locking it or closing it tightly. I left it ajar enough since we never locked our bedroom doors, just closed them and trusted. A door shut tightly would have betrayed my presence.

With the door closed, I breathed easier but this was just the beginning of my ordeal. Now I had to figure out how long I could remain silent and what if he came up the stairs and remembered that the door was not closed when he went down to the kitchen. A lot for an eight-year-old kid to think about. I reached down and felt around beneath my bed. That's where my brother and I preserved our library of books, comic books mostly, since my old man did not permit comics, not even Marvel Classics, which were Cliffs Notes versions of great literature with illustrations. I moved my hand furtively since I did not wish to knock over a whole pile of books; that would be heard. I could tell by the binding when I hit something memorable and appropriate: The

Hardy Boys Series, *A Figure in Hiding.* Yeah, that was me, a kid in hiding.

I opened it up and thought about the story, my two stalwart heroes, Joe and Frank Hardy who were out there someplace in Long Island, having adventures, following and tracking down criminals with a little help from their father. Here I was, not on an official adventure, but plenty of terror and I didn't have to leave my house. Paul and I always envied Joe and Frank because they had a cool boat called *The Sleuth* and a hot rod jalopy. They drove to high school, went to the malt shop, knew a few girls and hung out with their friends a lot but still did their homework and got good grades in school. Yeah, this was a life to fantasize and envy. There was nothing bad about the Hardy Boys; my brother Paul said there was a dark side to Joe and Frank Hardy, but I defended them to the death. Yet I did have some doubts. Every now and then I would see that expression, *nigger in a woodpile,* and think it was a printing mistake. Paul told me gleefully that the Hardy boys were racists one day, the day he first found the fated words. I looked at it carefully and was positive that the writer meant *Negro in a woodpile.* It was baffling for a few reasons. First, how could that word appear in a book written for American kids? Number two, what did it mean, *nigger in a woodpile?* Why would a Negro stay, live, or hide in a woodpile? What benefit would there be to dwelling in a woodpile in any circumstance? My response to my brother was that it was a printing mistake and Franklin W. Dixon would never use such language.

Creaking steps—my old man was coming up the steps. He had to go to the bathroom, find something in his bedroom, do something upstairs. It didn't matter. He was coming up the steps, and they were creaking under his weight and he was climbing very slowly. I closed the book (no more time for niggers in woodpiles) and thought about the present predicament heading up the staircase. I had to just be perfectly quiet.

At the top of the stairs, I could tell from the sound of his shoes that he was bearing right, which meant that he would head into the bathroom, and that he would definitely close the door behind him. All I had to do was tiptoe past that white bathroom door while it was closed, head downstairs (not like a herd of elephants) and get my coat off the hook in the pantry and boom, out the back door and disappear down the driveway. Just tiptoe.

The door closed. I heard the toilet seat raised. That was the sign for my break for freedom. I hesitated. There were still two choices. The noise from urine going into a toilet was good cover but not quite as effective as the toilet being flushed. I decided to wait for the most propitious moment, one toilet, one flush. That would make all the difference this morning, this day. I listened for the urine. It ended. The handle was pushed down, and I made my escape.

Old Man's Trains and Planes

IT'S A SUNDAY in the late 1950s, and my old man is feeling inventive and creative. He asks my brother and me if we want to have some fun. This word is used so infrequently that we're not quite sure what it means or what is involved. Fun. What sort of fun? And is it my father's notion of fun, which means to study, read and study and discuss things? We take a chance and enthusiastically yell, "Yes, sure, yeah, let's go." He says that he'll have to get dressed but we're accustomed to that. He's dressed up on Saturdays and Sundays; he always wears a sport jacket or suit when he goes on small errands. He's had years to train us, especially with his weekly excursions to Aqueduct and Belmont Park. Then, of course, he is well dressed, impeccable: raincoat, Bogey fedora, shirt and tie. As he gets dressed for this fun excursion, we run upstairs and tell our mother in a blithering-idiot manner that we're "Gonna have some fun with Dad. Bye!" She's happy. She wants us out of the house, and we have been pretty sour kids now since the television has not been working for months. They're happy, and we're insane but we find plenty of friends to go to see an occasional football game or some other sporting event.

From my mom's room we fly into a room adjacent to hers but separated by a linen closet; it has two windows with a bunk bed. There are two dressers, one new, one old. My brother and I put on our school clothes, which are pretty dressy, considering it's only a Sunday drive. Sneakers are tossed off and black and brown shoes come on. I hate black shoes and demand insanely that I will not wear black shoes under any circumstances. My mother has given up because it is not important

52

to her. As long as we're warm, that's the extent of her involvement in our clothing. I'm dressed first and out of the door down the steps to the living room and my father grabs me with a "Whoa, cowboy, aren't you going to tuck that shirt in?" I mash the shirt in between the suspenders and that's good enough. My brother already wears belts and looks sharp coming down the stairs. My father smiles and says, "Very good, very good."

Outside in the driveway is his 1956 Studebaker Champion with a new engine. He put it in himself, and we watched and helped. The engine came in a wooden crate from a brown truck. I was there that day and watched the deliveryman help my father carry it up the driveway. It sat in the garage for a long time. I asked my father when the car was going to be fixed many times. "When I have time, partner, when I have time." The engine stays in the garage for about a year, and every now and then he asks me if I want to help him so the engine won't freeze. It's the summer and I know already certain patterns of the physical world. Things do not freeze in the summer, even in that place that is thinking about becoming America, called Alaska.

"Pop, I don't think things can freeze in the summer."

"Oh, yes they can, kid. Yes, they can."

"But Pop, for something to freeze it has to be cold degrees outside. Right now, these are hot degrees."

He doesn't answer my observation but says we have to go down in the basement to get some tools. Our basement is a craftsman's dream come true. My father built a workbench with a ten-inch radial saw, his pride and joy, at the right end. All of his tools are placed in order on a piece of plywood that is mounted to the wall above the bench. Screwdrivers, hammers, drill bits, tap and die sets, tools that have no meaningful names to me, all clean and shiny. Next to the workbench on the left is a six-foot stand of shelves that hold all of his car repair tools from his days as an automotive mechanic. Ratchets, drivers, sockets, reducers, more tools, which have no names but are fascinating to hold and touch but we are not allowed to do either. We touch and play with them when he is not home, and we always remember to take them out one at a time since this is the only sure method of knowing which size holder held a certain tool. The basement is also the place of punishment. Here we are ordered on occasion to wait for our *discipline*. Three whacks with the strap is the standard punishment for the standard offense. I've already figured out that if you obey the rules, you'll only get three licks here and there and that's because you made a mistake. My brother has already figured out that it doesn't really matter how many whacks he gets; nothing can stop him from misbehaving, violating my father's rules, talking back to both my mom and dad, and hating himself.

"Carry this socket; you're in charge of this socket, one-and-one-half-inch socket."

"Pop, you're forgetting the torch blower. I mean, blowtorch. Remember, the freezing?"

"No, we won't need the torch. Come on. Let's go through the cellar steps. It's faster." I'm scared of this part of the basement because it is the darkest part. My brother claims that a little man lives in the corner and is liable to leap out at any time if you're by yourself. This seed has been planted and grown into a full-fledged specter in my head. Hardly any light ever gets back from my father's work area; there is just a little radiance from one lone bulb that's way in the back. I don't even like the word *cellar* because it rhymes with the word *hell*. My old man opens the basement door that leads to concrete steps. I don't like these steps either because I slipped and fell on them one day playing hide-and-seek and hit my chin dead on. No teeth were lost, but I had a bruise that lasted forever. I stay close, almost crashing into my father's legs because I don't like that feeling of being left behind in the basement. Unfastening a homemade lock consisting of wood, and a nut and a bolt, he raises two arms straight up, pushes those two wooden doors open, and then light from the sun comes right through, and I breathe easy.

"So Dexter, that's what I mean when I use the word *freeze* in regard to motors. Do you understand?"

"Huh?"

"Don't say 'huh.'"

"Pop, I was thinking of something."

"I can see."

"I was."

"OK, take it easy. When an engine freezes, that means that the oil had not done its job and the metal is sticking together so tightly, that the little parts will never move again. Like ice. If we turn this crankshaft, every now and then, this engine will never freeze."

We turned that crankshaft with a giant socket and a ratchet as long as a policeman's billy club, and my father has a special vocabulary for us anytime he desires our help. The instructions from the garage to the basement are always explicit. He mentions every turn, curve, left and right, up and down. These directions always end in exquisite details like, "The biggest screwdriver that has a chip on the yellow handle." Or, "Get the hammer that doesn't have a cat's claw on the end. You'll see the difference when you look at both of them." Or, "A Phillips screwdriver looks like a star—it has points on it." My brother and I are his most appreciative audience since he allows and encourages us to learn everything about cars, carpentry, plumbing, and electricity. "You guys don't want to be bums when you grow up, right? That's why I'm showing you all these skills. Whatever you do, you have to be able to take care of yourself and your family, if you ever have one."

We know patience because putting a new engine in a 1956 Studebaker Champion is an epic production. We watch entire Saturday mornings blur into Saturday afternoons and our little friends say the words, *Still busy?* so much that it becomes one sound after a while. We're covered with grease; our foreheads have that streak that was casually rubbed on while we were watching and thinking about nothing. We are amazed the first time our old man pours gasoline on our hands and the dirt and grime magically disappear. My favorite job is tool and part cleaner. I am handed nuts, bolts, tools, things that are wheels with hard edges that must be cleaned. By making one, ten, maybe fifty trips to the basement for tools, gaskets, nuts, open-end wrenches, closed-end wrenches, snap-on sockets, we feel like we understand this world. When my brother is eleven and I'm eight, we feel a kinship with the world of machines and cars already. We learn that sloppiness and negligence can in no way be tolerated. Some of the tools are used just to measure inches and millimeters and carelessness is frowned upon. These weekends never stop and our friends like to watch. The jobs on the various used cars are never over but it is inevitable that the days draw to a close with coming darkness. My brother, with a genuine air of concern, mentions that we should put the tools away.

"Dad, don't you think we should put the tools away? Someone might steal them."

"Paul, don't worry. Negroes don't steal tools."

"Dad, the neighborhood is changing. Some of my friends . . ."

My ears have perked up because I've heard a word that is important. Negroes are the new people who are moving into the neighborhood. I've heard about them but mostly in phone conversations at night during dinner. The phone will ring, and my mother will answer it, rushing from the dining room to the kitchen. It's not a pleasant conversation and even the quips I hear mean nothing. "Mrs. Kellogg, this is Mrs. Diaz; don't you understand that if we don't stand together, the neighborhood will go. He's offering you a low price, and he will charge the Negro a higher price, and the real estate agent is in a no-lose situation." I don't know what this means, but my mother always returns to the dining room table perturbed and sad. My father doesn't ask what's happened. She just says, "another one moving out" and my father seems to know what this code means.

"Paul, there's nothing to worry about. Spooks don't steal."

"Dad, you don't know what's going on."

"Look, Paul, Negroes don't steal tools."

My brother is holding his own and doing all he can to maintain a rational conversation with a man who is really not rational.

"Dad, anyone can steal."

My brother's last comment makes the most sense. I'm not even sure what these words mean: *spooks, Negroes, spooks, Negroes.*

"Let me tell you something, Paul. Spooks don't steal tools; if they did, they would have to go to work and that's what they're trying to avoid. Stealing tools and going to work is the last thing on their mind. Most of these southern Negroes, they're right out of the cotton field. They don't even know what a ratchet is for. Let's go get some dinner." With this he laughs to himself, and we're quiet. I start to ask my brother what this means, but he waves me off. He's not going to explain. He can't explain.

The day the 1956 Champion is finally started for the first time, the whole neighborhood knows about it. We're finally dismantling the wooden hoist that's held the block and tackle in the middle of the driveway so long that it looks like some piece of modern art. It's a Saturday morning; the V-8 without exhaust manifolds roars and bellows and a few neighbors walk up our driveway and shake my father's hand. Everyone is showing pride and respect. My old man calls us over and says that Paul and I helped, and he would have never finished without us. He's installed a starter button so no key is required, and Mr. King admires this. The motor is cut off and the shouting ends and normal conversations resume. We take Sunday drives in the car, and this is going to be one of them.

We're all sitting on the front seat. The leather interior is red and the place where the radio should go just has a piece of metal there with the letters, R-A-D-I-O. We back down the driveway, and my brother has to move a bit as my father's arm comes across the front seat for a better view of the driveway. We move down Westgate Street toward 140th Avenue and my father says, "Feel that?" We're both baffled and don't know what he wants us to hear. He doesn't tease us more than one more stop sign. "That's a V-8, a lot of power in the motor and it's not even broken in yet."

I'm hoping too that the engine is not broken in; that would be a terrible thing for the motor to be in the car only a few days and for it to break.

"Fellas, trains or planes. What's it's going to be? Planes or trains?"

My brother and I smile at each other. This is going to be a great ride. Our father has just offered us our favorite activities, watching the planes take off from Idlewild Airport or driving over to the Sunnyside railroad yards to view the trains as they are cleaned, inspected, and switched from one engine to another. Passenger cars of all types are being serviced there before delivery back to their current scheduled runs. I whisper, *Trains* to my brother, he nods his head, and I talk first.

"Pop, Sunnyside yards, maybe we'll see a GG1 getting its trucks greased."

My father turns to me and says, "You recall that expression." I answer incoherently since I don't know what this means. All I did was copy an expression that I heard his friend the train mechanic use. Anthony, his friend, who lets us get right up into the cabs of the trains, said this the last time we were there. As he put a new bulb in the largest flashlight in the world, he had said, "Hey Stan, gotta grease the trucks on that GG1 electric." I just remembered. I have a good memory.

We drive toward Long Island City, and my brother tries to get me to laugh when he whispers something about the Sunnyside Arena where wrestling matches take place with men with names like Bobo Brazil and Bruno Samantino. I start to giggle and try to conceal it because my father hates it when we "horse around" in the car, especially on the front seat, right next to him. I control my urge to laugh as I think of more names: Haystack Calhoun, Buddy Rogers, and Gorilla Monsoon. We get to the yards without any outburst. As we drive from Springfield Gardens to Long Island City, I keep track of all the construction that is occurring as Robert Moses massacres and improves New York simultaneously. We start to see the factories with steady clouds of steam coming out of them even on a Sunday. My brother and I are thrilled as we watch the neon signs that reveal the type of activity that goes on within these large fortress buildings. Swingline Staplers has a giant stapler that keeps on stapling, up and down, up and down, up and down. It's easy to figure out what Eagle Electric sign means; they have a big eagle that keeps on waving his wings on top of the factory building. Silvercup Bakery is obvious. Giant letters show us our favorite bread that comes in wax paper, and if you put Miracle Whip between two pieces of it, and nothing else, you've got one of the most wonderful sandwiches in the world. We're excited and sitting on the edge of the front seat, and we haven't even arrived at the main attraction yet.

Even though Long Island City is relatively empty on Sunday with every factory on a reduced schedule, the Sunnyside yards are bustling with activity. Men with lanterns walk from one track to another. Some casually stand on the last car, foot hooked nonchalantly in the last rung of a ladder, waving the engineer on, getting him closer and closer to the car that they are going to couple with. He signals that they are very close but no matter how slow the train is finally going, the crash is shattering. Crashing sounds come from all over the yard. It does sound like bombs going off. The passenger trains that have been washed inside and out shine and glisten. The Pullman cars are made out of steel cars so they will reflect the sun. We are dazzled by the light and the noise, and my father has left us alone to go and look for Anthony, or Tony.

We can stay on the overpass that straddles the entire yard and gives someone the impression that they are watching a movie in the latest craze to hit movie theaters; 70mm Panavision. My father told my brother, "Two places, the overpass or the old roundhouse. Don't come near those tracks, you understand? I'm going to look for Anthony, I mean, Tony." Looking down, we realize that this is better than TV or the movies or playing army in the "Woody-Woods." We both place our arms on the railing so we can rest our heads and just look and watch and look. We stay there until over the cacophony of noise we hear my father's "retrieval" whistle, which means that we better come running on the double after the second call. We look down into the yard, and he's standing near a man in overalls with an engineer's cap. We run to the end of the overpass and start heading down the stairs, as quickly as we can. My brother yells something at me, and the next thing I know he jumps the last third of the steps without hesitation. I'll never catch up, but on the next set I jump and skip the last quarter of the steps.

Anthony and my father wave us over once we hit the bottom of the yard. My father puts his arms around us and says, "What do you think, Anthony. Handsome, right?" While lighting a cigarette, Anthony nods his head a few times, and out from behind the smoke we hear him say, "Beautiful, beautiful boys. Look at 'em! Hey, whatta you guys want to do today? Get up in the cab or check out a caboose?" The words *caboose* and *cab* are shouted in unison so much that Anthony playfully puts his hands over his ears like he's going deaf. We smile and my father says, "Take it easy, fellas. Take it easy." He turns to Anthony and as he lights his Pall Mall, he points to a caboose that is only a few yards away and says, "Anthony, put 'em up right there. That way we can watch and talk."

Anthony bends down to talk to Paul, tells him something, and Paul smiles. As we walk away from them toward the Pennsylvania caboose, I also hear Anthony say, "Stan, that was a good tip you gave me 'bout the eighth race at Jamaica. Those balloons really came pouring in." We keep walking since there is nothing that Anthony and my father could ever talk about that would be more interesting than examining an old caboose up close. We climb up the stairs, and as I start to spin the emergency brake wheel, my brother almost shouts, "No, I'll tell Anthony. He said, 'Don't touch anything.'" I'm agreeable and understand that this is a very extraordinary privilege. Opening the door, we're both surprised at how neat and bare the cabin is. In the middle of the cabin there is a stove and on it, it says CHUBBY. This evokes laughter, as we think of fat kids in our classes, but we quiet down out of respect for Anthony. Next to the stove there is a black bucket with black rocks. My brother sees that I don't understand and he says, "Coal, dumb-dumb. That's how they get the stove going."

"I know what coal is. It makes heat."

"Well, you didn't know when you first looked at it. That's the truth."
Besides the centerpiece stove that burns coal with a coffeepot on top, we

look at the beds, bunk, and start to fantasize about living in the caboose. It would be so great. You can have your own house; it's on wheels and you get to go to places all around the United States.

"Paul, do you think we can get this job someday?"

"Sure, you don't have to be really smart for this job. It's a good job. I think these guys make a lot of money and you're in the union, for life. Anytime you're in the union for life, you've got it made."

"That's the kind of job I want. I would work all day and then climb up that little ladder and go to sleep. Hey, where do you go to the bathroom?"

"I don't know. Must be a little bathroom in the corner. Yeah, right there. You see that little curtain? That must be it."

"Paul, how come Negroes don't steal?"

"I don't know. I don't even know if that's true."

"I was going to say what you said, that everyone steals."

"Dex, Dad says things which are, which are . . ."

"What do you mean?"

"I can't explain it."

We continue looking in the caboose and like the vantage point of being able to see Anthony and my father talking, and because we're in the caboose, we're higher than they are.

About ten years later we're taking long drives on Saturdays, but we're not going to see trains or planes. We're accompanying my father as he pursues playing the horses. The rides are packed with tension from start to finish since my brother is developing the most recalcitrant traits imaginable. Heroin is his master, and he and my old man have a lot in common. They're slaves to things that they hope will bring about some sort of peace. Driven, obsessed, and mad to a certain degree, I now see the bond between them and why they hate each other so much. They've both taken stances that leave them in one head-on confrontation after another. My father is more irrational in his maniacal analysis of black people. As his own life starts to assume its natural decline in his late fifties and early sixties, he possesses no real strategies for adapting to the new world around him. As laws change and social and economic opportunities are open to American blacks for the first time, he can't grasp why there are no real demonstrable positive reactions in Springfield

Gardens, Queens, or New York City, for that matter. He searches for corrections on a macro scale in regard to the historic position of the Negro people in the United States; on the micro level, he longs for Paul to alter his course. He mentions Congressional laws and Supreme Court decisions and can't fathom why my brother is not making any progress, why his friends are mostly strung-out junkies who fear my father enough that even when they make an appearance at 137-78 Westgate Street, they straighten themselves out. If their noses are running, they stop sniffling. The urge to scratch their crotch area loses its urgency. Junkies roll down their sleeves so the telltale tracks are temporarily hidden. My father surveys them after they knock on the door and enter. They tense up, and my father suspects some type of criminal activity, but his guess is way off the mark. I can't fault him because I'm more than stupid. I'm so involved with political romance that at least my dad suspects some criminal activity having to do with automobiles and theft. Not bad. Me, when I see my brother stealing eggs from the back of the store, I compliment him and his companion, Carlos.

"Great, this is just what we need for the next demonstration."

"What the fuck are you talking about?"

As I talked they kept relaying the crates of eggs—144 in a gross—like soldiers passing ammunition boxes.

"Paul, I mean, we can use those for the next demonstration." Carlos is a good-natured guy and smiles. My brother is malevolent, crafty and crude, and most of all guilty, and has nothing pleasant to say in response to my inanities.

"Look, why don't you get the fuck out of here? What are you doing here anyway?"

"Man, you're a real jerk. All I said was we could use these for the next demonstration. I'm getting tired of the right-wing guys who are always on the other side of the street, throwing crap at us. Tomatoes, eggs, paper bags filled with shit."

"So, Dex, you really think that's why we're taking these eggs, for an anti-Vietnam War demonstration. Man, you're really fuckin' stupid."

He was right. I thought that my enthusiasm for politics, cultivated by my mother and father during the civil rights movement, had already grabbed his soul because he was older and had been to even more demonstrations. Paul had accompanied my mother to the most famous one, the March on Washington, Martin Luther King Jr., August 1963. I missed it. My compensation was to be there at the first anti-Vietnam War demonstration, Washington, 1965. But I was wrong. There was no commitment to political activism, just small-time crime, and being a hooligan. Carlos and Paul were robbing an old man's store and his eggs so they could get a little pocket change, no more, no less. I thought my brother might care that the old man was a Negro. He would have laughed at that the way he mocked my notions about the demonstration.

There we were in the car again, heading to Washington but not for a demonstration. My mom goes to D.C. for demonstrations in the1960s. My father knows that the tracks in the Washington, D.C. area are open during winter for thoroughbred racing. Sometimes he wants us to be with him and sometimes I think he really wants someone to split the driving. My brother has his license first and loves to drive. I like to ride and look forward to driving someday. I know how to fix cars and am anxious to buy one. I save my money from Higby's Dry Cleaning store and sit in the back of the Newport, jealous that my brother can already take possession of this big, red convertible with a black top.

We come out of the Holland Tunnel and really start to roll down the New Jersey Turnpike. My father pulls over at the first rest stop and asks us if we want anything. My brother accepts a cup of coffee, but I don't drink coffee and just stay in the car with Paul. My old man returns with two cups of piping hot coffee in those little gray cardboard trays, and for a second I'm reminded of the eggs. I look at the back of my brother's neck and smile as I review the stockpile of all the crimes he's ever committed that are either unknown to him or the rest of the world. It's a good thing to have for backup, a whole tally of misdemeanors and felonies. He's tougher but I'm smarter and ruthless and never feel threatened by him once we are teenagers. He can be undone and I know that. Looking to his right as my father knocks on the window, he slides over as my father motions that it's his time to get in the driver's seat. My old man gets in and closes the door. He hands him the keys.

"Paul, look, keep it between 65 and 70. For me 68 is the perfect speed and she likes it. Got it?"

"Yeah, I got it."

"OK, remember, this car is a big cruiser and the speed can really creep up on you. So, be careful."

My brother is so sullen that he doesn't speak and I like it when he's quiet. Everything that comes out of his mouth is ugly and mean. Sometimes I give him a break because I figure it's the heroin that's eating him and reducing him to a skeletal existence. Yet, it's hard to hear him disrespect my father. We drive, and I'm still in the back, and my old man is on the front seat with his *Morning Telegraph*. I ball myself into the back right-hand corner. It's December and even though the car has plenty of heat, it's just a cold day. We're really rolling.

"Paul, I thought I told you to try and keep it between 65 and 70."

"Dad, I was. I was doing 70."

"You're a goddamn liar. You were just going 75."

"OK, Pop, I'll slow it down. Like you said, it got faster without me noticing it."

"OK, take it easy. You have to drive safely."

Whenever I watched the two of them, it was like being in the theater and watching not only the same performance, but also the same scene with the same actors, night after night. After being a guilty onlooker and voyeur, at the age of seventeen, I can predict what they will say, how the course of the argument will proceed and how it will climax. Because I'm in the back, I mouth word for word what they will say a second or two before their human voices give voice to their inhumanity.

"Paul, what the hell is wrong with you? Twenty minutes ago, I told you to take it easy. Now you're going 80, 80 goddamn miles an hour."

"Pop, I have to tell you something. The person driving the car is the person . . ."

"Would you slow it back down to 65, goddamn it to hell."

My brother slows it down to the speed limit of 65, and my father is not as angry. It could stay like this and we could make the rest of the trip in silence. But my brother won't have it nor can he have it any other way. He starts to talk with that high junkie nasal pitch that he has when this stuff is traveling through his brain. "Dad, I was just trying to say something real important," comes out like he's talking through a piece of wax paper. The air is vibrating between him and my father and I shut my eyes.

"Paul, what are you trying to tell me? Is it about the horses?"

"No, I'm just telling you, the person driving the car is the person who is in charge of the car."

"What?"

"Dad, the person driving the car, in this case it's me, even though I'm not the owner, is not only in charge of the driving, but no one else can tell him how to drive, when he's driving, even the owner."

I roll myself up into even a tighter ball. This is junkie logic, the same logic that dictates you robbing your own house, your own family. There is no bottom line—a junkie can even strike a few rungs below "the ends justifies the means." I wait in silence and keep my eyes shut.

"Pull the car over. Pull the goddamn car over right now."

"Pop, what's wrong? I'm going 65 like you said, even less than 70."

My father turns toward him and now roars, "Pull the sonofabitching car over to the shoulder, right now."

My brother puts on the blinker and starts to nose the car over. With both hands at ten and two he expertly brings the car to a nice stop on the shoulder of the New Jersey Turnpike and for safety, nudges it over a few more inches so the big trucks will clear it with a large margin for error. He shifts into PARK and waits.

"Get the hell out of the car."

My brother opens the door, gets out, and reaches in for his coat. The door is closed gently because he does have a respect for some machines. My father slides over to the steering wheel. I've had my eyes closed all the time. I hear the buttons of my father sports coat hit the metal rim of the horn as he puts his hands in the ten and two position. I hear the car shift into DRIVE and know that my brother is still walking around the back of the car. A 1967 Chrysler is a long car. You can count the seconds it takes to get around it. With the car in DRIVE, it starts to move forward and I hear a little surprised *Hey* and know that we're moving and he's staying. The little blinker starts to blink and I know that we're getting ready to enter the turnpike. I open my eyes after keeping them shut all that time and look at the speedometer: thirty, forty, fifty, sixty, sixty-five. We're rolling. My old man is shaking his head. We are in traffic, and my old man heads for the median that is for cars only, no trucks. The speedometer is right on sixty-eight. There's nothing to say.

"Dex, I had to leave him. He's crazy."

"I know, Pop."

"Dex, he's really crazy. I had to leave him."

"Pop, I know. I know what you had to do."

"Your brother's turning into a real spook. He just wants to be like his spook friends. Got some sort of investment in being a geechie. I don't understand it."

"Pop, yeah. I understand what you're saying."

"Dex, in a little while I'll pull over so you can sit up front; it's warmer."

"Thanks, Pop. That'll be nice."

Dick and Jane See Spot Run

"Two, FOUR, SIX, eight, we don't want to integrate; two, four, six, eight, we don't want to integrate. Two, four, six, eight . . ." September 1962. A yellow school bus with eight Negro children. Outside the bus is a sea of parents with signs, placards, some on sticks so they can be shoved right up to the windows of the bus. Others are handheld and wave flimsily in the air. The bus driver keeps the door closed, not sure as to what he should do. He doesn't know what to do with his human cargo but opening the door is not an option. We look out the windows. Each of us has one because we're only eight so we don't have to crowd. We can get right up there and see what awaits.

The women, they are mostly women with a few men, are adamant. "Two, four, six, eight" is just abstract enough and cute enough that we don't quite understand what they want from us. But when the school bus windows are pulled down, things are made clear. When a woman sees your visage and says, "Go home, we don't want you here Milky Way. Chocolate Bar, get the hell out of here," you know that you are not welcome. My favorite foods were being used to degrade me. New names come my way and my dictionary expands quickly.

"Sambo, we don't want you here."

"Negroes go home, Negroes go home, Negroes go home."

"Hershey Bars are no good."

Back to the chocolate theme.

I look out the window to the left, toward the entrance and just as my father had predicted, someone is there to protect us. One police car, that's all. Doesn't seem enough against those odds. They are standing outside the car, arms folded, tall, but not doing anything. It would be nice if they would take a few steps closer to the bus and move these people away. But no, they stand there.

We are scared: Arthur Roberts, George Allan, Helen Travers, Alonzo Jordan, Olin Phillips, Howard Aikens, Joyce Galloway, and Dexter Diaz. We are scared enough not to talk but feel secure as long as we are on the bus. I know that worse things can happen. I've seen enough news reports with the kindly Walter Cronkite to know that sometimes they throw stones, rocks, bottles, and garbage. Sometimes they even set the bus on fire. Walter Cronkite is like the police officers. You know he's on your side, but he has to stay on the sidelines until the last second. The only problem is waiting for that last second to come. No one is talking. The seven other kids all know each other because they attended the same public school, from kindergarten through third grade. Months before this September, during the spring of 1962 there was a test administered to them and to me. They got theirs at P.S. 161; mine was given in a small room at P.S. 37, rhymes with 1927, the year the school was built.

I remember the exam because it was made to order, as far as making a young lad feel special. A very competent and official woman came into our third grade room and called off a few names. We walked down the hallway, past the boys' and girls' bathroom, past the white porcelain water fountains and came to a room that you always wondered about. The room was not a classroom. It had the word TESTING on it, but this was a special branch of testing since regular tests with Number 2 pencils and a little hand at the bottom of the booklet saying: STOP. DO NOT TURN THE PAGE UNTIL TOLD were given in regular rooms. This was the secret chamber. We were now in it, and it had a waiting room within the small interior. A few of us sat on chairs. We were told that we were going to be asked a few questions and would wait our turn in alphabetical order. While waiting, we could read the magazines that were in abundant supply, but to please keep quiet. Chills went up our spines.

My name was called sooner than later being pretty close to the beginning of the alphabet, and I jumped up. I walked into the smaller room and sat down next to a kind and intelligent-looking woman with a small batch of papers on her desk. "I would just like to ask you a few questions. I'm going to show you some things, pictures and objects. I want you to answer quickly but clearly. This is a special type of test. It involves only a little bit of writing; it is mostly oral. Do you know what oral means? My first question, and I aced it quickly with, "Yes, oral means to talk, not to write." The reassuring words flowed from her mouth, "Yes, you are correct. That's a good way to start our test."

On the basis of that test and questions about shapes and figures, those seven and I were selected to be the first children to integrate a school in Laurelton, Queens, in the early 1960s. We had a label, which we wore proudly: I.G.C., *intellectually gifted children.* This name was repeated over and over again once we were informed of our impending transfer from our neighborhood schools which in two years had gone from white to black. And with that change, anyone who remained behind was doomed and anyone who got out would have his or her life potentially changed forever. We didn't know it then, but a decree of death was quickly and resolutely being passed over a generation of New York City schools that had successfully served two or three generations of native born and immigrant students. Among those native Yankee and Irish there were blacks. They had reaped the benefits of this fine educational institution as long as they were in the minority. Once that balance tipped, once there were more blacks than whites, those children were slated for a diluted education. These schools had done their jobs for many years. That era was over. Once a school became black at this point, education ceased. A combination of racist teachers and apathetic teachers who were beholden to Daniel Moynihan's theory of leave them alone and they'll either rise or sink, were executing this policy with a vengeance.

My mother tried to explain it to me because I didn't want to be transferred to a new school. I loved my school. My brother went there. It was the perfect walking distance. Coming home to tuna fish sandwiches on toast with a glass of chocolate milk was my idea of heaven. I liked being an I.G.C. kid but didn't want to leave my home. Words like *opportunity* had little or no effect. "You're going to have a better chance there," she said a few times at the dinner table. My mother turned to my father who looked through history, old and contemporary, and put forth a different type of argument. "Dexter, you have a right to go to this school. People have fought for this right and have suffered. You know, like the Jackie Robinson demonstrations?" That set off a key feeling in me. My parents had marched and walked and picketed to ensure that if Branch Rickey wasn't sure of doing the right thing, a few thousand pickets would help him in making that ultimate decision which made Robinson the first Negro in the major leagues.

"You see, you're going to be like Jackie Robinson, the first Negro children to enter an all-white school. You have a right to do this. The U.S. Constitution says this. The Constitution is on your side. What do you think of that?" By this time, my heart had swooned, and I was bedazzled. Shades of Daniel Webster. The *U.S. Constitution* was with me. The Constitution of the United Sates of America was on my side. That's a lot of power. I felt taller, bigger, and all of a sudden staying at P.S. 37 had no appeal at all. I was going to prove something to someone. I had a document, the Supreme Court, Ike, and the 82nd Airborne behind me if necessary. I was going to make history. For once, I would be important.

Maybe that was why I was the first person to pipe up with any authority on the bus that morning. Others had whispered, but I started to talk so others could hear. "Don't worry. Don't worry. They can't do anything to us. What we are doing is legal. They are wrong. We are right. The Constitution says that we can be here. They are wrong. Integration is right. Segregation is wrong." These words came out a little forced because I was scared, but compared to everyone else, they sounded pretty encouraging. The seven kids looked at me and stared. In answer to their silence, I just repeated my speech again, with a few changes and with a different tone. "Look, they do not have the law on their side. We have the law on our side."

There was an affirmative rap on the school bus door and everyone jumped. So far, none of the parents had come into contact with the fragile yellow school bus. Now, with this banging we felt vulnerable. The police had not moved a step. Another rap and the door opened and we all looked to the front of the bus in fear. A hand with freckles moved into the bus. When I saw that the hand was attached to a man with a suit, my fears turned to a neutral kind of hope. The man was about sixty, avuncular looking and asked the driver to close the door when he was at the top of the stairs. The first words out of his mouth to the driver were not *good morning* or *hello* but a command. "I want you to keep this door closed until I tell you to open it. Do you understand?" The bus driver nodded and mentioned something about "the dispatcher didn't mention anything about this to me this morning." The man whom I was later to find out was the principal of the school, Mr. O'Hanlon, also nodded. The driver looked into that giant oversized mirror that school buses always have and probably saw something he had never seen in all his days as a driver. Even with all the shouting outside I heard him say, "I think they're pretty scared." Mr. O'Hanlon took a cursory glance at us and just said, "Who wouldn't be? This is Queens, New York, not Oxford, Mississippi." Then it became time for whispers.

With Mr. O'Hanlon leaning closer to the bus driver he started to talk into his ear. The driver's eyes were again in the mirror. I could see him, and he could see me. He listened at the same time and shifted uncomfortably in his seat. Despite his fidgetiness, he was still able to nod *yes* after the whispering concluded. His expression was concern but I couldn't tell what for. At least part of his anxiety was made clear when he uttered, "OK, but call up the company and tell 'em I'm gonna be a little late." Mr. O'Hanlon turned before descending the stairs with those rubber treads on them and said, "And you don't open this door under any circumstances. I'll be back." With that, the door was flung open like the arm of a mail train picking up a bundle of letters. The noise of the crowd came barreling in with more jeers than ever. In a second, they were muffled because that door had slammed closed, just like that mail car.

By this time our curiosity was gone. Looking out the window had stopped being fun some time ago. Three or four kids had returned to their original seats that faced the street that just had cars as opposed to the sidewalk that held the crowd. I had nothing to say. Some checked their pencils, sharpeners, and composition notebooks. One adjusted his glasses, and I could see that he was sweating, just on his nose. This made me smile since it was so odd. No sweat on his forehead, just his nose.

We were immersed in our own thoughts when the pitch of the crowd went up a few octaves. No one could contain his or her curiosity. We all went to the windows facing the picketers. The crowd had turned away from the bus and released its anger on a new target. The fury was heightened and the police had moved toward the nexus of rage. We could hear names of people being hurled around. The teachers were silent and listened. "Mr. Klavens, you should be ashamed. Mrs. Roth, I can't believe you're doing this. Ron, I mean, Mr. Rausch, you can't take their side. The first meeting of the PTA is coming up. We'll remember all of you who are out here." The crowd was yelling at about ten or twelve teachers who were marching in two ranks behind Mr. O'Hanlon. They too were crisply dressed, and they had a sharp and professional air about them. They formed two files going from the door of the bus to the gate of the school.

Boom, boom, boom, that authoritative rap on the glass of the school bus door. The driver swung the door open, and Mr. O'Hanlon came on, but this time turned to us. He signaled that the door should be closed. With a smile on his face, he said, "Good morning, children." Silence except for the catcalls and jeering outside. "Good morning, children." This time he got what he wanted. We all responded, *good morning* with that singsong manner that children possess when they say things in unison. He continued, "My name is Mr. O'Hanlon, and I want to personally welcome you to P.S. 156. As you can see, there are some people who don't want you to be here. They are not important. It is important that you know that we want you to be here. Those teachers that you see have formed two lines. You are going to walk in between those two lines. When I say, go, you are going to walk one by one straight to the gate. Don't look to your left or right. Hold your head up high. Just look straight ahead. No one will hurt you. There are two lines of teachers to protect you."

He then asked us to stand up and form a single file down the middle of the bus. My heart was beating, and the kid with the glasses now had sweat on his forehead and his nose. I was next to last by chance. I felt good that I wasn't the first one. I held my books in my left hand and a brown paper bag with my lunch in my right. The door flew open. The howls made me look down to the rubber treads that ran the length of the aisle of the bus. The word *go* was heard simultaneously with the slap of the door being flung open, and the first of eight stepped off the bus. It was slammed closed before the really maddening curses and catcalls came into the bus. I looked up. The crowd surged toward the rank of teachers, and they had their arms intertwined with each other. By holding their arms like a chain, the crowd couldn't break the line. They held. They held seven more times. There was one scary moment; right before I embarked I saw an adult drop to her knees; she tried to go through the legs of a teacher who closed them like a vise. With an outstretched arm she attempted to catch the left leg of the kid before me. She just missed.

My turn—the door slammed open, and I took a breath. I stepped off and heard the crowd yell but not as loudly. I figured they were just tired since they had done this seven times before me. I quickly walked through the guarding teachers and made it to the gate. Women with makeup and rollers screamed at me to go home, and I did exactly what Mr. O'Hanlon had told me. I kept my head up and made it safely to the gate where another group of teachers was waiting to escort us singly into the building. I made it. I was in my new home for the next three years.

What Is Hell?

———

WHAT IS HELL? We all have our definitions of it, and that varies based on our life's experience. I think it comes down to the terror we might feel, or the pain, be it physical or psychological. Of course, there are infinite permutations of this analysis. I know one thing. I never experienced it. I've had faint traces come in and out of my life, and they lasted a few weeks, maybe a few months. Real hell? I don't think so.

"Get that nigger, get him. Did ya see what he did? He punched Charlie! He decked Charlie, goddamn no-good nigger bastard. Punched Charlie? Hit a white man. Joe, too. Go get the car. Get who's ever around. We'll catch him!"

Those words, yelled and screamed at my father in 1931, that's hell. And once he told me this terrifying story, I knew what most relatives and friends of veterans of wars readily acknowledge. They, the veterans, puzzled, never talk about the wars that they've seen. Not a hint, not a story. How many children of World War II veterans don't have one war story to tell? There were fifteen million men who served in World War II, the good war, and there is not one child of those soldiers, marines, sailors, and airmen who can recall their fathers telling them a story of combat, a story of being in the line, fighting and killing Japs or Nazis or Ey-ties.

Even if you begged them, no soap, no dice, no nothing. They were able to sit in their 1950s La-Z-Boy chairs with an ice cold six pack on their left, ready to lean forward and grab the channel with their right. In those days televisions were small, and you had to sit right up close to them to see or hear what was going on. As they sat and watched, they were settling in to the last routine that they would ever need to know.

My father was just as laconic about the World War II he fought in the Pacific as he was about the civil wars he fought back home in the United States. He did have a lot to say with an undercurrent in him about what had occurred in Albany, Georgia, of all places; that's where he was stationed when he was at Fort Benning, Georgia. That was a most terrible experience for him. To go from freewheeling New York City, Harlem, Greenwich Village, to head south on that troop train into Dante's Inferno, that was hell on earth.

World War II was a mystery; my Dad spoke in those classic cryptic terms of *yes, no,* and *that was a long time ago.* The greatest event of the 20th century was reduced to monosyllabic responses and silence. I badgered him time and time again about the smallest details, friends, weapons, buddies, names, places, and it was as though I was interrogating him about some event that had occurred fifty years ago. It was the late 1950s, I was asking him about something that had occurred approximately twelve years ago. The only retort that he ever evinced and this was after my harangues, was "the real war wasn't against the Japs; it was with the white guys in the outfit." Another one: "Those crackers were worse than the Japs." Now, what the hell did that mean to a seven-year-old kid who wanted to hear a story about storming the hot sandy beaches of Iwo Jima or moving stealthily through some monstrous jungle on Tinian in the Mariana Islands? Whew! That became a ritual unknown for me. Ask my father a question about history and receive some indecipherable message in return. Ask my dad a question that could invoke energy and precocity, make me a better student and citizen of the United States and instead get these riddles, codes, anagrams, and crossword puzzles. Threaded throughout all of those enigmas, something dark and intangible; and then the smile on his face that transformed these question and answer periods into something more of a conundrum.

In order for my dad to talk about race and the pain of it, he could only present me with metaphors and images. I suppose he did not want to scare and frighten me, and that was rather noble of him. There were so many other ways in which he brutalized my brother and sister, but here he was, tender and caring, trying to protect my psychological welfare. It was either that or the pain was too much to talk about events approximately twelve years later or thirty years later. I think what I really heard or what he made me privy to were just the seminal events of his life in terms of race. He had, after a careful review of things, gleaned the incidents which left lasting nightmares. He had arranged two or three in a hierarchy of pain. He presented me with impressions of that pain, and I was a detective-therapist. He was able to unload his terrible burden to a priest who had no power to forgive or offer succor. Alleviating his racial encumbrances in the presence of a listener who had no insight, he knew there would be no judgment. The only possible reaction would be one of neutrality, and maybe that is all he wanted. Like writing a journal which you know will never be found until after you're dead, there's consolation in that envisioned scene where someone flips through the pages of your life and nods their head in the affirmative. I was a little boy. He did have my ear, and he knew I was listening. It was perfect for him. All I could say was *oh* or nothing and maybe that was all he wished to hear. And because my sagacious skills about life's labyrinth were so inchoate, what could I have possibly discerned about his painful experiences from thirty years ago?

This was our relationship as far as his personal history was concerned. It's difficult to tell one story without merging it with another, and when the theme is race and racism, they definitely seem to blend and blur together. He had grown up in the South, but Northern Virginia isn't really the South that we know and think about. Even during antebellum days, slavery in Virginia and in the area of Washington, D.C. was rather benign. Slaves didn't labor in endless fields of cotton, picking from dawn to dusk. Front Royal is about seventy miles west of Washington and on the edge of the Shenandoah Valley. If you keep on heading north about twenty-five miles, you will soon cross over into West Virginia. That's the section of Virginia that actually seceded from itself because it saw little benefit in maintaining an allegiance to the landed gentry and tidewater class of Richmond folks like Robert E. Lee and George Fitzhugh. No, Front Royal was a small town that found itself in the middle of things. It had a name that gave the impression that people with pretensions dwelled there. Front Royal. Whether they deserved this or not, I don't know. The few times I went there I was only impressed with how small it was. It was quiet, and if I were going to be a slave, this seemed like as good a place as any.

Because this was his South, he was unprepared for what happened to him during World War II. He and an entire generation of northern blacks were quite unprepared for what lay in those small army camps and bases that were located outside of civilization. I'm not sure if anything could have readied anyone for that. Richard Wright understood this concept and knew that he was shocking northern audiences—white and black—with his stories about what it meant to be a black in the South when he wrote *Uncle Tom's Children*. However, those were stories. Northern blacks heading south to army camps for basic training or permanent duty were broken by what they were to see, hear, and feel.

My old man had met a southern reality before, ten years previous to his experience in the United States Army Air Corps. It was 1931, and he was walking through a neighborhood in Queens called South Jamaica. He was walking up New York Boulevard saving a nickel during the height of the Depression that could have easily been spent on a bus. South Jamaica consisted of black and Italian immigrants. Poor people coexisted and if Mario Cuomo's stories are half true, people were too poor or didn't have the energy to be antagonistic toward each other. There were Italian-American fruit and vegetable stores. To see a butcher shop with an Italian guy behind the counter, filled with black and white patrons, was normal. My father kept walking north to the main mercantile district that ran along Jamaica Avenue. At the time the stores along Jamaica Avenue were its pride and joy. Black people shopped in large department stores and frequented banks made of marble. A noisy El ran above it, but this urban contrivance that usually functions as a blight on any sort of development had nothing to say to Jamaica Avenue. It thrived another thirty years until the late 1960s. By that time the big anchors of Jamaica's economic stability were decimated within a few years: Macy's, Mays, and Gertz went bankrupt.

Three blocks south of this bustling commercial district was a street that ran alongside the Long Island Railroad. Archer Avenue was an atavistic roadway that hinted back to a time when local merchants could set up their wares, very conveniently, right next to the railroad. There was a station named Union Hall Street. Peddlers, hawkers and yellers and barkers sold their wares from pushcarts and horse-drawn wagons. My father was familiar with these peddlers because his mother had cultivated an economic relationship with them that at least gave her the impression and perhaps the illusion that she was getting the best deal possible, even a better deal than could be had in a store up on Jamaica Avenue.

Solomon Cohen was a Jewish peddler, and my father knew him as Solly. He had grown up watching his mother haggle with this Jewish peddler year after year, sometimes acquiescing to his persuasive form of trading and at other times, abruptly turning north, which meant that some large department store was going to benefit from her most recent defeat at the hands of Mr. Solomon. To my father he was Solly or Uncle Solly, and to his mother he was Mr. Solomon. It was difficult or impossible for her to call him by his first name because she had come from that Virginia that taught a Negro to be respectful of whites in regard to social interaction. My father asked her once, and she became very angry trying to explain why she couldn't call him by his first name. It was too complicated. It was more important that in her pocketbook was her proudest possession, her official membership card from the NAACP; there was a very low number on it which proved she had joined in its earliest days. This was the way she spoke. That card mitigated not being able to make the linguistic transition that my father could not comprehend. Solly understood. He treated Mrs. Diaz with the utmost respect. "Good morning, Mrs. Diaz," he would say with a thick Yiddish accent. "How are you?" and "I hope you are fine" would pour out as one clause. He sang his English; he didn't speak it. "And how is Stanley, he is getting bigger and bigger, a very fine young man?"

My grandmother knew what it was to be polite. She worked for the Vanderbilts of Grand Central Railroad fame and was more than accustomed to being courteous and respectful. She appreciated those who respected her and knew how to reciprocate. My father saw Solly in the same way that I saw my mother's Jewish parents from Odessa on the Black Sea. People who spoke a language that was difficult to understand. People who between smiles and cajoling sentences that ended with questions even when they weren't, who would express themselves in a new and strange way. My father knew one thing: Mr. Solomon was a decent man. You respected him, and he treated you fairly.

"Come on, cotton candy, candied apples, step right up. Hey, yes, you, step right up and take a ride on the 20th-century marvel, the Ferris wheel. Is it as big as the one in Coney Island? No sir, but then again, I'm not charging you Coney Island ticket prices. That one is ten cents, and this one is five cents, and kids are free. Step right up, yes sir." A travel-ing carnival had come to South Jamaica. All a carnival needs is some open space, and there was plenty of it between Jamaica and Archer Avenues. A traveling carnival from the South with trucks and rides and lights had set up tents, stages, and stirred plenty of excitement for the young people in the neighborhood.

It was 1931, and my father was a little too old for the rides. He was twenty, and had already walked past the carnival several times which was remaining there for one week and one week only. He knew that the people running the carnival were a special lot. They were a cross be-tween circus performers and vagabond migrant workers. The carnival was from the South, and the men operating it were black and white, but my father, angry, had no trouble discerning who was in charge, who was working, and who was giving out all the orders to work. There was nothing overtly racist about it. It was worse than that. There was some-thing deceptive and disingenuous about the carnival. There was a mask. Someone was holding back, and an outsider could pick up on the fa-çade. It was analogous with William Shirer's perceptions of the manner in which German people conducted themselves during the 1936 Olympic games when they were held in Berlin. He and other journalists could not help but be conscious of how for public relations and propa-ganda reasons, German people toned down their virulent anti-Semitism and outward demonstrations of how vile things had become. They even took down some of the more offensive signs like NO JEWS WELCOME or DON'T BUY FROM THIS THIEVING JEW STORE, or a caution sign on a moun-tain road, DANGER, CURVE AHEAD; GERMANS 40 KILOMETERS, JEWS 100 KILOMETERS. For two weeks, Shirer, author of *The Rise and Fall of the Third Reich*, stated that the citizens of Berlin kept themselves in check.

These southern white men were doing the same. But my father was not angry about that. My father's anger revolved around the observa-tion that the black men who were doing the work and carrying out these orders did not have to do it this way. He felt that they somehow were volunteering for punishment. These men lived in the South and were beaten by it. My father was a northern Negro and had not acclimated to this regimen of exhibiting an appropriate deference to white people.

The carnival was in its last weekend, and Saturday was going to be a smashing success since so many more people would attend this last op-portunity to have fun. This coincided with the peddlers who had their wares set up near the railroad. They too had benefited from the carnival's presence and hated to see it go with the same sadness as the children who wanted one more merry-go-round ride and one more dunk for an apple.

My grandmother had afternoon chores for my father. Go to the peddler's market. Buy some items. A routine. My father walks north. It takes only about ten minutes to reach Archer Avenue. There was an old abandoned graveyard on the corner of Liberty Avenue. The gravestones were covered with weeds, and the Dutch names pointed toward a very ancient past of New York, of patroons and Peter Stuyvesant. He kept walking. When he turned the corner looking for Mr. Solomon's cart, there it was, turned on its side. Four or five white men were kicking and trashing all of his wares. Mr. Solomon was on the ground. They were kicking and punching him. He tried to talk the whole time that they were beating him. These were men from the carnival. Real white men. They taunted Solly with, "Old Jew peddler who always wants to make a deal, huh?" "Hey, Hymie, how much does this coffeepot cost?" then stepping on it to make sure it would never cost anything again. "Where's your horns, boy?" Mr. Solomon, even after being knocked down a few times, still tried to talk and plead and explain. "Look at the Yid; first thing they wanna do is talk with their hands. Goddamn, Izzy, stop talking with your hands and fight." Maybe those were the magic words. Stop talking with your hands and fight. My father was an amateur boxer. It was a respectable way to pick up some extra cash during the Great Depression. He had achieved some lower ranking in the Golden Gloves competition, Madison Square Garden. "Stop talking with your hands and fight." My father said nothing and started boxing. Punching, jabbing, right crossing and feinting. Five against one had just become five against two. Blocking, light on his feet, he was bobbing and weaving, stepping over pots, spools of thread, calico, and tablecloths. Two down, three to go. An uppercut catches another in the jaw and tobacco juice comes squirting out mixed with some blood from a mashed tongue. Two left. They flee.

"Get that nigger, get him. Did ya see what he did? He punched Charlie! He decked Charlie, goddamn no-good nigger bastard. Hit a white man. Joe, too. Come on! Get the car. Go get the car. Get who's ever around. We'll catch him!"

My father watched as the two white men scooted back to the carnival. Two men lay on the ground groaning. One bent over and kept spitting blood. My father started to set the wagon up, but Solly grabbed him. "Stanley, Stanley, you must run. You must run like the wind. You're colored. They are bad men. They are the bad men from the South. Run. Stanley, run. You must run before they come back. These are the bad men who are against the colored people." Not wanting to leave Mr. Solomon like that, my father started to pick up yarn and some tools off the ground. No one was coming, but Mr. Solomon had expressed an urgency that he had never heard before.

"Please, Stanley, I will fix this up. You must run away from here. I'll be all right. OK, okey-dokey, I'm OK but you must run." With this second plea my father started to move off. He turned the corner of Archer Avenue and New York Boulevard and started heading south. He walked briskly and then started to run a bit. He looked behind him toward the carnival, and there was nothing. No men were following him, so he started to walk. In the hollow of a railroad underpass everything is amplified, so when he first heard the Ford Model-T chugging down the road, it already sounded closer than it was. He turned around to his right, and there was a car with white men standing on the small running board. The men were waving sticks and pieces of tent poles out of the car and yelling, cursing, and swearing. Bottles were thrown. Pieces of metal and wood came flying out at him. None of the throwers was accurate, but the car was getting closer. Then my father saw something that made him run. A white man on the running board, looking like Will Rogers or Buffalo Bill, was twirling a rope around and around. He yahooed, "We're gonna get you, nigger. Boy, you in trouble now."

The car gained on him. The only thing that helped my father's escape was that the oncoming traffic heading northbound prevented them from crossing over to his side of the street. He ran and ran. He hit Liberty Avenue, and now the Dutch graveyard was on his left. The Model-T, rickety, gained and a tent pole caught him in the back. It really hurt. The man with the rope kept on twirling it like a cowboy looking to lasso a steer. The yells and shouts got closer. Insane with anger, the car and its driver finally disregarded all caution and swerved into the oncoming traffic and got up on the sidewalk. My father could feel that the car with all of its rattling springs and fenders and the screaming men was right behind him. The car knocked over small trees and shrubs and tore down a picket fence. With a large maple coming up, it was forced to go back onto the road; my father kept on running down the sidewalk and got a temporary reprieve. At South Road he made a left. The car didn't miss this sharp turn but by running on a diagonal he had gained a few feet on it. He cut across South Road and burst into a bar and poolroom known as the Bucket o' Blood. The car pulled up right onto the sidewalk.

Inside this neighborhood bar were black men with applejack hats and turtleneck sweaters. Some of them had a block V on their sweaters which stood for Vagabonds. Cigarettes hung from lips; pool cues were held in chalky hands. Mugs of Knickerbocker beer were grasped in sweaty fists. My father poured out his story, "I'm in trouble, big trouble." No other details were given because there was no time. The white men knocked through the swinging doors sweating and breathing. They had their clubs and rope. My father moved behind the semicircle of men who had closed before him. This small horseshoe of black men stared at these southern white men. Nothing was said and all that could be heard was the breathing and the fear. Ten against one had become ten against ten. "Nigger, ya lucky; ya real lucky." One of the pool hustlers muttered, "Go back to your carnival." A few more moments of silence and breathing and terror, and the white men filed out. The swinging doors creaked slowly as open hands kept hitting them before they could close completely. *Boom, squeak, boom, squeak, boom, squeak.* Then silence.

The Model-T started up, rumbled, and rattled off. My old man was catching his breath and trying to answer questions about the incident. He was told again that he was lucky, but this time it came from a black raspy voice. He nodded and talked about how if that old maple tree in front of Mrs. Henderson's house hadn't forced the car back onto the road, he might not have been so lucky. "Yeah, Ford Model-T ain't no match for that ol' maple. That's for sure!" A few laughs and the cues started to be spun into chalk to make that shot just right. The Bucket o' Blood returned to normal. "Hey, Stan, looks like you could use a beer. Rupert, give this man a beer for settin' the world record for runnin' from Archer Avenue to South Road." Laughter and another voice, "Stan, take that beer; that's Rupert's last nickel." My father demurs and mentions something about chores not being done, and his comrades are impressed with his fidelity to his mother. He only says one thing: "Don't mention this to my mom. You guys have to promise that." The heads go up and down and the applejack hats all agree that this is to be kept a secret. My father saved a white man's life, and it was going to be kept a secret. If Mr. Solomon revealed the story to Mrs. Mercy Diaz, she would only be privy to the triumph, not the terror, the victory, not the dread. She would hear that her son Stanley had done a heroic thing, and she would feel even better any time she displayed that NAACP card with the low number.

Sailboats in Central Park

THIS WAS THE second time I saved a white man's life. By age ten I was pretty adept at this and prided myself at possessing such adult skills when I was really only a little kid who happened to be smart and curious and knew how to listen to everyone's words. I understood their cues, their gestures, and all variations of body language. A sigh could be separated into so many different categories. And most of all I was patient. This quality played a big role in my life and my capacity to read people and be silent as I watched. Inadvertently my father had already taught me on so many occasions how to wait, and wait, and to wait in silence. Another trait, trick, and strategy that would come in handy years later. But saving white people was also one of my fortes.

The first time I intervened I did nothing. I was just me. I was about seven and my dad had asked me, "Dex, do you want to go for a little drive, not a Sunday drive, just a little one." I ran to the car, and the rule was if you got there before my dad, you could honk the horn one time. I pushed the Ford medallion that was at the center of the horn one time. When my dad got in, he replied, "You're so fast, like Jesse Owens."

We drove from Westgate Street and headed up to Merrick Road going past the big Times Square Store. As he said, we only drove a few more blocks and made a U-turn and pulled into a small gas station. The magic bell went off when our tires hit the hose that was on the ground. This signaled the mechanic that he had a customer. A man in dirty coveralls came out, rubbing his hands with a rag that he placed in his back pocket by the time he got to our car. He came around the front of the car, leaned over and said something to my father. In just a blur, my dad's car door flew open, and he had struck the mechanic. The punch sent him into the pump. Falling next to the gas pump in another blur, the mechanic knocked over the bucket with the window wash water as he slid to the ground. My father hopped back in the car. He had never turned the Ford off. There was a screech of tires, and I turned to see that the man was holding his face; he was on the ground, sitting upright but holding his face. There was dust and gravel. I didn't say anything, and my dad spoke first. Holding the wheel tightly, he said, "If you weren't here, I would have killed that guy." We drove back onto Merrick Road, heading toward Laurelton now and another gas station.

"Pop, what did he do?"

"Look, what I did, never do in the South. That fella called me *boy* and that wasn't necessary. That's why I punched him." The word *South* had meaning. This was the bad place. I wasn't sure why you couldn't do what my father just did in that bad place, but I was pretty scared. We got the gas and he knew I would never tell anyone, and I never did.

This was the second time I saved a white man's life. My father had bought my brother and me two beautiful Eldon sailboats. Fine non-toys which were the only toys that he would ever purchase. A toy had to possess an educational function so this inherently placed a severe limit on all the purchases he ever made for Christmas or birthdays. A.C. Gilbert, the famous toy manufacturer that made erector sets and chemistry sets was the perfect company for my old man. All their products were functional and edifying. These sailboats were in that instructional tradition. First, there was a faithful reproduction of a Yankee Clipper ship—you could see Donald McKay beaming with joy at the attention to detail. Second, and not to be outdone in features, was an oceangoing yacht with sails that responded to the wind and a keel that kept the boat afloat under all prevailing winds.

The sailboat pond in Central Park was large; to walk around it takes a few minutes and with kids' legs you're really embarking on a journey. My old man brought us there. We had taken the classic Sunday drive from Queens to Manhattan. Belt Parkway east toward Brooklyn, the Van Wyck Expressway north toward mid-Queens, the LIE toward the Midtown Tunnel and then proceeding a few blocks over to the park. The tunnel was our favorite part of the ride since it gave us an opportunity to play a game or two. We always wanted to be able to estimate when we would see daylight again after taking that initial plunge under the East River.

"One more turn."

"No, it's around that next bend."

"Hey, Pop, how much longer?"

"Why do they have those green and red lights in the ceiling?"

"Hey, Pop, why is that guy sitting in that booth?"

"Hey, Pop, is that a good job?"

"Can I do that when I grow up?"

"That's a nice job, right, just counting the cars!"

"Hey, the light, there's the light. You see, I was right. It was right around that last bend."

And then the light of Manhattan comes smashing down on the windshield of that old Ford. Our mouths would quickly shut as we were stunned into silence by the awe and beauty of the architectural ballet that the Manhattan skyline always conjured up. We looked up and up and the Midtown Tunnel seemed pedestrian in our memory. More questions.

"Pop, how do they build buildings so high like that?"

"How do they get the girders up that high when a crane can never be that high?"

My father shifts the car into second as we hit a little traffic. His brown hand remains on the white knob of the shift with a Pall Mall cradled between two fingers just gently enough that it won't be crushed. His left foot hits the clutch effortlessly, and the car responds. He responds, "How would you construct something that is taller than your biggest crane? I want you guys to think about that for a while. Think. How would you use that crane to help you when the hoist can only go a certain height?"

We were silent since we knew that these types of questions were of a serious caliber, and he didn't want us to just blurt out whatever stupid answer was on the tip of our tongues. He gets to a red light and that brown hand with the cigarette comes off the white knob and he takes a nice long and relaxing drag off that butt. "Well, what's the most constructive plan to build these skyscrapers?" My brother blurts out the correct answer, "There must be a way to get the crane to higher floors after it reaches its limit." I'm glad that my brother spoke first because I was going to mumble something about a "super-duper" crane that can really reach that high and go higher and higher and higher than any crane in the universe. My father nods his head in the affirmative, and the foot comes down on the clutch, cigarette between two fingers returns to its resting place on the column shift and we're headed toward the park. "You're correct; they use the cranes to lift each other. That's how they get to the top of the, say, the Empire State Building."

Central Park strikes you as this magical place if you grow up in Queens which is the suburbs in the 1950s. Just the fact that there is this moatlike wall all around its perimeter, you know beforehand that there is something very special on the other side of it. The cobblestones that are embedded around the trees make you walk unevenly and you must watch your step. Everything about the place, even the water fountains with their sturdy little helmet-shaped steel covers are something out of *The Wizard of Oz*. We jump out of the car and run without the boats; that's how excited we are about our day in the park. My father whistles his famous recall whistle, and we run back to the car. He says quietly, "Take it easy, take it easy," as we start to run with our prized vessels.

This time, as always, my father will only participate as casual observer and instructor. He presented the initial lesson about sailboats and sailing. This involved theory, method, the antithesis and always the proscription, "Under no circumstance do the following." After that twenty-minute lecture with time for questions that are never asked, we are let loose on the pond. He sat down on a bench and took out an old copy of the *Morning Telegraph* to review the charts, the records, and the dreams. My brother and I immediately departed each other's company being that we were sworn enemies when out of my father's sight. This pond with its great distances and long radiuses meant that we could ideally practically be out of sight of each other. I can tell from the perimeter of the pond that if I engineer my position just the right way, I won't even have to see him. I don't want to see him or his stupid yacht.

I walked away from the two of them. To be out of sight and sound of both of them was heaven. My brother represented cowardice and injustice. My father stood for the future which could be bad or good. I knew that failure with the execution of boating theory that afternoon would result in another lecture in a stronger and more pronounced voice and the possible removal from the activity. For my old man, failure indicated and proved that there was a combination of incompetence and a lack of interest in the project that was at hand, or worse, stupidity. I had no desire to fall into any of these categories and would rather confront the indignity of defeat in private.

I walked away and found my bench. As I hoped, I was out of sight of my brother and I could see my father reading his newspaper. I launched the *Flying Cloud* under a fair sky and with a good wind in her sails. She took off, and I immediately wished I had the string I had asked my father about during the twenty-minute block of instruction.

"Don't you think it would be better to have a string attached to the boat?"

"Why a string?" he asked a bit startled.

"In case the boat goes out too far and we can't catch it."

"This won't happen; the boat will sail on its own until it reaches the other side or it returns on its own."

"Oh, but what if the wind dies or it just gets stuck?"

"That won't happen; that can't happen."

"But the middle is so far from the wall."

"You have to have more confidence in your equipment. That's a good thing to know in life. You have to be confident in what machines can do. This is a machine. I know it's a boat, but it's also a machine. It was designed to do certain things. It will do them."

As I watched my clipper ship sail out, I was thrilled and scared at how fast it took off once the wind filled her sails. Then, flip-flop, just like that, she had turned over. I wasn't sure if it was just a gust of wind or me not placing enough ballast in the keel; there was a small device for filling the keel with water for extra weight. I knew one thing. The *Flying Cloud* was no longer flying and Donald McKay was looking for help. The ship sank very quickly, and my heart beat rapidly as I watched her go under. I looked and looked, and because the ship was brown it blended right into the murky pond water.

I walked along the walk which is about a foot higher than the sidewalk. I walked only a few feet one way or the other since I wanted to be able to report this disaster with some accuracy. I scanned the water. Other boats, especially the remote-controlled ones, cruised effortlessly and adroitly up and down, across and back, all within the vicinity of the sinking. They didn't even know that a disaster had occurred. They just kept going back and forth without a care in the world.

Flip-flop and from the two-foot depth of the pond, up popped the sunken *Flying Cloud*. It was my clipper ship. Her masts and white sails poked about an inch or two above the surface of the water. I could see her brown hull. All was not lost. I rejoiced privately at my good luck. Of course, I still had to deal with the problem of rescuing the ship but at least there was something to rescue. I studied. That was the first thing to do. Just look and look at the position of the boat and study it. Immediately I went into my mathematical mode which meant I would count methodically until ten and check if the ship's position had altered or whether or not it was still capable of sinking any lower in the pond. After a few of these accountings, I was assured that she wasn't going to sink any further and all that needed to happen was for a friendly adult to come along or a good breeze or a combination of both, and the *Flying Cloud* would be retrieved.

I stepped off the wall and sat down on a bench and relaxed the best I could. Every now and then a breeze would erupt, and I would see the foundered clipper move a few feet toward the other side of the boat pond. Far enough from my brother and father, this would only be a question of time. I got up, knowing that I had the time and with confidence walked over to the hot dog and pretzel cart. Most of the carts were strategically set up a few feet from another so no one businessman was being unfairly treated when it came to the free and open trading of hot dogs and pretzels. My guy was an old man with an applejack hat, tilted to the side in that cocky way. The smoke from the pretzels that were starting to burn a bit came to me and really whet my appetite. I never really knew about that chestnut smell that is supposed to inundate New York in the fall, but that blackened pretzel smell, that was unmistakably special. I counted out ten cents—two nickels—and asked for "a hot one, please." The man pulled out that metal tray where they keep the pretzels close to the flame, pulled down a sheet of wax paper, wrapped up the cheap lunch and gave me a napkin. With that in hand I journeyed back to my bench to wait out the salvaging of the *Flying Cloud*.

The wind picked up as the afternoon dragged on, and my ship started to come in, as I had predicted. I kept counting and predicting. It would only be a matter of minutes. The foundered ship got closer and closer to the concrete rim of the sailboat pond, and soon I knew it was just a case of reaching over and pulling her in. I got up. As I walked over to the spot on the wall where she would dock, a man—sports jacket, nice slacks, no tie, New York 1950s Sunday wear—walked in front of me. At the most he was one yard ahead of me. I could see what was happening. He had noticed the downed ship and was going to pick it up for the owner. I was more than grateful since at some point I would have to lean over the side, get wet, worry about wet clothes and explaining how that happened to me. He got to the rim, put one knee on it and reached over for the ship. Up she came letting out a ton of water. The shower from my ship sent many ripples out away from the edge of the pond that would eventually make their way to the center. I got adjacent to this Good Samaritan and had already said *Thanks* before he even acknowledged my presence. "Thanks a lot" I boomed one second after the first "thanks." He turned toward me with little or no expression. As the boat dripped dry, he said, "Thanks for what?" I quickly replied, "Oh, my mother told me that whenever someone does a favor for you, you are supposed to say Thank you."

He now turned to me and my outstretched hands. "You're not trying to say this is yours, are you?" With confidence that I possessed more than enough proof of possession, I informed him that this was my boat; it had turned over about an hour ago, and the name of the boat was the *Flying Cloud,* which he could see, if he looked on the bow. In addition, this was a model of a clipper ship, the fastest sailing ships ever designed, designed by Donald McKay for going from America to the Far East.

"This isn't your boat. How could a Puerto Rican ever have a nice boat like this? There is no way this is your boat." These words tumbled out of his mouth, and I understood everything except *Porto Rickan.* But those two words, *Porto Rickan,* when repeated in my mouth after the pause of being relayed from my mouth to my brain, and then back again, had been completely rejected because there was no place to file them. They would eventually be logged into that very special cabinet drawer that existed in my consciousness, that long list of words and expressions that crushed and terrorized, but right at that moment, they meant nothing. Nothing. I looked at him, baffled, not angry, not mad, just baffled. Why wouldn't he give me my property? I had thanked him. I had given him technical proof. Why was he holding on to my boat? He did not feel obligated to hold or continue a conversation with me. After a pause, he said, "Why did you let it sink? How come you weren't at the edge of the pond waiting for it to come in? I've been watching it for fifteen minutes, and you just sat down with a pretzel. I saw you." "Mister,

I've been here all afternoon. My brother is sailing his boat." I started one more sentence with the words *my old* but caught myself. I knew that from this additional information concerning myself nothing good would come of it. Futilely, I added, "If you look over there, you'll see my brother with that yachting sloop." The man had already concluded that I wasn't worth listening to and just shook his head in amazement that I would engineer such a paltry scheme in order to get something that wasn't mine. I was bereft of any other plan. I just looked at him in bafflement that someone would not return my clipper ship after I had just judiciously waited all that time.

We both sat down on the bench. He cradled the boat in his lap. It was dry. He repositioned the sails and admired the craftsmanship that went into it. I sat jealous and proud at the same time. This was not satisfactory. I was frustrated to the point of tears.

"Where are you going? I thought you said this was your boat."

"It is. I'm just going for a walk."

I headed toward my father who was sitting where I had left him. Nothing had changed.

"Little Eva—Our Kretchen by Crafty Admiral; Little Eva, ran last race, June 3rd, Santa Anita, mud, closed up, but not enough. Time, 1:09 for 6 furlongs."

I announced my presence.

"Hey, Pop"

"Yes."

"How's it going?"

"Studying and keeping careful records. That's the key."

I paused since there was no connection other than the physical. "Oh," was all I could say. He noticed that I did not have the boat with me. "Where's the *Flying Cloud?*" he said, remembering the name and sounding interested.

My prepared speech came out with genuine feeling and a bit of remorse. "It's like you said; the ship can sail itself. It doesn't need me. It's just sailing on the other side of the pond. It does everything you set it to do." A response was forthcoming since he had been vindicated. "If you follow the directions, things are always easy. Set the rudder and the sails in the same direction, and the boat will maintain an arc."

I sprang up with "That's exactly what it's doing now. I know exactly where it's going to stop."

With the paper raised back to "Morning Line and Jockey" before I even could turn back toward the new man with his strange words, I still felt better. I hadn't involved him. That was important. He would stay there, literally for hours studying and figuring. To involve him frightened me. I walked back and thought about new problems that were a bit more complicated than placating my father and having him sit with his *Morning Telegraph* for a few hours. Would this man have other reasons for keeping the boat? What if this man had a nice son whom he thought deserved a great and fine present? That was possible. Was it? Would this man just steal a boat and give it to his kid? I started to walk faster, frightened at the possibility of having the *Flying Cloud* survive her first ocean voyage and falling prey to a human being's avarice. I walked very fast now since this was a terrible possibility; it meant that everything I had just done, would be undone. The lies I had just given to my father about the clipper ship taking care of herself would be revealed if I dared to return empty-handed. I would have to tell him that a stranger had taken my boat. This could not happen.

I came around a long sweeping turn, and there he was, sitting on the bench. I increased my pace since he was an adult and an adult can get away anytime they feel like it, even at the last moment. Coming into view he looked at me with a blank face. No words were exchanged as I sat down. There was no visible triumph since my power and presence was the same in his eyes; I was still a strange entity to him, but I had exhibited the ability to keep my word. I had returned like MacArthur coming back to the Philippines. I felt good about that. I sat on his left with my arms folded. He had to look at me.

He coughed to initiate the contact. "Well, no one has come for this boat the whole time. I don't know how it could be yours, but I guess it is. Here." With that disclaimer he placed the boat in my hands. He got up, brushed himself off a bit and walked away. I sat with the boat in my lap trying to understand. At least he hadn't said those two words, *Rickan something*, no, *Porto something Rickan*. I would remember those words since they were important. The boat felt good and cold and fresh. I picked it up by the bow and let the remaining drops of water fall from the stern. I was comfortable. The rest of the afternoon would go well. Nothing could really upset the equilibrium I had just established. My brother could wander, find true and other sorts of mischief. I had survived mine. I got a sunken boat back from the depths, an ocean. I had returned, and I had saved a white man's life. This time it wasn't just because of *me* being. I had done something. I had made plans. They had worked.

Atomic Home

———◄◦►———

IT WAS OCTOBER 1962, another fall and I was loving school after getting past that rough September with the parents who did not like us. After a month, they could see that we weren't monsters and weren't going to ask their daughters or sons for dates. We made friends and enemies through team sports and labored mightily under the protective wing of Mr. O'Hanlon and his staff. "If anything, no matter now big or small, occurs that you think is wrong, come tell me immediately," were the comforting words he left us with one day in his office. We felt special because anytime we went to the "principal's office" it was because someone was in serious trouble, not us. His door was open, and he meant it.

It was a tricky landscape to negotiate. The problem with facing racism or any other hatred that has an ideology built into it is that ultimately someone will make the mistake of acting human and the contradictions commence immediately. Initially we were given the treatment. This meant that children avoided contact with us since they did not wish to pay the price of their own ostracism from the larger community of white children attending the school. For weeks and months we were not bothered but at the same time we did not exist for them. The teachers could see what was happening but they were hamstrung as to just how far they could go in socially engineering an educational environment. In the 1960s everyone, especially northerners, had their measure of what was liberal, conservative, what was feasible, and what was ideal. We were there attending classes. The classes were incredible. We had advanced math, composition, French every day, and science courses that always included experiments and labs. This was a fourth grade class in New

York City and a public school. No resource eluded us. Our assemblies were far different from Mr. Mack-New-Mara. Instead of being browbeaten into submission, we had guest speakers, even if it was just a teacher who had some special interest in a particular discipline. Routinely, we were given art and music appreciation. Operas, symphonies, and sonatas were played for us, and it was the equivalent of being with Leonard Bernstein on a Saturday morning when he led the Young People's Concerts. George became interested in Verdi because we listened in a trance to *Aida* one Thursday. Ravel's *Bolero* was just as hypnotic; I hummed it, looked in my *World Book Encyclopedia* to get more information about the composer. Our fine art periods were devoted to working with new materials in imaginative ways. Last, our physical activities were extremely well organized. Team sports, individual competitions were regulated; points were given for blue and gold teams and school esprit de corps was high. Ironically it was there that we suffered the most.

We discovered that because of the interaction incumbent on you to perform as a team that this was the one place where the *treatment* had a devastating effect. Mr. O'Hanlon and Miss Trusty, Mrs. Nicholson, and Mrs. Schwartz were able to guarantee a safe and enriched classroom environment. Monitoring the inner sanctum of a classroom was possible and they did that magnificently. It was in those few areas like sports and recreation that they and we were vulnerable. When it came time to choose up teams for sports, we were never chosen. The circle was made and two captains had been chosen. They now were in the lofty position of picking their warriors, their athletes. Of course, their favorites were selected within seconds and did not have to even make a gesture of supplication. The best punch ball hitter, softball fielder, or runner, they were guaranteed a spot on the team. Then there were the rest of us. I would jump up and down with my hand in John or Howard's face yelling, "Me, me, me, I'm really good." I started to use the word *please,* a word that children don't really use that often with each other. Then I saw other boys putting their hands together as though they were praying, and I saw that work for a few kids so I tried that. The combination of jumping, praying, and just begging got no results. We were never chosen. The teams would be chosen, and the games would commence. We would sit on the sidelines, leaning against the fence, standing in a circle.

Our bonds grew deeper and became all the more stalwart because of this isolation and excommunication. We had our own grandiose response. We contemplated starting our own "league," a version of the Negro baseball divisions. Of course, our Negro league would be different since anyone would be welcome. Little did we know that with eight kids, six boys and two girls, it's a Herculean feat to start a team, let alone a division. Our attempt at starting our own "New York Black Yankees" failed.

Even though Mr. O'Hanlon had said come to his office in response to any slight, no matter how small, we had some reserve, call it kid pride, that eliminated seeing him for a redress of our grievances. We thought about sending one of the girls, Helen or Joyce, to complain for the group, but they were being treated better than we were and the ploy would have been detected. We did not want to attract any more attention than necessary. During one gym period, a major breakthrough occurred due to the systematic surveillance of one teacher. Mrs. Hayes interrupted a game that was already in the first inning. This was a sacrilege. Time was sacred and to have to stop for even a few seconds was a deprivation of the most painful nature. In response, blowing that piercing whistle that cut the air with a bitter sharpness, we all froze. Our freezing came easier since we were leaning against the fence watching and talking. The other kids actually had to put down their bats, gloves, and the ball. Mrs. Hayes strutted onto the playground cement with high-heeled shoes that made the official teacher sound of *clomp-clomp, clomp-clomp,* one heel mark one decibel higher than the other. Those *clomp-clomps* got her to the pitcher's mound. With a blue serge suit, blond hair, she stood on that little white painted stripe that marked where little Sandy Koufaxes or Whitey Fords should wind up and hurl the ball. "Children, children, stop in your tracks." She didn't need the whistle. She had so many bracelets on her wrist that every time she waved her hand, it was louder than the clanging of a farmer's triangle and the call to breakfast. "Children, gather around me this instant. All of you. You, standing near the fence, come here also. Everyone listen. I have seen that certain children are not chosen to play and they want to." I listened to her speech but also couldn't help looking at all of those golden bands around her wrist. *Clang and bang, clang and bang,* and, "From now on they will be chosen." She pointed at us and continued,

"Starting tomorrow, I am going to be the captain. Yes, I will be the captain, and I will choose the sides. Is that clear? Is that clear? This is a democracy and everyone is equal."

There were groans and sighs. "If I hear another *sssss* sound from you Mr. Fabiani, your mother and father will be in Mr. O'Hanlon's office so fast that you won't know what hit you." Alonzo and George, my two best friends were beaming. I was pretty happy since I loved sports, was fast, and was thrilled with competition. Not all of us rejoiced since Mrs. Hayes had done for us what we had hoped we could bring about on our own terms. Yet, we weren't going to turn down the overture. The white kids were reluctant and already were conjuring up methods to circumvent this new edict, but at least as of tomorrow, we would be on the field.

"Tomorrow" came, and we were forcibly chosen to be on either David or Barry's team. This was a breakthrough. With a cabal officially in place, Barry, David, Bruce, and Neil had met after school and had prearranged a boycott of us that would be subtle enough that no one could be accused of any racial antipathy. We would be chosen as the *law* required, but we could be so far down the batting order, that the chances of us getting up in time to hit in a brief forty-minute period were nonexistent. And if we were about to get up, a small argument regarding the score or whether a man was safe at first or not delayed things enough that the dreaded buzzer would sound and the words, "Line up children," would bring to a close any chance of us getting that bat on our shoulders or hitting that ball with our fists. Sometimes they would just forget that we were there in the dugout. Although we were already the designated nonplayers who never got up, seventeenth or more in the order, sometimes they returned to the top of the batting order and number one was up again and when we questioned the accountability, they would say "Oh, we forgot." How could they remember when they had all of us playing in right field, four outfielders in right field waiting for that solitary ball to reach our reservation? Something else had to happen.

I can't remember his name or who it was, but there was a kid, some white kid who could see the way things were. He didn't have the appeal of an authority figure. His sway had to do with being a bit surly himself. He was by no means the smartest kid, not at least, academically. Common sense was his specialty. Mrs. Hayes did her job. That was as far as she could go. Race relations is a tricky business. Too much force can produce a negative quotient. Retardation can occur after all of the good intentions have been set down on paper with appropriate codes, numbers, paragraphs, and subparagraphs. No, you need a kid who on one cold afternoon in October, just when they're getting ready to play the World Series in real life, sees the connection between the New York Yankees vs. the San Francisco Giants and white vs. Negro at P.S. 156. The game had already begun. The *forced sides* were chosen, and we were 15, 16, 17 in the lineup, accordingly. Leaning against the fence again, we had to admit when asked by Mrs. Hayes whether or not everything was OK and we had been chosen; "we're just waiting for our turn." She turns and clomp-clomps away, and then just as the inning is at its end, when the opposite teams are taking the field and another takes to the dugout, this kid, with all the heroic sedition of Huck Finn, says, "We orta let dese colored guys play; dere pretty good sometimes." When he's censured and castigated for being a defector, he whips out a half dozen baseball cards from the back pocket of his sloppily cuffed dungarees and comes back, exuding more hubris than ever with, "Ya see dese cards? No, not dis one. Dis one, yeah; ya see dat guy's recud? He's hittin' .356. Dat's his recud. Dat's the back of de card. Now look on de fron. Is he white? No, he's colored. Ya know what dat means? Dat proves a colored guy can play as gud as a white. Right? Finito. Finished. My fadda sez some of ya guys are cafones for not lettin' the colored play. And ya know something? I dink ya cafones too." That was it. From that point on, we were really integrated into the school. After-school activities took on a new dimension since we weren't relegated to departing for our alien neighborhood and life as quickly as possible.

The Jewish kids at P.S. 156 had inadvertently taught me a great deal about my mother's religion which had been neglected or even trounced upon by my father. On a school trip to the zoo in Central Park, while eating lunch in the cafeteria, I found out that Jewish kids didn't eat everything and anything. As I munched on my ham sandwich and downed a small half pint of milk, I noticed that they were looking at me. I wasn't sure as to the source of their consternation since in the ranks of sandwiches, a ham sandwich was near the top. The night before the school trip I had pestered my mom, ensuring that I wouldn't be given a cheap sandwich like bologna or spiced ham when going on such a first class school trip. My mom was of the firm belief that A&P was good enough for us. We endured all Ann Page products and no matter what we said about those products, there was no convincing my mom that there was a difference. Even when my brother and sister showed her the difference between Skippy peanut butter and Ann Page, with the latter ripping the white bread to shreds, she stuck to her principles.

Then there was the chunk bologna controversy. There was nothing more humiliating than having large pieces of unevenly cut meat drop from your sandwich onto the lunchroom floor with a bounce. I started my campaign about this particular request weeks before the trip. Giving in to my badgering she went out and bought the Boar's Head ham and I was assured of retaining some dignity when I opened my brown bag the next day. That's why I couldn't explain the stares. I asked Julius what was causing the stirring. He quietly told me that I was breaking the law. I looked at him and gave a little jump. Because this was a new school and I knew that Mr. O'Hanlon and the rest of the teachers had gone out of their way to ensure our safety, I had already figured out that the least I could do, to pay them back for their protection, was obey all rules of conduct.

Julius was serious, and I asked him again, just to make sure I understood him. He replied without any hesitation that I was breaking a law; you can't have ham sandwiches and milk. I took a quick look around and could see that he was right. Every kid at the long lunch tables had juice or soda. Not one kid, boy or girl, had milk. He was right and I was wrong. I quickly decided that the sandwich with the Boar's Head ham was more important than a small container of milk, so I got up and threw the container into the tough looking metal garbage can. I came back a little regretful that I had no change to buy something to drink but felt better that I was not violating any rule or regulation. This routine went on until I finally noticed that in the school cafeteria, there were a few students eating ham sandwiches and drinking milk, simultaneously. An Irish boy from Rosedale, one of the best softball players, explained, "That's for them. You're not them. Eat whatever you want." I was confused about *them* and who he now was. But I respected John Massey a great deal for his softball prowess and decided to follow both rules and just switch back and forth depending on how I felt and whom I was sitting next to.

At three o'clock my Jewish schoolmates had another strange ritual. We all loved softball and punch ball and nothing was more important than our after-school contests. We always wanted to start immediately, as soon as we came flying out the brown exit doors of the building. Running down long concrete staircases to the yard, flinging our coats into a big pile behind home plate in a blur we changed from shoes to sneakers as quickly as possible. Then we had to wait. Our Jewish friends could not play until four o'clock, one long hour of waiting. They had to go to "after-school study center" in the synagogue across the street from the school. It was next to another building which I was curious about too, Home for WW II Jewish Veterans. I figured out from the graying and rusting artillery piece outside of the *home* that it was a place for wounded men who would never be completely all right. John, George, and Alonzo watched as Larry, Barry, Howard, Julius, Eric, and Richard crossed the street. Sometimes we walked right next to them and waited outside the door. As they filed through the doors, we saw them place small black hats on their heads and pick up books. The doors would shut and I wondered what would happen if we ever tried to gain entry. John Massey's theory was, "It's like a church—they have to let you in." None of us ever attempted to accompany our forlorn buddies as they went to "extra school" as we called it. We would practice plays, throwing the ball around, warming up, trading and inspecting baseball cards and if you were a professional like Bill, you actually oiled your baseball mitt.

At four o'clock they flew outdoors again, their second time that day and when asked what they had learned, at least Eric or Barry would show us books with strange writing. Not only were the letters strange but they told us that you read from right to left, not left to right. *Backwards* I said and they weren't too happy with that remark. I had one more question, "If this is school, how come we never see girls come in or out?" John Massey backed me on this one with, "Yeah, even if it's Catholic school, there's separate entrances for girls and boys. What's going on?" They replied that girls weren't allowed and we all admitted that this wasn't a bad idea and wondered why P.S. 156 couldn't have the same policy. From that point on, it was *play ball* and we always stayed until darkness. Inning after inning, run after run, outs, strikes and home runs and we just played competitively and in a gentlemanly fashion. Anytime there was a dispute the names of the greats were invoked. "Babe Ruth wouldn't do that," or "Willie Mays would have called that a strike." These were our largest concerns. Sports had performed a social and spiritual feat, bringing us all together in one dugout. Now our only worries were which IGC class was the best in softball, not mathematics or reading. I started by collecting baseball cards and lost myself in averages, runs scored, and pennants.

My father stopped worrying when he saw the bubble gum and cards on my study desk. After being reassured that although there was no phalanx of troops to protect us, like Little Rock, Arkansas, this protective ring of teachers sounded like a sturdy enough wall. In September my father was still concerned with what was occurring at the school, but after four weeks of official and unofficial reports that all was quiet on the Laurelton front, he stopped asking on a daily basis if any of the kids had been bothering me. He was moody, and I was later to find out from my mother that fall was his worst time of year. It had been that way since they were first acquainted back in the mid-1930s. I associated fall with good things. Raking leaves on a Saturday or Sunday was exquisite fun since it meant that a fire would be made later when it was dark. While the fire was at its height, my father would go in the house and bring out potatoes wrapped in aluminum foil. This was a treat. He knew how to bake potatoes in a leaf fire, and he knew just when to take them out. It seemed like everything was timed perfectly; just when the fire was smoldering, he would take the heavy steel rake and gently pull the spuds out. By that time it was too late to stay in front of the house. The extras would be distributed to the other kids who had patiently watched this miracle. We went inside and enjoyed this feat and feast.

Other autumn chores were not so magnificent. Exchanging all of the screens for storm windows was a labor of pain and boredom. These duties provided some relief for my father, but there was one week, however, that I could see something was bothering him, and it wasn't just his annual gloom and despair. From our *Weekly Readers* most kids in the fourth grade were aware of some sort of trouble that had started way back in September, a month ago, a long time ago. We kept reading about trouble in a place called Cuba. Whenever I looked at the map and instantly saw how small it was when compared to the United States, my worries quickly evaporated. The United States was a big country; Cuba was a small country. There couldn't be too much trouble in a contest like that.

My father was working a regular lithography job, which meant a routine eight-hour shift, eight to four, and he was home by five. This automatically cut down on playtime for my brother and me since with all our chores and homework, accomplishing those prerequisites between 3:30 and 5:00 was rather difficult. But my brother and I tried. Even if we could just go out for fifteen minutes, we were pretty happy. When I found out that Mr. and Mrs. Jordan did not allow Alonzo out for any amount of time on weekdays, I was very happy. Yet, there was gloom in the air for a few late afternoons as my father came home in his sports jacket and freshly pressed pants. He always wore a blue or white shirt with his varying jackets, and it was my job to take those shirts to the Chinese laundry on Farmers Boulevard.

One day my father came home earlier than usual and shocked Paul and me. We had done our chores. No crimes had been committed, but we were just shocked to see that his routine had changed, and he was home at four o'clock instead of five. Homework was done. Chores were completed. We were in the vacant lot practicing our pitching when he walked up the driveway with a *New York Times* folded in his arm. He went in the back door and whistled for us to come inside about ten minutes later. We never had to hear that whistle twice, and it was fun being hailed that way instead of with words.

My father sat at the dining room table with the paper spread all over it. In a somber voice he started, "You guys been following the news? Do you know what is going on?" Making sure to get the jump on my brother I quickly shot up my arm in the way I did in class at P.S. 156, I.G.C. Class 4-401, I passionately yelled, "Cuba, Cuba, there's something wrong with Cuba." He shook his head and told us to look at the pictures that were unusually large for the *Times.* I already knew that the barbershop paper, the *New York Daily News,* was filled with pictures, and the paper that my mother and father brought home each evening, the *New York Times,* employed pictures sparingly. The pictures were big and showed hazy ships. Not battleships, but hazy ships with unrecognizable boxes on them. Another series of cloudy pictures taken from the air showed a series of obscure buildings with little or no significance to my brother and me. We were not impressed. There was silence since there was no other place for us to take this conversation. My father kept quiet.

"The world's going to end," he intoned quietly. There was a pause, and my brother and I laughed since only kids used expressions like that. "The sky is falling down, the world is gonna end," and "See ya later, alligator." We waited for him to laugh, but he didn't. He continued in his quiet way: "The world is probably going to end in the next few days. Kennedy won't back down. Do you know about H-bombs?" This time my brother answered and used the word *hydrogen* which I knew but didn't know the meaning. I knew that H-bombs were bigger than A-bombs, but only as a kid knows that a cherry bomb is more powerful than a firecracker, and they're better to have on the 4th of July. He told us to sit down and started to explain the differences. As we sat, he explained why one was more powerful and then let us know that if one of them were dropped on New York City, it would flatten the entire city in a few seconds. "Like a pancake?" I asked. He nodded and said that it would be flat from Central Park to Jones Beach. I started to chill. My brother started to move uneasily in his chair. With all this information about being attacked and destroyed, not once had my father mentioned how we were going to defend ourselves against this very real menace. He hadn't smiled once. He meant it when he said it, that the world was going to end. I was silent. My brother couldn't take it, the quiet and the idea of not fighting back.

"Dad, who's going to live?"

"No one, no one can survive the blast or the heat. Those that do will die from radiation sickness in a few days."

I piped up with, "What's radiation sickness?"

"Radiation is a by-product of nuclear fission. It can kill more people than the blast. It doesn't go away."

As he talked, I started to think about where I had heard most of this information in dribs and drabs before this fateful day. This stuff about radiation and sickness started to come back to me. My mother already had taken me to many demonstrations and at some of them, the adults had signs that said, BAN THE BOMB. Sometimes they had a few pictures of what the bomb looked like, and sometimes there were accompanying photographs of places called Hiroshima and Nagasaki. Pete Seeger would sing songs at these demonstrations and rallies, and I remember always being cold; they always seemed to be within close proximity of the United Nations buildings. All of these images were coming back to me, including the hot dog I managed to persuade my mother to get me if she wanted me to keep on holding our sign that said, MONEY FOR SCHOOLS NOT BOMBS. They were all bits of a puzzle that never made sense. Now it did, and I started to whimper.

My father was really going over the details of the Cuban Missile

Crisis. He was just dealing with the reality and what it meant to us, and what would happen to us during the next few days. I had tears in my eyes and was distraught. I thought about my mother working in Manhattan and not being able to make it home on the train. It would be just my brother, my old man, and me. My sister didn't exist because she was far away. I couldn't worry about her if I had wanted to.

"I want you guys to go out to the garage and get some shovels. There is something we can do before this happens." My brother and I looked at each other with hope and excitement. This was action. This was taking the offense. Before we even asked to find out what our charge would be, we were out of the house heading toward the garage. We pulled open the white door and snaked our way around the side of the car to get to the lawn implements that were always buried in the back of the garage. I had a short one; my brother had a long-handled one. He said that was fair since I was smaller and could handle the little one better. We talked with restrained hope.

"Dex, I think I know what we're gonna do."

"Yeah, fallout shelter. That's what's we're gonna do."

"I just wonder if there's enough time to build one. We'd have to dig fast."

"Paul, me and you and Pop will help. We could do it. Come on."

As we neared the back door, my father came out with our two jackets. We had run out so quickly that we were just in our shirts. As he handed them to us, he asked if we knew what we were going to do. With optimism and excitement we both spewed out little fragments of our television-provoked imagination:

> Fallout shelter . . . duck and cover drills in school. Get under the desk, turn away from the window . . . *Twilight Zone,* a man makes a shelter and won't let people in . . . fair because he built it . . . unfair because . . . canned food is good and lasts a long time . . . if deep enough we'll live for a long time.

My father shook his head. "No, I want you to dig but not a fallout shelter since that wouldn't help. You would just die slower. You see, when the radiation is in the air, it can last for days, weeks, months, even years. When you finally come up to see what's happened, you'll have to breathe the air or drink the water and both will be contaminated." Our hands slipped from the shovels and fell to our sides as our last hopes of survival and life were crushed.

"But there is still something we can do; that's why I want you to start digging some holes in the back yard. They don't have to be very deep, about two feet." We were baffled. Everyone knew, even the guy from the *Twilight Zone* episode that a fallout shelter had to be about ten feet underground, the deeper the better. What could you save with a two-foot hole?

"Look, start digging and I'm going to start to gather up some important books that are in the house. We're going to bury some important books and some very important jazz records. That's the one positive thing we can do. Just because we are going to die doesn't mean we can't help others out. If we bury these books, we can help others who come after us who can benefit from certain information. I think a few science books would be a great help to people from another time. They won't have to take the time to make all of the discoveries that we've made already. Books about biology and chemistry. A book of paintings too, so they can see how we looked. Duke Ellington's music will also prove that Negroes made a contribution to civilization, to America."

My brother and I were too stunned to say or do anything. We turned and started to walk into the backyard. I started to dig, and he started to dig. Normally, we would try to dig right next to each other and start a fight about who was digging in that spot first and who thought about it first and who was a better digger. No, we just walked to different parts of the yard and stayed clear of each other. We couldn't even talk. I pushed down with my foot and removed a measly clod of grass and topsoil. My brother did the same. Neither one of us were that energetic. The holes were skimpy. Even though my brother had the longer shovel and was stronger, his hole was not much deeper or wider than mine. Quiet, just the sounds of shovels. Darkness came early because it was October. We heard the back door swing open, and my father came out with books and records that were wrapped in rags and cloths. Because it was dark, we couldn't make out the titles, and they were wrapped for protection.

I whimpered as I dug. After setting the books and records on the ground, my father walked to the garage. He came back with a hoe and started to help us finish the digging. As he hoed the earth, he asked me why I was crying. "Dad, 'cause Mom isn't home. How is she gonna get home from the city?" He didn't answer but my crying or words set off a reaction in my brother. He started to sob in silence and shake his head to and fro. Without breaking his pace my father replied, "You guys shouldn't think about that. Just think about the good things that we're doing. We're going to help people." This answer just brought about more tears and sobs from me. I finally asked the most important question.

"Pop, why do we have to die? We never did anything wrong. Why do we have to die?"

"The capitalists would rather destroy the world than let an idea grow. It's hard to explain."

"But Pop, we're just kids. We never did anything to anybody."

"That's why, I said, it's hard to explain."

My brother asked why couldn't all three of them just fight it out in the ring, Kennedy, Castro, and Khrushchev. My father had now borrowed my shovel because of my useless digging. Since he had started to help I noticed how neat the hole had become. Even his pile of dirt was neater than the ones my brother and I had made. "Say, that would be a novel idea and it's a good suggestion." My brother looked at me with a little smile, "Dex, imagine them with wrestling clothes." I started to smile a little too. My brother kept it up. "Dex, imagine Bobo Brazil fighting Khrushchev. Ya see, Khrushchev would have to have a cool name, like Moscow Bruiser." I laughed and picked up on the idea. "Paul, listen. And Castro, the Havana Smoker."

"Dex, that's good, the Havana Smoker. One more, we need one more. Kennedy, the Boston Brawler. That's it, in this corner, we got, at 300 pounds of flabby meat, Khrushchev, the Moscow Bruiser. In this other corner, hey, no cigars in the ring. The Havana Smoker and finally, without any further delay, the Boston Brawler." The laughter started and wouldn't stop. Images of wrestling matches and refs in gym shoes abounded in our head. We almost didn't hear my father say, "We won't bury them now. We'll wait until we hear something more definitive."

My brother and I were already grabbing at each other. The hole became a new part of the wrestling match. "Dex, whoever gets thrown in the hole, has to stay there for ten seconds."

"Wait, Paul, tag team. Me and the Havana Smoker versus you and the Boston Brawler. And the Moscow Bruiser can be the guest referee."

"Great, and the hole, you have to stay in the hole instead of going to a neutral corner, right?"

"Yeah, and if the Moscow Bruiser gets the tag, he has to go to the hole first, he just can't jump right into the match."

"Great, and it's possible that two guys might have to stay in the hole together . . ."

I chimed in, "And they have to fight to the finish, they have to stay in the hole until one comes out alive and one is dead."

In unison, excited at the prospects of reincarnating the Sunnyside Arena, we yell, "and as Tony the Tiger would say, 'this is Grrrrreeeeeaaat!'"

Just Some Driveway Thoughts

THE TIME THAT my father was thinking about killing my brother, I mean, really thinking about it, impressed me. It was memorable. I should say all those violent times and occasions were, but the time he had the M-1 carbine—souvenir from World War II in the Pacific—pointed at his head, right at his temple, man . . . His brown hand was on the brown and aging wooden stock, his finger on the trigger. My brother had said something. That was what was unique about many of the battles in my home. You were in conflict with the masters of your fate over statements, platforms, sayings, expressions, and ideas. Other kids were getting their licks for what they did. In my house, Springfield Gardens, the 1950s, the beatings which were mostly mental, not physical, were for what you thought or said, not what you did. That was an important aspect of my house.

How did things get that way? It must have been the Commie thing, no more, no less. That played such an important and an equivocal part of my parents' lives that they couldn't shake it out of their private existences even years after they were disengaged. Even after being "in the party" was a memory from twenty or thirty years ago, it still lived. Every American generation can pinpoint the day they give up on their dream. For mine, it's May 4, 1970, and the shootings at Kent State. For my mother and father, the execution of the Rosenbergs took away their illusions and vision. There is a difference. Our participation, maybe due to the lack of longevity, was quickly squashed by May 1970. However, the debris of my parents' aspiration landed solid and sound. They could still assemble parts of the puzzle with what remained even after June 3,

1953, and hearing that the Attorney General was going to accommodate left wing protest and the Rosenbergs being Jewish by executing them earlier. Those days of rousing marches, fighting pamphlets, and self-sacrificing men and women just melded into one blur; it traveled with them as they made their trek from Union Square rallies on 14th Street to southeastern Queens and Westgate Street. Crossing the East River may have added some curious toxins to their plans for overseeing a concoction of politics blended with child rearing. When we finally arrive at our brick house near Idlewild Airport, a world is tactically created with intellectual and political questions that not even our favorite television heroes would have attempted to answer. Pa, Adam, Hoss, and Little Joe Cartwright may have been able to run the Ponderosa empire, but they were totally vanquished at the hands of my mom and dad, the grand inquisitors. My mom and dad repeatedly pointed out that Hop Sing, the Japanese cook, was being exploited and racially caricatured by the Cartwrights and that was one more reason not to watch the show. While millions of other American kids were reminded to eat all the food on their plates because children were starving in India, we were reminded that Negroes here in the South needed help and those CARE packages should have a new destination: Mississippi, Alabama, and Arkansas. Walt Disney was subject to extra scrutiny because he had strayed from his early days as a socialist and had wound up being a supreme anti-union fascist who inculcated reactionary ideals in American kids through the dastardly use of Annette, Cubby, and Darlene. Why weren't there any Negro children in the Mickey Mouse Club my mother would ask in a serious manner? As usual, these questions could never be answered in a satisfactory manner.

So that is what was happening to my brother that night. They had visions of how children were to be brought up and my brother was an offense in ways he never could have imagined. He was not taking the party line or any line for that matter. He was a James Dean who had played chicken once too often. We were in the kitchen, yellow paint, the color of corn flakes on the wall. The tiles were a strange checkerboard configuration; something that the average person would have been reluctant to experiment with. I think because my father was an intelligent and overachieving Negro, he was always subject to proving something to himself that he was special. Therefore, the house presented him with numerous opportunities to prove just how special he was. In turn, that was the way he saw us, Vivian, Paul, and me. Experimental material waiting to enter his lab. My brother was a failed endeavor who had not reacted positively to changes in temperature, humidity, and pressure.

That's how my dad's political background stretching back to 1936 and his membership in the Communist Party came into play. I'm not sure if he was even aware of the ideas he had brought forth from attending party meetings in Brooklyn and Harlem but he confidently felt that our lives could be different just as he felt that the world could be changed by embracing the Marxist dialectic, Stalinist politics, the works of Lenin and Engels. He was going to prove that we were very distinguished. We were going to be smart and intelligent Negro children living in America in the 1950s with a world of opportunity. The world, no, the universe, was there to be picked and mined. No one would have to settle for second class citizenship as my father had to when he was a young black man in the 1930s. We were free to do what we wanted.

Me, I went along with the laboratory testing and found it interesting. It definitely built up your confidence, and I needed that since I was the most diffident person in all the five boroughs of New York City. It's hard to be confident when you don't exist. It's hard to be confident when you are not sure about some of the most basic questions in the world: Who am I? Where do I come from? What am I doing? Where am I going?

"Stanley, Stan, Pops, no, not like this." My mother can scream pretty loudly when she has to, and this was one of those instances when some sort of divine intervention was required. Anytime a father is prepared to murder his offspring, on the verge of taking the life of his son, one better shout and scream as loudly as they can. They have only one chance. How many times did I watch this scenario and how many times did I smile with a smirk that connoted one thing: "You're gettin' what you deserve, just what you deserve."

"Pops, please, Pops, please, please, let him go. Kick him out of the house. But not this. He'll go away and never come back. He can't learn anything from this; he's sick."

My heart always fluttered since this was happening only about a foot or two away from me, and that little M-1 carbine looked liked Davey Crockett's *Old Betsy* and since it was right next to his temple, making a physical as well as psychological impression on my brother, I too, was impressed. This was a war I was witnessing, all-out fratricidal war. My father against my brother for the ninety-ninth time. Good versus Evil.

God against Satan. The Americans against the Germans. The Americans against the Japs. Light against dark. It was a magnificent righting of all wrongs. Freedom was coming. A day of liberation. The signing of the Emancipation Proclamation. The Declaration of Independence. The lifting of the Nazi heel on Europe. All these things were manifested as I watched my father take action. V-E Day was being reenacted. Little Rock schools were being integrated. Let freedom ring.

Paul; he was silent throughout the incident with the rifle, and it ended with the carbine being stowed away in its secret hiding place. He always had a lot to say. That was his specialty. However, at times like this, he tended to be silent. And that was how this entire episode had commenced in the first place. My brother had said something, not done anything, just said something that indicated he wasn't happy with his place in the home.

Silence; that was all my father wanted. He asked little of Paul, but it's sad when you can't even do that for your father or your mother. They ask a little and you purposely don't give that in return. Strictly looking for a reaction and guaranteed by heaven and hell to get it. What do you do when one won't be quiet? Stanley's routine was simple and direct; everything he did possessed some sort of mathematical formula or equation to it. He was definitely into three chances. Three strikes. Three opportunities. Three moments in time. My brother, I think, was a competent practitioner of "unlimited strikes and chances." Bad luck for him. This evening, he had violated that three twinklings theory of existence, and he was going to learn another lesson. A father can crush a son, even an unruly drug-infected one who thinks he's ready to go all the way.

All the way. That was what this lesson revolved around in a succinct way. My old man had given up on traditional methods of quieting a truculent son. He had acquiesced to extreme measures. Of course, there had been gradations within this scale of escalation.

Alonzo noticed it. He was my best friend from the fourth grade on through adulthood. We had gone for a bike ride, going to unknown neighborhoods, far enough that we became thirsty. We had explored Laurelton, where the semifriendly Jewish people lived and Rosedale with the dastardly Irish and Italian people dwelling in ignorance. We had taken chances. Now we were home.

We were walking our bikes up my driveway when we heard shouts of anger. The screens were in, it being summer. Screens are funny; you can't see through the mesh but you can hear everything. The conversation had a ridiculous singsong-y phrasing to it, and Alonzo shook his head. It was that classic pattern that most linguists have identified as possessing no real substance or content. Just emotion. Raw emotion. It's a song; it goes like this:

Stanley: What did you say?
Paul: You heard what I said!
Stanley: No, I didn't hear you. What did you say? I just want to make sure.
Paul: You heard what I said. I just said it.
Stanley: No, I didn't hear you. Say it loud and clear.
Paul: You really want me to say it? You're ordering me to say it?
Stanley: Yeah, I'm ordering you to repeat it.
Paul: OK, I just want to make sure that you are forcing me to say something.
Stanley: OK.
Paul: OK, I said that a guy would have to be less than a chump to keep on arguing with you.

The tinkling of a broken wine goblet and I press my face right up to the screen and peer through a little hole never repaired. My father now has the shattered shard right to his throat, and I see a little blood, not a lot but enough to impress Alonzo and me. My brother is scared. His neck is arched all the way back, and he looks like some sort of circus freak who can elongate certain muscles at will. He can feel the blood.

My father pressed a little harder, not cutting the big one but pressing with authority. This was a different type of song though, not as predictable or known.

Stanley: I want you to apologize for what you said.
Paul: Sure, anything.
Stanley: All I want is an apology.
Paul: I apologize. I apologize. I apol-o-gize!
Stanley: Good, get out of the house for now.

Misbehavior in my father's eyes was an impossibility because left-wing politics had imbued him with the concept that human beings, like economic conditions, could conform to theory. What was stated in a textbook had concrete and tangible parallels in reality. During the early years of my father's attempts to correct my brother's behavior, he quoted from the greatest works of the premier theorists of all time. It didn't matter whether it was Engels, Marx, Lenin, or Trotsky; he took theoretical models, which had been applied to nations, communities, and idealized individuals, and applied them to human beings. That's what's my brother was up against.

Alonzo and I quietly walked our bikes back down the driveway, hopped on and rode through Springfield Gardens for the rest of the afternoon.

Growing Up

—=≫•《(•)》•≪=—

I WAIT FOR you, every Monday night, at 6:30 PM because it is your line that I want to be on, because you are the best teller in the world. I have five dollars for my bank account; I just spent eighty cents on two hot dogs with everything, and now I'm on your line and in love. You are a brunette and would have won the Miss Subways contest for sure. I would have pulled off thirty or forty voting ballots from the little tab on the E train for you. Your teller plate says S. LEWIS, but I made sure to diligently listen for your first name. One evening I was rewarded, and I heard one of your teller friends call you Sally, straight out of that reader when I was a kid. "Sally, Dick, Jane and Spot." My favorite heroes. That Sally lived in a neighborhood that was somewhat like mine. Whenever I looked at the illustrations of what you were doing with Spot, I said, that looks just like Westgate Street. Right down to the picket fences around the homes. Dick wore black shoes; sometimes brown but always blue jeans with cuffs. Jane had common sense and warned both Dick and Sally about their little tricks and games. Sally and her little jumper, dropping rocks and sticks into puddles of water to make a mess. Swept up and swept away with them, as though they were real, I lived in their house and I was sure they would like mine. Now I see a real Sally.

"Yes, how may I help you?" These were her words every Monday night at 6:30 PM Jamaica Savings Bank was open only one evening a week. I made my pilgrimage each Monday night because I had collected money from my paper route on Friday. Some people did not pay until Saturday, but eventually I got my money for delivering the *Long Island Press* to my sixty-five customers. I was proud and happy. It was September

1967. The war was on, and I had my eight dollars a week. The routine was an excellent one. I came home at about three o'clock, and the papers were already there, a big bundle of newspapers bound in bailing wire. Bob, the route manager, drove an old beat-up station wagon which when fully loaded, barely took the weight of the thousands of papers that he picked up at the central office in Jamaica. Bob liked me because I was dependable, and I liked him because he was an adult who regarded me with some importance. He was still sporting a crew cut when most guys his age were going hippieish. He was for the war, "bombing Hanoi back into the Stone Age," and let it be known that he was a hawk. I had already been to the first large-scale anti-Vietnam War demonstration in 1965 down in Washington, D.C., so I avoided that topic with him and stuck to papers and trying to make money. But I could already see the complications of knowing and liking people and not siding with them about the Vietnam War. Luckily, my primary interest was increasing the size of my route, putting my earnings in the bank and being free of my parents. My life at fourteen took on all the trappings of an adult with school, work, money, and love, even if Sally didn't know that I pined for her.

I felt that I deserved her love since I labored all week for it. After changing out of my school clothes and eating a quick peanut-butter-and-jelly sandwich, I sat down with a pile of rubber bands on one side of me and sixty-five copies of the *Long Island Press* and started folding. Those sixty-five newspapers had to be folded just the right way so they would fit into the basket of my truck bike. They couldn't be stuffed in too tightly because you only wanted one to come out at a time as you hurled them to glory. I was good. Well, not at first. As a matter of fact, I was amazed at how bad I was at throwing the papers. The first few weeks I watched papers sail uncontrollably hitting swans, cars, one time a window (a big bay one) and I was so grateful that it didn't break.

There was a routine. Once all of the papers were folded, I went out to the garage and got my bike out. I checked it out, the tires, especially the front one, since that was the one that carried the weight of the basket. Carefully packing the papers, I had already learned never to use rubber bands twice even if a nice customer returned them to you. That first time you saw that disassembled *Long Island Press* floating through the air, you knew never to do that again. Page two was in the gutter, page fifteen in a hedge and the sports section was draped like a drop-cloth on the sidewalk in case of a sloppy paint job. On rainy days the company supplied you with brown waterproof bags for protection. They cost a penny, and I discovered that they were durable enough that they could be used again. However, the customers always threw them away. I enlisted my mom in my work and told her that I had an idea. First, the question. How could I inform and remind those people that I wanted the bags back? How could I retrieve them? My mom listened and came up with an idea that predated recycling and being ecologically sound by twenty years. There had to be a way to inform people on rainy days that they should not throw away the protective bag. There was no way to contact them each on an individual basis since practically no one was home at 3:30 in the afternoon. Within a day or two of hearing about the dilemma she performed one of her miracles. She was always capable of one or two. The first one was that every now and then she would actually bring home a pizza, after work. We were amazed. She had ridden the train all the way home from the Lincoln Building on 42nd Street, opposite Grand Central. Getting off at Hillside Avenue, next to the last stop on the train, she walked upstairs and ordered a pizza. She then waited, got on the bus with the pizza and rode for twenty-five minutes to Springfield Gardens. She then walked from the bus stop to the house, and we were in heaven. Her other special feat, not as grandiose but just as much appreciated, was to bring home a product that we knew only as "the special cupcakes." There was a company that only distributed their product in Manhattan, so anytime we got them, they were a real treat. The name was in script, and I knew that made it more exotic. There was nothing like hearing my mom come in the back door with a box of "Entemens." We mispronounced the name, but it didn't matter. When she came home with the plan of saving my rain bags, it was just another case of her showing me how resourceful she was.

"After dinner, I'll tell you how I think I solved your problem," she said, coming in at about 7 P.M. I was happy and waited through dinner for the surprise and the solution. With the dishes dried and put away, my mom started going through her bag. She was never really content with a pocketbook, and I took note that in summer it was one type of bag, and in the winter there was another slung around her arm. Out came a manila envelope. As she opened the packet she said, "I'm pretty sure this will solve your problem with the rain bags." I moved over to the dining room table beneath the three-light chandelier. My mother, in an imaginative fashion had typed a message on one piece of paper and then made almost fifty copies. On the original it said:

> Please save this rain bag and I will pick it up on Friday nights when collecting. Sincerely, your Long Island Press paperboy.

This was repeated about fifteen times from top to bottom. With fifty copies, I had already calculated that I had over six hundred messages if I cut them up carefully. I looked at my mom and said, "You're a genius. I can't believe you came up with this idea. It's really great." I hugged her. I couldn't wait for the application of the theory which normally would not have occurred until the next downpour and ran into the pantry and got a discarded newspaper. Downstairs was where I kept my supplies of rubber bands and rainproof bags. I skipped up the basement steps to the kitchen, talking as I went, "Mom, all I need is the scissors." "Dex, don't use my good scissors for sewing on this paper. There has to be others lying around." Normally, I would have ignored this plea and explained that cutting a few pieces of construction paper was not going to damage a pair of industrial garment scissors. However, this time, I had to relent. She had just done this terrific favor for me, and I could oblige her small request. In a drawer in the kitchen were some single-edged razor blades. I gently drew and cut one message from the piece of paper. "Watch this," I said and proceeded to fold the paper with the message inside; I then handed it to her and said with an air of pretense, "Here's your paper, Mr. Anderson." My mom played along and said, "Thank you." She opened the bag, unfolded the paper and picked up the little message and read:

> Please save this rain bag and I will pick it up on Friday nights when collecting. Sincerely, your Long Island Press paperboy.

I hugged her and told her that she would get any three wishes she desired of me; from her fourteen-year-old sometimes unpredictable son, they were hers. Her Aladdin wishes were pretty banal, but I stuck to them because they were important to her: walking the dogs, taking out the garbage, and she never even got to three.

I became the most assiduous paperboy due to my attention to details.

I started to wake up as though I were in a dream for the past few years. Fantasies, even elaborate and constructive ones had kept me out of the fray. There had to be some precision in my life. I just couldn't be the sloppy and careless person that I had become. Not that I was proud to be disheveled. I just think I wanted to be the opposite of my brother. The worst fate that can befall someone, at fourteen, is to be conscious of a proper role model but one loathes the person so much, that you reject the behaviors that are implicitly being offered to you. My brother already had a sense of himself as a public figure and dressed accordingly. Nice expensive clothes from shops that catered to young men on Jamaica Avenue. The shops had legendary names for black youth and he proudly said, "Kings, only Kings carries these types of suede jackets." That's one sort of model. It never took hold. Social presentation left me feeling phony and awkward.

Having my customers chastise me on Friday night for their papers being discovered in bushes, on awnings, or under their cars was another type of model. This connected you to the world of work, obligation, and responsibility. When I walked up to the door of a person, I was to learn that people could be dissatisfied with my performance.

"Young man, the paper was wet on Thursday; I'm subtracting for that."

"You misplaced the paper. I asked that you put it in the storm door."

"You're the worst guy I've seen. I wish the other kid was back on the route."

Almost all my customers were black. The neighborhood which had been ninety-nine percent white in the early 1960s was now one hundred percent black, but there was no difference. Black lower-middle-class people had replaced white lower-middle-class folks. They had exchanged houses and locations. The whites had moved farther east on Long Island and the blacks had moved farther east from Manhattan and Brooklyn. For a few years Springfield Gardens was a proud black neighborhood that held up its houses and lawns and backyards as proud displays of what black people could accomplish. The churches, the schools, and the Boy Scouts and the Girl Scouts contained a sense of accomplishment. There were civic associations that met regularly to coordinate social and political goals and agendas. Springfield Gardens was a decent place to raise a family.

* * *

"Yes, how may I help you?"

"Hi, I would like to make a deposit."

But Sally and my mom didn't look like the people on my paper route, and I loved both of them. An incident occurred about a month before freshman year in high school that woke me a bit from my solipsistic coma of Aurora racing cars and baseball cards. I had been asleep. My brother and I had gone to visit Nanny over in South Jamaica, 107th Avenue and New York Boulevard. We had spent the afternoon with her eating a nice lunch and watching a baseball game with Antonio, her Cuban husband. It was a fine time. We left with five dollar bills each from Antonio. He was a retired redcap from the Pennsylvania Railroad, the type of fellow Malcolm X had known when he was first getting started, the type of man that Malcolm X mocked for staying with his job, his place in the world. But Malcolm X was dead and Antonio was alive, and the crisp five dollar bills were in our jean pockets. Malcolm X's book had come out in 1965 and that stuck in my mind for obvious reasons.

> *You laughed and mocked someone like my grandfather, working hard on the railroad, a good job for a black or Cuban person in 1940 but he's alive and you're dead.*

As we walked from their house to the bus stop on Merrick Road, we noticed five black kids our age on the other side of 107th Avenue. They were walking in the opposite direction toward New York Boulevard. They eyed us with a sense that we weren't exactly intruders, just unknown quantities. We passed each other. There was nothing ominous about them since we were all about the same age. Even though we had passed each other, they then cut back on a diagonal crossing to our side and came up behind us. They caught up to Paul and me and were quickly right next to us. "Hey, where are you guys going?" one of them asked. Paul gave a neutral monosyllabic answer, "Home." This left them dissatisfied and I could see that. Now there was something threatening since they had surrounded us. To let them know that we somehow belonged and weren't a threat to them, I said, "Our grandmother lives in that big yellow house up near New York. You know it, big yellow house with a green roof." I was relieved when I saw a nod of the head of one of the five.

We started to walk, and they quickly caught up to us and asked if we had any money. My brother said *no*. They then asked me. I said *no* also but they knew I was the one to push. "All I find I keep," came at me from one of the band. I didn't know the expression due to living in that dreamlike world. He repeated it with an explanation. "Whatever I find on you, I keep." I thought instantly about that crisp five dollar bill and came up with my own crafty reply. "You have to let me keep money for the bus; how are we gonna get home? We told you we were walking to the bus stop." My long-windedness just angered them and one of them yelled, "OK, just gimme a dime. That's all, a dime."

I was relaxed and smiled inside. I reached into my pocket, took out a dime, and dropped it into a black hand. Paul said, "Come on," and I acted like being given an order from a higher authority, as though I had no other choice but to rush along and say, "Bye." We started to walk and Paul quickly whispered without turning to me, "We're gonna have to run for it." Just as quickly I whispered, "No, don't run; they know we're OK." As a rock sailed past my head, I could see that I was wrong. "Get those white boys!" was yelled, and I knew that we were in trouble. "You white honky bastards, you can't run." My brother and I took off with our new Chuck Taylor Converse sneakers. Sticks, rocks, and cans kept hurling past us. Fortunately the gap and our running was just enough to keep them from achieving any accuracy. We ran for our lives. As we got closer to Merrick Road, we knew we might make it. However, our escape depended on whether or not a bus was coming. We hit Merrick Road and unconsciously we knew that any bus, the Q3A, Q4, Q4A, Q5, or the Q5A, any bus heading east on Merrick Road would be a godsend. We turned around, and they were right behind us. A rock ricocheted off the ground and just skimmed my pants. There was a bus, the Q5 to Rosedale, not ours but our emergency escape. My brother flagged the bus, and it pulled over with the door already open. We hopped on and watched the enemy stop dead in their tracks. They couldn't get on the bus. That wasn't an option.

The doors closed and the light was green and we pulled away. We moved to some seats near the rear door and were breathing and sweating. The little gang became smaller as the bus lumbered away from them, and they yelled and hooted at our escape. Despite our gasps, I asked my brother why they had attacked us. We had been coming and going through that neighborhood for years. "Paul, it's either because we had money or they think we're white or Puerto Rican." He was out of breath and paused, "Take your pick. Important thing is we got the hell out of there." I reached in my pocket for the five dollar bill. It was there but offered no solace. I was upset at not knowing the answer. I wanted to be attacked for having money, not for being white or Puerto Rican. We didn't talk and thought about how we were going to have to get off and walk the rest of the way home at some point since we were on the wrong bus. I started to think about colors, that black hand, my mom, and Sally. Sally, the woman I love is white, and I've never thought about that. Sally, who on nights when it's cold in the bank, wears a green high school warmup jacket over her business suit with the words *Andrew Jackson*, is not my color, whatever that is. How can I ask her for a date? What will I say when she asks who or what I am? I'll hesitate. The answer will seem clumsy. I'll seem even clumsier than ever. The jacket's too big for her, and I know it's from a boyfriend from times past. It's 1967 and white kids don't go to Andrew Jackson anymore. Only a few. Andrew Jackson, one of the premier schools of the Queens secondary system is changing and neither I nor Sally nor Vivian would be welcome there. At one time, parents made sure that their sons and daughters were accepted to Jackson, because it wasn't that far beneath Bronx High School of Science, Stuyvesant, or Brooklyn Tech.

The words, rhetoric and language of the summer of 1967 started to resonate also: Black power, black militancy, SNCC, Martin Luther King Jr. versus Malcolm X, long hot summers, black upheaval, black violence, black urban violence, Detroit, Newark, black, black, and black. And I loved Sally.

Wake-up Call

⟫⟪◉⟫⟪

In the movies the police make pretty dramatic arrests. They're usually camped outside the drug suspect's home, waiting for the signal. Walkie-talkies, little speaker phones in their ears, flashing lights, and even secret coded messages. The tension mounts as the forces build ensuring an arrest without any chance of a last-minute escape. Ready, go, and in they pour, officers, agents, guns drawn, combat shooting poses and they all look pretty impressive with their battle gear. When the police and agents from some federal enforcement bureau came for my brother, it was nothing like that. In real life most arrests are made in the morning, and there is no need for that much drama because when you come between five and six the criminal is usually sleeping. You can count on that. With little or no drama, these officials rang the bell. It was a weekday. I'll never forget. You forget the other arrests, but that first one always leaves the biggest impression.

It was a spring morning, as pretty as they come in New York. We were both sleeping in the same twin beds that once had been linked together as a bunk beds. With two windows on the north and west side of the room, there was always plenty of light. The northern view gave us a panorama of the neighborhood climaxing in the 19th century dome of a wooden schoolhouse, P.S. 161. This school and its prodigious pitched roof with red shingles dominated the small hamlet that I grew up in. On the other side, facing west were the tracks of the Long Island Railroad. Commuter trains blasted through, a few an hour. During rush hour they were more frequent, but that only lasted from about five in the afternoon to seven at night. For a time, the trains ran on the ground, so one really had a bucolic setting of a train station, commuters getting off at the end of a tiring day in the city, and walking or driving from the station. Some drove but it really wasn't necessary. Springfield Gardens was idyllic in that sense. However, when they elevated the train and it paralleled our second-floor window, it completely lost its rustic ambience. Then it was like living next to an El in Manhattan. Noisier and uglier, the Long Island Railroad became a nuisance. It shook the house. When a superfast model car became standard issue in 1968, the train flashed by so fast you were literally only getting a small glimpse of aluminum and a lot of noise. The rural railroad vanished and became a suburban commuter train that transported people to their bedroom community.

For a kid the grandeur of a train dies hard. However, there was one last bit of glory that the LIRR retained; once a month, and twice a month in the winter, coal trains would come trudging through. My brother and I romantically imagined that they had plowed a path all the way from Pittsburgh, Pennsylvania, or even farther west and were preparing for the final run to Nassau and Suffolk counties, the end of Long Island. We knew when they were coming. The rolling thunder of a coal train with its 150 cars was unmistakable. The rails forecast its impending approach long before you would even see it. At a minimum, three great diesel engines, sometimes five, would come honking and blasting their horns. If you were fast enough and started to wave, the engineer would give a blast just for you, and my brother and I would argue incessantly whom the engineer had honked for. "It was for me; no, he didn't even see you. Did you see him wave? That was because I waved." Once this argument remained unsettled but settled enough for other activities to commence, we began an activity, which we considered the highlight of not just the day, but the weekend. Counting and identifying the coal cars or if we were lucky, and it was a freight train with cars from the most exotic places, imagining and dreaming about those strange and distant lands. The contest always began in earnest.

"SP, that stands for Southern Pacific."

"Yup, UP, that stands for Union Pacific"

"That's too easy. Everyone knows the Union Pacific,"

"Wabash, do you think that's a place?"

"I don't know, don't want to live there, Wasbash something."

We would laugh as our editorial commentary provided us with another source of entertainment.

"B&O, that stands for Baltimore and Ohio."

"CP, Canadian Pacific, that's from far away."

"M-A-I-N-E, what does that stand for? Missouri, Alabama . . ."

"That's Maine you idiot. Boy, what a jerk."

"Oh, yeah, but the way the letters are spread out on the sides of the car make it look like . . ."

"Maine, one of the most important states in the Union. All our lumber comes from there."

"And fishing. On that board game they always have fish for Maine."

"You're right. A lot of fishing."

And it would go on and on for perhaps 118 freight cars. The morning the police and other authorities entered our home they could still see a little of that boyish stuff in him, in me. They walked in wearing very nice suits, and I saw how my brother was cuffed within seconds. He was lying facedown, so it was ideal for them. They knelt on his back, grabbed the right hand, then the left, two snaps, and that's it. I'm not even sure my brother woke because in those days he slept to twelve or one like it was nothing. My father had to dump the bed with him in it many a morning just to get him to go to school. Now his head was in the pillow, and he finally figured out what was happening while they were reading the search and arrest warrant. They actually had their paperwork in order, and with their blue and gray suits you could see how professional they were.

I looked over at him.

> Weeping, don't weep, don't show weakness. Show 'em how tough you are. Don't weep now. You've been dealing heroin of the lowest grade to the lowest grade scum imaginable. You're tough and these are feds. Show 'em; James Cagney cries because the priest Father O' something asked him to cry. I'm not asking you to cry so don't. Take it.

He turned his head toward me and started to really cry. He couldn't make that much noise because of the pillow and that knee in his back. My parents were in the hallway, innocent bystanders. I was never quite sure what they were thinking. They had to be baffled to say the least. My brother represented a new sort of sociological species that never existed before. Neither the psychological community nor the social scientists had ever dreamed him up. The chapter in the psychology book had not yet been written that presumed to explain how middle-class environs could produce this sort of contradiction, but it can, did, and will. You can have a backyard, little swimming pools, cookouts and summer camps, and that won't ensure you don't have 200 glassine bags hidden in some books (you can even have a small library in the home) ready to go. That's why my mom and dad stood there. Heroin selling and addiction was something that went on in Harlem, Hollywood Harlem at that. Drug addicts nodding to the slow rhythm of heroin dwelled in places like Bedford-Stuyvesant and Southern Boulevard in the Bronx. It was in the movies. It was exotic. "That first generation of parents was to freely admit their naivete when they attended thousands of psychotherapeutic meetings. They told facilitators, ex-drug addicts, mediators, counselors, negotiators, "I just thought he was sleepy because of homework." Or "I wondered about the clothes, but she did work after school." Or, "I found the needle and thought it was a prank." Or, "This was something for the colored people to do, not my son." Even Mario Puzo's *The Godfather* cultivated this notion that only one group was prone to drug use: "Keep the traffic in the dark people, the Coloreds. They're animals anyway, so let them lose their souls." More than you knew, Mario. More than you ever dreamed.

The agents tried to be helpful because this was Springfield Gardens, not 137th Street and Lenox Avenue. If anything, they were downright cordial and pleasant and could see from my parents' faces and demeanor that they were truly engaging in social intercourse with their peers and in my father's case, because of his intimidating carriage and vocabulary, their unequal.

"Sorry to break in on you folks like this but your son has been dealing narcotics for at least six months. We've had him and the house under surveillance for quite some time. He finally . . . sold, hey, Eddie, come here for a second. Tell Mr. and Mrs. Diaz what's going on and what happened. They probably don't understand what's happening. Yes, Mr. and Mrs. Diaz, you see this? Your son sold me this the other day. Do you know what that is? It's heroin, smack, shit, excuse my

French, horse. He's been dealing this for about four or five months, all out of this house. You probably noticed the new clothes, the new stuff he's been bringing in, right? You didn't? Well, those are the first signs of something going on with the illegal distribution of narcotics. Here's my card if you have any questions."

I've propped myself up on one elbow to get a better view, and I've been gloriously ignored the entire time. That's the only way to take it all in. Now the covers are pulled off him, and with a quick yank, he's on his feet. He used to weigh a lot more but heroin, smack, shit, will make a scarecrow out of the most robust seventeen-year-old kid. I don't care how much he eats. That stuff eats you and you're reduced to the bare basics. He's told that he can go to the bathroom to get dressed. The agents are thorough though. Everything he gestures toward is inspected. The tears run down his face as they take him to the bathroom. Up come the sheets; the mattress is turned over. His shoes are bent inside and out. The nightstand on his side of the room is quickly emptied. They're quick and efficient and are able to keep a conversation going among themselves or with my parents as they do their job. I want to be a part of this but don't have anything to do. A guy that looks just like Clint Eastwood finally includes me in the drama, "That's his dresser right? I don't want to go through your things. It's not necessary." Finally, I'm engaged; I'm there and present and talk. "Yeah, that's his." Not a lot but I said something.

They are not careless or negligent. Now it's time to dump his dresser drawers, but they do it one by one, onto his stripped mattress. Before they empty number two or three, they place number one back in its place. Nothing is left in doubt. They even unroll his socks, and I have to smile. My smile stops when a few bags drop out of the blue ones. Everyone is doing his job. They ask if they can use the phone, and my parents are happy to say we have one upstairs and down. They'll use the one closest to them. Everyone is on the ball except I finally notice that Clint Eastwood is in a trance. With his neck craning upward, he's finally noticed something that can't help but be noticed: my more than fifty model planes that hang from the ceiling in a dramatic re-creation of the B-17 raid over Schweinfurt, Germany, back in 1943. Clint is engrossed as he looks at the attention to detail. The Flying Fortresses are all flying in a tight formation. From all different directions the Me-109s come slashing down at the B-17s. By using fishing wire so it is practically invisible, there are suspended Focke Wulfs attacking the underside of the formation. He looks and stares and is not there.

"It's really something. The fishing line, that was a great idea. Who did this?"

"Me."

"Incredible, it must have taken you hundreds of hours, not just making them, but studying photographs or maybe paintings. Have to admit that I've never seen too many paintings of this sort of battle scene."

I perk up and say, "I have this great book from the American Heritage collection. I think it's called *Air War Against Hitler's Europe.*"

Clint hears half of what I'm saying because he's thinking more about my brother getting dressed in the bathroom than the B-17 that is fending off a head-on attack from three Messerschmitts. Pulling a chair from our study table he gets on it for a closer look. His finger gently flicks a propeller, and he spins it. His chiseled face is a curious series of twists and turns. He gets down from the chair and waves his hand indifferently as one of his colleagues says, "You think there's something up there with the planes?" He looks at me and whispers.

"I don't understand."

"I thought you said it was pretty authentic."

"No, no, this is beautiful, wonderful, it should be in a museum. I just don't get it. You did this, and your brother is into selling smack in the neighborhood. It doesn't make any sense."

I'm just as dismissive of his last remark as he was of the suggestion from his friend that there might be some glassine bags hidden in the bomb bays of my Flying Fortresses. Years of training, practice and obedience cause the following words to flow out of my mouth just like an actor who has received his cue from the director.

"He's a bum. My brother's a bum. He doesn't want to work. He's a lazy bum."

Clint doesn't have answers for this either, and I want to change the subject.

"Were you in the war?"

We're interrupted by an agent who has come out of the bathroom. "Hey Bill, what's up? Chief in the bathroom says he wants a blue-and-white sweater that's hanging in the closet. Get it for him but check it first."

"Sure, be right with you."

He walks over to the clothes closet and examines the vast array of clothing that my brother has amassed over the past few months. Stylish pants, sweaters, shirts, and many pairs of shoes. Everything is of the finest quality and exhibits true taste and a sense of class. Outfits consisting of everything from shoes, socks, suede sweaters, accompanying dickeys and turtlenecks, they are all there in abundance and overabundance. The blue-and-white sweater is finally spotted and removed from its hanger. It's neatly folded and pressed. Clint walks with it to the bathroom, and I notice that he does feel the creases and other various folds in the sweater. When he comes back, he goes straight to the closet and starts to flip through the rest of the wardrobe. As he rustles through the clothing, he talks to me with his back in my direction. "You shouldn't call him a bum. He's your brother, remember that." His voice has moral overtones to it, and I can discern that I am being chastised.

"You were in the war, right?"

"Yes, I was there."

"You were in the air corps, right?"

"Yeah" and that's followed by his whistling a few notes from *off we go, into the wild blue yonder* . . .

"So, were you a pilot?"

"No, I tried but washed out. Became a navigator."

"So you were on B-17s?"

"No, B-24 Liberators down in Italy."

More training and practice has taught me that you never ask anymore questions of veterans once you reach this point. He broke the awkward silence.

"Still hard for me to understand. Nice home, nice parents . . ."

I have nothing to say. I lie back down and wait for my brother to be brought out of the bathroom. My parents go downstairs and I can smell the brewing coffee. Their old beatup coffeepot with a fresh batch is the only comfort they'll have this morning. Coffee and cigarettes are going to have to go a long way. My father smokes Pall Malls and my mother puffs on Parliaments.

An Unhappy House

IT WAS AN ugly summer, notwithstanding all the good and decent hippie things that were going on all across the United States. Things were booming from New York to California, from Texas to Michigan. The war was on; week after week WNEW Channel Five would broadcast the Honor Roll of the dead from the New York Metropolitan area. The names would scroll across the screen, and each week it got longer and longer. An unrelenting drumbeat and a funeral procession trumpet played as the names rolled. It quieted you down. You had to respect the dead, no matter which side of the war you were on. So many young guys died. It was the summer I started to come apart. This was the summer that I would never forget. Everyone has one. I always figured mine would revolve around falling in love and falling out of it. Instead it was about fractions, parts, and no common denominators; there was going to be some crying and dying. This was the season that my life truly became ugly and in a way that I would never forget. The scarring, like bad adolescent acne that leaves those swatches of purple on a person's face, would always remain.

Bruce Glickhouse, that's the name of my Doctor Faustus whom I encountered, with the cardinal difference being that there was no deal I could make with him so he would cease and desist in his torture of me. He wanted my soul. He wanted my soul, and there was nothing I could do to stop him. He got my soul and practically a lifelong sentence without parole.

There's a place, a nice place, a great place, the 92nd Street Y. It's also known as the Young Men's Hebrew Association. This place is a cultural landmark and gathering place for the New York Jewish community. I knew it well because of all its cultural activities and affairs. I had understood the importance of the synagogue and the after-school center since my days in Laurelton. Aware that there were so many more Christians than Jews, I understood the need to create a refuge also from a Christian dominated society. It was reassuring that Jewish people had their own place, especially after what had happened to them during World War II. Their own place. It made me respect them and think about how they had created their sanctuary. It let them know that they were equal to their sometimes sworn enemies.

My connection with the 92nd Street Y was my forced attendance at a poetry reading here, a piano recital there, things of this nature. My mother arranged these affairs in a surreptitious manner, as she had to. If I had known what awaited me after she said, "How about dinner in the city? Meet me at the 666 Building at about 5:15," the fight I would have mounted would have vanquished any parent, except my father. Once he found out that the money had been paid, a check had been made out, there were no more questions. I attended initially in pain and was almost always joyful for the coercion at the conclusion of the event. I inevitably found myself clapping the loudest or sitting around to listen to the question-and-answer period. A few times, I even wangled an autograph or two.

I had another connection, not so esoteric or academic. The hosteling, and Bruce Glickhouse, that was it. A word that I had never heard before, strange enough for me to think at the outset that this was really *a Jewish thing*. The first time I heard *hosteling* I was positive that it was something peculiar to this group of people who wouldn't have a glass of milk with a ham sandwich (one of my favorite combinations), took off days from school and work because they were sad, and even when they did eat, it just didn't seem like they savored steak and potatoes. A thin burnt cracker without salt was sufficient. Because I had heard my mother speak Yiddish with her mother, Jenny, I always put words that I didn't understand into that lexicon. Jewish words, Yiddish words, Russian words; no question, *hosteling* reminded me of Jenny Kravitz and her kitchen in Brooklyn and a woman who said *good boy* and *nice boy*. Then the Yiddish would begin and the strange foods and smells that went straight up my nostrils. My mom and her mom would converse in this secret code that had its own systematic rhythm of pauses and continuations; this language had declarations that always sounded like questions. In the Flatbush section of Brooklyn, which in the 1950s was predominantly Jewish, Jenny lived with her aging husband; she was a retired seamstress. She was that first generation of Russian Jewish immigrants who hit Ellis Island in the early 1900s and embarked on a trail of tears and transition. Little did she know that she was following and embracing America's dream for all of those who were enchanted by a statue of a woman holding a torch. The fire in that torch can lead or burn. For that generation it did both. Sometimes I wonder if blacks had had the same light, would their lives have been different, then and now? Would that light have made a difference?

With black shoes, blue dresses, white blouses, she had this puritanical manner of dress, and she would look down at me and smile. The road from Odessa on the Black Sea stretched a long way. After Ellis Island you end up on Chrystie Street on the lower East Side. You pay your penance there and work fourteen-hour days in factories sewing and sewing until your eyesight goes bad. You earn, save a few pennies here and a few nickels there. Cookie jars and mattresses and finally the step of opening a bank account. Of course, you don't do it yourself since your English consists of *hello* and *good-bye* and *good* and *not so good* and a lot of smiles. When the strangers speak their native tongue, which you do not understand, you take off your glasses as though that will improve the lines of communication. You lean forward with your glasses in your hand and nod your head hoping that this intricate gesture will be perceived in a neutral fashion, and this in turn will make *the Yankee* think that you do know what is going on or what is demanded of you. Your oldest child accompanies you on this important mission to the bank because he *speaks good American English.* When you first enter the bank, you think of the Czars and a pogrom for a second, but that little boy with knickers who "speaks good American English" keeps pulling you to the desk that says NEW ACCOUNTS and Sammy Kravitz doesn't see Cossacks on horseback or drunken Ukrainians on foot. He sees NEW ACCOUNTS and knows that this is the way to do things. This is the secret to America. NEW ACCOUNTS. The weekly visits are made and because your "little Sammy" can't keep missing school to go to the bank since the bank is only open from nine to three, you gather up that special courage and go alone. In response to "How can I help you?" and other small linguistic pronouncements, you know to politely pass the little maroon book with three American dollar bills under the bars.

Those three American dollar bills add up and another neighborhood that sounds like some mixed-up American words—brown and ville—starts to haunt you. Other neighbors on Chrystie and Delancey and Rivington and Hester Streets have already embarked on another trip across a body of water. This time it's not the Atlantic, but a river called East and you think, *This brown village, everyone goes. Brownsville, Mama, not Brown Village. Mama, say it, Brownsville.* You do hear *Brownsville* and think, *American people always want to shorten and make something faster. It's a Brown Village, not Brownsville, ach, these American people and their fastness.* On the corner of Sutter and Saratoga, you open up a candy store and luncheonette and live above it with your family. A store; in Odessa this could not have happened to even the richest and smartest Jew and here you are with a store and four children who "speak good American English."

Hosteling in the late 1960s at the 92nd Street Y and I misconstrue it as Yiddish. My mother asked me if I had any desire to go on a hosteling trip with the 92nd Street Y, and I envisioned more people reading on a stage with a spotlight and a foodless affair that comes after the applause. This had no appeal; I was never going to eat, not if I didn't have to, hard-boiled eggs and a piece of celery, when I should be eating hot dogs and apple pie and driving Chevrolets. Yes, sir.

I'm dragged to the office of the director of the summer hosteling program and meet Max, and I don't know that I've been signed up already. I'm perturbed until I discover it's just a question of choosing which trip. Trip? I look at the brochures and am intrigued with the pictures of long lines of bikes threading their way through the Pennsylvania Dutch country and three-speed English racers tooling down the coast of Massachusetts. And this is how I met the man who ruined my summer and my life.

A toilet, a large lavatory in the men's room of the YMCA in downtown Boston is where it starts. We had just ridden from Cape Ann on the coast all the way to Boston, a magnificent ride. I had done not just well; I had been behind the group leader at all times. He was first, and I was second. The ride was over and we were settling down in rooms with real beds and bathrooms that had showers. I was in the bathroom. I was in one stall and he was in the other. The toilet with its tightly wound grade "C" toilet paper that came off in shreds only added more depravity to the humiliation that I was about to endure. Rounding off this disgrace with just the right touch of baseness, my stallmate was doing a certain something that possessed a certain rhythm which alarmed me. I said to myself, "He's doing that now, that close to me." He was able to talk and maintain his rhythm. It was Bruce. He was sharing a room with me, and I knew his red sneakers. He eased my self-consciousness with, "I love to read in the bathroom. Do you?" This struck me as being very open and juvenile at the same time, but it did relax me. "Sure, there's nothing like a good crap and a good book." He used the black vernacular of the day and pounded the stall with a "Right on!" I knew he had made the clenched Huey Newton-H. Rap Brown-Eldridge Cleaver-Bobby Seale fist. I laughed and said, "Right on, brother!"

There was a silence, and his other fist continued. Then he said, "What are you?" I said "huh" because there was no connection between the last thought. He repeated, "I said, what are you?" I was quick and just said mindlessly, "What do you mean what am I?" He kept on now without taking a breather. "No, I just said, what are you? Where do you come from? Or, where do your parents come from?" Now that he was being specific I felt better and reeled off the answers that came to my head. "Oh, I'm from New York. I was born there. My mother was born in New York too. My Dad, he's from Virginia but he's been in New York City since he was a kid. So, we're all from New York. Good old New York City." Still feeling uneasy about the other activity because the rhythm had increased, I devised a new strategy and decided to turn the question around. "What are you?" came from my stall. "I'm Jewish; what the hell did you think?" he answered. He kept going, "This trip is out of the 92nd Street Y; it's for Jewish kids." I was unnerved for a second but saw my out and took it:

Me: *Well, yeah, but this Y isn't just for Jewish people. Anybody can join.*
Bruce: *I know. It's open to everybody.*
Me:
Bruce: *Like I said before, what are you?*
Me: *I don't know what you mean.*

Bruce: Look, I don't know what you are. Are you Spanish? Your last name is Diaz. That's a Spanish name. Just say you're Spanish. I don't care.

Me:

Bruce: Well, say somethin'. What are you?

Now I was in trouble and didn't know what to say or do. I didn't like to think about this topic. And I hadn't thought about it enough to even present and develop an acceptable subterfuge. I pulled some toilet paper and the sound of unrolling sheets of paper, tearing one by one, signaled that this conversation was coming to an abrupt halt. "Where you going?" came from Bruce's stall. I pushed the cool metal handle and was relieved to hear an avalanche of water, enough to drown out my answer and my leaving. Over the cascading water he heard me say, "Meet you back in the room." With a loud yell that echoed against the clean white tiles, he said, "I need a little more time to finish this," and I heard his rhythm start to increase and rushed out of the bathroom. The hallway with its dark brown floor was pleasant. The doors were oak and solid, and I took out my DO NOT DUPLICATE key out of my front pocket. I walked down to my door, opened it and walked right to the window. I threw it open and looked at downtown Boston which was sweltering in the August sun. It was hot, but there was a breeze up on the seventh floor and it felt good. I heard another DO NOT DUPLICATE key opening the door and knew that Bruce had returned from his double session in the lavatory. "What are you?" came out of his mouth before the door was even closed. I turned around quickly with the curtains blowing on either side of me like a shroud. "Look you have to stop fucking with me. You understand? Stop fucking with me. I don't know what you want from me. I answered your questions. Just stop messing with me."

He was a little surprised that I had cursed at him and even appeared hurt. We had been bike buddies for the whole trip which meant that no matter where we were on the road from Cape Ann to Boston we were supposed to look out for each other. We had shared a tent and if there were bunks, he got the upper and I got the lower. He had treated me fairly when we couldn't settle an argument about who was to get the last piece of a Hershey Bar that we both coveted with equal avarice on one long stretch of road that had depleted all of our stamina. Bruce Glickhouse had suggested that we flip a coin. I objected only because I knew he wouldn't agree to maintain the bargain if I won the coin toss. We flipped calling heads and tails as the quarter sailed through the air. My heads won and he gave me the Hershey Bar. I stammered, "You're really going to give it to me?" Without a pause, he replied, "Sure, you won, didn't ya? Fair is fair. You won. Fair and square."

This same kid whom I thought really did possess this special code of fairness and doing things by the rules and not rewriting them in the middle, was now making my life miserable. I was desperate.

Me: I'll buy you another Hershey Bar.
Bruce: What? Who said anything about a goddamn Hershey Bar?

I started to whine, "Well, what's wrong with you, all of a sudden? I thought we were friends." He plopped himself down on the neatly made bed and said, "Sure, we're friends. Who said anything about not being friends?" I flopped down on my bed and tried to steady myself. It wasn't any good. I sat up on the edge of the bed and stared down at my Converse sneakers. There was a moment of silence or rest. I couldn't tell. Maybe if he saw that I was really upset about these questions, he would leave me alone. But when you're fifteen, it's just the opposite. It's like seeing your boxing opponent with a small cut above his eye. You start tagging that cut over and over again and if you can rub the laces of the glove right across that cut, ribbing it with each lace, then you know you're on your way to victory.

He stayed in the prone position, stared at the ceiling and said, "Look, I believe you when you say that you're not Spanish. A person can have a Spanish last name and not be Spanish or Puerto Rican. I even believe you when you say you can't speak Spanish. I believe people when they tell the truth. I'm fair, like with the Hershey Bar back on Route 128 heading toward Boston. I know you're not Spanish, but you're still something. You have to be something."

Those words dwelled in my ears like the ringing of some big bells that are on the verge of cracking.

You have to be something.
You have to be something.
You have to be something.

I was muddled and bewildered. I thought about one more attempt to please him, offer him an answer that would force him to cease and desist but nothing came out. I was going to say "American" but that sounded so ridiculous at the time. "American" would have just reinitiated the interrogation on another level and there would be one fewer answer in reserve. His voice crashed in on my two minutes of sanctuary. "Just ask yourself about your parents. What are they? Whatever they are, you are. Simple as that."

I started to think in response to that. What were my parents? They were my parents. I had never thought of them as being anything but. The name Diaz had confounded me before, but I was always able to convince people that I wasn't Spanish. I didn't speak any Spanish and I didn't understand any. You could jabber at me all day, and I wouldn't understand one word that was being spoken to me. Puerto Rican kids had tested me many times before by cursing at me or talking about my mother and they could tell from my blank reaction, that I hadn't comprehended one word that they had said. All those times, all those instances, it was sufficient to find out what I wasn't. Now, for the first time, I was engaged with someone who was not satisfied with knowing what I wasn't. He wanted to know what I was. He had to satisfy a new desire. He wanted to feel secure about himself and if I gave him the right answer, he would calm down because knowledge of someone's race in America is a cardinal issue. It indicates and governs so many things. Sometimes one's very own life depends on it.

I thought about my parents, literally. I created pictures of them in my head and reflected on their physical appearance. They weren't Spanish. My mom looked like Claudette Colbert and I loved her. My father looked like no one else that I had ever seen in the world and I loved him. I was never quite sure where my father got the name Diaz but it seemed to fit him. No one ever asked him to talk Spanish. Why? How come people were always asking my brother and me to talk Spanish? If we all had the same last name, then there should have been logic to the consistency of our treatment. But there wasn't. Looking back I now understand something that is frightening, reassuring, and uncanny. My parents were black and white and everyone but me knew that, saw it, and perceived it. To me, they were just Mom and Dad and they had no prescribed color that could ever fit or be applied to them. I didn't see them that way. I was color-blind. In attempting to answer Bruce Glickhouse's questions, I was attempting to do the impossible. Up until that day, they were just two people, good and bad, insane and sane. Now I was being forced to look at them for the first time in my life. Glickhouse kept hammering away at me but I decided to lie on the bed and look at that ceiling. He didn't know that I was prepared to do this for the rest of the afternoon. Years of preparation kept me in shape for this sort of ordeal. I was in pain but looking at the cracks in the ceiling encouraged me to make diagrams, clouds, and other shapes. I let my eyes wander and his voice drifted off into the background.

When I got home from the trip, my mother met me at Grand Central Station. I was stronger and the two weeks of continuóus bike riding and camping had made me leaner. My mom could see that I was happy and we got on the subway to take us home to Jamaica, Queens. It was the E or the F to 169th Street and Hillside Avenue. I was proud of my pack and my biking cap. I wore it at a jaunty angle and felt good. Within a day or two, I took the opportunity when answering my mom's questions about the trip, to ask my own questions. It took some time because I had never talked about anything of a personal nature with my mother in my life. I was fifteen and we hadn't discussed any issues or problems. I started with the question, "What am I?" My mom hesitated, thinking about all the possibilities that lay behind the words and the question mark. I asked the question again and modified it a bit, "What am I in terms of race?" Again she hesitated but she was curious as to the origin of the question. I told her that there was only one problem on the entire hosteling trip and it had to do with this guy who kept harassing me about "who are you?" I could see by the expression on her face that she was uncomfortable having this discussion and I could see that she was overwhelmed by the inevitability of it. My mother said, "Well, what did you tell him?" I grew surly since this was going right back to square one. If I couldn't tell Bruce Glickhouse about who I was and only who I wasn't, nothing had changed in two days that had given me some insight into who I was. I could only reply with a little anger in my voice, "I'm me, that's who I am." My mom looked at me and asked why wasn't that good enough. I twisted and turned in the kitchen while she sat down. I paced across the black-and-red tiles and they seemed so unfriendly and ugly at the time.

I crossed my arms and leaned back on the kitchen sink. The silence lasted a long time. "Mom, I'm tired of this Puerto Rican thing. People have been asking me and Paul for years, 'do you speak Spanish?' 'Are you Spanish?' 'If you're Puerto Rican, why don't you speak Spanish?'

And sometimes they make fun of us for being Spanish." I stopped and then immediately started talking again before she could give a response or an answer, "This is messed up. Dad's father is Cuban but he's not Cuban. Right? How come Dad doesn't speak Spanish if his father is Cuban?" My mom got up and walked to the stove and lit the burner under the coffeepot. I had seen this act many times before when she was discussing something serious with my father and felt odd that I finally had raised some subject with her that forced her to reheat the coffee. My parents made one big pot in the morning and kept reheating it. Their coffee was good to the last ground. She sat back down and said that she didn't have an answer for me but she was very happy that I had been honest and spoke to her about this problem. "You know, you're not the only one in the family who has thought about this or has had to deal with this. Vivian and Paul, they both have had problems with this and I think you should do what they did," my mother said while walking back to the kitchen table to sit down. I wasn't as angry as before and was certainly intrigued when I found out that this problem ran through the family; others had had it before me and they had successfully dealt with it. This was my conclusion. My mom didn't tell me that I had reached the wrong conclusion. I was under the impression that just because someone had *dealt with a problem* that indicated that it was solved. I started to relax and unfolded my arms and slouched against the sink. My body eased and the tension dissipated a bit. My mom, however, didn't look at me and this left me feeling that things were not as simple as I thought. When they *dealt* with this problem of being Spanish and other things simultaneously, what actually happened? Did they get shots for it? Did you swallow a sugar cube with the polio vaccine as we did in grade school when that miracle was discovered? My mind spun at a furious pace. My sister wasn't home and she lived a life foreign from mine, always in Europe, Mexico, away. My brother's life was a mess. Constantly fighting with my father, doing poorly in school, running around with hooligans and petty thieves, I hoped this wasn't an example of how he had dealt with the problem.

I straightened up, a little alarmed at any cure that wasn't direct and simple and long-lasting. I already didn't like the manner in which my mom had even framed this situation. She had structured it as a problem that was more like a disease and her words hinted at some sort of medicinal solution as opposed to a social one. I blurted out, "Well, what do I have to do? Tell me because I don't like feeling this way, like I don't know who I am." Getting up and walking toward the stove so she wouldn't have to look at me, quietly she said, "You have to talk to someone." "What?" came blasting out of my mouth. She turned the burner off and repeated herself, "Yes, you have to talk to someone, a doctor." I was so angry then and there that I could have shoved her and her reheated coffee away from me. Here I was, suffering a stage of consciousness that I never had before, struggling with it and baring my soul and she mentions that I have to talk to a doctor.

"Mom, I'm OK. I'm just a little confused. I'm a little mixed up about this Spanish thing. This kid, this damn kid, made me all confused and crazy because he mixed me up. Kept on asking those stupid questions over and over again. I'm just mixed up. I don't need a doctor."

"Dex, you know what type of doctor I'm referring to, right?"

"Sure, Mom, sure, shrink, a psychiatrist."

"OK, I just wanted to make sure."

"Look, there's no way I'm talking to a doctor, any kind of doctor about this problem. It's a little thing; I can solve it on my own. I just wanted to talk to someone about it because it never came up before."

With her coffee cup between her hands she nodded and said OK but that I should talk to her if this problem bothers me too much. I agreed that I would. I thanked her for talking to me and for being the kind of mom that a teenager could come to if you had a problem. I went upstairs to the bedroom that I shared with my brother and flopped on my bed. I found myself staring at another ceiling with just about the same number of answers. The rest of the month was a hellish one. I was tormented about being something and not being something. Words like *white* and *Negro* continually haunted me. The only solace I had was taking the handball court over from dawn to dusk with Alonzo. We dominated the courts behind Springfield Gardens High School from 9:00 A.M. to 7:00 or 8:00 in the evening. We were the perfect team; he was left-handed and that gave our doubles pairings an extra advantage. It was hard to get something up the middle against us. Alonzo had his "killer" balls that were impossible to pick or scoop up, and I just had strategy. I returned serves that hit the upper reaches of the wall and then bounced over my opponent's head. They watched as they hoped that the ball would either go over the wall itself or would bounce over the "long line" on its return. Our only break was for lunch and we would hop on our bikes and scoot down to Alonzo's house. Alonzo's mother was from South Carolina, the country, and her version of lunch definitely did not revolve around a sandwich and a glass of milk. Large pieces of cold fried chicken came out of the refrigerator and heaping portions of potato salad were placed on our plates. The oven was turned on for a few minutes to heat up some of last night's biscuits. Then you got your glass of milk. With that refueling, Alonzo and I were more than prepared to take back what we had temporarily given up when we unlocked our bikes from the fence around the handball court a half hour ago. We vanquished team after team, always with the refrain, "point game" and an official announcement of "21–10, slaughter, or 21–3, massacre, or 21–18, good game, good try." But that wasn't enough.

A few weeks into September 1968, I went back to my mother and asked her about talking to that guy, that doctor. School and its onset had proved too much for me. Bruce Glickhouse's questions remained with me, and as I looked at all my Jewish friends in my sophomore year, I wondered if they too might ask those unanswerable questions and what would I say when they did. I couldn't take the anticipation of the questions and the faltering answers. It was time to make a move. I said, "Mom, I think I should talk to that guy, that doctor." There were no further questions, affirmations, or validations. She made the appointment for a Saturday in late September; Dr. Kirschner's office was in Forest Hills. I was so angry and resentful about going that I tried to balk at the last second. I respected the fact that my mother had made the appointment and I felt a little better that it was her doctor, her psychiatrist. I took the bus from Springfield Gardens to Jamaica to catch the E or F train to one of the more respectable neighborhoods in Queens. I tried to get lost but the address was only a few stops from the exit of the station so ignorance of location would not have been a convincing excuse for my mom. His office was on the second floor of a Tudor apartment house. Tudor sets a dark and gloomy tone and the exterior of the apartment house made me feel like I was entering a dungeon. I was nervous as I took the self-service elevator up to the second floor. Dr. Kirschner had already opened his door as he heard the elevator move from the lobby. Opening the door I looked right and then didn't have to look any more since he had opened the door and my mother's description of him was more than accurate. Glasses, studious, kind-looking and wearing a brown sweater, he quietly said, "You're in the right place; I'm Doctor Kirschner."

I walked in and did not like the apartment; it had that quiet psychiatrist look and I felt that this was where the *crazy* people went and talked about being *crazy*. There were abstract paintings on the wall, abstract sculpture on the tables and bookcases. It was dark and very somber. "Would you like something to drink?" These words with a foreign accent had no appeal to me whatsoever and I quickly turned down the offer of juice or soda. His short hair revealed a large forehead which showed how smart he was and his glasses, added to his shrink appearance. I looked for the portion of the room where the interrogation was about to occur. I couldn't help but notice his large swivel chair and a couch that was opposite it. *That's where the crazy people talk and that's where he listens.* Again his words, despite his kind demeanor and the foreign accent that always made American people feel pity and sorrow for refugees from Europe, were cloying: "Please, have a seat." I had a light jacket on and did not take it off when I sat down. We made small talk about my mother seeing him and how she had made the appointment at my request. I agreed that it was my idea but I wasn't crazy, just a little confused. He took note that it was about the sixth time that I had used the word *crazy* and what did I mean by that. I was glad he had finally asked a question, even a meandering one. I spoke with confidence and in an aggressive manner. Not only wasn't I crazy, I really didn't have to be here. I was just confused and it was making me feel bad. I quickly relayed the anecdote of the hosteling trip incident and he listened very carefully. When I talked, mentioned something, he took it down in his head. I could see that he was doing that. Everything was going along fine until he asked me if it was OK that he asked me to do something. Because I had spun the bicycle trip with so many details and so much truth, I said, *sure,* without any hesitation whatsoever.

"Dexter, do you like to draw?"

"What?"

This question had caught me so off guard that I didn't think he had actually said the world *draw*. All the word that rhymed with *draw* throttled through my head and I felt stupid for not listening closer. I was silent and my expression said more than any of the stupid words that might have come from my startled head. He repeated the question:

"No, I just asked you if you like to draw. I think your sister is an artist, correct?"

"Yeah, my older sister, Vivian, paints, she paints and draws."

"That's why I thought you too might draw something for me...."

"Yeah, but my sister's an artist, a real artist with an easel, oils, brushes, I mean, she can really paint. That's different."

He placed a hand on his chin and took a deep but nonjudgmental breath and continued.

"Yes, I don't want you to paint, just draw a picture, if you can, that's all I'm asking." With that soft request from a voice with echoes of the Warsaw ghetto in it, I gave in and became complacent. I thought to myself, *You want a picture? I'll give you a fuckin' picture. What you do with it, that's your problem.*

He didn't have to get up to get the materials; they were right next to him on a small, dark mahogany table. He had planned this and I didn't like that. I'm not sure if there was any test that he could have administered that would have made me feel good. Perhaps, if he had asked me to show him how to serve a hot one that just crosses the "short line" on a handball court, that would have been different? I don't know. As he gathered up the materials, I could see that I was going to have choices: crayons, pencils, and different types of paper. I thought, "Why don't you give me some construction paper and a scissors and I'll make some cut-out figures." I was mad.

I said, *thanks,* as he handed me my choices and started to look at what would be best to try and draw or paint. He coughed smartly and said, "Dexter, I want you to draw, or paint, whatever you feel comfortable doing, a family." I looked up and I just couldn't be angry with this refugee from a country where we were sending CARE packages as late as 1965. I coughed too, not quite as smartly and asked, "What do you mean? A family of what?"

"People. I would just like to see what is your idea of a family. You could talk about it, but I thought it might be easier to draw one."

"OK doc, I mean Doctor Kirschner."

I started to draw. I choose a classic Number 2 pencil and a sheet of white paper. I didn't plan that much of the drawing because I soon realized that I had started in the lower third of the paper. Damn, there wouldn't be enough space and I would have to start again. Now I was nervous.

"Doctor Kirschner, could I have another piece of paper?"

"Surely, take your time."

I had a new sheet and felt better. This time a little planning. Thoughts of how Vivian could draw ran though my head. I started to concentrate more on how she would have done it than myself. She would always start with large swirling circles, no matter what the subject of her paintings. Trying to swirl was far more difficult than I could have ever envisioned. I scratched out my swirls. Before I could ask, Dr. Kirschner had handed me another new sheet. I looked at him and said, "This time I'll get it. Didn't think it would be this hard. Harder than I thought." He smiled and nodded. I folded my leg and used it as a desk and the magazine was my pad. I draw three stick figures. As I was drawing, I talked. The light from a lamp struck the fleshy part of my leg that always appears between your sock and the bottom of your trousers. My skin was tan in the light but made to appear even more yellowish in this 60-watt bulb. "Doctor Kirschner, I don't know if my mom told you what I came here for."

He smiled and said nothing and I got nothing from his smile. I kept on drawing and talking. I didn't look up when I talked but I wanted to make sure he had the right guy. I spoke in a monotone voice. "Doctor Kirschner, I just want you to know that I'm OK and don't have a problem with my parents. I know a lot of kids my age have problems with their parents. They hate them; they can't love them. They want to kill them. That's not me. I'm OK with my parents. I . . . ." I had started to say love but that didn't come out and I wondered why I hesitated. I kept drawing without a break and hoped that my nonstop movement had distracted him enough that he hadn't noticed my stumble. I gave him a side look and started again, "My parents are really great. It's this thing about me. I don't know what I am. I know that sounds funny, but this kid made me think about something that I never thought about before. I just want to be able to give someone an answer when they ask me."

He nodded and asked me if I needed any more time. I blurted out, "Yeah, it's going to take more than a few minutes to describe what I'm going through. It's . . ." He pointed at the drawing and said, "I meant the drawing. Are you almost finished with the drawing?" I looked at my spartan stick figures, two big ones, one little one in between, and said, "Yeah, this is about the best I can do." My two adults and one child in between them didn't hold that much of a challenge for him to get the picture. However, one thing was becoming clear. There weren't going to be any questions answered today. Every time I asked him a specific question about identity and my current problems of August 1968, he gave me a look as if neither one existed, neither me nor the time of year. It was frustrating since I couldn't get angry with the guy. After talking about five minutes about what I perceived to be my problems, I could see that no answers were going to come my way anytime soon. Surprised when I looked at him, I could see that he was studying that measly drawing I had made. Three stick figures, two big, one small, and he was examining and studying it the whole time that I was talking.

"Dexter, can you explain what this means?"

"Sure, that's a father and a mother and a kid in between."

"And this means what to you?"

"Oh, just the average family; I mean, I know there should be two point five kids, but one kid sort of tells the story."

He became pensive and I knew I was finished when he went back to the drawing. I decided on one more try. I didn't want to leave that office without being able to tell my mother that I gave it an honest try . I coughed for attention and Dr. Kirschner looked up. This was it. I kicked that ball as hard as I could, stating, "Doctor, I met this kid Bruce Glickhouse and he kinda made me think about things that I never thought about and when I did it really put me in a lot of pain, so I told my mom, and here I am. I'm ready to give you any information that you feel is important about my case." He picked up the drawing and instead of answering, asked me, "Why is the child in between the parents?"

Higby's Dry Cleaning Store

As MUCH AS I loved my father and knew he was a hero to all of my friends, he still wasn't enough. Because he was perfect, that automatically meant that we could never talk about or discuss the important things in life like sex, women, and having sex. That world was *verboten* for us. Drugs had to be addressed because of my brother's addiction, but that again was from a practical and sociological point of view. My brother was a textbook case of something, and therefore he played no part in my life. Since my father couldn't talk about those issues with me and since there was another man in my life that could and wanted to, well, that was the ideal situation.

Mr. Higby, who owned Higby's Dry Cleaning store, was going to be the most important man in my life. I know you're thinking I already told you who was the most important man in my life, and it's not that I'm deceitful; it's that we don't have enough words in the English language for these circumstances when you have competing people, men and women in your life whom you really do love more than anyone else. You truly imagine that you will never imagine loving anyone better, but then you meet this other human being and you end up saying, well, he or she was almost the most important person in my life, and you catch yourself because you just said the same thing a few weeks, months, or years ago, and you're not lying. You're just. . . . You're just trying to tell a complicated truth. I know that there still were other *most important* people in my life. It's the language, not me. If we had a word like, *gooleypitushwahghjlov,* this would solve the problem. Because if we had that word, that long, strange sound would capture the idea of a person whom you love body and soul, and you are one hundred percent certain that you will never, ever love or praise anyone else, but this isn't true. If we had that word, then you would know what I'm talking about. But we don't have *gooleypitushwahghjlov*. I'll just have to make do with what's in Webster.

Higby was going to make me a man, and because his wife could not have children and he always wanted a son, it was perfect. My father had his topics and areas of specialty: racetrack, cars and carpentry, communism, history, and jazz. Higby had his: work, sex, business, drinking, and exposing me to another world. I was fortunate. If I hadn't had this bad Virgil in my life, I would not have known that other world existed.

He drafted me the same way a scout goes looking for a big league ballplayer. He invested time and energy, about a year's worth, and offered me a contract that I couldn't refuse. I went straight from the farm team to the major leagues, and I paid Higby's Dry Cleaning store back tenfold. He had been searching for a replacement; George Lewis, counterman and presser had worked there for years. He was friendly, adored my sister and always said hello to Vivian and me. The world had other plans for him. His draft notice came, and the next thing I knew he was saying good-bye to Springfield Gardens and us forever. He wasn't killed but never came back. The war needed an ever-increasing army, and in 1968 the army needed him. Mr. Higby, looking for a replacement, drafted me. The last time I saw George he was sporting a khaki uniform with a few yellow stripes on the side of his sleeve and seemed content with his new position. I had his job. I was content too. It was a fair trade.

For the past year I had done something rather innocently that had attracted Theartis Higby's attention on a daily basis. I didn't know that future employers wish to examine your past work record, and they have many ways of getting your résumé whether you know it or not. I was fifteen and wasn't even aware that there was a record that could be scrutinized. I suppose even this unconscious selection process was what made Higby loom larger than life from that first day onward. He had his own sayings, his own little aphorisms, his philosophy built on life, Harlem, getting the combat infantry badge in Korea, being black, and being a black businessman. His perspective on life and things exuded a different brand of confidence that my father did not employ or rely upon. My father had books and articles. Higby had life, and it was raw and crude, but on occasion he refined it enough to make it palatable and appealing to a fifteen-year-old lad from the neighborhood.

I had gone to the dry cleaning store to pick up an order. My mother or father had left some items there, and I was doing the Saturday chore of getting their clothes before he closed at seven o'clock. I walked in unconscious to his machinations and plans. He had been planning this for some time. With his olive brown skin, balding head, he leaned against the counter and said, "Mr. Diaz, Paul or Dexter, right?" He paused and I spoke up. "Yeah, Dexter, Paul's my older brother" came out in my interrogated voice. "Let me see your ticket" and he turned away walking up a long aisle of clothes, disappearing into the back. He returned with the plastic encased clothing. Putting the clothes on that ubiquitous hook, I gave him the money, and he started to make change. "How would you like to work here?" Those words, *work here,* struck me like lightning. The paper route was held in high esteem but to work in a store! To work in a store with a cash register for holding the receipts instead of my right-hand pocket where I stored all of my nickels and dimes, this was a tremendous change.

"Are you serious, Mr. Higby?" I said rather incredulously. "You want me to be George's helper?" He started to shake his head. "No, George is going, got his greetings from Uncle Sam. Going to get a new set of clothing courtesy of the taxpayers, three hots and a cot and . . ." and from that point on I had to learn that this was how a black man talked. He just didn't say *yes* or *no.* He said things that sounded like a song, a poem, a story, a fable. There were no simple yeses or noes. Everything had a rhythm to it, and the rhythm was so appealing that he changed my speech pattern. This was how I started to speak like a black person. I would never be the same again. I would be the same inside, but my way of talking, my sense of the potential that language had for making music was born the summer of 1968. When people heard me talk from that summer on, they knew that there was something definitely black about me. I didn't even know it was happening, but it did. I would not carry any parental linguistic pattern over from my mother and father. I was going to be black and black and black. He made me black. It happened. I wasn't black before 1968. I was from then on. People noticed it and asked me what happened as if I had attempted some new weight-lifting program or had decided to start exercising. I hadn't done anything. It was osmosis.

"So, what do you think? You should probably talk to your parents. If you want, I'll speak to them the next time or call them," he said with a genuine parental concern. My blasting retort hit him quickly, "Yeah, I'm one hundred percent sure it's alright. I'll still talk to them, sure, but I'm fifteen and can do things." I grabbed the clothes from the hook, totally exhilarated that this incredible thing was happening right before my eyes. Visions of work, importance, and money came tumbling into my head. The *Long Island Press* was a good job; having customers remember me and tip me extra at Christmastime was fine, but Higby's Dry Cleaning store, with a neon sign and an awning in the summertime with his name on it; this was a dream come true.

I was out the door and walked about half a block. I turned around and walked back to the store. There was something that I wanted to ask him. There was something swirling in my head that just had to be answered right then and there. Why me, what was so special about me that I should be picked from all the young boys in the neighborhood. "I checked out your work record," he said, and this again was an example of him saying something in that special way. I had no work record so what was he saying? But he was serious. How can an adult say something that is not true and yet be serious and truthful? "But Mr. Higby, I don't have a work record. A work record is a paper that shows all of the jobs that you've had. I don't have one," I said.

"The hell you don't! You got one of the best work records of any young man in this neighborhood. Don't tell me you don't have a work record. How else do you think a person can get hired if they don't have a track record? You know what a track record is? Your dad plays the horses. What's a track record?"

I was stunned for everything made sense, but I wasn't prepared for quick questions and answers like this. Everything in my house had a different pace. When you talked about Marx, the Second Front, and the mistrial of the Rosenbergs, you were quiet and methodical. I looked at him and said, "Sure, I know what a track record is!"

"Good, I know you do. You better. Now tell me what a track record is." I smiled inside because I was going to talk about something that I knew and was confident.

A track record is a recapitulation of all the past performances of a thoroughbred race horse. It is a complete history of all races whether mud, turf or the flat. It will have races national and even international. It will have all of the horse's times for different distances. For instance, at Aqueduct Racetrack, two horses hold the record time for a six-furlong race; Near Man did it carrying 112 pounds on July 17, 1963; Beautiful did it on December 6, 1964, carrying 121 pounds. That record-setting time was 1:08:2:5. That's one minute, eight and two-fifths seconds.

Mr. Higby looked at me, and the smile that had been growing for the last few seconds just got bigger and bigger. He was shaking his head. The smile didn't stop, nor the head shaking, "Ya see, boy, that's one of the reasons I'm hiring you. All that information in your head. Just like a little encyclopedia. But let me tell you something else. Besides that, I have been checking you out. You just didn't know it. You were too busy doing your paper route job. That's good. You were so busy that you didn't even look up to see Ol' Higby looking at you." That was another thing that he did which was startling and new and exciting. He talked about himself when he was talking to you. He would casually say, "Ol' Higby knows; that's for sure." Or, "Don't fuck with Higby; whatever you do, don't fuck with Higby. Ain't nothin' in a drugstore will kill you quicker than Ol' Higby once you start fuckin' with him." If you asked him a question, he would proudly say, "Higby knows; just gimme a second and Higby will tell ya right off." The music was there and rolled out of his mouth like a player piano. I listened.

I listened some more. I had heard it somewhere before. Somewhere I had heard this type of talking, making yourself into a character because you weren't satisfied with what society had done with you. Louis, sure, Louis Armstrong did this. He would conduct conversations with himself during those early recording sessions when he was really feeling his oats, back in 1931 and 1933. Louis would be in the studio for Columbia or Okeh and would just start conducting his own monologues. He had nicknames too, and he talked in that special way that made you want to laugh and laugh and laugh.

"Now, good evening ladies and gentlemen; tonight, looks like we have a little argument between the saxophones and the trumpets, 'cause these cats just said that they're gonna get away, and the little trumpet just said the same. Ain't that right little trumpet? That's right, oh, you little devil . . ."

The steam from the press in the back hissed. "Now, little did you know, goddamn your soul, I've been looking at you for almost a year. That's right. One year. And that's how I know you're a good man. Every day, now listen, talk to me now, look at me, look at Higby. Every day I know exactly what time it is when you ride by with that bike. Every damn day. Every day you come with that newspaper bike and go across those metal cellar doors. Crash, bam. First I didn't like it. Crash, bam. Every damn day at 3:15, crash, bam. Then I got to liking it. Because it was you and it was the exact goddamn time every time. Do you know that? Yes sir, every day at 3:15 you and that damn bicycle hit those metal doors, boom-boom, and I look up and say, that's that newspaper boy, right on time. Right on time. Like *The Crusader* express train coming out of Jersey City. No, more like that train they call the . . . damn, way out west, fast goddamn train, what the hell is its name, the, *The Zephyr*, like the goddamn *Zephyr* heading from Omaha, Nebraska, to Denver, Colorado. Never 3:10, never 3:20. Day after day. Paper route, hell you got to be dependable for that. Paper comes out every day, right? Saturday, even Sunday. I don't see ya on Sunday but right again on Monday, crash, bam, 3:15. So Ol' Higby figured, that's the man for the job. I need someone who is very dependable and reliable. Need someone who is going to be at work on time. Need someone that I can trust. Trust with money too. If you were cheating the customers or the paper, you wouldn't have lasted more than a week. That's the kind of business that is. Yes sir, I got an honest and hardworking man right in front of me, and I know you're the man for the job."

The steam hissed again, and someone hit the right pedal of the press to hold it down on the pleat of some skirt or the crease in a pair of trousers. I looked at him. He was so real. So brown, so penetrating. The music had stopped, but my breathing hadn't. It had all flowed out like one big mighty river of love and affection. "Well, I guess all I have to do is ask my parents, like I said before."

"That's right. Go ask 'em, Zephyr. Go ask 'em."

One-Quarter Mile

—◦((◦))◦—

AT THE BACK of my old high school, there is an athletic field. It takes up almost more space than the main buildings of the school itself. Large, expansive; when Springfield Gardens High School was built, there was more than enough space. The southeastern section of Queens consisted of large tracts of swampland. The early farmers who cultivated their rich potato fields on Long Island had never been able to tackle the problem of drainage in this remote section of the borough, and it remained dormant until the 1960s. When it came time to build another high school because the classic and stately ones, Jamaica and Andrew Jackson, were far too crowded, 1965 was the year and Springfield Gardens was the place. My high school was constructed with plenty of available land; those of us who knew about how schools were built, kept on asking, how could you build a brand new high school without a swimming pool. Building a high school without a pool was a sign of the general decline in how the city was unable to provide for its own children. A symbol of that negligence demonstrated that one generation of immigrants deserved pools and another generation of immigrants, did not.

However, there was a track, football field, baseball field. With the elevated Long Island Railroad as the ultimate goalpost or wall for hitting a home run, you could lose yourself there. The complex was so big that, due to underutilization, you felt the barrenness of the place, the school, its lack of resources. Some students waited for a pool; others waited for a football team that took almost ten years to materialize. Everyone, from the principal, the head of the PTA, to the student council leaders knew that the authority of the state was being undermined in some basic and fundamental way. No one could have told us that America was changing forever, or at least the America of the 1950s that had nurtured us with some pretty grandiose baby bottles overflowing with an abundance of mother's milk, was starting to dry up and we weren't quite prepared to be weaned from such plush cribs. I had grown up making fun of products made in Japan and using them as evidence of another kid's economic deprivation; now I heard of a company called Toyota and that the Japanese, who were no longer Japs, made more than decent cameras. I too was now wretched and it didn't have to do with rising Japanese economic fortunes or being a greedy baby who reluctantly lets go of its mother's nipple.

Glickhouse had undone me, and I couldn't seem to recover from his poison. I had seen the psychiatrist two times and was through with that. It just made me feel officially crazy. The school year commenced with me insanely aware of being cut in two. I never felt more black and white. I started to spend long periods of time looking in the mirror, at my face, my complexion. My hair took on a special meaning. I now began to think of those barbers and how they had praised my hair, my *good hair* and started to pull at it. If I had good hair, why wasn't that enough? Why couldn't I just be a little lighter, to match the good hair and therefore, just be taken for one thing? White. Or, the opposite, how about the proposition of having *bad hair* and just being a few shades darker like my father, therefore eliminating any other racial possibilities but one. Black. The mirror in the vestibule became my torture chamber. With arms dangling in the usual awkward high schoolish way, I stood in front of that glass and examined my imperfections: skin color, hair. Hair, skin color. Grotesque. A whole new language that had no meaning now had meaning. The language of color, which had sauntered in and out of me for years absolutely without one shred of nuance, now rocked me, shivered me, shriveled me:

Light-skinned, yellow, red, high yaller, Chinese Negro, mixed, mutt, mulatto, half-breed.

I couldn't turn my ears off. It was as though I had developed a pair of elephantine ones, picking up all sounds, real and unreal.

In a daze, I hoped school would rescue me and it did. For the first few days just the routine of new classes and new teachers removed me from my madness. Then something happened. All the teachers in New York City went on strike. This had occurred before, but those strikes centered on money, wages. New words were being tossed about, and I knew that this disagreement just wasn't concerning a teacher's salary. Community control, hiring and firing, race, racism, anti-Semitism. A place called Ocean Hill-Brownsville, Brooklyn, was in the news and became the focal point of the dispute between teachers, parents, and the board of education. Day after day, this neighborhood was dramatically filmed on TV; day after day, you saw large photographs in New York's picture newspaper, the *Daily News*. Parents and teachers were yelling at each other. The argument was new and strange to me. The parents felt that black children should have black teachers. I had never thought of that before in my life. Odd to me since my P.S. 156 experience had shown me that for three years white teachers had taught us, taught the eight of us well, and we were eternally grateful for their care and attention. To kids, teachers were teachers and they could be painted black, white, or purple; if they were mean or nasty, you were in a terrible prison, and it didn't matter what color they were.

These parents felt differently. They were committed to an agenda that said a black teacher could inherently teach black children better than a white. If it were just a theory, no one would have cared. But at some point, this community decided to apply the theory which meant firing certain white teachers so new black teachers could be hired to replace them. This was the cause of the strike. This strike was to cause a rupture in the city that I knew and loved, and it erected lines between two groups that had traditionally shared their pain and suffering, Jews and blacks; it was to break lines of communication and cohesive bonds that went back to the 1920s and the early days of the NAACP. A Jewish couple, Amy and Joel Spingarn, had funded this organization when W.E.B. DuBois knew it was on the brink of bankruptcy. Julius Rosenwald, a Jewish philanthropist and one of the major shareholders of Sears Roebuck, had contributed 4 million dollars during and after World War I for the construction of a few thousand elementary schools in the South for blacks. He also funded the creation of twenty-five YMCAs in the north, which were segregated at that time. This special connection between blacks and Jews would never be ameliorated. This strike in the fall of 1968 was bad for the city, bad for the civil rights movement, but good for me because I met another Jewish guy who was going to intervene on my behalf and rescue me from that torture chamber with the mirror. His active participation in my life would prevent me from committing a series of some self-destructive acts. Even then I knew that if it weren't for him, I might not have made it through being black and white and being sliced and diced.

Jack. Weinstein. Jack Weinstein. I even liked his name when he introduced himself to our sophomore English class. Young, athletic, handsome and intelligent; I was struck by his energy and wit. Already on the first day, he had made contact with thirty-five kids, all races, all groups, and us. Springfield Gardens seemed to be a sociological experiment in integration and balance. If an ethnographer had desired to fashion a laboratory with the perfect blend of humanity, this was it. With a student population that consisted of whites, blacks, Jews, and Italians, with whites making up seventy percent and blacks approximately twenty-five percent, according to the sociologists of the day, Springfield Gardens was ideally integrated. In terms of class, all were represented, from the blue-collar Italian kids of Rosedale to the middle-class Jewish kids of Laurelton and Rochdale Village; the black population was even more diverse with children from middle-class homes in St. Albans, Springfield Gardens, as well as those whose parents were blue-collar and civil service workers.

Jack Weinstein stood in front of his class and me and was excited about the books that we were going to read. We were to meet him five times a week, and we would be reading the classics. With a tweed jacket that somehow made him look cool, sweater vests, and wing-tip shoes, he turned and started scribbling notes on the board. Our loose-leafs broke open; we thumbnailed our way through our indexes of tabs and found English. I had already put English first, feeling that this was a show of allegiance and loyalty. I copied the notes and noticed that he had saved filling out the Delaney cards for last. How could he forget something that every teacher in the school always did like an automaton? That was interesting since most teachers accomplished these first-day bureaucratic tasks in a rather perfunctory manner. Data, information, bureaucracy, boredom, listlessness, and disinterest. Jack was already asking us about our favorite books and to hell with the Delaney cards. He wanted to know us, not numbers and addresses. He was light on his feet and startled us when he assigned boys and girls to get books from the book room. Girls never performed this task because they were too, too, too something; of course, we had never thought about why girls couldn't get books and that was the way Jack was. That was his magic. He was always doing the thing that no one had ever thought about or asked *why* to. This teacher just wouldn't be satisfied with the most innocuous and prevalent answer of all, *Because.* I watched the girls and boys walk out of the room and thought, "That's a first. Girls are going to carry those big books all the way from the storage room back to our class." Anytime he saw that incredulous look on our faces, he would just say, "What's wrong? You never saw————doing———— before?" Before we could utter our stupefied *yes,* he had already gotten out, "Well, these are new times and new things are going to happen."

That was going to be his pace, his rhythm. With his sandy colored hair sometimes falling over his forehead, brushing it back up with his hand, he bounced and rarely sat at the desk. Intent upon accessing our reading skills, he asked everyone to read a paragraph or two from *Great Expectations.* I sat in the second row and quickly calculated that I was going to be about the tenth person to read. I waited with anticipation as I heard some people read flawlessly and others stumbled or just read in that monotone voice that overtly implies that there is no connection between the audience and the text. When my turn came, the words flowed out:

> You bring me, tomorrow morning early, that file and them wittles. You bring the lot to me, at that old Battery over yonder. You do it, and you never dare to say a word or dare to make a sign concerning your having seen such a person as me, or any person sumever, and you shall be let to live. You fail, or you go from my words in any partickler, no matter how small it is, and your heart and your liver shall be tore out, roasted and ate.

As I started to read another paragraph, unauthorized, Jack stopped me with a "Whoa, slow up. That was great reading. Terrific reading." I looked up from my hardbound green book, *Adventures in English Literature,* and smiled. He was smiling too. Because of his approach to teaching us, everyone knew that he cared, was fair, and was going to make learning a pleasant and wonderful experience.

Then came the strike. About two weeks into the fall term, the fires of Ocean Hill-Brownsville had ignited the full fury of the teachers' union. A guy named Albert Shanker had his name in the media every day. The two groups, teachers and the school board, were inalterably deadlocked and opposed to each other. Worse, charges of racism became twisted into that other malignancy, anti-Semitism. It was clear to the parents. *The same people who own the stores that steal from us, the same people who own the apartments who charge us unfair rents for miserable living conditions, are the same people who teach our children. The "Jew teacher" must be expunged from our community schools.* Shanker, tough New York labor leader who came up through the ranks, was not going to back down. He knew his rights and that of the union. They struck and went out on the longest teachers' strike in history: 68 days. Some students rejoiced. I was heartbroken. In addition to meeting Jack Weinstein during those first two weeks of school, I had also met my first love, my first princess and that was her nickname, "Princess." Her name was Adeline Moore. She was brown skinned, beautiful, had long black hair, and dressed perfectly. Her skin was dark enough that she was worried how certain parts of her body would become *ashy* on occasion. I liked those parts of her body. I liked her entire body. I was in love with the most beautiful girl in the sophomore class, and no one could understand, especially me, why she had even talked to me during those first ten days of school. But she had. All the boys knew about her, dreamed about her, wanted to talk to her, if she would only give them an audience. I had gotten that audience, that five minutes of her time.

I was sitting in the lunchroom, fluorescent lights beaming. With the school only two years old, everything was fresh, clean, and sanitized. The rectangular table was four by three, so ideally six students could sit on the sides and two more at the ends. I was there by myself eating my favorite lunch, a tuna fish hero with potato chips. I wasn't alone by habit, strictly coincidence. Then she appeared through the door and looked around for a place to sit. As she paused to survey the cafeteria and strategically set herself up in a commanding position, two more of her friends practically bumped into her. She looked, sighed, looked at my table and me. She made no facial expression other than one of relief that there were places available and she and her best friends would not have to be split apart. I stared and thought, *Princess, Negro girl with good hair. Everyone loves her. Dreams. Princess, don't even know her real name. What would it be like to talk to her? Hear her voice? I would do anything for you if you would just talk to me once.*

"Do you mind if we sit down?" I looked up and the Negro girl who would have been voted Miss Springfield was talking to me. I nodded my head *Yes.* She was surprised.

"I asked, do you mind if we sit down?" I was never quite sure what this meant, when a person asked you "if you minded something." It was one of those strange expressions that revolved around being courteous but that didn't mean anything to me, so I kept nodding my head "yes, I mind if you sit here." She looked at me and laughed.

"You're sitting here all by yourself, and you mind if we sit down? Are you sure you know what I'm asking you?"

No words from me, just more nodding of my head. One of her friends became decisive and said, "Well, we're gonna sit down anyway." I smiled and said nothing. I didn't think they would sit near me since they were girls, and I didn't know them, but they sat at my end of the table and Princess was directly opposite me. I couldn't believe my luck, my incredible good luck. I said nothing but took in everything that was being said and found out within a few seconds that Princess had a name, Adeline, and her friends were Barbara and Roxanne. As I ate my tuna fish hero, I noticed that my table was a magnet for male eyes and attention and felt good about that. Even if I never saw her again, I could say in the locker room, in the bathroom, or in the parking lot, "Princess sat opposite me one day."

"What's your name?"

"Me?"

"Whom else could I be talking to?"

"Dexter. I'm Dexter."

"That's a nice name, unusual. This is Barbara and Roxanne."

"I know. I mean I heard you say their names, when you were talking, in the last few minutes, you said their names because you had to, in order to let them know that you were talking to them."

Barbara and Roxanne rolled their eyes, and I started to explain a little more, but Princess took it all in her stride and repeated, "You have a nice name. I think you're the only Dexter in the whole school. Right?" Her friends nodded, not too impressed with my claim to fame and started to talk among themselves. The clock moved toward the end of the lunch hour, and I kept quiet. The warning buzzer rang, and we gathered up our trays. I offered to take Adeline's tray and she shook her head *no* while she still had a straw in her mouth and was sipping the last drop of milk from those little pint containers. She kept on sipping and at last, said, "But that's nice of you."

Being that I was officially in love from that point on, it was incomprehensible to me that there was going to be a strike and the school was going to be closed. Impossible, that because of a batch of stupid teachers and parents, I was going to be inextricably cut off from these two people, Jack Weinstein and Adeline "Princess" Moore. When I first heard the news flash, that the teachers' union had voted to strike, the only hope I heard in that news account was that the vote was not unanimous. There were some union members who for very intricate reasons were not going along with rough-and-tough Shanker. I didn't know why but they had voted *no* in a demonstrable and visible fashion. The unified wall of support that Shanker had hoped to present to the city and Mayor John Lindsay was not exactly made of reinforced concrete. Picket lines went up immediately around every school and students were told that the schools were open. Open? When I heard this little rumor that the schools were open, I turned on the radio and listened for the latest news and details. I was rewarded for listening to my little transistor radio with an earphone. The board of education had determined that there were enough nonstriking teachers and administrative personnel to keep the schools open and that education would continue.

It was a long and listless weekend as I hoped and prayed that the school would be open. My prayers were the most complicated of my life, so far. I had never really been aware of any sort of need besides food, water, shelter, until this summer. Glickhouse had made me realize that my life was complex and painful. Dr. Kirschner had intimated that whatever solutions existed for my peculiar problems, they were not readily attainable. Within a month of that despair I had met two possible saviors. Jack and Princess. Even though I had only known them for literally a few minutes here and there, I could see vast possibilities. Sanity and love; love and sanity. That's all I wanted after that crazy and miserable summer. Maybe I just wanted love because that usually takes care of the other problems but that's a pretty obscure concept for a fifteen-year-old kid. They were right there, one in an English classroom and the other down in the cafeteria. To have them ripped away from me by a guy named Albert Shanker seemed grossly unfair, and I took to hating his name, voice, black-rimmed glasses, and face. If black parents want to have black teachers, great, give them purple teachers, just re-open the schools, so I don't have to be crazy.

My frantic prayers were partially answered when it became official that the schools would be opened on a limited basis. Alonzo, friend from the days of integrating P.S. 156, called me and asked me if I wanted to see what was going on at the school. He explained that since being an SP student and skipping a grade, school was important, and he couldn't afford to miss any of his advanced placement or honors classes. I had one honors class and agreed that we should find out in person what courses the school might be offering on a limited basis. We made a plan to meet the next morning, first at his house, which was closer to the school, and then walk over. The news had stated that some schools would have picket lines, and that any teachers who felt duty bound to their jobs, principles, or salary, would have to endure the damning cries of their former colleagues who were forming ranks in front of certain schools. That worried me a bit. Anytime I thought about picket lines, signs on thin pieces of wood, people milling about, that brought back memories of demonstrations, rallies for me and against me. We decided to try to enter the rear of the school since that was the closest entrance anyway. No luck. We walked around the perimeter of the school, cautiously poking our heads around the corners to see how much of a fracas there might be if we attempted to enter the school.

From three hundred feet away, it did not seem as contentious as we had imagined. Since it was the 1960s we were accustomed to seeing in real life or on television violent demonstrations with people clashing with each other and police. Clubs flailing, tear gas, soldiers with fixed bayonets, these were everyday occurrences and images back then. As the three hundred feet dropped to two hundred and then one hundred, we could see that as demonstrations go, this was low key, peaceful, and more a battle of words than a battle of fists, bats, clubs, and rocks. First of all, some teachers had arrived so early that they had skirted the picket line trial completely. Others were entering through the side and back entrances. The tough ones, tough either by principle or just human resolve, walked right in front of their fellow teachers and kept their eyes straight ahead as they heard, *scab, traitor, rat*. A few actually stopped and shook hands with longtime friends, said a few words, and then kept walking.

When it came to students who were going around the police barriers, the teachers demonstrated that this wasn't about us and didn't say a word. As Alonzo and I walked through and waited from some deprecatory remarks, there was just silence, and we were glad of that. I whispered to him, "Not like that day at 156, right?" He said nothing and kept looking right in front of him. I nudged him again, "Alonzo, it's great, not like 156, right?" Again, he kept silent. As I started to talk again, he whispered through gritted teeth, "I thought we agreed not to talk until we entered the building. Can't you stick with a plan that you made up?" I was stung with this rebuke, but knew he was right. We had made a contingency plan about what to do under these circumstances and dignified silence was always one of the most important criteria to embrace at times like these. We had watched Dr. Martin Luther King exhibit this on many occasions and had even seen a short documentary about how the Freedom Riders and the students who were going to sit at segregated lunch counters and restaurants; they were instructed to remain silent and to practice nonviolence no matter what the stressful circumstances. They actually practiced this before embarking on their journeys and had to pass tests where role-playing antagonists pushed them to the limit of their youthful student exuberance for a cause. Alonzo was right. I had broken discipline and had to learn.

Once we got in the school, we couldn't believe how silent the whole building was. We were asked for our program cards and parted ways since he was a junior and I was a sophomore. We were happy to find out that there would be only one lunch hour, so we would meet at noon. The administrators who were there were more than prepared. They had set up parodies of schedules and classes and with only a few teachers on hand, we were informed there would be limited choices. When it comes to performing a radical triage, eliminating the miscellaneous was rather easy. It had been decided that the most important classes, English and math would proceed. I wondered how they were going to pull that off with so few people, but when I saw the names on a portable blackboard, I realized that these teachers at Springfield Gardens High School were either very talented or they were pretty damn resourceful. Viewing the names of teachers whom I had known during my freshman year, I was impressed as I saw how many were teaching three subjects. I went down the list with a hope that I would see one name in particular. W is way at the end but there it was, J. Weinstein. Damn, goddamn, I was rejoicing. He was teaching English and math in room 312. The classes were at odd times because of the makeshift nature of the programming, and they were longer than usual. Sophomore English was starting in about a half hour. They didn't want students barging into classes that were under way so if one arrived in between classes, there was a music teacher in the auditorium who was teaching a nonstop history of musical instruments, Western masterpieces, and choral singing. I was entranced as I watched Mr. Meyers pick up each instrument and play scales and then a solo. Clarinet, saxophone, trumpet, he just picked them up and brought them to his lips and played, put it down, picked up another one, and then put it down. His audience, about fifty strikebreaking kids gave him a round of applause that he would never forget.

Buzzzzzzzz. The warning bell rang and I headed out of the auditorium for the third floor and Jack Weinstein's makeshift English class. It was an eerie quiet since the halls were so empty, the way they were known to be on certain important Jewish holidays but this empty rang hollow. Out of five thousand students, there were only about three hundred of us. You could hear our penny loafers, Playboys, and Converse sneakers in the hallways and it didn't make one happy. I was happy though. I was heading toward room 312 and English. When I got to the door, there he was, already writing something on the board. I knew I wasn't late. He was just being efficient. The only real surprise was that there were students younger and older than me. Even with five thousand faces, you knew who was in your particular sophomore class, and I didn't recognize one other student. Before I could waste any time wondering why these older and younger kids had come to the class by mistake, I heard a brassy voice say, "Magwitch, come on in. We might need you to read again." I glowed with the attention and the literary nickname that I had been blessed with. He had remembered my reading about little Pip meeting Magwitch in the graveyard, despite the strike, the tension, and the fear. "Sit anywhere for now and then I'll tell you the deal," came out of his mouth in a rapid-fire manner. That was his style, and I was to learn that his staccato speech pattern was a mirror of his rapid-fire mind. He tended to repeat himself but you didn't care because you may have missed it the first time due to speed, precision, and the lack of listening skills. "OK, look, this is the deal. There are four hundred of you and about thirty of us so for those of you who are good in math, you can figure out that we are going to have to double and triple up on things. Take this class for instance. Just from looking around you can see what's happened. I'm going to teach a generalized English class. With the math, as you can also figure, you will have to be separated. I can't teach trigonometry to those who need calculus and vice versa. So for the time being, we're going to talk about writers and writing and how authors best convey their message. Everybody understand?"

We all looked around and nodded. A few people raised their hands to clear up any last minute questions regarding attendance, Regents exams, and if we should bring our lunch with us. We were nervous and a little scared, but we all felt safe with him, in the room, behind the walls, and on that side of the picket lines. The class commenced. Jack Weinstein wrote some words on the board like plot, character, setting, tone, style and theme, asking us to define the terms, if we could. There was plenty of participation and the class was in Mr. Weinstein's hands ten minutes later. I was jealous, jealous that I had to share him with thirty-nine other people, some who I felt needed to be chastened because they were seniors and saw fit to make faces and an occasional whispered stupid remark. At the end of the class, with the sharp piercing buzzer, made more acute because of the lack of bodies in the building, almost everyone agreed that he was great. They mentioned how he rated on their one through ten scale. I was proud and noted to someone that, "He's my regular teacher. English. He's my regular English teacher."

I walked out of the room, and he smiled at me. The day was half over. Next class was math—geometry—and then lunch. That was it. A real intimacy quickly developed for two reasons. First, there were so few of us in a school that usually housed five thousand students. Second, no one could deny that we felt like the privileged few. We were defying the odds. It was the 1960s and challenging the status quo was normal, but it still had the potential to endow one with a special nobility no matter how many times this was experienced. By the third day of the strike all of us knew, from the news reports, TV, and reactions from our parents, that these teachers were the rebels, the radicals. They were revolting against their union; they weren't necessarily in favor of community control and parents having the power to hire or fire teachers, but they were against the method of asserting that this new experiment was wrong. Going on strike was an extreme tactic for demonstrating that community management of schools was wrong. There were less expensive ways to make this point. The more we heard the news, the more we heard Albert Shanker call our teachers who were crossing the picket lines *scabs* and worse, the more we looked at them as heroes. They were. That was the other factor that made us feel unique. We were keeping the schools open and education did not come to a halt. We were showing New York and America that we were noble.

Lunch came quickly and I painfully found out that I couldn't sit in my special room in the cafeteria. It was senseless to open up a cafeteria for a thousand when there were only about eighty kids. However, I was fortunate that I was able to find a table with only one person and I could be by myself.

"Hello Dexter, remember me?" came from a voice that was familiar to me but still new. I looked up and there she was, stretching an awkward leg over the bench seat to make herself comfortable. Princess, like a vision, was there, all in white, white stockings, white dress, and a white ribbon in her hair. With my lips pursed to call her Princess I quickly transformed my mouth and formed the word Adeline.

"Adeline, I can't believe it's you. I thought I never would see you again because of the strike. It's really you. Man, this is great. Where is Roxanne? What happened to Roxanne? Is Barbara here, back on the lunch line?"

"No, it's just me. They're not coming. I called them and asked them to come with me on the bus because I'm a little scared."

"Sure, I know exactly what you mean. I was scared walking up that long path between the teachers, but I was with my friend Alonzo. He's my friend from a long time ago, public school days. We planned the way you wanted to plan it with your buddies, I mean, girlfriends."

I looked at her and she was more beautiful than the last and only time I had seen her. Everything, her brown face, her straight black hair, smile, everything. And she was talking to me, and now I could hear every word that she was saying since the cafeteria was short nine hundred other human voices. I smiled, and she could see that there was something different about my adoration. All of the males in the school loved and worshipped her, but I adored and respected her.

"Adeline, what time do you get out?"

"The same as you, everyone gets out at 1:00 P.M."

"Do you have to go straight home?"

"Yes, my grandmother would be pretty worried but . . ."

"Adeline, but you'll have a few extra minutes before you have to be there."

"Sure, meet me out front where the buses for St. Albans are lined up."

That was all I had to do. I had prepared some long-drawn-out speech about how I wanted to talk to her and it didn't have to be today, this time, but it could wait until next time. Instead, Adeline knew that we could be friends and saw no need for me to grovel as I had planned. If anything, our little relationship was dreamlike. Not just because I was walking down the hallway with Princess but also because she was like me and that was comforting. I could sense that we had a certain other kind of bond. I thought about her incessantly.

There was no way you could have such straight and good hair without having some white blood in you, and my calculation was correct. On our first date, which was at the Valencia, the art deco movie theater on Jamaica Avenue on a gray Saturday afternoon, I found out about her family. Adeline's father was Italian and her mother was black. Just like me but in reverse. She asked me about my family and I held back. I said, "I'll tell you later. It makes me feel a little funny." After the 15¢ buttered popcorn and the 10¢ Cokes, we walked out into that sunlight that even when it's gray, blinds you if you go to the movies in the daytime. We walked slowly to the Jamaica bus terminal, and I asked her if she wanted to go to the penny arcade where I would pay for her to take a few shots at the targets. She declined. "Don't be sad." That was all she said and I felt my chest heave. I was about to cry but held it down. We got on the Q5A and sat on a cushioned seat for two near the back of the bus. As the bus plowed down Merrick Road, making stops here and there, I knew that Baisley Park was the deadline. Linden Boulevard came with Baisley Park on the left and I placed my head on the backrest in front of our seat. I looked straight down at the floor and said in a muffled voice, "My father is Negro and my mother is white." I kept looking at the rubber mats that were on the floor of the buses in those days. I had revealed my secret. She touched my head and said quietly, "I know. It must be bad for you since you're so light; the kids must mess with you. White and Negro. You can be anything. Me, I definitely have good hair but I'm too dark, right?" I looked up from the rubber mat with those little waves in it and told her that she was the most beautiful girl in the world, and she was beautiful because she was this perfect combination. "Adeline, don't say that. You're not too dark. I don't see that. I don't see any color. You're just beautiful. All I see is you, and you are the prettiest girl in Springfield Gardens High School, and I will do anything for you."

The semester that possessed fear and anguish was transformed by fate and fortune into a very wonderful one because of Adeline and Jack Weinstein. Even my brother was impressed with my good luck. "Adeline, who lives up on Merrick Road? Go ahead with your bad self. About time, about time little brother," Paul said. I beamed. Because the strike was going to last "forever," I had the dazzling opportunity of seeing these two people not only on a daily basis but for everlasting periods of time. When school finally recommenced on November 18, 1968, I had to go through a bit of a withdrawal. The weaning process was painful and I immediately became disdainful of all the students who hadn't gone through what we had done. They had been home, watching television or working. Now Roxanne was back; Barbara was back. The lunchroom was filled to capacity, but I was satisfied. Adeline was my girlfriend. We went to the movies, museums, and kissed on the couch.

Classes were in full swing. The regular English class resumed, and I was well prepared for sophomore English. Jack Weinstein had made us competent writers and readers. I felt great about my writing. We had read *Great Expectations* after all, and I identified completely with Pip. He was an outcast and made every attempt to connect himself with decent people in a not-so-decent society. I felt the same way. I was haunted in December with the same questions that had plagued me in September after that hosteling trip. Adeline made me think more about it because she was black and white but God had made her dark enough that you would not doubt her lineage. Despite her good hair, she had no sides to choose. She admitted feeling funny about having two different parents but I could see from our long talks on the E train heading toward Manhattan that she was free of the oppression that still dogged me. I still needed to talk to someone; when I looked in the mirror I felt like spitting on the image. I looked and looked and never liked what I saw. I needed some answers, and I was going mad since I didn't even know what the questions were or if anyone could take a chance at answering them. I didn't like being in hell. It's not for heroes. It's for those who suffer. It's for those in pain.

I was counting the days again. I knew that once the semester was up, I might never see Jack Weinstein again. I tortured myself as I wondered if he could be as insightful with me as he was with a piece of literature, a novel, or poem. I knew that we had read and analyzed a lot of books but that was all theory, that was in the classroom. What about real life?

Mine was the first generation to make flagrant use of the expression *the real world* and anyone who employed it knew school was not *real*. Estella and Miss Havisham were real in their own way but they never had to worry about the color of their skin. I made a decision that somehow I had to approach him before it was too late. I was completely bewildered as to how to speak to an adult, a teacher. I was terrified of all the negative contingencies. If I talked to him, he could just summarily brush me aside. He could have politely informed me that I had made a mistake in approaching him and that he could still do me one favor: refer me to the counselors on the first floor, opposite the principal's office. How do you talk about stuff that has nothing to do with school, homework, being late or absent? I was sick with fear.

Near the end of the semester he assigned a composition entitled *The American Dream*. It was a great topic for the class. With the Vietnam War at its apex, the civil rights struggle taking new twists and turns that would modify its character forever, everyone was questioning what America meant, now that Dylan was talking about "The Times They Are A-Changin'." I saw my opportunity and jumped on it. I thought to myself, *Write about this topic in such a way that you let Jack Weinstein know you want to talk to him, about things other than school.*

We prepared for a week by discussing the topic in class. I thought about the assignment at home every moment that I had. The day of the composition came and I wrote with all the conviction and passion that I possessed about my American dream. It was a place where a person like myself could live with dignity and pride, a place where I would not have to embrace an underground existence and feel triumph because I hid well for a week or month or year. It was a place where Adeline wouldn't have to say, "I'm a little too dark, right?" Exhaustion was the result of my metamorphosis into an invisible man. There I was, fifteen, and already drained of good raw teenage energy, which could have been relegated toward the arts, music, girlfriends, books, politics, life.

I prayed. It's hard when your parents have instructed you with, "Men create gods, gods don't create men." Yet, I gave it a go. I prayed that he would receive my message through my essay. I hoped that as he graded the composition he would hear my plea for understanding and compassion. I did not believe in God and felt a bit hypocritical but I still prayed. My parents loomed large in the background. Their assumptions that if there were to be a solution in America to the problem of race in

America, it would be political, economic, and social reverberated loudly. I still prayed. My God was neither the Christian God nor the Jewish God. I laughed to myself as I thought, "I'm lucky, got two guys listening and batting for me." He would listen. He had to because he came to the aid of everybody and anybody who was persecuted by a harsh world afflicted with injustice. He missed nothing with his omnipotent vision. His memory was excellent too. My God would always remember the look on the small Jewish boy's face as he was herded out of the Warsaw ghetto by an arrogant Nazi soldier. He saw the Negro battered by Bull Connor's deputies with clubs, then set upon by German shepherds. And he saw me, not every day, but on special days when the brutality that I was subjected to bordered on the absurd, harassed by militant blacks in the morning because I was too light to be accepted and then assaulted with a slingshot by some white ruffians for being a "nigger" in the wrong neighborhood in the afternoon. He listened.

Jack Weinstein heard my story and understood that I was trying to communicate to him through that composition. He did not turn away and even though a few other faculty turned their heads in consternation the first time I walked into the teachers' cafeteria to talk to him, he took the same kind of stand as he had done during the strike. People come first; gossip and backstabbing come further down the line. We ended up becoming friends for life. We spent many an afternoon walking around the athletic field behind Springfield Gardens High School talking about blacks, Jews, and what I was supposed to be. I felt better just because I had finally found someone to confide my feelings of rage, anger, but mostly confusion. That's what we talked about more than anything else, just being confused.

It took a few weeks of me avoiding the topic, talking about my brother, Adeline, even doing poorly in math. The day arrived when I decided to tell him the ugly side of my life. Now I was doubly inhibited because in those weeks that had turned into months, I now had a friend, not just any old friend. An adult, a teacher, a man whom I respected and adulated. George and Alonzo were amazed that this had happened. For Adeline, it was as though I had betrayed her a bit and the rest of the student body by being friends with the enemy. I held back on what I wanted to tell him since the first day that we had started to talk. In those days, I always felt that I was misleading people, especially those important to me. We always walked early in the morning. I would meet Jack in the cafeteria at least one hour before classes commenced. He has already had his cup of coffee and was working on the *New York Times* puzzle. No longer sheepish, I just walked in and sat at his table for a second. Folding the paper in that special way that *New York Times* people do, we would get up and exit at the rear of the school. Then we would start to walk on the track.

I always had a lot to say. I started to talk in an oblique fashion.

"Mr. Weinstein, I was just wondering, you know a lot about history, right?"

"I think I have a fair handle on it."

"Good, you know how in Germany, they had these laws that if you were Jewish and you had a certain job, you would have to tell a German citizen if you were Jewish?" We never would break our stride when we walked. His wing tips were hitting that tarmac and my Converse sneakers were symmetrically aligned. Even when we paused with our thoughts, the shoe and sneaker sounds were always there.

"Let's see, those are probably under the provisions of the Nuremberg Laws, 1936. They probably had a law that if there was contact between an Aryan and a non-Aryan, the Jew or Slavic person had to inform the German of his background. Pretty perverse, it's hard to think that it was only thirty years ago."

I had what I wanted. The idea was planted and all I had to do was have the courage to carry on with what I had been contemplating for weeks.

"Please, Mr. Weinstein, whatever you do, don't tell anyone this. I've got enough trouble already, but this thing has to be kept a secret. If anyone ever found out, I'd be done for. Jesus, I shouldn't even tell you but I have to talk to someone because I'm going out of my head."

"I'm right here. How many laps is this?"

"Er, about the third. We've done three, almost a mile."

"This is great; we're really killing two problems with one stone. I'm getting my exercise. You're getting your exercise. I wouldn't call it therapy since I don't have a shingle to hang on the wall."

"Mr. Weinstein, I have to tell you. I've been lying to you, well, not really lying. But what's it called when you lie by not offering the information, even when you have it? Lying by . . ."

"Omission. Lying by omission. You're making this sound pretty bad. What did you do? Hang around with the Manson family when they were plotting their dastardly deeds out on the West Coast?"

"No, it's . . ."

He knew when to be quiet and just walk.

"Mr. Weinstein, you see, I'm hiding who I am from everybody. Some of the kids, they think I'm white; some think I'm Negro, and some even think I'm Spanish."

"Must be confusing."

"Yeah, that's it. That's it, that's it. Right there. That's it."

On the turns I had to speed up a bit because if you're in lane number two walking adjacent to someone in number one, you have to take that extra stride on the turns. It's imperceptible to the eye, but it's there. I was grateful that we were on a turn because that gave me a legitimate excuse not to talk, just walk.

"Mr. Weinstein, I went to a psychiatrist, a few months ago, to talk about this thing that I'm trying to talk about. I'm not crazy. Just had to talk to someone."

"Dexter, plenty of people see psychiatrists every week, maybe even a few sessions per week and they're not crazy. They're just trying to learn about themselves and their relationship to the world."

"Well, that's me. I was just trying to figure out some things, like what you said. Some things about me."

"Dexter, did you learn anything?"

"No, I only went twice; I didn't like it too much."

"That's normal."

A Long Island Railroad train came by and we geared our breaks to the noise of the train. This was an express, Lynbrook to Jamaica, no stops; she roared by.

"I'm mixed. My mom is white, Jewish; my dad's Negro."

"*Mazel tov,* the best of both worlds."

"What?"

"Dexter, that means great. You've got the best of both worlds."

"Mr. Weinstein, didn't you hear what I just said? The train was going by, but didn't you hear me?"

"Didn't you hear me? That's great. I thought you were going to tell me something terrible. Jewish, Negro, what a mix. Let's see, jazz, sports, intellect. It's not fair. You're going to have the jump on the rest of the kids at school. You're going to do well in high school, SATs, college."

The sounds of the wing tips and Converse sneakers were no longer synchronized. That clip clop sound reverberated. It was the fourth lap and our time was drawing to a close, one mile, four times around the track. The Long Island Railroad and the school just seemed to disappear. I just heard the little insignificant sounds of feet.

"Dexter, look, I know some things are going to be tough, but when that happens, the tough get going. You have that in you, too. You can take it. I know you can."

We walked beneath the goalposts of the unused football field because it was a shortcut that gave us another two minutes to end our conversation. I looked at him but said nothing. He smiled and asked if I was OK. In those days, my only response in a clumsy attempt to articulate confused feelings was to say, "I'm OK, just feel a little funny." I did feel better. I just was not prepared for the depth of the plunge I had just taken. I wasn't ready for the dive and his answer as to how to pull out of it. I was still spinning when we got back to the rear entrance of the building. Not as fast, but still pretty fast.

Lucky's Dream

———◦((◦))◦———

CLOTHES PRESSERS ARE a strange lot. In my four years at Higby's Dry Cleaning store I was to meet a vast array of them. Some of them were truly iconoclastic individuals. They were a roving band of men who moved from job to job. Just the fact that I met so many of them was a sign of their transience. Robert, Big Paul, Clark, another Robert, and Al. Then there were others who just showed up on Saturdays to help with the big rush that occurs in the dry cleaning business. Last, there was Lucky. Even now I can't say what his real name was. He never told me. I must have badgered him once a week from three to seven. Adolescent curiosity. Teenager stupidity. I would get to Higby's at three o'clock sharp. Classes ended at 2:30 so I had enough time to go home, drop off my books, get on my bike and ride over. I would say, "Good afternoon Higby." He had taught me that and demanded it. Because I was so withdrawn and self-absorbed I didn't talk that much. I wouldn't even say, *hello*. He told me that this was not acceptable. I had to say, *good afternoon* on weekdays and *good morning* on Saturdays. In addition, I had to talk to the customers. I was paralyzed most of the time people came in and also had nothing to say. What was wrong with being quiet as long as I did my job?

After that ritualistic greeting, I would put my bike in the back and say, "Lucky, what's your real name?" A squat and tough looking man would wave his hand at me in a sign of disgust. Our war commenced for the three hundredth time. Lucky had joined us in the winter of 1970. As usual, he came out of nowhere and would disappear in the same way. Higby never told me how he searched for pressers. They just showed up

170

one day when I came in at three. I hadn't seen them interviewed. Had never heard of them before that fateful day. Higby never mentioned them as historical figures from his former life or past. They would just be in the back bringing that press down, stepping on the pedals, tapping the black knobbed handle to release a burst of steam, then releasing the brake that kept the press down. I would meet them when I went over to pick up a batch of clothes that needed to be placed in plastic bags. They worked on the piece system, which meant that they got paid for each skirt, dress, trouser, or shirt that they pressed. They kept careful track of their work since every pleat counted. There were no hourly wages. Neither benefits, nor Social Security. Higby paid them daily if they wanted it or all at once on Saturday night. It was up to them.

With his one hand, Lucky was a marvel to look at. I had tried my hand at pressing the clothes once and failed miserably. Higby looked at me and shook his head after trying to teach me for fifteen minutes. "It's good that you're book smart because you ain't going to make a living at this." I asked him to teach me one more time, and he tried. We placed the trousers on the press. He showed me the controls and the order that they were used. I didn't have a problem with the mechanics. As always my problem was with sight. I couldn't see what the object of the pressing was. "Nigger, don't you see that pleat? The crease, nigger, right there, the crease, put the pants so the press comes down on the crease." I would sigh and acquiesce rather quickly. If one doesn't see the line, the curve, or the right angle, they're lost in worlds that demand this as a rudimentary jumping-off point. That was one reason I couldn't learn how to be a presser. The second reason, I didn't want to get burned, and if you're scared to be burned, you can't press. Robert had taught me that.

Robert was our most interesting and subdued presser. Tall, thin, with a well-sculpted forehead, wonderfully groomed mustache, and light skinned, he was a handsome Negro who was in his mid-thirties. We had the same sort of hair although he would say, "You got that extra softness; it's a subtle difference, but it's there. Something from way back, maybe the master, maybe an overseer, something small. But it's there. It's all in the blood." I went home that night and looked up the word *subtle* and was struck that this was an SAT word. He used a word that I didn't know. Robert became one of my good co-workers, and I never thought twice about doing a favor for him. Lunch, I would go out and get him any kind of sandwich. I would ride as fast as I could on my bike. If it were a hot meal, I would ride as quickly as possible so his chicken and collard greens would still be hot when I returned.

"Come here, I'll show you how to press. You're smart. Higby just doesn't have any patience. Watch. Watch. It's like dancing. Do you dance?"

"No." My monosyllabic answers left no avenue of reproach. When I said, *no* to something back then, people knew it meant *no*.

"Well, forget about that. Just watch. You know the order of the knobs, right?"

"Yes."

"OK, now just watch the way I set up these pleats on this curtain; you take these pins and start a pattern. Once you have the pattern established, you just duplicate it over and over again. Now, that's not too hard, is it?"

"No," and Robert's patient and protracted presentation of pressing for dummies was just the right approach for me. No yelling and no grandstanding. I liked his manner, and it was the only one that I could tolerate at the time for learning. I didn't know that my own intolerance was sometimes interfering with me learning things that I didn't quite understand at first. I was frustrated easily and didn't like things that didn't come easily. Pressing was definitely on that list.

"That's it. OK, you've got the pleats in this curtain set up perfectly. Mrs. Henderson will appreciate this. Now, think about how happy this old rich lady will be when she sees these curtains perfectly pressed." I was gone as soon as he said "Mrs. Henderson" since an abstraction like a customer who lived in some big house in St. Albans was far removed from my reality. Who cares how a rich lady felt about some dumb old yellow curtains that should be burned in the first place? That's why they invented Venetian blinds. Well, the people from Venice invented them.

"OK, Dexter, now here goes. Bring it down like you mean it. You don't mush; you press. Drop it like you mean it. Now run your hand along that last pleat."

I placed my hand carelessly along the last pleat in the stupid way I had of doing things once I was officially uninterested and felt the searing burn of scalding steam.

"Jesus, watch out what you're doing. Here, run to the faucet and put that hand under the cold water. What were you thinking of?"

I ran to the dark water closet we had that only contained one old deep tub and an industrial-size faucet that poured out gallons of water. I placed my hand under the ice cold water. I heard a "How are you, boy?" come from Robert as he finished Mrs. Henderson's pleats and was glad that she would be happy, since my hand had been sacrificed for her Saturday night black bourgeoisie party that everyone who was anyone attended. I backed out of the closet into the light and saw a red line on my hand, very red but very straight.

"Damn, that thing is hot."

"What were you thinking about?"

"I don't know, pressing, I guess."

"Well, you have to concentrate more."

"OK."

Robert was going to attempt to teach me one more time just like Higby. In the real world you don't get three chances, three strikes, three of anything. It's really about two. You foul up two times, and the real world just doesn't have the time to give you that third opportunity. Every time you foul up, that time and money is gone forever and no one can afford that. Three strikes and you're out? No, it's two, and that's if you're lucky.

"You'll never be a presser because you're scared!"

"Robert, what do you mean? I'm not scared of anything."

"You don't understand and might not understand for a long time. When I say that you're fearful, it's not something you just conquer in one day."

"But I'm not even scared. Let me do it again."

"No, it's OK. You're scared of being burned and that's why you can never be a presser. Nobody becomes something when they're scared like that."

His words were cryptic enough. I liked what he said because it did sound like a movie or a play. He used words as though he had seen something that I would never see or wouldn't see for a long time. What I never got to hear in the barbershop, Negro men speaking with wisdom and wit, I definitely heard in the dry cleaning store almost every day. Higby, Robert, and the taxi guys from the local livery service were my teachers and embracers of black culture. They were from the North, the South, and even California, and I can still hear my naïve remark to Teddy,

"Man, I didn't even know there were any Negroes in California." Teddy, a thoughtful and very light-skinned man with glasses said, "Sure, a lot of colored jazz musicians were out there after the war. I've seen 'em on Central Avenue." Places that had existed only in the pages of a book were now alive. These men had lived in Rocky Mount, North Carolina; Louisville, Kentucky; and Biloxi, Mississippi. No matter where they hailed from they were now in New York City living and working and talking.

Our official time for philosophizing was Saturday night, after seven. At five to seven I would go outside with the keys to the large Master Locks and start pulling the gates over the windows. A few customers would rush as they saw that this was their last chance to pick up some article of clothing. The gate over the door would be left halfway open for the tardy customers. I waited outside until Higby gave me the sign and yelled, "Shut 'em down Dukeschank." Dukeschank, what a nickname but that is what he called me. I found out this was one of the most basic principles of black life. Whatever a thing was named, whether it be human, animal, or object, had to be renamed. Dexter was "Dukeschank." Lucky, we didn't even know what his real name was, but we knew he had been renamed. Theartis Higby was "Ol' Higby." They compressed their entire lives of forty and fifty years into a few quick expressions that reflected who and what they had seen.

Lucky was a sawed-off version of Floyd Patterson, Negro heavyweight boxing champion of the 1950s. He had Patterson's short haircut, and he himself was stocky and pugnacious. He had his own style of pressing due to only having one hand. He would lay the pants or skirt down and just use the palm of his hand like one big index finger. He knew he had my attention since I couldn't make adequate use of my five fingers. The pleats just sat right; the crease in the jacket was perfect and he would bring the press down with a thump, hit the pedal for the blast of steam. His button-down shirts were always opened to his stomach because of the heat, and he routinely wore a threadbare pair of gray slacks. I made eye contact with him every so often in praise of his work, but he didn't need me. I was only qualified to run the "Suzy Q," which was the brand name of a steaming device for simultaneously aerating garments with steam. It was a human form like a mannequin without arms or legs. You placed the dress or jacket over the top and threw a corset of metal brackets around the whole body. You worked three red knobs; one took care of the left arm, one the right and the last one steamed the dress front and back. No skill or finesse required, just motions which prepared the garment for the pièce de résistance, the pressing. I was an underling in Lucky's universe and therefore had to take and absorb his abuse.

We stood next to each other for hours and said nothing. Lucky stayed focused on folds and creases, and I pulled suit jackets and evening dresses out of a large cart of clothes fresh out of the dryer. Machines steamed and pressed to a certain rhythm and a human voice wouldn't have fit in. An industrial-size fan drew out as much heat and steam as possible into the backyard. Its whir was constant, and its one speed was monotonous. The machines for the cleaning and drying of the clothes were noisy, and Lucky had that maddening quality about him of being inured to men and machines. I couldn't get his attention even to pick a fight. He knew how to mess with me and made sure he made me feel his lashing once or twice a day.

"Cap'n, de clothes is ready," he would announce. I looked at him. I said nothing. "Cap'n, can't you hear? De clothes is ready." I had made the mistake of asking him not to call me that, *Cap'n.* I had never figured on an adult having the need or even the urge to tease someone younger than himself or herself. In Lucky's case I had been wrong. He teased and tortured, tortured and teased.

"Lucky, look, I don't like being called that."

"Why? You de cap'n here. You in charge. You goin' to high school and all. I'm nothing, just Lucky. I call you to take clothes out. You de boss." That was the other name that Lucky threw my way: *Boss.* Of course, this got just the reaction that he had hoped for, and my frustration made him feel more than successful. I was in pain. I was no captain or boss, and I knew how he was using these words. It was just to mock me. This went on for many months. I told Higby that I really didn't like this name-calling, and I was mad about it. He told me that Lucky was simple and stupid and from South Carolina, so why give a fuck about a fool nigger like that. I told him that this thing was really getting to me and that he would have to do something about it someday. He would say, "Dukeschank, don't take it so hard; you're too sensitive." With that redress of my grievance I knew that there was nothing else to do.

I timed my attacks. I had five choices since dry cleaning establishments were open Tuesday through Saturday and closed on Mondays. Five choices but my routine varied little. It always started with a question. "Lucky, I always wanted to ask you something." I said, as I started picking through some clothes, getting them ready for the Suzy Q. I knew what reply was coming. "Yes, Boss?" I fit a woman's sleeveless dress over the Suzy Q body form and started working the controls. Now I knew I had to shout. "Lucky, I want to ask you one thing. Why do they call you Lucky?" Because of the noise, he cupped his good hand to his ear and indicated that I should yell louder. "Lucky, why do they call you Lucky? I always wanted to know." He looked serious, first from making the effort to listen and then to coming up with an answer. "I'm lucky, that's all," he said.

I yelled again, "Oh, like that song by Duke Ellington, *I'm Just a Lucky So and So.*" Lucky looked up as he adroitly caught a dress with his one good hand and flipped it down onto the press. He nodded his head. Just to make sure he knew that I was instigating a fight, I yelled, "Down in South Carolina, they've heard of Duke Ellington, right?" Lucky shook his head in disgust at the question and took a drink from his jelly jar, the one he always used for water. Pressers all keep a vessel for water, especially during the summertime. Some have regular glasses, but I've seen some pretty arcane devices employed for this purpose. Milk containers with the tops cut off, wine bottles, beer bottles, and even an aluminum pie pan shaped in a V for the water to collect. Lucky's jelly jar made a childish statement about him. He would always close it tightly after each sip and tell me when he needed more water for it. He wouldn't say *Boss* and he wouldn't say *Cap'n;* he would just motion with his bad hand, the one that only had a thumb, to get him some water. Since he hadn't antagonized me verbally, I didn't think it was just an objectionable chore. It was hot. Damn, it was hot and a little cold water meant a lot to anyone in the back of a dry cleaning store pressing clothes in August.

"Why do they call you Lucky?" I started up again. He stared at me with this hand resting on the pressing bar. With his forehead on top of his arm, he looked toward me and shook his head. I spun my sleeveless dress with a little flair and brushed off any offending hairs with a whisk broom. The next step was to bring it to him for pressing. I pulled the dress off the form, placed it on a hanger and walked it over to the rack where he took the clothes that were ready for pressing.

"I'm a lucky man, dat' why. I am a lucky man. I am a lucky man. Dat's why."

"Why are you so lucky? Tell me what happened in your life that makes you so lucky?"

He concentrated on what he was pressing and didn't look up to answer. I knew this was the conclusion of our conversation, at least for today. He didn't look up for the rest of the day as I brought him jacket after jacket, dress after dress, all on hangers and racked them neatly for him. He worked methodically, and I studied his one-fingered hand just as methodically. I wondered and let my imagination run all over the place as to what happened to the other four fingers. In some ways, this feature, one thumb, made it difficult to look at him seriously. How many people approach you and have only one thumb on their hand? One doesn't know whether to admit their squeamishness or their guilt by avoiding eye contact or by making eye contact. There was one last thing regarding Lucky's dress and demeanor that transformed him into a cartoon figure. He always wore slippers around the place. A dry cleaning store has a factory atmosphere to it, so it was just incongruous to see a man with one thumb on one hand and wearing slippers approach you. You couldn't look at his face because he possessed that pugnacious boxer expression about him. You definitely couldn't look at his feet without laughing because of those stupid slippers. Finally, his hand with one thumb made you wince and turn away. You spent most of your time talking through and around him. But he had a presence. And he knew how to break me.

"Higby, Higby, " I screamed in anguish. "Higby, Higby, I can't take it anymore. "Lucky keeps fucking with me." I heard the chair slowly being pushed away from the sewing machine, and I knew that Higby was heading from one side of the store to the other. He walked with a dual air of exasperation and also relief. How many cuffs could he put on trousers in one afternoon without a break? My screams had at least offered him that solace.

"What the hell is goin' on over here?"

"Lucky is messing with me. I can't take it anymore!"

"What's he doin' to you?"

"Higby, you know what he's doing. He keeps on calling me Boss and Cap'n. He knows I hate it."

"Lucky, didn't we talk about this a little while ago?"

Lucky kept pressing. He had a nice rhythm and decided to pace his answers with that of the press. He spoke as the press went up and down, "Yeah, you tol' me not to call him dat a little while ago. I 'member."

"Then why do you keep on doing it?"

"Do what?"

"Why do you keep callin' him Cap'n and Boss?"

"He white."

"Light, motherfucker, not white" came hurling out of my mouth. I had clenched my fists.

"Dukeschank, you watch your mouth. You're talking to an adult."

I said nothing in response to Higby's remonstration. He waited.

"Well?" I said nothing; he waited. "Well?"

"I'm sorry. I shouldn't have cursed at an adult."

"Good, now Lucky, look, this boy is sensitive. He asked you not to call him Boss and Cap'n a few months ago. I remember. You remember?"

Before Lucky could speak I butted in, "He's mocking me. He's doing that to mock me."

Lucky said nothing. The whole time Lucky's press had spoken for him; he kept bringing that press down to a rhythm that was all his own: set, press, lock, steam, release; set, press, lock, steam, release. I knew this was part of his answer. Higby wasn't one to repeat himself and waited with Lucky the same way he waited for my apology. For a few seconds all you could hear was the press.

"I remember. A few months back, he tol' me, he don't want to be de Cap'n or de Boss."

"Well, why do you keep callin' him that?"

"I won't call him dat no more."

"Dukeschank, is that OK with you? Lucky said he won't call you those names anymore."

I nodded yes with my fists still clenched. I was thinking of striking Lucky and how he might whip out his knife that he kept in his back pocket and how he would mess me up pretty good before Higby could even stop it. But it would have been worth it in some way. Higby walked out and left us in our angry silence. I didn't want to make any eye contact with him. It was that awkward moment where both parties feel a little silly and ridiculous. I looked at him. Lucky, with hands on his hips, then stuck his tongue out at me, and I thought this was another characteristic to throw into his immaturity repertoire. I eyed him and shook my head and sighed as loudly as possible. Lucky's mind, his raw and crude unformed conscience scared me, but I wanted to smile at the same time. How could he stick his tongue out at me? That was such an adolescent thing to do. Was he really a child in ways that I didn't want to contemplate? Up until that moment, he was just a thing, an object to me without any degree of human sentiment or kindness. From the pugnacious and brutal forehead, down to the slippers, he was a puppet person to me. His ugly manner of mauling English yoked with grunts and hoots only further proved to me that he wasn't human.

It was that, the way he spoke that obliquely revealed Lucky's past to me. Every time he spoke he linked me to a world that I wanted no part of. Every time he spoke it was impossible for me not to feel as though I was being hurled back and intrinsically linked to some befouled and debased world. Every *dat* and *boss* and *cap'n*, double negative, *he have* instead of *he has*, made me question what he was truly capable of feeling or thinking. I became certain that a land called South Carolina controlled and monitored his emotional and intellectual being. He responded to things from 1930 that I could not imagine or had any desire to think about. He dreamed strange and distorted bucolic notions that I only knew from books and films. With a black consciousness mutilated by southern white racism I refused to see him as anything but a mutant. He was an experiment that had gone awry.

The words *boss* and *cap'n* and *boy* faded from his vocabulary. He never called me that again. Now, when he wanted my attention, he would just yell *Hey* at the top of his lungs. I would bring him a batch of clothes. We said nothing more than that for months. I kept track of him out of the corner of my eye. I noticed that he started carrying a Bible with him, and he read passages, moving his lips. Whenever he had a break, which in reality meant that there just weren't any clothes ready to be pressed, he would sit up on the long table and start reading his Bible. He never read anything else but the back of the sports page to see what the winning number was.

"Lucky, you promised me something a long time ago. I was wondering if I could cash in on it now."

"What? I promise you somethin'? Why? I ain't never promised you nothin'."

I lied but had him convinced because of the tone of my voice. "Lucky," I continued, "you told me that you were going to tell me how you lost your fingers. Don't you remember? You said, 'Cap'n, some day I'm gonna tell you how I lost my fingers.' You remember now, right?"

With him convinced he put his Bible down and became thoughtful. "OK" came out of his mouth with a little air of contrition. He had meant to tell me. I just had him persuaded that he had taken an oath and was standing on my rights. "OK, you see. I got caught stealin', and dey cut my fingers off. Dat's it. Dat's the truth. The Gawd's honest truth."

With an incredulous smirk I said, "Lucky, you gotta be kiddin' me. You expect me to believe that? You were caught stealing something, and somebody caught you and then they cut your fingers off. Who's gonna believe that story? Don't start that South Carolina stuff either. This is a bunch of bull. You said you were going to tell me what really happened. That's not what happened."

"Dukeschank, you ain't asked me the most important question. You ain't asked me what was I stealin'."

"OK, I'll make it official. What were you stealin'?"

"Pussy."

"What?"

"Yeah, yes, yes sir, pussy I was stealing."

"White?"

"No, dey kill you for dat." No, young colored girl I shouldn't been messin' with. Father caught me; very mad. Very young girl. 'William, I teach you lesson' and smack no more fingers. Dat's all folks, like Porky Pig," and he hummed the closing music of all those Warner Brothers cartoons. He was free as he talked and didn't notice that he revealed a name to me. However, I didn't believe this "William." It was just the way he said it. The other part, the finger chopping, that was true.

I kept my thoughts to myself after the only soliloquy that he would ever recite to me. That was his longest speech. He had never spoken so long or so freely before. He acted things out and had even added some musical accompaniment when he hummed those closing bars of the cartoon. I tried to look into his eyes as he was talking to see what kind of light would be there on this very special occasion.

"You believe me, right, Dukeschank?"

"Yeah, I do; I really do."

"You know people can do somethin' like that?"

"Yeah, sure, I just thought that maybe white people had done something terrible to you."

"Dey could and dey do. All de time. But not dis time. If I mess with a white girl, big trouble. You know dat?"

"Sure, I know things are terrible down there."

"How you know?"

"Shoot, read about it, read a lot about it."

"What books you read about de South?"

"You ever hear of a writer named Richard Wright?"

"No, I ain't never heard of him. I just read de Bible."

"Yeah, that's right. I guess we better get back to work."

Lucky agreed that our time out was more than enough and that a return to pressing and Suzy Qing was in order. I walked back to my machine. He reached into the large laundry basket for another pair of pants.

Christmas, months later. There's an air of festivity in the place. Higby has gone all out and sent me to the little hardware store to buy a can of spray frosting for the front windows. While there I take the initiative to buy some Christmas lights and Higby compliments me on my business sense. "Customers don't mind being reminded that it is Christmastime by their most frequented commercial establishments." I looked at him, smiled, and recalled how he had *Dry Cleaning Journal* on his lap the other day and he was probably mimicking something straight out of page 45 or 48. But he's right. People are happy. They come bustling in and drop off large amounts of clothes and party dresses and even a tuxedo here and there. Men and women whom I barely say *hello* and *good-bye* to, start to talk about a tip that is coming my way for being the best delivery guy or the best counterman who has never lost any of their clothes.

I beam and dream of an extra dollar there and an extra five dollars there. Higby has already mentioned that I'm getting a bonus and the fantasies about what to do with an additional thirty dollars has made for some grand schemes in my head. This will be the first Christmas I'll be able to buy friends and family exactly what they want or exactly what I think they want. The list goes from one item per person to two or three. It strikes me for the first time to get Higby something, and I'm proud of myself for coming up with this idea on my own. Then it strikes me hard. Lucky, get something for Lucky. Lucky has no friends or family. Never once has he received a phone call from anyone at the job. He never makes any calls from the phone next to the cash register. No one has ever come to visit or stop by and see him. Yeah, get Lucky a Christmas present. But what? What could this man who lived in a room in a boardinghouse want or need? He shared a kitchen with other roomers, which meant that all of those kitchen utensils were already in supply. I pondered this question laboriously and thought about how Christmas was not always going to be fun if situations like these occurred with any frequency. I thought about asking Higby, but I wanted to surprise Higby too so that wasn't an option. Lucky, though, since we really weren't that friendly, just peaceful antagonists in a manner, would take my question about a Christmas present in the right way. In addition, just discovering that someone was thinking of him and his life would make him feel pretty good at that time of the year.

I take care of Higby first. I talk to the most dependable livery driver, Teddy, and ask him to do me a favor and get a bottle of Johnny Walker Red from Mulholland's liquor store and to make sure it's in one of those fancy Christmas boxes that has a red ribbon on the top. He knows what I'm up to immediately, saying, "Getting something for the old man, huh? That's downright thoughtful of you. Gotta be eighteen to get whiskey though, so I'll do that little favor for you." I fork over the money to Teddy and remind him about the red ribbon on top of the box. He nods his head and says, "I'll sneak over some time next week; sooner or later Higby will make a delivery in the truck and I'll be watching." Teddy walks out and I'm happy. Higby's favorite drink is Johnny Walker Red mixed with plenty of milk so "it goes down smooth, silky and easy." He's going to be happy when he sees this box next to the cash register December 24th. Lucky, got to get something for Lucky.

I walked away from the front door, watching Teddy scoot across Farmers Boulevard. When I saw him enter Mulholland's before going into the taxi stand, I could see that half of my Christmas plan was under way. I didn't want to hesitate any more about the next step of my mission and sauntered into the pressing area. There he was, slippers, white T-shirt, and gray slacks, pressing away. "Hey Lucky, I want to ask you something?"

"What's de matter?"

"Lucky, no, nothing is the matter, I just wanted to ask you something good."

He frowned a bit but could tell by the quality of my voice that I wasn't attempting to commence the cycle of fratricidal warfare that we were so familiar with.

"OK, ask me somethin'."

As I got prepared to talk, I heard this Mickey Rooney–Andy Hardy tone creep into my voice. It went up an octave. Why? I don't know. But I could feel my throat tightening a bit.

"Lucky, I was just wondering . . . I want to buy you a Christmas present, and I want to buy you something that you would want, instead of something that you don't need. Lucky had kept pressing all through the conversation. A serious look came on to his face and he shook his head.

"No, you can't buy me nothin'. Don't buy me nothin'."

"Lucky, look, everyone is getting a bonus. I can buy you something. Just name it."

When I said this, I thought to myself, *name something that costs about five bucks*. There was a pause, and all you could hear was the hissing of the press and the pressure building up in the pipes. Lucky shook his head and reiterated that there was nothing that I could get him for Christmas. I took this the wrong way and wondered if Lucky felt insulted by a teenager desiring to buy him something for Christmas. I started to anger a bit but reminded myself that this would not make things better.

"Lucky, look, I have to bag a whole batch of clothes. Gonna be at least an hour. When I come back, I'll ask you. Just think about it."

Lucky stopped the press and leaned forward so as to hear what I had just said. I repeated my request and he said, "OK, Dukeschank, you come back in an hour."

I walked back to the customer side of the store and started to bag hundreds of clothes in all combinations. Sweaters, skirts, vests, and suits. The Christmas rush was on. People holding social gatherings wanted their drapes and curtains just the right way. Some household items were so large that I had to use two or three hangers to hold the weight of them. Remove tags, put pink fluffy paper on women's clothes, place bundle on metal holder, pull the plastic down over bundle, karate chop plastic at perforated edge, place finished product on rack. An hour of this goes by, and I'm finished. In between I take care of a few customers, either taking in dirty clothes or dispensing clean ones. It was time to talk to Lucky.

"Lucky, I just wanted to talk to you one more time."

"Oh, about de . . ."

"Yeah, I want to give you something for Christmas."

Lucky brought the press down and placed it in the neutral position so it would hold the garment on the bed but not steam it. With his bad hand, he wiped his brow. He then backed away about a foot from the press, stared at it, and then moved back to it. He placed both hands on the controls. He then bowed his head. He kept it down. It was quiet since no steam was hissing from the press. He spoke with his head down to the press, saying, "So you want to get me somethin' for Christmas?" Just from him keeping his head down, I could see that my generous offer and request had caused him to become somber. The fun was gone. I was anxious that something good had become something bad without me doing anything.

"Lucky, look, it was just an idea . . . it was . . ."

He cut me short and raised his head. He was crying. My stomach reacted first and tightened like a Slinky spring that's become all screwed up. There were no sounds. It was that kind of crying. Just steady tears rolling down that tough face with a square head. He looked up into the fluorescent lights that were directly above his head and murmured, slowly and with creakiness in his throat, "For Christmas, I want, all I want, all I want you to give me is de strength to stop drinking dis liquor. Dat's what I want for Christmas, for Gawd to give me de strength to stop drinking dis liquor. Dat's what I want."

He reached into his back pocket, took out a small bottle of Canadian Club and took a drink. He shuddered as it flushed through his body. Nothing made sense. I had seen him take a drink from his jelly jar water on the press a thousand times, and I had seen him take a drink from his back pocket a thousand times and then it hit me; *a thousand times you've watched Lucky take a drink, straight from the bottle and never thought about it.* Slowly things started to gel. Lucky was an alcoholic but that word still meant little or nothing as I silently said it. An alcoholic was a person who sits in a corner in a bar with a bottle for himself. *Lucky is in a dry cleaning plant with a bottle and he's by himself.*

After that last shudder, he put the bottle back in his hip pocket. He moved the press out of the neutral position and hit the knob for some steam to come down. He had to yell now, "Dat's some Christmas present to ask for, right? Right, Dukeschank? Dat's some dream." I grimaced and just shook my head in agreement.

Trouble in Paradise

———ᐅ•(❶)•ᐊ———

WHATEVER INTEREST I had in drugs, experimenting, flaunting, exploring with my friends, was killed off at an early time by my brother. Paul started smoking pot when he was a young teenager; heroin was running through his veins by the time he was a junior in high school. He sat in a chair in the living room nodding out, unconscious to me and my minor requests about turning down the music, or shutting down a record player that had already worn a groove into the LP because he was in a daze. He sat and nodded. I looked and shook my head. The only excitement was the money. Heroin was such a lucrative business, and the money poured into his hands. Big wads of ones, fives, tens and twenties in dirty rubber bands were all over the house. My job was to count and recount. For accurate accounts, a ten dollar bill would come my way. Ten dollars was a lot of money for a high school lad in 1967.

It all started with a lie. I was later to find out that junkies are the scourges of truth. Maybe it has to do with the word *junkie: Junk, trash, garbage, refuse.* You sometimes asked yourself how did you ever expect this person to tell you the truth about anything when the social tag, their label, reeks of untruth. "Never trust a junkie, even when they say good morning or good afternoon; they're already thinking about how to scrape up two dollars here and five dollars there and if it means taking your television set when you're not looking, that's a given." The phenomenon of the drug addict entered my life via my brother's world and all of its spidery webs. Once you're in the world of junk, shit, horse, dope, you're aware of how fast and widespread a social infection can be. My brother's boyhood friends were afflicted, and I was hurt to see them rubbing their watery noses, scratching their arms, sniffling, nodding. Guys I had played softball with, roly-poly, teenagers who had taught a generation of kid brothers how to ride bikes, play army in the woody-woods, remove a lawn mower engine and mount it to a bike, converting it into a motor-bike, all of them flopped and disintegrated by the time I was fifteen. I never had the opportunity to say thanks for their earlier gestures of kindness and help. Now they were in my house, thinking about stealing from my little coffeepot where I kept my savings from my paper route. When you ask them naively, "Did any of you guys see my money?" They say, "No, Little Paul, what's the problem? Wasn't it just there the other day? You just showed it to us. Where could it go?" The junkies lie in the morning, the afternoon and at night. They lie about the simplest things and the most complicated things. They lie and lie and lie. They are born liars.

It's 1968 and New York City endures one of the longest teacher strikes in history. Albert Shanker and his powerful union holds New York hostage and there's nothing that the city can offer as a ransom that will satisfy his demands. Community control, something that sounds like a righteous democratic concept that involves parents in educating their child for the first time in history, has a negative side to it. Black anti-Semitism starts to corrode the community board of Ocean Hill-Brownsville. If you sided with the parents at first and, in addition, were turned off by Shanker's sullen bulldog appearance, you throw your partisanship back to the union once you hear those classic phrases: *you know, the ones with the hats, you know, the chosen people, Jew teacher, Hymie teachers* and other derivatives. Black people readily exhibit that being in the United States since 1619 has done them more than one disservice. This one they wear on their sleeve like any other good redneck from Louisiana or Tennessee. When their masters imbued them with Christianity, they also infected them with a righteous hatred of Jews. I suppose one just goes with the other.

That fall, in New York City, school does not start until late October, and every class schedule is lengthened at Springfield Gardens High School, so as to meet the state requirement for a minimum number of hours spent in the building each day. I'm joyful when I discoverer that sophomores won't start classes until noon, and we'll be in class until about six in the evening. All morning off. Really a half day to myself. Other students commence their classes at seven and are out by eleven-thirty. My brother has already been left back so he's spending an extra year in high school. I'm slowly catching up with him and am proud of my record and ashamed of his. I'm a freshman and he's a senior; I'm a sophomore and he's a senior; I'm a junior and he's in jail.

He's not interested in attending his early morning classes. He leaves before my parents go to work. No books, no pads, no pencils. By nine o'clock he's returned, and I know that he wasn't let out early. He's cut classes and is going to stay home for the rest of the day. The doorbell starts to ring. Sometimes simultaneously the phone starts to jump off the hook. The business is open. The gates are up. It's time to sell heroin for a few hours from a house, a house with a driveway, a backyard, barbecue, and a garage. It takes me weeks or maybe a month or two to figure out what is going on because as my brother said, "Junkies are the best liars in the world." He should know. It's such a tricky and deceptive little world made up of liars, thieves, and cutthroats. If the house had ten guys milling around on a Wednesday morning in November 1968, not one of them was to be trusted any farther than you could throw him. Heroin makes you hungry, and it's a special sort of craving that must be met or it eats the user first.

The atmosphere in the house was special. These were strung-out junkies, but they were special. They were the first generation of people in that post-World War II era who were going to be crushed and swallowed by something that was mythological, a legend. There were legendary junkies that literature and cinema conjured up: *The Man With the Golden Arm*, Barney Ross, the boxer coming back from war in the South Pacific and an addiction to morphine that surreptitiously metabolized into accepting other more hideous substitutes. But those things were far away in books like Burroughs' *Junkie* and *Naked Lunch* and Hollywood. There was the connection made between blacks and drugs via jazz, but that was also illusory. We were in that little hamlet Springfield Gardens, protected and isolated from those worlds. The fledging black middle class had fled Lenox Avenue and Putnam Avenue for this insular suburb, and there should have been security in Eden. Springfield Gardens should have functioned as an asylum, a safe haven. Maybe due to the illusions that are refined in refuge like this, the truth is even harder to bear. Maybe because of the illusions, that is what makes the lie bigger, fatter, and more digestible. You don't want to see something so badly that you don't see it. But I could smell it. Books had developed my sense of smell, and I knew something reeked in paradise.

Claude Brown wrote *Manchild in the Promised Land* and Piri Thomas wrote *Down These Mean Streets*. These were my primers, my guidebooks for the decay that was inundating my house, my home. Of course, the parallels didn't always jibe between these classic portraits of urban life in New York City and what was occurring in Springfield Gardens. That book hadn't been written yet. Thomas and Brown would have been shocked if I had somehow contacted them and said, "In the southeastern section of Queens, New York, there is a neighborhood with tree-lined blocks, single family homes, libraries, church organizations, and Boy Scout Troops all over the place, and young men are dealing junk out of those nice homes." Notwithstanding their inability to make sense of things, I still was saved by those books from being in the dark, my own little world of ignorance and naïveté. Because their chilling portraits left such an impression on me, I started to put two and two together. I came up with four every time, even when I didn't want to. Every time my brother walked to the door with nothing and came back with a handful of bills it was because he was exchanging a small glassine bag filled with dope. The bags are so small that you can hide them in the palm of your hand. If the police approach you, discarding them is sometimes as easy as one, two, three. Only a veteran cop would know that if you punch a junkie hard enough in the stomach, you shouldn't be surprised if he starts to expel a few bags of high-priced heroin at the same time he's coughing up his guts.

Hiding the drugs for Paul wasn't too much of a challenge either since their diminutiveness helped in this endeavor. An entire stack of glassine bags can be concealed in an obscure crevice, corner of a drawer, nook in a closet. This is the junkie world: small petty thoughts and small clever coyotelike tricks that keep them alive. My brother's wits start to develop a finely honed edge since every junkie coming to the door isn't necessarily a legitimate customer. He bends the eighth Venetian blind from the bottom of the windowsill so many times by peering through it, that he gives it a permanent dent. He tells me nothing. He gives me no information. Just does his business.

It's hard to study with the commotion, action, and constant activity. The junkies themselves are not loud. Heroin smooths things out, and there are plenty of moments in the living room when there is nothing but stoned junky silence. Sometimes I get a lot of studying and reading done. Sometimes none. Even if they're quiet, it's uncanny and one never knows when the doorbell will ring again and even when they exit the house, that eighth Venetian blind gets bent again. Ronnie, Delmare, Bobbie, Joey, and Paul all nod out in unison once the shooting and sniffing is over. They have their favorite chairs and positions. While still conscious, they place a record on the turntable with the arm left off, so it will repeat inexorably. They also have their favorite records: the Doors' *Strange Days,* anything by Cream, the Stones and maybe with a sense of mockery, Bob Dylan's *Rainy Day Woman.* For some reason The Beatles' *Hey Jude* strikes a chord with them, and for a bunch of young black guys, I'm always surprised at their musical taste in 1968. No soul. No R&B. Just solid rock.

I used to look at and study them and wonder what was going on. They didn't seem particularly happy or particularly sad. They looked sleepy, and they slept the morning off. When they awoke, everything proceeded in slow motion. They smiled and winked at me. There's a certain way a junkie awakes from his slumber. Grabbing the arms of the chair that he's fallen asleep in, he pulls himself up from his slouch, wiping the snot that has dribbled out his nose. Or he scratches his arms. They all grab and rub their crotches in a Freudian manner, reassuring themselves that it's still there. Or during the initial phase of consciousness, because there's some residue of junk on one of his nostrils, there's one more snort, one more glorious whiff and he smiles. Whatever manner of arousal it may be, Dutch used to smile at me as he became conscious of my presence. Duke used to wink when he realized that I was studying him. My brother looked sullen and surly when he saw me looking at him. I smiled.

The hard thing was withholding all of this information. There were more than enough reasons to let someone know. Once your house becomes a public place, a bar that dispenses drugs instead of alcohol, you feel as though there is a need for something to make this new enterprise legitimate. It's difficult to describe. I was always hoping that somehow this whole activity was legal, and I just didn't know about it. My brother and his friends were such good guys. They were funny, athletic, and caring. In Springfield Gardens High School I had so many *big brothers* who called me *Little Paulie* or *Paulie Junior.* To walk down the halls and be greeted during the passing of classes was thrilling and exciting. To watch them nod out to oblivion because they just ingested this little white powder made me wonder just how powerful this little powder could be. It took strong men and made them into little babies, quiet, docile, sleepy. It brought together young men who normally were boisterous, argumentative, and there was so much to argue about in those days, and transformed them into rather passive dozers. A handout from the Black Panther Party, which had a branch in Jamaica, Queens, lay unread or the message unheard. There was a branch of SDS in our high school; their leaflets and calls to action melted in the haze of these opiate mornings. Even their differences of a racial nature were discarded. Here were whites and blacks, who at least possessed a casual mistrust of each other, sometimes almost practically lying in each other's arms. No more sports, no more tension, no more struggle, no more growth.

I wondered about telling my father. His reaction of course would have been swift and violent. That was the problem. When you went to him for a solution where mediation and understanding were demanded, where a plea for new ideas was required, my father's conventional and expected response would be honored. Fortunately, I wasn't the messenger that time. The closest I came to the role of informer was when the house was robbed, not the first time, but the third time. I could see that there was a pattern.

Anytime we bought some new appliance or item that really had some value, that television or stereo was gone within a few weeks of bringing it back from the store in the back of our 1965 Fairlane 500. Junkies need heroin, and that costs, and there is only one way to meet that need and that's crime. Springfield Gardens was ripe. Everyone worked hard to pay for their homes and to maintain those cars, lawns, and backyards. This first generation of black middle-class people journeyed to Manhattan every day on ninety-minute trips, taking a bus and subway. They were gone from seven-thirty in the morning to seven in the evening. More than enough time for a junkie to enter that home, search, pilfer, destroy, examine, evaluate, and steal. These junkies were confident in their information since they were sometimes robbing their own homes. They knew that everyone was working and that these homes were like small stores just waiting to be opened.

Our house was pillaged and after the second time I knew that these weren't strange marauders or innocent kids from out of the neighborhood as the police first theorized. The white police officers shook their heads as they surveyed the damage. We never called them until the evening because no one knew until about dinnertime. As we prepared to sit down to dinner, they would answer our call and enter through the front door. An apology for the delay but we were number ten for that day in a small five-block area. My father would give them a detailed list, an inventory of what had been stolen. My mother cried when she lost her fox furs that my father had bought as an extravagant present to celebrate one of their anniversaries.

The food would get cold, and you never felt like eating; as a matter of fact, nobody ate, except him. As the red juice from the steak congealed and became white and disgusting, he ate with relish, and I knew he knew. He would look at me across the pile of Silvercup bread that waited to receive pats of butter, and he knew that I knew. It was at that time I pledged to myself to crush him in whatever way I could and to pray for his quick demise. Anybody that would violate the sanctity of his or her own home deserved a severe chastising. My type of punishment for my brother was going to be severe; in later years it involved disowning and shunning him. It would take many shapes, but the most frequent was to insulate myself from his life and circumstances. There were to be no consequences for this excommunication since between feigning ignorance or absentmindedness, he was in the dark as to where I stood. For a time, in his eyes, he had a normal brotherly confidence that I was in league with him and his devices. Counting on my silence because he was giving me an education that I could never get anywhere else, he had allowed me to enter this special place of the cool guys who were junkies and no one knew but a few special envoys who were permitted to enter that world.

This did buy and earn my silence but not cooperation. My parents' suspicions were doomed since their vision of what could occur in Springfield Gardens had inherent limitations. There were limits to how low they could drop their expectations of their offspring. Pranks, foolishness, mischief, that was where they were bound to end up as they attempted to figure out what was going on in their home and neighborhood. Relying on a buffoonish analysis that just connoted how much denial my father was in, he would break down the problem into racial stereotypes, his own very special racial stereotypes that existed nowhere else but in his head. "Lazy spooks that don't want to be constructive and make a contribution to the community" was one refrain. "Too many spooks from the South" was another one. It had taken me some time, but I finally ascertained that a *spook* was a Negro. My father would never use the word *nigger* when making derogatory remarks about Negroes in those days. That word carried too much weight and pain to be used in any manner. One thing was clear. He kept on hinting that my brother was somehow connected to this community that was opposed to any form of positive progress. In addition, he was enlisting in the band of destructive people on his own accord. Basically, Paul was volunteering to be bad when he should have been, according to my father, joining the useful social movements in the community.

It was a puzzle. There was a rubric here, and it took years for it to become concretized in my consciousness. By the time my brother was arrested for some crime other than a prank, my old man interrogated him in such a way that I finally realized the complexities of the racial dichotomy assembled in his mind. For my old man, when you are *bad,* this means that you are overidentifying with your black half. Simple as that. It's implied that this isn't a mandatory corollary into my brother's existence, because since you are half white, you could ward off this strain, this incessant demand. "Do you want to be a constructive Negro who makes a contribution to society or do you want to be a lazy spook who belongs on a plantation?" My father's words started to chill us and even in my brother's junkie daze is ripped away, and his glassy eyes lose their sheen for a second or two as he listens to the implications of his actions. Lashed with these words, expressions, and sayings, we're both crushed. My father is unrelenting now that we are old enough to understand, and we're mature enough that he's worried about our welfare. All aspects of human achievement or failure are placed in his paradigm. "Paul, Dexter, listen. Do you want to be like W.E.B. DuBois, Duke Ellington, Langston Hughes, or do you want to be like some lazy southern Negro sleeping on a stack of cotton bales, waiting for the boat to come to the levee?"

My father, a sardonic man of few words, never has conversations with us. He only presents chilling anecdotes that are to illustrate just how determined one's fate could be if they make one fatal mistake. Principles of his personal philosophy abound through stories that haunt me to this day.

Paul, Dexter, come here. I want to speak to both of you. I saw you playing in the yard and was reminded of a story. Did I ever tell you the story of Sam? He was almost the first black train engineer. Listen, sit down for a second. You probably know that Negroes are not allowed to do that much. That's right, Paul, due to discrimination and racism. It's hard to . . . almost impossible . . . to get in that union, the Brotherhood of Locomotive Engineers. The whites have that one sewn pretty tight. Anyway, there was a black fireman. Sam. Worked on the Southern Pacific. According to the white engineer, Sam was the best fireman he ever had. Best in the world. Shoveled coal into the fire like no one before. Kept the train in tiptop shape. Never late, always on time. Perfect. One day the engineer said, 'Sam, I know things are bad for Negroes but I'm going to give you a chance. I've been noticing how you watch my every move, watch the gauges, the valves, the throttle. I do believe you know how to operate this steam engine, so I'm going to give you a chance.' Well, Sam can't believe it. He's been shoveling coal for chicken feed for years and this is a miracle. He jumps down from the coal tender and thanks the engineer. To make everything official, the engineer hands him the gloves and his hat. The engineer says, 'Sam, take her out of the station; she's all yours.' Sam puts on the gloves and hops up into the seat to look out the window. He takes the hat, sets it on his head and then turns it backward. Before he can even touch the throttle, the engineer grabs him and pulls him out of the seat and says, 'Boy, you can't run this train until you learn not to wear your hat backward. You don't wear something backward, when you're trying to run the train forward. This train is going forward, not backward. Get your shovel and go back to that coal tender.'

My father laughed and laughed at the end of this small story. "Can you imagine getting that close to what you always wanted and then boom, you just kick it away because you had to be a spook? Sam just couldn't leave that hat on his head the right way," my father would intone with a sense of sadness, now that he had stopped laughing. These stories and many like it had some special meaning for him. We weren't quite sure what they meant but the older we got, the sadder they became in terms of plot, the twist, and the irony. What realities hid behind these tales we never knew nor did we want to. We would find out soon enough.

My father has to yell because of all the airplane noise, "Dexter, I'm going to check up on Sam." He points in the opposite direction of where I'm standing. I nod that I understand. It is too loud to hear anything. Jet after jet with only about thirty seconds between them keeps taking off. He cups his hands like a bullhorn and shouts, "You stay here." He starts to walk away from me in his gray raincoat without a liner and fedora hat. It's a slow walk. I turn around to check out the planes: United, Delta, Northwest. They are lined up as though they are in a traffic jam, all waiting their turn. From Rikers Island, you're so close to LaGuardia, that you can see the rods that pull the aerilons in the wings and the flaps in the tail. This is probably the closest I'll ever be to the planes. It's great. I'm close enough that I see how the turbine blades start to spin, and how the nacelle extends during the test of the engines. When you are under the flight pattern, you can feel the heat and whirl of the turbines.

Plane after plane, I've devised tricks and counting games to keep myself occupied. It's going to be a long wait. To enter the jail for a visit is a long process with a few last minute unexpected delays. It's a hot, clammy day in June or the summertime, and I'm waiting as always, patiently, very patiently. Years of life have taught me not only how to wait but to wait in silence. I read something once about Beckett and how he knew what it was to be truly silent because of his experience during World War II in the French Resistance. Whether you were waiting in hiding or waiting to be questioned by the Nazis, you developed a cult of silence. Quiet with little or few expectations. That's the way I am especially when I wait for my father at the racetrack between races. He's quiet and between each race he studies the paper for the allotted name making little notes and notations. He likes to pen and scribble little addendums to his formulas about horses who are older than five years old. Horses that haven't won a race in ninety days. Horses who are switching from the turf to the flat. He doesn't talk and I don't either. Perfect.

Now I'm waiting again and the guards look at me without any interest. They joke and follow their routine making some of the visitors uptight and relaxing others. My father has already passed through the fenced enclosure, has proven who he is and has disappeared. I'm too young to go to jail, even as a visitor. Either that or he doesn't want me to see the hell that is there.

I'm mad, pretty mad thinking about how I have to wait for Paul who has committed some more crimes and never wants to take what's coming to him with any sense of decency or grace. He always calls from the police station. He's the opposite of me. He does not know the beauty of silence. My mother is starting to learn it. This was the time she hung up. I had answered and heard, "103rd Precinct." I put the phone down and didn't listen any further. I walked to my parents' room and knocked on the door. I lied and said it was for my mother. She got up and looked perplexed being that it was about seven o'clock on a Saturday morning.

"Hello, who is this? Where? Stay there," and with that she hung up the phone and went back to bed. I suppose my mom just got tired or maybe bored. How many times can you listen to, "I didn't do anything; I swear." He invokes morality and the guilty parent syndrome by saying, "You never believe me because it's me. Anyone of my friends and you would believe them but if it's me, nothing."

Rikers Island is adjacent to LaGuardia Airport, so I have some solid distractions, some of my father's favorites and the ones that he trained my brother and me to pay attention to. This used to be the choice for a Sunday activity, to watch the planes land at Idlewild Airport when we were little kids. Now I'm as close to LaGuardia as I could ever desire, and there are plenty of planes to watch and plenty of time. Before my old man leaves for the jail, he notices that I am thoroughly focused on the planes and cautions me about watching too close. I got outside of the car. I ask him, "Pop, what are you worried about, that a plane might crash?" He's too serious for any joking asides and keeps looking at some directions that he has in his hand and talks without even looking up, "No, the exhaust. It's not good for our health. Every time one of those jets takes off, there must be a few hundred pounds of exhaust in the air. It's gets on your face. There, feel it. Do you feel it?"

I raise my hand to my forehead where his brown hand had been only two seconds ago; I feel with mine and he's right. There's a clammy film on my skin, and it feels very dirty. I watch a few more planes take off before getting in the car. I stay there for the rest of the afternoon.

I Find Religion

I SPENT MANY years without God or gods. My parents, anytime we asked the dreaded question, "Is there a God?" answered the most profound question of all time in a matter of fact manner, usually not even turning away from their coffee or whatever duty they were attending to with, "No, man invents gods because he needs them due to his ignorance. When you're not ignorant, you don't need God or gods." Simple enough. When kids asked my sister, brother, or me why we didn't attend church, we mimicked this answer except there was one difference. We affected an air of superiority and contempt for our little companions. It was implied in our retort that we were above them and them being ignorant, should follow our lead. I'm sure there were plenty of parents who would have shooed us out of their homes if it hadn't been for our other admirable qualities. We were quiet and intelligent. In retrospect, I suppose it wasn't fair to them. We were trained in the art of debate. We knew how to hold our ground in a contested discussion. We were schooled and trained to fight with words. There were hours of training, training at home, and training at camp. Every summer we went to camps, very special camps.

In the movie *Dr. Strangelove or How I Learned to Stop Worrying and Love the Bomb,* General Jack D. Ripper lives in dread as to what lengths the Soviet Union will go in order to brainwash and propagandize the American public. Not being satisfied with undermining every major institution of our society, General Ripper's obsessive paranoia has him convinced that the postwar Communist conspiracy will employ the most unscrupulous means in their possession, including contaminating

the water system. Few people acquainted with the film can forget
Sterling Hayden's monotone voice as he indoctrinates Peter Sellers with
his theories.

> Mandrake, have you ever seen a Commie drink a glass of water?
> Vodka, that's what they drink, isn't it? Never water. On no ac-
> count will a Commie ever drink water and not without good
> reason. Water, that's what I'm getting at . . . water . . . and as
> human beings, you and I need fresh pure water to replenish our
> precious bodily fluids . . . Have you ever heard of a thing called
> fluoridation, the fluoridation of water? Well, do you know what
> it is? Do you realize that fluoridation is the most monstrously
> conceived and dangerous Communist plot we have ever had to
> face?
> Mandrake, do you realize that in addition to fluoridating
> water, why there are studies under way to fluoridate salt, flour,
> fruit juices, soup, sugar, milk, ice cream . . . ice cream, Man-
> drake, children's ice cream. Do you know when fluoridation first
> began? 1946. 1946, Mandrake. How does that coincide with
> your postwar Commie conspiracy? . . . The fluoridation of water.
> Ice cream. Little children eating ice cream.

Persuaded that these are the diabolic means that the Soviets will
apply, he orders an apocalyptic nuclear assault on the Soviet Union,
ending the world in fire not ice. However, he really didn't know that it
wasn't ice cream, the fluoridation of water, or anything of that nature.
His paranoia was completely directed in the wrong direction. Summer
camp. Yes, innocent summer camp. Some parents were worried about
their children being abused, lost, or drowned at summer camp. While
McCarthy is wasting his time and energy purging Hollywood, right
under his big fat nose, is the biggest, fattest Commie plot ever hatched.
However, only a few Americans really knew that the true terror was
Commie camp, the camps that thousands of us were sent to during the
1950s. As other children sat around campfires and sang songs, like
Home on the Range and *This Old Man, he played one, he played knick
knack, paddy wack,* so did we but our songs always possessed some politically conscious messages in them. In the 1950s many left-wing parents sent their children to camps that not only offered traditional
activities but also encouraged and cultivated progressive and liberal
ideas. "Red Diaper Babies," as they are now known, admit that these

experiences were sometimes the landmark moments that motivated and inspired a lifelong commitment to social activism. I was one of them and it was always the music that left the biggest impression.

Our songs were intended to raise consciousness. If they didn't, there was something wrong with them. The music we were exposed to at camp always harkened back to historical struggles for freedom, democracy, and justice. Slavery, resistance of the Native Americans against being conquered, workers fighting for a living wage, land for farmers, civil rights, the music always addressed these topics in a spiritual and rousing manner. When you sang these songs at night with a counselor playing a guitar, *This land is your land, this land is my land, from California to the New York Island,* you were moved. All of the songs espoused how America was the only place that could ever be the best place. America possessed the basics in abundance and overabundance. It just needed refinement. With a little economic redistribution of the wealth, as described in *The Banks Are Made of Marble,* or with a response to the symbolic nationwide call for social justice in *If I Had a Hammer, I'd Ring It in the Morning,* America could truly be "the land of the free and the home of the brave." For future political rallies and demonstrations of the sixties, I can see where thousands of kids were imbued with their fighting spirit and high esprit de corps. As someone said, during the 1960s the right-wingers may have had the food, but we had the songs. Our songs ran the gamut of Pete Seeger, Joan Baez, The Weavers, Oscar Brand, Woody Guthrie, Buffy Sainte-Marie, and Josh White, and of course, Paul Robeson. Their songs were sung at our camps. I went to one of these camps, Camp Calumet, in upstate New York.

The camp was great and as far as Communist subversion goes, well, kids just want to have fun and if you want to say that singing a few songs by progressive people who believed that artists should take stands on issues of the day, well, I guess we were all guilty, kids as well as counselors. I loved my bunk, my bunkmates, my counselor, Howie, and on the day I had to leave, I cried and cried. I learned how to swim in a lake, camp out at night with a bedroll under the stars and most important of all, to be quiet while Howie sneaked Sandra into his bunk at night and made her laugh and cry late into the night. My parents' finances only permitted one month so when I had to say good-bye to James, Mike, and another James, I was heartbroken. These camps that catered to children who had come of age during the late 1940s and early 1950s were the few that were integrated, staff as well as campers. This was important since if you were ever to feel like you belonged and were not different, you would have to see and interact with living things, people, schools, and camps. In order to have faith, one, even a young person, must be able to witness the manifestations of the theories that were being espoused since July 4, 1776. This camp was one of those manifestations. It was there I got to view that America could embrace its most innovative ideals in a most unique manner. That's what Camp Calumet meant to me. It gave me weapons for defense, not offense. When I returned home, I started to listen to a record that I had heard played at the camp. It was in my house but now it had new meaning. Hearing Paul Robeson's voice now echoed in a new way:

Who are you? Are you an American?
Am I an American? I'm just an Irish, Negro, Jewish, Italian,
French and English, Spanish, Russian, Chinese, Polish, Scotch,
Hungarian . . .

This was Paul Robeson's famous reply in *Ballad for Americans*. Who are you? Whenever I was asked this question, because of a summer at Camp Calumet, I was now armed with two answers. It was clear that I was confidently either an Englishman as Mrs. Roth had told the class during the story of Thanksgiving or I was an American. According to Paul Robeson everyone was included under this grand umbrella. No one was excluded. The list went on to pull in groups that I had never met:

. . . Litvok, Swedish, Finnish, Canadian, Greek and Turk, and
Czech and double check American.

That was such a great answer, Paul Robeson's reply to an anonymous speaker from the 1938 recording for Columbia Records. After patiently telling the story of America, a tale reincarnated by John Latouche and written by Earl Robinson, he finally explodes (with Paul Robeson you sometimes had a feeling that he was imploding) and states emphatically that he represents every group that has ever come to the shores of America. No one is left out and the last line *and lots more* lets the listener know that this list is never really complete. Robeson spoke for me anytime I was harassed, attacked, and ridiculed. I always heard his strong and manly voice and that two-record set inspired me and kept me strong. The background singers had a nice and simple name, the American People's Chorus; they were regular people and you could hear this in their amateurish but very penetrating voices. In the world evoked by the chorus and Paul Robeson, I belonged, thrived, and lived, and my fantasies grew and were spurred on by the playing of these two 78-rpm records on a daily basis, sometimes two or three times a day.

We had a gigantic Magnavox television and hi-fi system whose scale captured my imagination just because of its opulence. Huge, bigger than little me, white birch wood, a piece of furniture with doors, cabinets, some sliding, some opening toward you. I would run and drag my chair over, causing one of my parents or an older sibling with some degree of parental authority to state in a controlled and slightly irritated voice, "It's better to carry your chair instead of scratching the floor." Finding the record in the vast archives of my father's two thousand plus record collection was always an odyssey. There were two thousand records of which ninety-nine percent were jazz albums that he had collected in the 1930s, '40s, and early '50s. They were in order, some sort of library discography that meant everything to him, but when you're little and can't make distinctions, you identify things by color, pictures, and paintings, even smell. The bindings of record albums in those days had identifying symbols that were the clues that you were on the right track. RCA Victor had a dog that sat next to an old fashioned phonograph. Columbia had a little microphone; DECCA just had the letters D-E-C-C-A. Another clue might be roman numerals. Since records were at times issued in sets, there were volumes so if I saw VOL., with IV or VI next to it, yes, I was getting very close.

Ballad for Americans was a two-volume set with a red, white, and blue cover, a photo of Big Paul smiling and gazing intelligently in front of an American flag. Opening a record album possessed the same mysterious quality in those days as opening a book. There were pictures and text and the fact that this was just the beginning of the adventure, made the entire experience sparkle with excitement. The ritual of playing a record had steps and phases and the steady buildup of tension was finally resolved with the climactic plop of a 78-rpm record down the spindle onto the platter with a satisfying thud. It was ready; I was ready.

Volume on, selector switch pointed toward phono; action. Paul Robeson's Shakespearean voice expounding the hypnotic words, easy to remember,

> In '76 the sky was red, with thunder rumbling overhead, bad
> King George couldn't sleep in his bed . . .

Every day, once in the morning, then when I came home. As my doubts grew about who I was, I knew I could run home, put on *Ballad for Americans*, and hear my story told. No matter how many difficult questions were put to me, Paul always sang my answer with courage and fortitude. I thought about believing in God but figured early on that he somehow had created the mess that I was in—if he existed—and that was already a strike against him.

Later when I could read, write, and understand the outside world a little better, I discovered that if one is to build an arsenal to defend himself against a racist or ugly world, the best weapons are books, music, and art. When the world is menacing and dangerous, a temporary retreat must be made but it is, as the generals say, a tactical withdrawal. Anytime I went home and put on *Ballad for Americans*, or later, as a teenager, read Mark Twain, Richard Wright, Thoreau, Ann Petry, Langston Hughes, and Gwendolyn Brooks, I was just getting myself in mental and psychological shape for future encounters, I was like a boxer hoping to stay in the ring one more round.

By the time I was in seventh or eighth grade, I stayed. I now knew that words, vituperative and nasty, could be countered with ideas that evoked strength and continuity. A racist could be outthought. Even five of them. True, physical confrontations would still leave one battered and bruised but that was on the surface. You triumphed on the inside and that is what was important and essential. In books by Dickens, Gorky, and Hemingway, there is one mutual connection. The individual has value and worth. I made the connection with middle class Englishmen and women, Russian peasants, and American outdoorsmen; despite our different backgrounds and the immediate circumstances of our lives, they included me in their world. Wretched people must appear in literature or else, as Tolstoy says, a poor little Russian peasant boy might be hurt to read a book where he is not included. He may reproach the author. The books I read never gave me that motive or impetus. I was lucky. I or someone like me appeared in every book and that was more than comforting. That is what saved me. That was life itself.

I wanted to believe in something or have something that would throb inside me when I heard or saw the outside world mirror my internal one. I was empty. I lived this spiritless life until July 6, 1971. On that day Louis Armstrong died, and from that day onward I was blessed with the spirit; I was blessed with the wonderful miracle of finding him and his music. My life and those around me was changed forever. It was midday, and I was listening to the radio, a news station. On the hour, they announced that Louis Armstrong had died. I was struck. I knew it would be important for my father to know about this event. I jumped up and ran downstairs to my dad who was in the basement, under the fluorescent lights studying and figuring which horse in the eighth race at Belmont might, if he switched from turf to the dirt, just might have an extra advantage. I flew down the wooden steps and told him that Louis Armstrong had died. He uttered, "Damn, Pops died? Pops died. Man, that's a blow. Why don't you play some records by Louis; that would be a nice thing to do. That would be a nice little tribute."

I walked upstairs and thought about the request. It certainly wasn't an order, just a request from a man who wanted to recall someone else in a certain way. I walked over to the massive record collection that always set the tone in the living room: two thousand 78-records, all cataloged by my father's esoteric discography system. Just as John Dewey had come up with a structure for placing all books in order, my dad had done the same with his jazz records back in the 1940s. I wasn't sure how it worked; it was based on numbers and colors. I looked at the records and didn't know where to start. I walked back through the dining room, through the kitchen and perched myself at the door to the basement. Down those wooden steps my father had returned to examining and studying his charts. "Hey, Pop, one problem: I don't know where to look." He leaned forward to make a notation next to a horse's name that was returning to the dirt after some unsuccessful attempts as a turf horse. Working at an architect draftsman's table, which always gave his obsession a mysterious scientific ambience, he said, "Green, 110 through 350, and then blue, 800 up to 875." I repeated the numbers to myself and walked back to the mammoth record collection. I had already calculated that I had over three hundred records to choose from. Since there were two songs on each record, that meant, over six hundred titles to decipher. Damn!

The record collection itself possessed a physical presence that instantaneously imbued one with the sensation that he was in the presence of something greater than himself. There they were, 2000 records flushed and tinged with brown sleeves. The hardened brown sleeves were firm to the touch. There were separate sections for the ten-inch records and then other sections for the twelves. The case was handmade out of mahogany and bamboo. A long piece of highly polished bamboo ran along the top of the case. I think it was the bamboo that gave the record case an exotic touch; that round piece of bamboo, two inches in diameter that your hand had to cross when getting a record, ceremoniously signaled that you were leaving one world and entering another. Inevitably the result was an awe-filled reverence with a twofold purpose. First, you were inspired and knew humility; your meekness before this massive collection of art compelled you with an urge to bow reverently. Second, because every one of these records was breakable, your obsequiousness was compounded with an inevitable and inexorable sense that if you dropped one of these records, if you cracked or splintered one of those disks, that transgression pointed toward a moral lapse in your character. You had ruined something for eternity. That record could never, ever, be mended or repaired. You had taken it upon yourself to outrage Duke Ellington, Count Basie, Mildred Bailey, and Rex Stewart. You had, without just cause or a rational reason, capriciously determined that the art of Oscar Peterson, Charlie Parker, Lester Young, Paul Desmond, and many other classical geniuses must be destroyed. That's what made the whole process a haunting and spooky ritual. To shatter a record from my father's prized collections meant that you possessed the effrontery to insult geniuses like Billie Holiday, Bessie Smith, Art Tatum, and Benny Goodman. Whenever a record was smashed by a lowly individual like my brother, my sister, or myself, my father wouldn't strike out in his usual way. No yelling, hitting, orders to go to the basement, orders about extra chores; no, he would just shake his head and murmur, as though cracked and ripped himself, "You just destroyed a great work of art forever; it will never exist again. Why did you do that?" You were left for the rest of an afternoon, morning, or weekend to contemplate your abject act in your room.

With all those choices and the living room very quiet with the blinds drawn due to the summer heat, I came up with my own scientific method. Find the blue series, 800–875 and just blindly pick a record. Don't look at titles. I was alienated from that massive library of music, because of the titles themselves. How could these titles appeal to an eighteen-year-old in 1971? *Lady Be Good, Nice Work If You Can Get It, Roll 'Em Pete, You Can Depend on Me, Am I Blue? Time on My Hands, I Want a Little Girl, Conga Brava* and *Don't Be That Way.* My spontaneous solution to the problem would eliminate all of that travail and pain. I knew from past experience that anytime I had previously attempted to choose a record, it was futile because the titles ended my desire to explore and discover something new. This time, it was a sense of now or never. With my father downstairs waiting to hear some music, something for this unofficial memorial service, perhaps that was the pressure I needed. I shut my eyes and placed my finger on a brown record jacket. I pulled it out gently without looking. I opened my eyes but purposefully did not examine the disc itself. I could see that I had a blue label.

With the record in my hand, number 814, I walked over to the turntable, disciplining myself that I wasn't going to look at the title because that potentially would force me to make another choice. Two titles, two choices. Keep it simple. I slipped the record out of the jacket and swung the turntable arm back so it could receive this unknown platter. My eyes were open, and I could see that not only was it blue, but it was the DECCA label. However, I refrained from reading the title. I placed the arm over the record and turned the switch for EJECT.

The platter started spinning, and the entire mechanism was out of my control. When you played a 78 record, everything happened at this accelerated pace. Your association with the mechanics of the turntable practically made you liable to having an aesthetic experience. When you saw those records spinning so fast that you couldn't even read the label, you felt that the music was to be fast and exciting. *Plattt!* It dropped down with a thud and the arm was already out of its resting place. Up, dropping down within a second or two. That high static sound came out of the speakers. I'll always remember that sound.

The roaring blast of a big band came out of the speakers. I'll never forget it. The energy, the zeal, the pronouncement. It was a large jazz orchestra playing as loud as possible, and the tempo had me breathless. After a few seconds of this raucous music, his voice, but not of *Hello,*

Dolly fame or even *Mack the Knife* days. No, this was a voice I had never heard before,

> *"My heart gets a chill, I feel such a thrill, my feet won't keep still, when they swing that music . . . I'm so happy as can be, when they swing that music for me."*

He had sung those words and touched me. I was shivering as he was singing. As he sang the last chorus of words, I could feel the dynamic of the music building to match the potent force behind his singing. He was building and the members of the band were attempting to match his vigor. After the last words of the song, Louis Armstrong put that trumpet to his lips, and my life was permanently changed.

I had never heard anyone play the trumpet like that. I had never heard anyone play any instrument like that. So pure, so bountiful, brashly playing a brass instrument as if to tell the world that this is the only way the trumpet should be played. The solo was so close to the words that he had just sung, that I couldn't tell which was mimicking which. When he sang, it sounded like the trumpet solo and when he played it sounded like his voice. The energy seemed uncontrollable. I couldn't imagine how this man could get so much sound and resonance out of that small three-valve instrument. I thought that maybe there were two or three trumpets playing but no, it was just him, just Louis, just God. The solo climbed and soared. Louis pushed his horn another octave and played in perfect pitch. I knew from being in the high school band, that being able to play high notes meant little or nothing if one couldn't maintain his tone and pitch. Here was someone doing it effortlessly. He climbed another octave and left the melody completely and just started to play rhythmically. No one had ever played a song like this. How could you just play the same note over and over again and make a song out of it. But he was doing just that. He was playing the same note with different rhythmic punches and making a discernible song out of it. He climbed another octave, and the band followed playing louder and louder. He kept pushing the limits of the trumpet. Finally, he was there. He was in heaven and so was I.

Everything had disappeared. The room, the two thousand records, my father's omnipresence down in his basement. There was only one thing: that trumpet. Even when the needle entered those last grooves of that 78-rpm record and the hiss jumped a few octaves, I didn't run over to eject. It idled in that elliptical orbit for many seconds. Back and forth in that crazy way that puts you in a daze if you stared at it too long. I was already in a daze. That trumpet, that voice. That trumpet.

Something happened that day that was to change my life and my sense of who I was and where I could go besides a psychiatrist's office for my troubles, for my pain. I had found a great deal of solace in talking to Jack Weinstein. Without him I wouldn't have survived high school. I had found none in Dr. Kirschner. Now I was to go to a new place that I never imagined would hold any succor or solace for a human being. That music, jazz, was to envelop my life in a religious sense. I was going to become a prophet, an acolyte, a disciple. It all happened in that summer of 1971.

The pilgrimage naturally commenced with a total immersion of body and soul into my father's jazz collection with a monomaniacal focus on Louis Armstrong. Satchmo, Satchmouth, Satchelmouth, Gate, and Dipper. Pops became my messiah. He had arrived, and I was waiting to be redeemed. I proceeded to cull through the Louis Armstrong section, making large stacks of records in prepared batches of six since that was the maximum number that would fit on the spindle. Six records and glory. The names no longer mattered: *Heebie Jeebies, I'm Not Rough, Chinatown, My Chinatown, Dippermouth Blues, West End Blues, Potato Head Blues,* the names became fascinating incongruities. The stranger the name, the more I loved the record. I played these records over and over again. I would take that stack of six and play it again, same order. Then I would flip those six over and play the other sides. *Muskrat Ramble, Struttin' With Some Barbecue, Dear Old Southland, Hobo, You Can't Ride That Train, That's My Home* and *Stardust,* the more arcane the name, the deeper in love I fell with the piece. I was in a reverie. Each side was approximately three minutes. For three minutes I was gone. A break, the drop of another platter and I was gone again. Maybe this was what it was like to be on drugs? Maybe this was what it was like to be in love? This was better than love since he loved you without reservation or condition. And he loved you first. You didn't have to do anything. Well, you did. You had to listen.

"Listen, Dex, listen to that note, you see how he holds it and bends it at the same time." My father's words were the only interruptions in this drugged orgy. He would actually come upstairs from his den of charts, records and figures to talk to me during certain records. His interruptions took the same shape and form, every time. A lesson. A quick little block of instruction.

"Listen, when he plays the cornet, you get the feeling that he's still in this raw stage of exploration and discovery. He's still developing his technique, aptitude. When he switches to the trumpet in 1928, he's making new types of discoveries, but they're all in his head. It's not a physical relationship that he's having with the horn. It's intellectual."

I was scared of my father, again, but for new reasons. The jazz had a certain sort of hypnotic effect on him too. He talked in the present tense about people who were dead. He talked about the trumpet solo as though he was listening to it for the first time and that he could, if he desired, talk to Louis and Louis would have responded, perhaps in the following manner,

> Yeah, Stan, I'm playin' with Earl Fatha Hines, or should I say, playin' tag with Earl Fatha Hines, because this cat is tryin' to do things on the piana that ain't never been done before, but little Gate is gonna show him a few things in about three seconds, just watch this . . .

His world vanished too. He dropped his obsession with the horses for a few minutes and taught me. I was filled with thousands of questions, and he answered them all. I was entranced as I found out that he possessed this encyclopedic knowledge of jazz. Names, places, and recording dates, were all filed away in his head. Amplifying this experience was his capacity to couple the music with actual places and events that he had experienced. "The first time I heard that cut, I was walking down 125th Street. Harlem. I was looking for a job, 1933. It was the depression so it was hard as heck to get a job. I had my favorite music store because he had a speaker mounted in the doorway, right above the door. Man, whoever it was, a Negro businessman that made me feel good because he was Negro, forgot his name, but he gave people a private concert. Sometimes, Dex, I'll admit, I forgot about the job hunt and just listened to Lee, no, William Patterson, that was his name. Great young Negro businessman when there weren't that many Negro owned businesses. Boy, he played Louis and Duke all afternoon."

His trance swallowed me, and this was a fortuitous process; I was listening to the same cut except that it was forty years later. Harlem, the Harlem of riots, 1964 upheavals, and oppressive poverty evaporated. Stanley Diaz' Harlem lived. To make the journey complete I would have to read everything written about jazz and of course everything ever written about Louis Armstrong. Libraries and sections that I had never ventured into, the one with the numbers 700 and above became my haunt. I would borrow the maximum number of books permitted on my card and then ask for extensions. Then another amazing thing happened. One day, while reading and making notes, Stanley Diaz, but it was Stanley Diaz of Edgecombe Avenue, the year 1937, saw me and asked a simple question:

"Why duplicate work?"

"Oh, I'm not sure what you mean. I'm just reading."

"No, I can see that you're reading. I'm not referring to that. I meant, why go to the library when you don't have to?"

"Oh, I'm still not following you, Pop."

"Get up for a second."

I followed his request and walked over to the other side of the living room where the bookcases lined the walls. They were very modern looking. No nails. Wood that was slotted and expertly fitted from the hands of a craftsman. Making only a few major purchases of material goods, he had bought a 10-inch radial saw for building cabinets, picture frames, train tables, and bookcases. This was one of his favorite projects, the bookcases. He asked me for the book that was in my hand. Examining the title, he then ran his finger across a long row of books, and then stopped. He pulled a book off the shelf by the sides, not the binding. There was some dust on it that he blew off.

"You see, *Hot Jazz* by Hugues Panassie."

I was dumbfounded and felt silly. I started to point out that it might not be the same book because mine was soft covered, and this one was hard covered but I could see that if the subtitle, *The Guide to Swing Music*, was the same, it was indeed the same book.

"Pop, where did you get this book? It looks like the original version of mine from the library."

Beaming with pride he said, "This is the original one, the first edition, so to speak."

"Wow, a first edition. That means you got this book when it first came out."

"You're right; I had to."

"Pop, what do you mean, you had to?"

"When you love something like jazz, or art, you have to study it. You just can't understand it from listening or watching."

I looked at the book. I flipped through the first few pages and saw two things: the sale price and the name of the man who had translated it from French into English. I studied the price for a second making some quick computations of an historical nature. After a pause, I said, "Pop, if this book cost $3.50 in 1938, wasn't that a lot of money? This was during the Great Depression, and you said that you used to walk places just to save a nickel on the subway."

"You can say that again daddy-o."

I thought about a nickel for the subway, meals that cost twenty-five cents and said, "Pop, this is like a guy spending an eighth of his weekly salary on something, anything."

He looked around the room as though he were checking to see if there was a blackboard for an illustration or some object from 1971 that would brilliantly illuminate what he desired to explain to me. I figured it out as he was doing one more visual semicircle with his eyes. He was guilty.

"Dex, I know it was an irrational thing to do. That's it. I was making about thirty-five dollars a week and you're right, or pretty accurate. I was spending a tenth of my weekly wages on a book. And things are really tough. Man, the winter of 1937 in New York." He let out a whistle that dropped a few octaves. "Goddamn." He continued, "But, you see, these books were celebrating or showing that Negroes could do something. Negroes were creating something that couldn't be taken away. No question, people are stealing something from Louis and Ellington on a weekly basis. White guys are listening, stealing and copying. But the Europeans, like this guy, Panassie, they're chronicling and keeping records that will never be eradicated. You see, when you're a Negro in 1937, there's not too much to be proud of. Things are different now . . ."

With that last line I know he would bring the conversation to a close because he wasn't one for clichés. By browsing through those bookcases I was to learn that he did have almost every major book, historical or critical about jazz. It was odd. Whenever I read a review from the 1960s or 1970s and saw books mentioned with a great deal of deference by the author and I would smile as I thought, "I have that book, a hard-covered edition, with an autograph." As I progressed in a mediocre fashion through my college studies in some subjects, I still felt ebullient about studying and reading because of this love and passion. I was becoming a specialist in a discipline without being aware of the time and energy and dedication relegated to his endeavor.

Alonzo and George were the first to hear about my secret life. I didn't know how I was going to reveal it to them. It was difficult to envision how not to alienate them since it was 1971, and the music of the times was important. People who were our age or just a few years older than ourselves were producing songs that spoke to us about the civil rights movement and the Vietnam War even if they accomplished this in an oblique fashion. I needed to show that there was a connection between that music and my music. It came to me one day when I was listening to Louis Armstrong and His Hot Five. Obeying the instructions of my father who had told me to memorize all of Louis's solos from 1926 to 1929, I was as usual listening. According to my old man, if you listened to the trumpet work done during these three years, you would never have to listen to any other jazz musician. There was something magical about this approach to learning about a subject so I took his advice with a robust enthusiasm.

It was early in the morning. No one was home. I didn't have to be at Queens College until one o'clock. The stereo was on. As I let *Muskrat Ramble* penetrate me for the seventh time that morning, I heard a connection. I walked over to the record player and played it again just to make sure. There it was. Country Joe and The Fish had borrowed this tune for their own purposes. Just like Duke and Louis being in the 1930s, it was still going on. I skipped over and put *I-Feel-Like-I'm-Fixin-to-Die-Rag* on, probably this group's most famous piece of music, a song that sent shivers down LBJ's spine, "One, two, three, what are we fightin' for; don't know, I don't give a damn; next stop is Vietnam." I put Louis's 1926 version of *Muskrat Ramble* on and now I was certain. This was the connection. This made me into a teacher, an acolyte, a madman with a gospel.

We always met at George's house on Friday nights, and I told them a few times throughout that week that I had made the most important discovery of my life, and I was going to show them something that they had no knowledge of. In addition, I added that I was the only one privy to this. With a pizza ordered, a large bottle of Coke chilled, I came in with a small package of 78-rpm records wrapped in newspaper. I carried the records like Sam Spade handling the falcon. I teased them a bit by not telling them what was in the package but hinting that I needed a special piece of equipment to make the evening complete. After dining on our slices of pizza, without any introduction I just said, "I'm going to prove something to you tonight. I'm going to teach you guys something that you never knew existed before. I'm going to prove that there is a connection between jazz and the music we listen to today. George, go get that old record player in the little case because we can't use your new stereo for the presentation of the proof."

I couldn't discern how they regarded all of this. I think I just overwhelmed them with my gushing energy. I had so far demonstrated little or no passion for girls, drugs, or alcohol. Sports still possessed some small thrill for me. This was different. I was out of control. George returned from his bedroom with a little box that he set on his kitchen table. With two latches on the sides for the speakers and one for the cover, it opened like a quaint contraption from another time. Alonzo was interested in the fact that George still had this old phonograph and his explanation that his mother wished to listen to old records every now and then was satisfactory. I carefully unfolded my *New York Times*-wrapped records and put them on the spindle. As I placed them in a particular order, I spoke and gave them my theory about Country Joe's song *I-Feel-Like-I'm-Fixin'-to-Die-Rag* and Louis Armstrong. They didn't laugh, but I can't say that they were convinced or impressed. I was going to have to let the music teach them as it had taught me. I put on *Muskrat Ramble* and watched their faces. The first few bars, nothing. Then they heard it, not the words, just the music that went behind, *"one, two, three, what are we fightin' for?"* The smiles were broad and when I saw them give each other five, I knew they were on my side. I started to talk in a nonstop fashion about Louis. Right before the next platter dropped, I had already given them a preview that raised their expectations to an even higher level. They were great listeners and George, in particular, started his own running commentary. "Dex, did you just hear what he did?" I initially took this as a reproach and answered, "What's wrong?"

"Nothing is wrong. Did you hear what he just did with his trumpet, Louis, your hero?"

"George, wait till it ends and I'll play it again."

When the record was played again and George put his hand up in the air to indicate this was the time, I leaned closer to the little speakers that extended off the sides of the phonograph. He was right. Louis had so many technical tricks that it was going to take months and years of listening before I could even come up with a structured way of chronicling them. Because George and Alonzo loved music too, they were to raise my consciousness to other aspects of jazz that I was missing. All three of us banded together to study Louis on many a Friday night and it was our way of getting high. We needed nothing else.

The climax of my passion for Louis Armstrong and jazz was to manifest itself within a year of that fateful day, July 6, 1971. At the end of my freshman year at Queens College another miracle occurred. I was just completing the course, "Masterpieces of Western Music" and the closer we got to May, the more excited I became. I was doing well and loved listening to the recordings and having the professor cement the connections with history, Italy in the 19th century or the influence of jazz on classical. We had worked our way from the 12th century to the 20th and I eagerly waited to find out what new places the professor was going to take me as she lectured on the history of jazz.

About a week before class, because she had made no mention of jazz being on the next lecture, I waited to speak to her after class.

"Professor Watkins, I'm really excited about your last lecture."

"Good. What sort of fireworks do you expect?"

"Oh, well, I just want to hear what you're going to say about jazz and what recordings you might bring in."

She looked at me with a strange smile and adjusted her glasses a bit.

"Dexter, I hope this doesn't disappoint you but there is no lecture on jazz."

I was hurt and she could see it on my face.

"But Professor Watkins, Bartok, Stravinsky, I figured it out already. Jazz comes next."

The same smile became bigger and she told me something that was more shocking than the lack of the last lecture.

"Honestly, I know nothing about jazz and couldn't speak with any authority about it to the class. I wish I could. I should know more about it."

I nodded my head that I understood but was very disappointed. I started to walk away when she said, "Are you interested in jazz?"

"Yes, it's the greatest music in the world."

"Dexter, let's go to my office for a second. Do you have a moment?"

We walked past the music library where students sat with headphones. Going farther back in the building, we were soon next to the studio rooms where one person could rehearse. Professor Watkins was small, the kind of small that you wanted to not just carry her books and papers but her also. She was probably only a few years older than me and with her glasses looked eternally youthful. Once her books and records were on her desk she spoke.

"Do you think you have enough knowledge under your belt to teach a class on jazz?"

"What do you mean? I just want you to do it. You're the teacher."

"But I was being entirely honest with you when I said I can't. I don't know anything. It appears that you do."

I looked at her as though she were playing a good joke or prank.

"Professor, do you mean, you want me to get up in front of fifty people and teach them about jazz? I'm just a student myself."

Her brunette hair was in a ponytail because of the warm weather and she moved it from one shoulder to another.

"Dexter, you can do it. I'll help. I'll play the records as you direct me. You talk to the class. You have watched me do it since January."

I told her *yes* I could do it and jumped and ran out of the building after setting the date. As soon as my father came home from work, I told him of this incredible thing that had occurred, that a professor had asked me to teach a class on the history of jazz. I asked for his help. Out came the yellow legal pads and within an hour, he had put together an outline for the class. Choosing records as he made the outline, we assembled the notes and the records on his racehorse desk in the basement. He agreed with almost all of my choices.

The night before my *class* I was excited enough that it was difficult to

The Jeffries family, Front Royal Virginia, 1918. My grandmother, (sitting) far right; my father, standing at her left

The Kravitz family, 1940; my mother, behind bride to right

Mother: political, compassionate, and intelligent, 1938

Father, with a deep love and respect for jazz, 1936

At a Manhattan
nightclub, war years,
1943

Manhattan nightclub, before going overseas, 1944

Father, Kings Park,
Queens, 1931

Mother, South Jamaica,
Queens, 1944

Mother's high school
graduation picture,
Franklin K. Lane, 1936

Mother, executive
secretary, 1944

Father and my grandmother,
1944, South Jamaica, Queens

Father in early 1930s, South
Jamaica, Queens

Stanley and Marilyn Diaz, 1946

My brother, father,
myself and my sister,
South Jamaica,
Queens 1953

My sister, brother,
myself, mother,
Bennington, Vermont,
1954

Father and myself,
South Jamaica,
Queens,1957

Myself and brother,
Springfield Gardens,
1955

Myself, Bennington,
Vermont, 1954

My brother, myself,
grandmother, and
my sister,
Springfield Garden
1957

In P.S. 156, fifth grade, second row from back, fourth to left of teacher,
Laurelton, Queens, 1963

Seventh Army, West Germany, 1977

Seventh Army, West Germany, 1979

Taxi driver, classic checker cab, 1976

My mother (left) and two friends, Manhattan, 1941

My brother, father, and myself, Springfield Gardens, 1972

Father, right of stool, Front Royal, Virginia, 1918

Parents' closest friends, Rex Stewart of Duke Ellington Band
with wife, Ruth, 1947

go to sleep. I had practiced my talk on the advice of my father and had even timed it. Everything could be played within ninety minutes. Professor Watkins had gone along with my request not to inform the class of the *guest lecturer*. That was a plus since I didn't need the additional pressure of knowing that people were doubting my ability for not just minutes, but a week.

I sat with the class in my usual seat and Professor Watkins smiled as she said, "Today, we have a treat because someone from the class is going to teach us about a subject that I know little about but would like to know more of. Dexter is going to teach the class about the history of jazz. So, Dexter, come on up." I walked to the front of the room. To the left of the desk was the commercial record player. Professor Watkins stood by it as planned. After giving her the stack of 78s and 33s, I got behind the desk and took a deep breath as I saw what fifty people looked like. I put my legal pad in front of me, but not directly in front. I started to talk. A few kids laughed and the professor put her finger to her lips. I half read and half talked my way through the notes. I turned to Professor Watkins and nodded that it was time to put on the first record. It was going to be *Muskrat Ramble*. It had worked on Alonzo and George and I hoped it would work again. At first nothing. Then about a minute into it, the faces started to change to smiles. People started to look at each other and whisper, Country Joe and The Fish. After the record stopped playing, they asked me if I could prove which was recorded first. I asked Professor Watkins to read the recording date on the record. In her authoritative voice she said, July 16, 1926. There was a hush in the class. "1926, that means that Country Joe and The Fish ripped Louis Armstrong off." I said it wasn't really ripping off and that musicians always borrowed from each other.

From that point on, I had a most wonderful experience as I talked, taught and proved. It was one of the special days in my life. I didn't know that I was going to be a teacher some day, but I got a charge from being up there in front of all those people, changing their minds about something important, important to me. At the end of the class, Professor Watkins and everyone else gave me a standing round of applause. I was sweating, smiling, and still pretty nervous. A few students came up to me after class and shook my hand.

"Well, how do you like being truly an assistant professor?"

"Professor Watkins, that was so great. So great to be up there and have the kids listen and learn."

"Dexter, you're lucky. First, that was a splendid lesson, and I learned a great deal. Number two, you are a natural teacher. The class was in the palm of your hand after the first few minutes of the class. Remember that, if you're ever thinking about a career." I looked at her half believing her but definitely not believing in what had just occurred and myself. I couldn't deny it though. I had done something great and victorious, and I was happy.

The X Factor

WE MUST HAVE freaked out Brother Willy X on several occasions. Even though he came on a weekly basis with his *Muhammad Speaks* to our front door, he never knew who was going to answer; he never could fathom what was going on. My black father, my white mother, and then me. We had a large solid front door painted green and white with three windowpanes at the top. I always knew when it was Willy X ringing the bell because I could see his hat, a sharp fedora which he wore during the winter months. In the summer he wore another hat made of straw. Winter or summer, he was tight: bow tie, suit, and highly polished shoes. Ninety percent of the time a representative of the Black Muslims had the upper hand because of their dress, appearance, and oratory. They hurled their wares into your house with a downpour of words and energy that made a Seventh Day Adventist seem like a Girl Scout making her shortbread cookie pitch. "How are you doing, sir? Good Morning, ma'am. Young man, have you heard of the glorious message this week contained in *Muhammad Speaks?*"

Yet, coming to 137-78 Westgate Street in Springfield Gardens, Queens, New York, was a stumbling block for them. Naturally Willy X was not the only door-to-door spokesman for Elijah Muhammad. There was Brother Adrian X, Brother Phillip X, and a host of other Xs. Notwithstanding Malcolm X's prefabricated and rehearsed speechifying to his disciples, there was nothing in his rhetoric that prepared one for his acolytes. The words came out with diffidence. The speech had pauses in it. The word *yes* was the most positive thing they could say as they eyed us week-to-week, month-to-month. But there it was. A white woman would come one time. A black man would come another time. And then there was me.

It was tough, and once I knew their politics and religious foundation from reading about their origins, I could understand why they were a bit flustered. They were selling a mixed message of Black Nationalism, heritage, pride and hate, and ignorance. They were also insane. Whenever I perused a copy and saw the small cartoons of Dr. Yacub, their scapegoat for the evil white race that had plagued black people for six thousand years, I knew that these people were irrational. Whenever I read their official plank on the last page of the paper, which was boringly the same fifty-two weeks a year, "What the Black Muslims Want," I knew these people could not be reached with logic. They wanted the federal government to give them seven states in the southwestern part of America. I looked at the map. Who the hell wants to live out in Arizona or New Mexico? In addition, who wants to live in a segregated society, voluntarily, no less. The message of the Black Muslims was so counter-progressive and reactionary that one really couldn't fathom it. Why would a black person voluntarily ask to remove himself from a heterogeneous society when so much time and energy has been spent on trying to integrate himself into that society? Not just time, blood, tears, split heads, and busted wrists. This was not an easy task. Going to demonstrations, getting knocked around, spit on, that wasn't easy. Where was the courage in retreating to Flagstaff or Albuquerque? Martin Luther King Jr., Joe Louis, Jackie Robinson, Adam Clayton Powell Jr. and Sr., what happened to their counterparts? Did black people run out of courage and stamina so quickly?

Retreat and withdrawal and acquiescence and fantasy were the main proponents of the Black Muslim movement, and most middle-class blacks had nothing to do with them or their program. I wouldn't be surprised if we were the only family that not only had a discussion with them but also purchased some of their products. By the mid-1960s Springfield Gardens was a solid black middle-class neighborhood. My neighbors regularly attended the Methodist church on Springfield Boulevard, the AME on Merrick Road, and Presbyterian church on Farmers Boulevard; the Black Muslims were the most alienated group of individuals that they could imagine. They had houses, Magnavox televisions, and Maytag washers. America was good and their children's admission into the local Jack and Jill association was living proof of that. The

Plymouth in the driveway that received that new coat of wax with a chamois cloth purchased at Times Square Stores was more proof of that. Finally, walking to their door, past their flowers and well-trimmed grass, were the ultimate symbols that no one in the house was packing up and moving to Tucson any time soon. Yet, they came, the brothers with their neatly folded newspapers and talked of liberation and the black man being free and how the white man was the devil, the true devil. They came for many visits.

"Your mother is very light." I saw that baffled look on Brother Willy X's face.

"What's in the paper this week?"

"Oh, there is a fine article by one of our best writers about the importance of African history."

"Good. I'll go get the money."

"Excuse me, young man, before you get the money, your mother . . . she *is* your mother, right?"

"Sure, that's my mother."

"OK, I just wanted to make sure."

"I know; you're worried that you're talking to a white person when you're only supposed to talk to Negroes."

"*Negro* is an artificial term for us. We prefer the word *black*."

"Yeah, I've read that in the paper. Well, she's a very light-skinned *black* person."

"Good! She is very intelligent as is your father."

"I'll go get the money; it's fifty cents, right?"

"Unless you like to order some of our products. I think your father prefers our fish."

Well, I couldn't say he preferred the fish for its taste or quality. My mother liked the fish also. The Black Muslims were entrepreneurs for sure. They sold their bean pies and loaves of bread, and plenty of codfish. The items were packed with their own label and markings that informed you beyond a shadow of a doubt that this was produced *by* a black person *for* a black person. In addition, the money from the purchase of the product would be channeled right back into the black community. It was simple as that and I respected that.

I came back with the change and made him smile when I said my father would like some of his fish. He left his copies of *Muhammad Speaks* and his clipboard next to the flowerpot and turned to walk to his car.

When the trunk opened, I was always prepared for the white smoke that would come out of the coolers holding the dry ice and the frozen fish. He took out two packages of codfish and closed the trunk. Putting the codfish in a brown paper bag as he walked up the steps he was beaming.

"This fish is good for you. A fine substitute for pork."

"You have to admit, every now and then a pork chop tastes pretty good."

"There is nothing filthier than a pig and that's where pork comes from."

"Smothered with some onions on top, it still tastes pretty good."

He nodded as I took the fish and handed him four dollars. Anytime we bought products, there was no charge for the paper and sometimes a few extra copies were given free of charge so I could "give them to my friends." I quickly learned that we weren't really having a dialogue. He had been schooled in answering certain questions with very prepared answers. Anytime you took him out of his Black Muslim Block of Instruction for dealing with the public, he turned to the sale of an item or perhaps signing up for a meeting on the clipboard that he always carried with him.

I was afraid of him and for him. To be that earnest, that confident, that misguided, and to hate, was scary. On a weekly basis he was telling me that my mother was the devil; all white people were the devil. There was no good white people. Well, my mother was not a devil. She had no relationship to Dr. Yacub or any of his 59,999 followers. She had probably been on more picket lines than Brother Willy X could have imagined. From 1936 to the present she never said die. She never retreated. She was not going to Santa Fe to live in isolation from the world. The world was a bad place. The challenge was to change it. You don't change things by creating lies and fantasies about things that have never existed. Whenever I saw the cartoon drawing of Dr. Yacub whispering into the ear of some "fool Negro" I knew I was dealing with people who were caricatures themselves. They had stopped thinking when they took the oath of fidelity to the demands on the last page of the paper.

Were they that angry? In my teenager consciousness, you had the right to be angry, but this was in direct correlation to what you had endured during your life. If there were circumstances of your existence that had caused undue hardship and suffering, being angry was a righteous thing. You should be mad at racism and other social and political injustices. When I looked into Brother Willy X's eyes, I'm not sure if I saw that defensible anger and rage. Maybe I didn't like it that he was calm now and whatever unwarranted slights he had confronted were behind him, and the membership in this organization had numbed him a bit. There was an edge to him, but I was never sure as to how far he would go in following the messages of the Honorable Elijah Muhammad.

Of course, the most frightening was their leader, Malcolm X. He was intelligent, charismatic, and funny. He had a manner of speaking that let the average black person feel he was their kin. Joking in that rhetorical fashion that makes fun of the speaker as well as his listeners, he had mastered the vernacular of the street. He knew the slang, jive talk, ranking out, and even possessed a bit of the Apollo stage performer in him. If anyone was the devil, it was him. I can still hear that husky and throaty laugh when he knew with certainty that he had his debating opponent on the ropes. What a laugh! Cunning, foxlike, and powerful. He turned things around. Talk about appropriating someone else's rhetoric. I specifically recall hearing him play with the words *sit in* as in *sit in demonstration,* which was one of the most effective tools that blacks had during the civil rights struggle. He laughed and said, "Sit in? There's something passive about that strategy. I don't even like the word *sit.* That's the problem with Negroes today. They want to sit around and wait for the white man to tell them that they're OK and let me tell you, Black Muslims are not going to sit. Black Muslims, and let me make this perfectly clear, I'm speaking not for myself, but for the Honorable Elijah Muhammad, let me say . . ."

Melville and Twain would have loved Malcolm. That famous line, "First, I would like to say that I'm speaking not for myself, but as follower and helper and representative of the Honorable Elijah Muhammad . . ." was one of the greatest con man lines in all of American history. Imagine, someone talks to you with all the sincerity in the world. The words truly emanate from their heart, their soul. You see the passion in the eyes. You hear it in his voice. You're swept up. You too start to have tears. You too start to have a tight feeling in your throat as it constricts with emotion. Then, the fervent speaker who has aroused all of this feeling, glibly, and strategically says, "Well, these aren't my thoughts. I'm really the mouthpiece for someone else? There he was. Shirt, tight tie, spectacles, and after a few words with him you reach for your intellectual wallet in your back pocket to make sure it's still there. Malcolm was slick. Malcolm was intelligent. He was a native born American genius who knew that the ultimate puzzle for the black American to solve was to apprehend that he was American. The ultimate challenge—to believe it. Uncanny, but near the end of his life, after experimenting with different forms of political expression, he realized the limitations of any sort of fundamentalism. Fundamentalism restricts and represses. Dogma stifles intellectual thought and Malcolm could not be stifled. The secret of America must have come to him like a fire bell in the night. Like that scene in *Catch-22* when Yossarian has his epiphany courtesy of Colonel Cathcart and Colonel Korn:

> *"Like you?"*
> *"Like us."*
> *"Like you?"*
> *". . . You just want me to like you? Is that all?"*

Yeah, Malcolm started to figure that out. It wasn't as crude as that, and there was some refinement to his ascertaining this same Zen-like moment. A crude version of this was his infamous statement that determined his premature expulsion out of the Black Muslim movement in reference to the assassination of President Kennedy. The *chickens coming home to roost* statement, that was vulgar. Insightful and penetrating but vulgar and unredemptive. However, once he returns from his mind-expanding journeys abroad, he comprehends the best way to beat America is to be American. His brilliant tactic of making sure that he could legally carry firearms, which is protected by the Second Amendment of the U.S. Constitution, would have made him a future candidate for the president of the NRA. Use America to fight America. The tools and resources are right there under your feet. Black people don't know the treasures they're treading on.

Malcolm, if he had lived, was going to embrace the country that flailed him and then flail back and the most conservative thinking American was going to be forced into a vulnerable position by the unassailability of his position. He had already come halfway with the wearing of the business suit. Black Muslims were what America prays we all will become: businessmen "like us." That's all. They may have started small with their bean pies and packages of codfish, but damn, you have to admit, they were on the right track. Be a businessman and you will never want. How many times did I hear Malcolm say, "Once we have our own business and we can buy our own cup of coffee, we will know a certain dignity and pride that has been robbed from us." He was right. Every immigrant group that has arrived since 1619 gets to do that. The initiation process starts with the store, everything from dry cleaning to the twenty-four-hour grocery. That's a good place to start. You hardly speak any English, but your children see people walking into the store and giving you money and treating you with mercantile protocol. What greater example for an immigrant child. From that point on he knows what Malcolm understood; he could see that the black community was devoid of that feeling, a sense that *I belong here because I am like you.*

I wonder if anyone will ever know what he was saying. Malcolm. I slowly became acquainted with him because he wrote most of the editorials and articles for the newspaper. It only took buying two or three copies for one to figure out that the Honorable Elijah Muhammad never wrote one article. His docile face was on the last page always with the same inflammatory and rhetorical message. In my neighborhood Malcolm X was considered a fanatic and a propagandist at best. Anytime I tried to distribute my few extra free copies of the paper, my black neighbors shook their heads vigorously and went into their own tirade. Mrs. Walton informed me that the Muslim didn't believe in God. I told her that she was incorrect. She looked at me and with fierceness said, "*our* God." The Black Muslims were considered a cult that had little or no influence on black middle-class life. He was like a gnat that kept on making that high-pitched whine in the middle of a hot summer night's sleep that tells you that the hole in the screen that you failed to repair, is going to cause you a night of unmitigated hell. That's what he was. It wasn't popular to like him and most people were eased when he was assassinated. With his murder in Harlem, everyone breathed a little easier, including the Black Muslims. Who knows how long they were rejoicing that cold winter night?

"Why do we keep on buying fish from that guy? Why do we buy anything from him?"

My mother was thoughtful and said there were "social, economic, and political considerations" to be understood. I listened carefully since

I wanted to know how she was dealing with the contradiction of buying codfish from a man who considered her to be the devil and a member of a species that should be eliminated.

"We should attempt to support all progressive movements around the world. Any nation or institution that is embracing socialism should receive out support and help. Every time we purchase that codfish, we are making socialism stronger." I didn't have a response because I saw absolutely no connection between the Nation of Islam and socialism. If anything, any time I saw them sporting their full dress regalia, which consisted of black leather coats and ties, I was reminded more of a bunch of fascist storm troopers at some party rally outside Nuremberg. All they needed were the boots and the picture would have been complete. They exuded that phalanx of macho militarism that bordered on fanaticism.

My mom could see that I was perplexed and told me to get a package of codfish out of the freezer. I walked into the kitchen over the checkerboard red-and-black tiles that my father thought was an avant-garde design and reached for some codfish. I brought the package that was like a frozen brick to her. I gave it to her. I didn't know what was going to happen during this lesson but I could discern it was going to be a subtle one. My mother was never one for dramatic corrections or public triumphs. She barely looked up from whatever she was doing at the time, switched to her reading glasses and said, "Here, read where this package of fish comes from. I mean, where it was caught and processed."

I took the package and turned it so I could read the print:

PACKED AND PROCESSED IN POLAND.

That was it. Staring me in the face was the answer that explained why we endured Brother Willy X and his fish selling. Somehow the Muslims had a contract with Poland and my parents saw a connection that I never would have made. I walked back to the kitchen and placed the codfish back in the freezer. I didn't like this explanation but saw the logic in it. My parents were committed since 1935 to endorsing and reinforcing progressive movements, domestic and international. To them this made perfect sense since the NATO alliance was one hundred percent committed to destroying the Warsaw Pact nations. The Soviet Union and all of its allies needed every bit of affirmation they could receive. And if it meant buying frozen codfish from Brother Willy X who is just as consigned to you being exterminated so he can go and live in seven Southwestern states of America, so be it.

Brother Richard X came into Higby's Dry Cleaning store once a week. Just like Brother Willy X, he was scrupulous in his appearance and dedicated to proselytizing the ideas of the Nation of Islam. Higby had told me to buy the paper from him if he wasn't there. When he was there, he could speak to Brother Richard X in a rather sincere tone about the importance of building a new nation. This was flattering to Brother Richard X and he was able to sell a few bean pies in addition to his newspapers. When I asked Higby what was his position on the Black Muslims, he explained that he bought the paper because it was good for business and Brother Richard X was free publicity for him and the store. He asked me what I thought of them.

"I think they're trying to do something positive."

"They've been around since the late forties. At first I thought they were crazy but I like the way they're trying to get black people into business. Black people need that sort of connection."

"Like I said, they're trying to do something positive so that's good."

Brother Richard X was a regular visitor to the shop until one week, when instead of coming on Thursday, he made an appearance on Saturday. We were closing the store. Higby and the pressers had been drinking since five and it was almost seven. In his buttoned up raincoat and hat, he dashed in at the last second. I was surprised since he kept a fastidious routine. I could tell from his smile that nothing was wrong; he was happy to catch us before the gates came sliding down. Since Higby was there, sitting on a fifty-five-gallon drum of dry cleaning chemicals, I motioned for him to come over and make whatever transactions he wished to conduct with this Brother Richard X. Higby stayed on the drum. I walked over and told him that "the brother from the Nation was there." He smiled and said, "Tell that boy I want to talk to him in my office." This was a breach of etiquette since only the elite few were allowed to pass from the clothing side of the store to the side where the plant was. Pressers, some of the livery drivers, that was it. Never a customer and not someone like Brother Richard X. I wondered what was up. Higby had been drinking, no more and no less than usual. He was his normally rambunctious self; it was Saturday and I was feeling a bit defiant and rowdy myself. I was only minutes away from receiving my thirty dollars and it was Saturday night.

"Did you hear what I said? Tell that boy to come back here. I want to talk to him."

"OK Higby, I just thought that maybe . . ."

"Come on Dukeschank, go get Brother Richard X. We all want to talk to him."

I walked back to the counter and let Richard X know that his presence was requested and that he was entering the inner sanctum of Higby's world. He beamed and grabbed a whole batch of papers off the counter. He picked up his shopping bags that contained the bean pies and walked over. I followed behind anxious and interested. He looked for a place to set his things down and Higby got up off the drum, cleared off the clothing table and told him to rest his things.

"You're lookin' pretty sharp tonight, ain't he, Paul?"

Paul, one of our replacement pressers agreed and said that all Muslims looked sharp. Brother Richard X took the compliment and mentioned that Muslim brothers had to set an example for the community. Higby went on to state that the Muslims had a real job ahead of them if they were ever going to really try and improve the black community. The prefabricated answers came out of Brother Richard X's mouth concerning the devilish white man and how the Honorable Elijah Muhammad was going to lead the black man out of the wilderness.

I kept quiet since I had heard this on many occasions from the other brother and knew the pitch through and through. I looked at the clock and saw that it was seven and told Higby that it was time to "shut the place down." "Hold on Dukeschank, hold on, we have to let Mr. X out of here first." I could see that the gates weren't going to be closed exactly at seven and the next thing I knew, a late customer took advantage of the gates remaining open for a few extra seconds and was at the counter. I attended to the breathless customer who was more than happy that she had caught us at the last second. Her party night would not be ruined because she was going to be able to wear her favorite dress. I rang up the bill, said good evening, and walked back to the other side of the store. Higby had gotten back on his drum, his throne, and was holding court about race relations and Martin Luther King, Malcolm X. I had missed some of the conversation, but everyone was

intrigued. Brother Richard X knew that it was unpopular to say anything negative about Martin Luther King, and he paid him some perfunctory respectful remarks. I was relieved because I knew that this
could have easily started some sort of raucous and violent debate about
who had the better answer, the best solution, the only solution for the
black man's problem.

Brother Richard X asked us if we wanted to buy any more bean pies,
any more editions of *Muhammad Speaks* and said that he was running
late. He apologized for missing us on Thursday but would be there the
following Thursday as always. He picked up his two shopping bags and
looked awkward for a moment as men do when they have a shopping
bag in each hand. Higby said, "I just wanted to tell you something before you leave." Reaching for a bottle of Johnny Walker Red he poured
some in a glass. Then he opened the container of milk, mixed the milk
with the whiskey ("it makes it go down a lot smoother") and took a
very satisfying sip. He let out an *awwrrrr* and slapped his belly which
protruded a bit over his belt. "I just wanted to tell you something that
I've learned about life. I've been around a bit, the South, Korean War,
got my own business, live a pretty good life. Are you listening to me?"

The shopping bags were placed back on the floor and Brother
Richard X straightened up. "Sure Mr. Higby, I respect you. There aren't
that many black businessmen. They are few and far between. I think this
is the only black-owned dry cleaning store that I've seen. That's in New
York. There are more stores like yours in Chicago and Detroit."

Higby took another sip and nodded his head acknowledging the answer.

"You've been to Detroit?"

"Yes, that's the center of the Nation of Islam."

"And you've been to Chicago?"

"Yes, I started there, a type of training. All Black Muslims must be
trained first. All Black Muslims attend classes and we're tested."

"Well, it sounds like you've done a lot of traveling and that you will
probably do a lot more before you finish things." At this point, Higby
was lost in thought and no one could see the thread of what he was
leading up to. Collecting himself with the aid of another Johnny Walker
and milk, he said, "You're going to travel to many great places, many
great cities: New York, maybe even London, Paris, and Moscow. I don't

know where you're going, but I'm going to tell you one thing, that no matter where you go, no matter how far you travel in this world, no matter where you go in these fifty glorious United States, always remember one thing, that you ain't nothing but a no good stinking black ass nigger."

Volcanic laughter erupted all throughout the shop. Lucky, Paul, a few livery drivers, they all united in one calamitous uproar. For a few seconds howls and shrieks of derisive laughter filled the air. I laughed for a second because the others laughed. Lucky almost had a fit as he jumped and turned and laughed. Higby stamped his feet and even though he bent his head to the floor he kept this hand outstretched for all the sympathetic "slapping of fives that were coming his way." Brother Richard X stared. There was nothing he could say. He picked up the shopping bags and took quick long steps to get out of this pandemonium that had been built at his expense. The laughter continued and they were already at the stage of assisting and measuring the joke and the injury it had registered.

"Did you see that nigger's face when I said that?"

"Spook thought you was gonna compliment him."

"Good, good for that nigger, nigger thinks he different from us. I say, good for every X nigger to find out that. Higby, you taught him lesson."

Higby eyed me since I had stopped laughing first. I felt guilty for laughing but it was hard not to when everyone else was so incredibly boisterous.

"It was funny but I don't think you should have insulted him like that. He's trying to do something."

"Dukeschank, you don't know what the hell you're talking about."

I defended myself quickly stating that I had encountered Black Muslims before, including Brother Willy X who came to my house with his fish.

"Higby, these people might be too religious but they're trying to do something for the black community. Don't you think it's good, this stuff about black-owned businesses?" I felt good when I saw Paul nod his head a bit and grunt, "He's right about that." Higby shook his head as he started to build another drink, a really big one. He was back on his throne and he balanced himself by holding on to both sides of the drum.

"Dukeschank, do you know anything about Muslims?"

"Well, not too much. But I know it's a religion."

"Hell, these people aren't Muslims."

Lucky, who rarely participated in any of our conversations, looked and shook his head. In his broken language he said, "Dukeschank right. Dey is a religion."

With his arms folded Higby said that we were both ignorant. I was growing angrier.

"Higby, look, I don't agree with this guy. But you shouldn't insult someone's religion."

"That's what I'm tryin' to tell you two fools. Paul, you know what I'm taking about?" Whether Paul knew it or not, he drunkenly nodded his head in the affirmative.

"Dukeschank, did you ever read the *Koran?*"

There was quiet and I knew I was on the spot. I waited for Lucky to say something about me being in high school and in something called honors classes and how I should know it. Fortunately, the whiskey had made his tongue too thick to say anything.

"No, I'm not too religious. Shoot, I ain't even read the *Bible.*"

"Well, listen to ol' Higby one more time. The *Koran* is the Muslim *Bible.* Lucky, what are the first words of the *Bible?*" Lucky was drunk but stumbled through, "In de beginning, there was . . ."

"Dukeschank, what's the rest?"

"In the beginning, there was light, and . . . look Higby, I really don't know. I'm not against the *Bible* or nothing, but I really never read it, but I'll take your word for it, or Lucky's word, that that's the way it goes."

"Good, now I'm gonna tell all you guys something. The first lines of the *Koran* go somethin' like this: In the beginning there was one god named Allah and he had one prophet named Muhammad. There ain't nothing in that book about some little spook with sunglasses from Detroit, Michigan, being the other prophet. There's one prophet. That's it. Get my meaning? That nigger got everybody fooled into thinking he's a prophet, and there is only one goddamn prophet in the first place. Paul, you ever think of that?"

Somehow Paul, despite the consumption of his favorite drink, rum and Coke, managed a pretty dignified answer. He said that Ol' Higby had a point and that if a book said that there was only one prophet, then there was only one prophet. We were all quiet.

"Dukeschank, you got anything else to say?"

"No, Higby, I believe you. Funny, I never thought about this prophet thing. It's like a regular guy on Merrick Road saying he's Jesus or something."

"Exactly, there's only one Jesus. How would you feel if a guy started saying he's Jesus?"

Lucky, in his own swirling stupor looked up and said, "Higby, Mr. Higby, Sir. Take it easy. I'm convinced. I guess dis Honorable Muhammad person is trickin' a few people."

"A whole lot of people, Lucky, a whole lot of people, Dukeschank. Little spook with shades got all these people conned into thinkin' he's from the Middle East. Shit, maybe East St. Louis. And niggers believe him. That's what gets me. Even this Malcolm X fella who seems pretty smart. Niggers believe in this crap because they have to. They have to believe that they're not what they are. I know; you want your thirty dollars. That's what you're thinking about."

I started to smile and confessed that it was late, and I wanted to get going and it would be nice to get paid. Higby hopped off his throne with a little jump, balanced himself by shaking off the liquor, and walked a straight line over to the cash register. Paul, Lucky, and the livery drivers were going to stay for rounds two and three, four, five, and six. Higby asked me how I wanted it and I joked, big bills would be fine. He must have felt guilty because he asked if I understood everything that had gone on that evening and that he really hadn't insulted the man's religion. I comforted him with "Ol' Higby is always right." I left the store a little more confused than I had been that morning or that afternoon or that evening.

Dexter and Eleni

THURSDAY HAS ALWAYS been my favorite day of the week since college days. It was on Thursday afternoons and early evenings that I became jubilant as I thought, *tomorrow I can see her.* Tomorrow I will see her, and everything will be all right. She loves me and I love her and to be loved and cared for by someone so special, so beautiful and intelligent, that is . . . At four, sometime in the late afternoon, she is going to take me to a new place again, and I will feel wonderfully free. She loves me more than any woman I've ever met so far and even though I waited freshman and sophomore years to meet that special someone, it was worth the wait. I love her, too. I'll do anything for her as she'll do anything for me. That's love. Most important, she isn't like the other women I've known. I don't have to lie about who I am. I might tell her other lies, but the most important lie of all will not be repeated. She accepts that I am black and white and blue all over.

In addition, the joy of Thursdays in my junior year was vitalized by the fact that my part-time job as a tutor at the Writing Skills Workshop brought so much joy into my life. New friends, Phil, Dominick, Frank, Doris and Woody, more people that I never would have met under any other circumstances. The Writing Skills Workshop was a bold experiment; we were going where colleges had never gone before as we met the needs of the new student, the nontraditional student who was deemed unorthodox exclusively by his poor and weak academic training. The new America was uncertain as to what to do with them. This first evidence of a deteriorating educational system started to make itself apparent as more and more young people graduated from high school who lacked *basic skills*. This euphemism meant that these people could not read or write or do basic math. But the U.S. was dealing with this the same way they had dealt with the Vietnam War; you just lie and create a rhetoric that covers the scab and hope no one at headquarters notices the hemorrhaging before you quit, resign, or get promoted for doing a good job.

Besides these ill-prepared students coming out of American high schools, there was another revolution occurring that would make itself noticeable in a room numbered 232 at Queens College. A new generation was coming along, many of whom were women, who found themselves before, during, and after Vietnam, after going to California, after going no place but into their heads, waking up at age thirty in some arbitrary job and saying:

> *I'm smarter than the boss. I know it. All he has is that college degree that's on the wall that says, "Awarded this day in 1962." True, it's not 1962; it's 1970, and I'm not 18, but couldn't I start that same process?*

Across the United Sates colleges were going to answer this young woman's question with a resounding and affirming *yes*. The college of the 1950s was going to be retooled and refitted. English departments, from New York to California, from Texas to Michigan, were reevaluating their goals and missions. Confronted with a new challenge that had never been tackled before, English teachers reassessed this new type of freshman who was intelligent, willing and able, but due to a break in their schooling, could not be thrown into a classroom unless that little bit of rust on their sentences and paragraphs was sanded away. Peer tutoring was envisioned as one of the answers, and Queens College was in the forefront of this movement to view students and the process of writing in a new light. I was part of a national movement that transfigured the way English was going to be taught in American colleges. It was big. Journals, free writing, experimenting with visual aids and music, collaborative reviews and critiques, all of this was experimented with at Queens, and I was there right on the cutting edge. I spent many hours at the tutoring center, learning my trade and craft. Supervisors, who were adjunct lecturers in the English department, cultivated an atmosphere by which the study of literature and poetry was encouraged and oversaw the tutoring process. They watched us work, offered help and guidance. They answered questions on everything from subordinate conjunctions to the importance of a lesser-known but important British writer named Wilkie Collins. Thursday afternoons were therefore very special to me. I was happy since the afternoon and the end of the day held more and more opportunity. So between those two new worlds, one revolving around the tutoring, which affirmed my skills and resources, and the other, the love of a woman, I was set. I was secure.

I met Hannah Sallinger when I was in love with another woman, and that seems like a familiar pattern in my life. When one relationship doesn't work out with your current spouse or partner, you confide your troubles to another woman, and she in turn becomes your new love. So that was the first cycle of turning to another woman who would shepherd me through the end of a relationship.

I loved Eleni Handrakos even though she was older than I. When she told me that she was Greek, I thought that was rather exotic. Greece, the islands of the Aegean, gods and demi-gods, Helen, Aphrodite, Achilles, Odysseus. Here was romance and adventure and an extension of that world of glory and kleos three thousand years later. However, that three thousand years makes a difference, like it or not, and this Eleni of Kew Gardens, Queens, was neither a muse nor elegant. She couldn't be. Her parents had come from Greece in the 1930s, and they were just ignorant immigrants who were about as closely connected to Homer as an American is to Cotton Mather.

We wanted to sleep together, oh so badly. Our necking in the supply room of the registrar's office turned physically violent as we knocked over boxes of office supplies, old manila folders of adolescents from the era when Queens College had been a reform school. We rolled along file cabinets, got dusty, brushed ourselves off, and then reentered the main office, timing our returns so no secretary would give us a second glance. This went on for months, commencing in a spring semester and torturing us until the final weeks of May when school drew to a close. When we finally did have sex during the summer, it was messy and unpleasant. With all that boundless energy and lust we were only able to turn our backs on each other and hope that the wall or clock radio would provide some solace. Except for the sex or our rudimentary attempts to *do it,* everything was fine. We loved each other a lot.

Our relationship was or seemed well rounded. We met after our classes, dined in the school cafeteria. On Saturdays or Sundays we went to Flushing Meadow Park, site of the World's Fair. We walked by the relics of the 1964 celebration; I noticed the rust and expressed shock that things as important as this were not maintained. She noticed that they were ugly, whether it was 1964 or 1974. She was right. We sat on green New York City park benches and reached into brown paper bags to eat tuna fish sandwiches. If there were any crumbs, the ducks and swans that patronized the lake in Flushing Meadow benefited. They would follow us as we walked, and it was cute, to have a flock of fans encouraging and spiriting us along. Eleni visited my home and met my parents. She came over and felt welcome. I was happy to be paired with someone, and knew that bringing her home several times lent that stamp of legitimacy, that badge of honor that had eluded me for so many years. Eleni liked my parents, and they liked her.

Because I was always asleep, *unconscious* would probably be a more appropriate word, I hadn't noticed that I never visited her house until we had been together for about six months. I brought it up in the most casual manner, "Hey, I want to see your house; I've never been in a garden apartment before." Smiling, Eleni explained that there was nothing special about a garden apartment and that she could describe it to me. My next question had to do with occupations and vocations. "What does your father do for a living?" I had asked, wanting to know how this man supported his family, spent his eight hours a day, five days a week, his life.

I was heartened when I heard the answer. He was a furrier. Immediately, my mind, the same mind that saw the relics of the 1964 World's Fair in pragmatic terms of maintenance and upkeep, knew that the furriers was one of the most progressive unions to come out of the labor struggles of the 1930s. Eric Foner's large encyclopedic study of how this union came to be occupied a prominent spot on my parents' shelves. Some people have the *Bible* and the condensed *Readers' Digest* version of things. My bookshelves were heavily laden with everything that International Publishers had ever assembled or thought about distributing. Herbert Aptheker's *The Negro in the Abolitionist Movement, The Negro in the American Revolution*. Pamphlets and magazines. When I heard furrier, I instantly made the connection, Furrier's Union, Foner, left wing, progressive, good.

That's the way my mind worked. I always took things literally, one to one correspondence, black and white, up and down, good and bad, right and wrong, left and right. This was to haunt me later, and the haunting always had to do with the idealized forms I placed over people because of some small piece of historical or biographical piece of information that I had heartily internalized. Ridiculous, but I suppose it was a way of ordering the world.

Perhaps I asked two or three more times, mentioned and suggested that I should get to know her parents because it's always good to know one's parents. I couldn't make a dent into her monosyllabic answers and retorts and gave up on my indirect approach. We went on like this with me in the dark and innocently thinking, he's a bad furrier, that's all, no more no less. Not every left-wing furrier has the time to meet his daughter's boyfriends.

We were in my car, very close to her home. I was driving her home after an afternoon at Jones Beach; it was summer, and we had ventured out to one of my favorite places, Jones Beach, West End Field #2. She had explained why she believed in God and how it was important to believe in something. I had been agreeable and had not fought or offered speeches invoking Marx or Lenin. Reflecting on her passion for the Eastern Orthodox Church, I smiled and said to myself, "These people really believe in this stuff. It's in them, deep." The drive back to Queens is always a long one on a Sunday afternoon in August. The sun beats down on the black vinyl top of a 1968 Cougar; your damp towel is spread on the black bucket seats to give you a little relief from the heat. The windows are rolled down, manual air-conditioning, and as you brush your arm on some part of the interior you realize that goddamn piece of the car is hot, especially when you're already sunburned. You smolder and wait.

"Eleni, aren't your parents home? It's Sunday, right?" These words came out in a dogged fashion. There was something about them that was going to build in pitch and volume. There was something about my words that was going to use the heat and exhaust and sun to their advantage. There would be some answers.

Eleni was caught looking out the window as the Meadowbrook Parkway merges with the Southern State, and the traffic snarl made everything seem like we would never get home. "Yes, they're both home; it's Sunday. They never do anything. They're home," she replied. This was the answer I wanted and proceeded not to hold a conversation as much as to conduct an interrogation. "Eleni, this is the best time for me to meet them. It's Sunday. They're there, and I'll just run upstairs for a second and meet them. No muss, no fuss." This sounded like an order. It wasn't a question, and I could tell by her face that this was unpleasant for her and whatever part of it I deemed cute, she found to be ugly and resented it.

"Dexter, you can't come up." This was brutally spit out; it sounded like an announcement of a truth or a fact. Whatever I was requesting no longer had any innocence. I could now see that I was asking for something that could not be imagined and anytime you do that, you are bound to end up in a place that you never envisioned either. There was a sound of finality in her "You can't come up!" I wasn't coming up to meet her parents because that scenario did not exist. Why?

"How come I can't come up? I've known you for almost six months and have never met your parents. This is a normal thing that happens. It just happens, don't ask me why. It just happens. How come I can't meet your parents?" With a face turned toward the scrubby grass and the small pines that line the Southern State Parkway, I saw her body bunch up. She crossed her arms on the window even though that spot was very hot. I knew. She placed her chin on those arms and gave another sigh, deeper, longer. She turned toward the front of the car. Now her arms were on the dashboard and she placed her face on them. The dashboard was hot but she took it. Rolling her head from side to side, I could see that she was crying. Some people make noise. Some just heave and sigh. She sobbed. With her head straight down so I couldn't see her face or eyes, staring at the floor mat, she said, "Dexter, you can't come over because you're black. My parents said I can bring anyone home, anyone. He can be Jewish, Irish, Italian, anything as long as he isn't colored."

The pain was bad, worse than I thought. Physically, I rolled my head toward the window first, then shook my head like a boxer who's just been given a solid shot to the temple but is still standing. The motion was slight, but it was there. I felt myself shudder and shiver simultaneously. I dropped one arm off the steering wheel and rubbed my bare leg as if to comfort myself. Rocking ever so gently, I held on, as the tremors streamed through. There was nothing to do but talk in a monotone voice that had no expression or emotion.

"You're probably wrong. I don't understand it. They've only been here a few years. I think you said they got here in 1939, 1940, so it's not like they've been in the U.S. all this time. They didn't pick this racial thing up in Greece, right? There are no black people in Greece right? Plus, your old man was in the furriers union; that's a pretty progressive organization. He was exposed to good ideas in that union. I know that. You're probably wrong. It is historically impossible for them to have said that or thought that."

My lack of emotion either baffled her, frustrated her, or she was just so ashamed of having to hurt me in that way. Maybe she was also embarrassed that she still did their bidding when it came to personal relationships. Raising her head from the dashboard and looking directly at me, she bellowed, "Didn't you hear what I just said? You can't come over to my house. You can never come over to my house. It doesn't matter how much you know about English or Louis Armstrong. They would die if you ever came over. Just die." She turned and put her head back on her arms. She uttered one more *die*. Her last *die* didn't even have a *just* in it because she was spent and exhausted.

The Southern State Parkway, as you head west toward New York City, becomes the Belt Parkway. A few more lane changes and merges and we were leaving the Van Wyck Expressway for the Main Street exit. The car seemed to labor under the heat but whenever I peered at the temperature gauge it was right where it should have been, 185 degrees, cool, for a blazing summer day of stop-and-go driving back from Jones Beach. I thought about leaving her a few blocks from her house as punishment. Make her walk with her basket and blanket, two or three extra blocks for, for, for not, for not being, for being, for not being . . . I couldn't even figure out what the crime was, but I was still smarting from its affliction. Then I thought about a last minute dash up her steps, ringing the bell and shouting, "Here's that colored boy you're so afraid of. Right before your very eyes, baby, what a big surprise!" In reality, I was too paralyzed and hurt to even contemplate moving my back off the bucket seat. The sweat-soaked shirt was on the verge of making that suction cup noise; if I had made a move, it would have held me down, would have glued me to the seat.

As I parked the car, I realized something else that was incontrovertible. This was not her house. She had lied about where she lived. All those drives home and I thought this was her house. I had created so many heart-rending fantasies based on 144-02 72nd Road when it was really 144-10 72nd Road or who knows. She really didn't want me coming home for that visit. I had just blithely driven away glad that I had ferried her home all of those times. Who knows how far she walked to keep her dark secret? How many extra steps taken so the lie would live for both of us, one conscious and the other unconscious. I didn't want to start so I just said, "Well, we're here."

"Dex, I had a good time, except for the end."

"No, me too, it was a nice day at the beach, except for the, like you said, the end."

"You have a little burn."

"Oh, yeah, you're right. No big thing."

"Guess I'll see you tomorrow at Jefferson Hall."

"Yeah, good ol' Jefferson Hall at nine o'clock. Right?"

"Right."

The next day at Jefferson Hall, the registrar's office, the college. We smiled and ran to the storeroom for our little coffee break. She was distressed and apologized for what had occurred on the way back from the beach. I was glad to hear that she had thought about things between us, hadn't given up and even wondered about the future. "Break's over" came from Mrs. Colletti, an old civil service employee whom we admired because her son had been killed in the war. She had recovered from that blow. If she could stand up to the meaningless death of a son in Vietnam, perhaps, Eleni didn't know this, I thought we were up to the task of confronting another ugly aspect of America, racism, past and present. Back at my desk, I filed tear-off applications from people who desired to be nonmatriculated students in the fall, attending the evening session. On my lap was the college directory of services on campus. I was positive that the school had a counseling service. Queens College had benefited from the ever-expanding baby boomer population and the taxes that their parents were able to pay. The state now returned those tax dollars in highways, new subway cars, and an ever-expanding City University of New York. This was the heyday of burgeoning growth. To meet the massive need of all these new students, departments had not only been expanded but also created and developed for the first time. The counseling department was an official department, with tenured rank professors who gave help to students who were first confronting school, drugs, and love. Eleni and I were in the last category.

Because we were part-time student clerks we did not have a traditional lunch hour so we took our second unauthorized break in the storeroom. I told her that I had a suggestion, an idea. There was some-one who might help us. I started with hesitation since I had my own re-luctance to therapy. Memories of Dr. Kirschner were pretty fresh. That was only five years ago. My father's voice about how shrinks were for people who were crazy was omnipresent. I started with, "You know the counselors, over in S.S. building?" She looked up with a lot of doubt and replied, "You mean, the people who help you with the advise-ment?" I was caught off guard because I had forgotten that there were two groups of advisers on campus. I told her the truth, saying, "You know, I'm really not sure. You're right. I don't know which ones take care of which. Maybe they do both, talk to you about courses and talk to you about your problems. Either way, it's better than nothing."

Eleni played with her Sioux cloth bracelet on her wrist and became thoughtful. Because we were in the storage room the silence was ampli-fied. Turning and turning that bracelet was the only motion. "Good, it's a good idea," Eleni blurted out. She continued, "But one thing; you have to take care of everything. The appointment, the arrangement, whatever they call it." I grabbed her and gave her a big hug, picking her up off the floor. She hugged me back as I held her up and we embraced passionately. Since she was higher than me, she hugged my head, ran her hands through my hair, and beat on my shoulders with her fists when I wouldn't let her down. I held her up, took a few more love punches on my shoulders, and let her down.

Within a day or two I walked over to the office for counseling and advisement. A student clerk asked me whether I wanted counseling or advisement. "Counseling is for personal problems, right?" came out, not in a whisper, but not in a normal tone either. A nod of my head told him that I wanted counseling. I made an apppointment, was given a lit-tle reminder slip, and told Eleni over the phone that we were going to see Dr. Hannah Sallinger next Friday.

I thought Eleni might change her mind, but she was positive about the upcoming appointment. If anyone wavered, it was me; I thought about the time, the effort. I thought about what might come out of this process. Convinced that we would only talk about ourselves, as a cou-ple, I dropped any last minute thoughts and trepidations. When that Friday came, we walked from Jefferson Hall to the Social Science build-ing. My greatest fear was that someone would see us entering and leaving, but once I saw that there were inner and outer rooms and that as you went past the secretary's desk, you were hidden from view, I was completely relaxed.

Sitting out of view, we barely waited a minute when a tall woman with dark hair walked up to us with an outstretched hand. "Eleni, Dexter, I'm Dr. Hannah Sallinger. Why don't you come in?" We shook hands and followed her down a small hallway that removed us farther and farther from the outside office. I loved this removal from the public eye and breathed easier and easier. Even my father wouldn't be able to see me here. He was at work, millions of miles away down on Canal Street, in lower Manhattan. I was very happy.

Dr. Sallinger's office was bright. There were posters on the walls. We didn't know where to sit or how to sit and remained standing for an extra uncomfortable second. Smiling and with a small laugh, Dr. Sallinger said, "Well, come on, there's more than enough room. Just choose a seat." We were still awkward and even though she was right, there was more than enough room, once we sat, we both looked at the floor, the wall, the window, any direction but straight ahead. When we finally did look up, there she was, looking straight at both of us.

"Well, why don't we get started? What would you like to accomplish? What situation do you have that you would like to make better?" Eleni was quiet. I was quiet. I looked at her, and she looked at me. Dr. Sallinger waited patiently. We both bumbled through an answer that possessed catchphrases like *relationship* and *problems*. I managed to mention one specific piece of reality, the fact that Eleni wouldn't let me come over to her house. Dr. Sallinger wanted to know how important that was to me. I didn't want to give her the details since this would be an indictment of Eleni, and as I saw her shrinking in the chair, in fear of every question, I wanted to protect her. She didn't like the process. We concluded the hour with Dr. Sallinger requesting to see us both individually and then a follow-up session with us as a couple. We agreed.

Eleni went first, and I was jealous. I was also scared. I thought about the fact that even if she didn't tell any lies about me, it wasn't fair. She was getting to tell her story first and anytime you have to tell the story second, you're at a disadvantage. I contained myself though. I didn't ask her about anything she said although I asked the innocuous question, "So, how was it?" Eleni made a face and said, "I didn't like it." I kept quiet and wondered what didn't she like, Dr. Sallinger or what went on. They were different.

When it was my turn, I practically ran to straighten out whatever lies and distortions Eleni may have told. I was a bit breathless when I sat opposite Dr. Sallinger, and she could see that I was agitated. This time no prodding was needed. There were no pregnant moments of silence. I told her that Eleni was a good woman, but she was crazy. I surprised her when she asked me, "What about you? Do you have any problems?" Because of my years of being black and white and in pain all over I didn't even hesitate and replied, "Are you kidding? I'm crazier than her, but I know it. That's an important difference." Wanting to follow up on my confession Dr. Sallinger kept on, but I stopped her. She said, "What do you mean, you're crazier than her? What does that mean?" I waved my hand at her. "It's not important, just trust me, I know I'm crazy, but it's about other things. Let's get back to me and Eleni." Relenting with a neutral face, Dr. Sallinger asked no further questions and just let me ramble on. She asked some questions about what we hoped to accomplish by seeing her. We wanted to have a good relationship. We had problems. We thought that she could help. With the hour near its end, I was relieved when she let me know that we were to see her on a regular basis and that she had good feelings about staying together and working out our problems. After inquiring about possible dates for regular appointments, I walked out. It was settled. Every Wednesday at eleven in the morning.

That next Wednesday while at work in the registrar's office, I motioned to Eleni to meet me in the storeroom. We followed our routine of one going back alone, followed by the other, with a minute between our covert retreats. I kissed her and happily proclaimed that we were only about one hour away from getting help, and that if we were happy now, we would really be happy after talking to this woman. Dr. Sallinger was going to help us be happier. I kissed Eleni and picked her up, but she didn't punch my shoulders.

"What's happening? What's wrong?" I said.

Eleni looked at me, and there was no smile, big or small. "I'm not going."

"What?"

"I'm not going. That's it. I don't like that woman."

"Eleni, you've got to be kidding."

"No, I'm not going. Like I said, I don't like that woman."

"What are we going to do? We're supposed to be there at eleven."

"Dex, I don't care how much time is left. I'm never going to talk to that woman again."

I was baffled and based on Eleni's resolve, I could see that persuading her was impossible. When she said that she wasn't going, it was the same voice that proclaimed that I wasn't going to her house to meet her parents. I shook my head in exasperation and disbelief.

"Eleni, you're not real. This is not real. We're supposed to see her because she wants to help us. Don't you want to be helped?" My voice had that strident quality in it that indicated fear and more fear. Her reaction to my fear was to start to cry. She made a fist and bowed her head into her chest. She asked me for some tissues. I started to feel bad and started to focus on concrete things. I acquiesced quickly. Those tears, the tissues and the deep heaves of her chest overwhelmed me.

"Eleni, OK, I'm sorry. Forget about it."

"I'm not going; there is nothing you can do to get me back to her."

"Really, forget it. We're not going. OK?"

"OK, I'm going back to work, Dex."

"Eleni, one thing, we should call to cancel. We just can't not show up."

"Dex, I know you hate phones, but I'm not calling. If you can't call, just walk over there."

I could see that Eleni was scared and frightened by the entire experience. Whatever happened when she talked to Dr. Sallinger had been bad, and I could only guess at what demons or monsters had been scratched from a long thorny sleep. I shuddered when I thought to myself:

Eleni must be really nuts. If that could happen after just one session, she really must be crazy. Glad I'm not that crazy. I would never like to be that crazy.

She was right about one thing. I hated to telephone and I sure wasn't going to call to cancel this appointment. I looked at the clock and saw that I could easily walk over to the office, cancel the appointment in person and still have time to do my work for the day. Filing applications for nonmatriculated students who wished to attend in the evening session was easy, and I had my little system of categorizing and alphabetizing at the same time.

"Mrs. Colletti, I'm going over to S.S. building to get something."

"Just save some time for those . . ." We both said "nonmatriculated evening applications" at the same time. She smiled and went back to her work. I walked out of Jefferson Hall and made a beeline for the counseling office. I felt embarrassed about going there whether it was to keep an appointment or cancel one. No one would ever suspect what I was up to. This was another one of my secret missions that kept my private world private. I got to the outer office and spoke to the student who was in charge of referrals. She waved me on when I started to mention, *supposed to see Dr. Sallinger at eleven.* She pointed with her finger at the door at the end of the hall and said, "She's in. She's waiting for you."

My plan of not having to see her went awry. I had hoped that the clerk would have intervened on my behalf, but no, that pointed finger meant I was going to have to take care of this myself. A pointed finger, a casual disinterest in one's job, and that is how I became acquainted with the most important person in my life. I walked down to the end of the hall, and the door was open, wide open. There she was, sitting at her desk.

"Hello, is Eleni behind you?"

"No."

"Oh, is everything OK? Is she ill?"

"No, I mean, she's OK but she's not coming."

"Oh, why don't you come in and tell me what happened?"

"Doctor Sallinger, OK if I stand right here? A man doesn't have to come in if he doesn't want to, does he?"

She laughed a bit and said, "Sure, you can stand there. I just thought you might be more comfortable if you sat down. But, no, it's no problem. What happened, though?" I explained that therapy wasn't for Eleni and that she really felt bad about their session. I apologized for wasting her time and that if we ever felt like we could both come back, we would. "Well, I'm sorry that you two won't be coming. I think we would have done some good work together." I looked at her since everything she had just said was so genuine. After meeting us briefly, once together and once individually, she cared about what happened to us. I started to hesitate as I prepared to exit the doorway which I had now been occupying for three awkward minutes.

"Well, I guess I'll be heading back to Jefferson Hall; that's where I work."

"You work on campus. I didn't know that."

"Yeah, student aide for the evening registrar, Mr. Matthews. You know him?"

"I know the name, but I don't know him personally."

"Well, I'm heading out. Thanks for talking to us, I mean, me, too."

At that moment she got up from her swivel chair, and I looked at her and wondered why she had moved. She stuck her hand out to shake mine. Her black hair and black eyes were right there, right in front of me. We shook hands. I turned and walked a few steps. I heard her sit back down in that chair. She hadn't closed the door. It was slightly open. I tiptoed back to her door. I wanted to ask her something. I waited and breathed and my heart thumped in my chest. With my eyes closed, I took some more deep breaths. I slowly pushed open the door. This was it. She looked up from her desk and said, "Did you forget something?" I said nothing. I said nothing and just kept standing in that doorway. She didn't mind that I said nothing and just kept standing there. I was frozen. My face may have said something to her. I can't be sure. But I kept looking right at her black hair and black eyes.

"It's OK if I just stand here?"

"Sure, does it make you feel better?"

"Yeah, I just want to stand here. I don't have to talk, right?"

"No, stand there. You don't have to talk."

I stood there for a good five minutes, and that's a long time to stand in someone's doorway and not say anything. We kept looking at each other, and the whole time she didn't back down. She just kept looking at me, not away, not around me or through me, just at me.

"Doctor Sallinger, I'm going to talk a little."

"Yes, if you wish."

"I'm not going to sit down because a man doesn't have to sit down if he doesn't want to. A man can talk and stay standing, right?"

"You're right. A man can stand up and talk to me."

"Good, I just want to get something off my chest."

"I'm listening."

I leaned against the doorway that I had now been standing in for about ten minutes. I was already exhausted, and nothing had happened. But I was fatigued. To lean against the door comfortably, I had to move a bit inside her office. I now was halfway in. It felt good to rest. I smiled as I put my head against the doorjamb.

"Dexter, do you feel better?"

"Yeah, I do. Funny, I'm really tired. I just want to rest. It feels good to lean after all that standing."

I was quiet again. It was nice not to have to talk. Silence and rest was what I wanted, and she was giving it to me. I could see that I didn't have to do anything. It didn't bother her, the silence and the breathing. I leaned against the doorjamb and slowly slid from the doorway to the wall. I was in her office, but I was still standing. I placed one foot against the wall the way guys do when they're hanging out on street corners.

"Doctor Sallinger, I'm tired, really tired."

"You don't mean from not getting enough sleep, not that kind of tired?"

"No, I'm tired of being crazy. It can get to you after a while."

"I thought you said that you were crazy, but because you knew that you were crazy, it wasn't so bad."

"I lied. It's bad. It's bad."

"Oh, how bad is bad? You're not doing anything bad to deal with this badness, are you?" I smiled and shook my head and said, "No, no drinking, no drugs; maybe I should. I just deal with it. It's not that bad."

She had turned completely around since I was standing in the back of her office, leaning against the wall. I had collected myself a bit and decided to explain my definition of bad.

"Doctor Sallinger, look, I know you're used to dealing with a lot of crazy hippie kids. This is nothing like that. My problem is very, very special, but I'm sure you psychological guys, if you work a little overtime, you can figure this one out too. I have this problem, something to do with identity. I'm sure you've handled many cases like it before with all these hippie kids goin' nuts. It's a little unusual, but like I said, I'm sure if you take some time and do some research, you'll find the answer. You see, I have a black father and a white mother, and I've had a difficult time finding myself, who I am, what I am, you know. Can you help me with this? How long do you think it will take? A few weeks? A month? Whatta ya think?"

"Dexter, what about Eleni?"

"The hell with Eleni, this is about being crazy, really nuts. That girlfriend boyfriend stuff is a lot of bullshit compared to this. This thing will make you nuts, absolutely fucking nuts. It can rip a man's head off; I don't care how fuckin' tough he thinks he is. Right off, right the fuck off his shoulders, you understand?"

My raised voice didn't scare her, but it impressed her. I didn't want to scare that black hair and those black eyes, so I quieted myself down and started to rub my head. I apologized for cursing. She said nothing.

"Doctor Sallinger, you see, this is hell. This black white thing is fuckin' hell for me, every day. I would do anything to get out of it. Anything." As I spoke, I noticed I had slowly slid down the wall to the floor. I had only one more question for her.

"Doctor Sallinger, OK if I just sit on the floor like this? I can't move. I'm really tired. Really, really tired. I know a man should be able to stand on his own two feet, but I am really, really, fuckin' tired. I just need a rest. Just a little break."

She looked at me and said nothing, but with her face and eyes told me that it was OK to do what I was doing.

"Doctor Sallinger, are you sure?"

Again, she answered the same way, with silence and just one human face telling another human face that she understood that I was tired, and it was OK to take a rest.

Down and Out But Not Beaten

"DOCTOR SALLINGER, LET me clean off your car. Been snowing all day." There she sits, and her winter boots are in the corner, making little puddles of water. Caked-on snow has slowly dissolved into water with little particles of dirt and salt. I watch and wait for an answer. She smiles and says, "That's the third time you've mentioned that. Aren't we going to do some work today?" That reply is frustrating since I want to do something for her. She won't let me. I've offered to get her things, make her things, walk her to her car when it gets dark; the Queens College parking lot is immense and is more like a car pound for vehicles that have been towed away. There are few lights and the gravel is so uneven that anytime it rains, large tidal pools of water are left standing for weeks. All I want to do is clear the snow off her car because it's 5:00 P.M., and it's been snowing all day Friday. I attended an English class, did some tutoring and ended up at her office at four. My car is covered too, and it would be so simple to do this little chore at the same time I'm cleaning off my car.

"So, Doctor Sallinger, can I do it for ya?"

"Dexter, you want to do things for me, and we've been over this before. I've told you. You've already done so much for me."

"Not really, I haven't done anything. You've changed my life. You made me a new man. You brought me out of the dark, the dark, a dark, a dark type of, a dark kind of slavery; look, I can't come up with a metaphor. A fuckin' cave, that's it. You've unchained me and brought me out of a dark cave. Do you know how important that is to someone? It's like freeing someone who's been trapped underground for years and now they see light, trees, stars, sun, moon, the whole thing."

Dr. Hannah Sallinger is pensive as she hears me. She looks at her fingers which she tends to keep under control except at times like this. Ninety percent of the time she keeps her hands clasped over her knee or just in her lap. Now, she clasps and unclasps and I know one thing; she's feeling and thinking. The hands stop and she talks. "Dexter, that is exactly what I mean. Therapists are like teachers. You're a teacher." I cut her off quickly and reply with emphasis, "Tutor, just a tutor." With a look of slight exasperation that I can be so stubborn and such a stickler for exactitude when it's important to me and unimportant to the rest of the world, she nods her head and repeats, "Tutor." This concession makes her readjust the seating arrangement. She turns her chair a bit, and we are facing each other.

She starts again. "So, therapists are like tutors. They get fulfillment out of the progress that they witness. And the process. Out of the process itself. They see the person change, feel better about themselves or gain control over some aspect of their lives that was previously out of their control, and that's how you pay me back. When I've seen what you've done in the last two years. It's incredible, remarkable. You've worked so hard, worked hard through so many things. It's not easy. Not everyone can do what you did."

She's right and it takes only a small retrospective journey for me to think of the incidents, past and present, that we've encountered. For every dark world I brought her, gray skies filled with threatening clouds and unpredictable wind patterns that she was not familiar with, she has always figured out where the storm hailed from, where it was going, and when it would leave the mainland and dissipate over the sea. I've walked into this office with the most wretched and confounding things spilling out of me, sometimes without any control or connection to what I had said just the previous week and her face always remained the same. I didn't care about the personal nature of some of the remarks either:

White people are racist.

You're probably not a racist but there's a chance.

Black people are racist.

White people suck; they really suck.

When I say white people suck, I don't mean you.
Black people suck; they really suck.
I could really kill some white people today.
I wouldn't kill you. You're really not white.
I could really kill some black people today.

All of my maddening fantasies and desires; she walked me through them and made me realize that these were just masks on top of other things and although legitimate, sometimes they only served as distractions. She's right about the process. It's long and thick, and I could see how one would gain a sense of pride and accomplishment from watching someone for more than two years. That's a lot of process. There might not be progress, but the amount of time and effort would have to be accorded recognition. Every Friday for two years, sometimes twice a week, all year except for small vacations and even then she gives me her number or someone else's in case there is an extra cry for help. She listened to everything. Everything.

"Doctor Sallinger, I have something to tell you. It's unusual. I never told you this before but I have definitely been thinking about it, and I can tell you anything, right?"

"Yes."

"I think we should sleep together. I know I'm younger than you, but I really like you a lot. I'm smart, kinda. It might be nice. No, it would be nice. Just one time. I'm just telling you the truth. I'm not making anything up. This is the way I really feel."

Instead of answering my question with a yes or no, she transformed it into something more useful. It was the same topic, but something had happened. That is the kind of power she had. I'm positive that she smiled a little bit or even laughed, but it was so short, and her next question had come out so quickly that I could not concentrate on whether she wanted to or not.

"Dexter, tell me what that would be like."

"Huh?"

"I'm asking you to describe how you would imagine it to be."

I woke up and sat forward in the chair. I had a tendency to slouch and with twenty minutes into the session, I usually slowly disappeared into the seat. My neck would touch the back of the chair. Sometimes pinched skin and hair on a piece of metal would set off some sort of alarm that I was slouching to the floor. Other times, nothing would stir mind or body except a question or a remark.

"Tell me, what do you think it would be like, to be in bed together?"

"Didn't you just ask me that?"

"Yes, but you didn't say anything."

"Who, me?"

"Yes, let's do some work before the hour is up."

"Sure, I was just thinking, daydreaming."

I told her that I wanted to make love to her, and it made me feel funny since she was only the second woman I had ever said that to, the first being Eleni. I knew she was older than me but not that old. It didn't matter. I had fallen in love with her after six months. I never tired of looking at her face, black hair, thin features, elegant clothes. In the summer, swirling dresses, paisleys and flowers. Light tan high heels to match her spring suits. Sometimes she would dress very formally, like a business-woman going someplace, and I learned that she was going to a conference. I inquired as to what the conferences were about, and they were always about psychology, trying to help crazy people like myself. I would look at her legs and study them. A medallion between her breasts always had a hypnotic effect on me. I liked her a certain way until she told me that she had a son and a husband and all my fantasies crumbled. Just another woman whom I wanted to sleep with who wasn't available. Still, it was nice to talk about it and have someone to talk about sex with.

"Doctor Sallinger, we're in a room and you're in bed and I'm in bed with you."

"Yes, good, how did we get in bed?"

"Whatta ya mean?"

"Just what I said."

I looked at her and shook my head. This was torture and I regretted telling her that I loved her and wanted to sleep with her. If this is what happens when you confess to a woman that you love her, I was better off keeping my romantic and lustful longings to myself.

"Well, Doctor Sallinger, look, I don't know. We're in bed and I don't know how we got there. But we're there, in bed."

"Do we have our clothes on?"

"Jesus, what the hell do you think?"

"I don't know. I don't know one thing that is going on in your head. This is your fantasy."

I was disgusted and shook my head. I stayed silent and breathed exasperated breaths that could be heard, even over the little air machine that created background noise so when you cried, no one else would hear but you and her. I was being incredibly honest with her considering that I had spent the first six months of therapy doing one thing and doing one thing only: lying. I lied about everything. I lied about my mother, father, sister, brother, me. At times I spoke truthfully about friends and personal interests. I could never forget the time she requested a record player from the audiovisual services so I could play her some Lester Young. I was trying to tell her how much jazz meant to me and how I had studied it, taught a class about it once and had made some very good friends based on this love, this obsession. I walked in one day, and there it was, a really nice piece of equipment considering it was a college operation. The two speakers detached from the main box, and it was true stereo. I had safeguarded this album all day Friday. I had kept it wrapped in cloth. It was a twelve-inch 78, very rare. The label stated, *Lester Young and the Kansas City Six*. The cut was one of my favorites, *After Theater Jump* and I always thought that Lester Young, Prez, that light-skinned dude who always suffered for his color, was working out his problems in another way. I was benefiting from the fact that he had never discovered Freud or therapy but instead, a tenor sax. That would have been a tragic loss. Prez might have talked to a therapist and never would have gotten to play obbligato for Billie Holiday on *Mean to Me* and *This Year's Kisses*. Man! No Prez blowing his way through *Shoe Shine Boy*. Some of the greatest jazz by a black artist would have never been created.

I put the platter on ever so gently. A twelve-inch 78 was always an extra fragile thing. They really broke easily. The turntable started spinning and the music started coming out. Prez played and took a nice long solo. I waited to see some reaction. Nothing. One advantage of a twelve-inch 78 was that it is normally longer than a ten inch. Ten-inch records were approximately three minutes in length. You got a nice extra thirty to forty seconds from these large ones. Luckily, this worked. She kept listening. I studied every feature, hoping that something would happen. I wanted to see a reaction. The platter kept spinning. I hid my foot and folded my hands so she couldn't see the tempo that I was beating out with both, hands and feet. Lester blew. I prayed. I leaned over to turn up the volume but sat back down like I had forgotten something. That wouldn't be fair. That would be cheating. Blow, Prez, blow so the Big S can hear your soul. Blow so she can understand what jazz has done for me in the past few years. Only a few seconds left, a few precious seconds. Ensemble, piano solo, Buck Clayton on trumpet, and then Prez. Thank the Lord, instead of a 16-bar solo they gave him 32 because of the record. I see it. She's starting to tap her foot. She heard Joe Jones hit that drum behind Prez, and she's tapping her foot. It happened. I look at her face. She smiles, nods, and says, "That has a nice beat." That was better than sex, and from that point on I cut down on the lying a bit.

I wasn't the perfect client although I knew I was special to her. One time she asked me if she could have permission to tape our sessions. I thought that she wanted to do this so she could remember what was going on but that had never been a problem. Alonzo and George would always laugh anytime she caught me in a lie with her perfect memory. Even though she never took any notes, at least notes that I had witnessed her writing during the session, she remembered each and every detail of our conversations. It was uncanny. I thought maybe she jotted down things after I left but, still, there was no other way she could recall the smallest detail. After a session and then a weekend drive to Princeton, I reveled with George and Alonzo as I showered them with the half-truths and lies that I had fed Dr. Sallinger, hoping that I satisfied her, fooled her.

A few weeks later, another drive down Route One and I'm going past the Seagram's plant on the right and Rahway State Prison on the left, cruising through New Brunswick; I drove into the Princeton Visitor Parking lot. They came walking from their dorms; they resided in Gauss Hall or Dodd Hall. I took the visitor's pass and put it on the dashboard of the car. Our rituals on Friday in the fall were to play some serious touch football. They could see that I wasn't really focused. In the huddle, making our plays, Alonzo blurted out, "Come on, what the hell are you thinking about? I said, run a buttonhook. What happened?" I kept my head looking at the ground the way football players do when they're getting instructions in the huddle. "Big S, Big S got me. Caught me. Caught me." Alonzo shook his head and said, "Fuck it, we'll talk about it later. Nigger, now put your mind on the game." The games were wonderful since Alonzo and George had been studying all week, and this was their release. Books, papers, seminars with recitations, they were receiving that classic Ivy League training, and they were pent up with a great deal of energy by Friday afternoon.

The football field for our games was well kept. The grass was cut and groomed. Autumn colors blazed on the leaves of the trees that lined the field. Coats and jackets were placed in nice piles and stood for goalposts. A few books placed in a straight line formed the perimeters of the field. We were set. All we needed was a football and eight to ten guys. Rus, one of Alonzo's best friends was the quarterback. He would call the play, "Huddle, huddle, come on, let's huddle." Alonzo was on to me as we stared at the ground.

"That's what you get for fuckin' with the Big S."

"I wasn't fucking with her."

"You were lying; that's fuckin' with somebody."

"OK, Al, let's listen to the play."

Within a few seconds we were back again, losing yards and now desperate.

"Dexter, Big S got the power and you're trying to lie to her. You can't."

"I wasn't lying. How the fuck does she remember everything? I told her that months ago."

"Dexter, I'm a psych major. These people are trained. Hundreds of hours of training and supervision."

Rus would finally intervene with, "OK, knock off the bullshit and the codes. Let's make a play." Once the game was over I could really tell both of them what had happened, and George would just have a puzzled expression on his face as he listened to my pathetic strategies and lies, and he had no sympathy for me. George, in softer tones, the opposite of Alonzo's harangue, would almost whisper, "Help, this woman is offering you help. You have to take it. Every time you lie, you're only delaying the process. Are you scared?"

I spend the entire weekend with them. On Saturday nights we had inaugurated another tradition of staying up as late as possible and then going to a deli on Nasssau Street for large overstuffed heroes that we would bring back to the room. These "subs" helped us stay up until the crack of dawn, and it's during these late night or early morning hours, they confess to me what they are facing at Princeton that's made them uncomfortable, uneasy, and isolated. We're only nineteen, but we all have an intersecting history that connects us with America and the civil rights movement. The lines run from Selma to Springfield Gardens. We've been through the racially tainted times of the early sixties that made for rough and challenging experiences at P.S. 156 in Laurelton; J.H.S. 231 in Springfield Gardens; and then on to the high school of our neighborhood with the same name. Wherever we go, racial tension and animosity is in the veins of the people. I figured it was something that they were familiar with. We already knew what it was like to be in the minority. If you could get through P.S. 156 where there were seven hundred white kids and only eight of us, . . . Just from scouring the Princeton campus on all my trips, it seemed like the same ratio: ten to one.

Alonzo has been holding back on his anger and lets go with some prefatory cursing, "Goddamn bastards. Not like I don't have enough trouble already with the classes, books. No, these people gotta start fucking with us." Alonzo had never cursed before in his life. All those years of Sunday Baptist school and Sunday services and sometimes an occasional service on a weekday night had kept him on the straight and narrow. The curses came out like a wondrous stream because he had combined the oratory of the black church, sermons and preachers he had heard, with blue streaking metaphors and similes. I laughed.

"Goddamn, whist playing California niggers who never heard of tough times, telling me and George what the fuck to do. Dexter, Dexter, remember that organization, A.B.C., Association of Black Collegians? I was almost the vice president? Goddamn, sonsabitches are tellin' me and George that we're Uncle Toms. Do you believe that shit? We integrated that school, 156. We did things when these California niggers were eating oranges or whatever the fuck they do out there. These motherfuckers got the nerve, got the nerve to tell me and George, 'cause we know some white people, we're Uncle Toms. Do you believe that shit? Do you? Do you believe that shit?" I started to raise my hand to ask him if this was the biased version of things and was he going to give me, midway through the night, the real truth later when he said, "And thank God you're not here. Niggers would be fuckin' with you too because you're light. Yeah! Philadelphia boogie niggers would look at your skin and your hair, Lord, that good hair is gonna come back to haunt you, niggers would look at you and say, 'high yellow nigger with good hair thinks he's better than everyone else' and then start fuckin' with you, too. These niggers would tell you that when we—get this shit—we, when we were on the plantation, someone like you was up in the Big House making everybody else do the work. Yeah, you're a house nigger, me and George are field niggers and we're supposed to be mad at you one hundred twenty years later. I ain't bullshitting, Dexter. A.B.C. niggers would run you off campus, and you've got splinters in your hands from being on picket lines when these Washington, D.C. niggers were hiding in their house, eatin' Kentucky Fried and you were fightin' for them. You and your mom invented the motherfuckin' picket sign."

George isn't as insistent, but he's upset and starts to nod his head. Just so we don't have to waste any time, I interject, "I figured the white kids were messing with you guys and you just didn't want to tell me. Didn't want to dash my illusions about Princeton, so to speak." George shakes his head and before he can answer, Alonzo bursts out, "No, no, niggers, the niggers are messing with us more than the white boys."

George finally talks. Quiet, he stops smiling and says, "These students are doing something that borders on psychological manipulation. It's strange and you would have to see it or hear it to understand it." I frown, and he can see that my dubious look is going to force him to speak with a little more sincerity. "Dexter, no, I'm not saying these people are evil or bad. But something's happened in the last few months, a year at the most. Organizations like A.B.C. and probably others like it are all over the country, all over college campuses and they're changing the color, no pun intended, of the whole struggle. Everything we did, fought for, the whole integration thing, they don't want any part of it." There are candles burning in the darkness of their room, and they've caught my attention, and I feel like there is something dark and ominous being revealed to me for the first time. The candles flicker and I shiver.

I also feel bad because I've been left out of this movement of reversal. At Queens College, there are so few black students that no political agendas of this nature have been developed or pursued. They've been suffering in a fight and struggle that I didn't know about and losing. We never lost anything to anybody, and I'm mad. I'm baffled too, and my words are halting and sound even more pathetic because it's five o'clock in the morning and our sandwiches are soggy.

Without more delay it comes out, "What do they want? They're against integration? That's what we've been fighting for since 1961. What do they want, to go back to the back of the bus?" Alonzo hasn't sat down during the entire conversation. He paces, and he's really mad.

Looking at him to make sure he won't interject, George sees that he has the floor. He continues, "It's more complicated than that, I think. They want integration; they want to be at Princeton. They want to be Princeton men. But they want to withdraw and do their own thing. They want to be here and not be here. They've got the white kids feeling so guilty that there's a distance developing between everyone on campus. We're not part of that so when they see us talking to white boys, white girls, or anyone else that isn't black, we catch hell for that. It's weird and alienating. At Springfield, when I was vice president of the student organization, I worked with white kids all the time. We were students, not black or white; well, Negro was the word then. We worked to make things better for all students. This is weird."

Alonzo comes back from the stereo after putting on a Doors album. He's calmed down and explains how he knows that he's not completely rational. The political situation changed in one semester. He's recalling the spring semester like it was a thousand years ago on another campus. Popular and intelligent with good oratory skills, he had moved in social circles on the Princeton campus, making positive impressions on people and the future was wide open. That's over now for him. With a subdued anger in his voice, he starts to curse but stops, "Look, this is what it comes down to. They're saying that all white people are racist. All of them, without exception. All white people are racist. They're so crazy, damn crazy; they'd say that even Goodman and Schwerner were not to be trusted. That's how far they've come unglued. White boys come from up north to help black people register to vote in Mississippi and their intentions are under a shadow. Schwerner, I think his brother is a professor at your school, right? He's a professor at Queens College?" I nod my head vigorously and somehow feel like this small connection makes me part of their world. "Alonzo," I say, "he's the dean of something. The dude is a dean at Queens." *Strange Days* plays in the background and we crash, me nodding out first.

I leave Princeton on fine Sunday afternoons as late as possible. Because the drive is only ninety minutes back to New York and if I did some reading assignments for my own classes, I stretch that afternoon into the early evening. Whenever I leave, I'm not the same. I feel chastened as though I've attended at a retreat for one or two reasons. They made me rethink how I'm handling my therapy and the lying that works at cross-purposes with getting well. The other reason that I feel like I've been to a monastery is the intensity of their lives. The center of that tension indeed Princeton itself. The campus is fraught with political and racial tension. *All white people are;* that line sticks in my head as I drive up north on Route 1, past dozens of signs of another new America, fast food places and swimming pool stores that sell white sand for pool filters; that confounds me since I don't see how white sand will keep pool water clean.

The trip back has the drama of going over the Goethels Bridge, through Staten Island and over the relatively new Verrazano Narrows Bridge to the Belt Parkway. I debate with myself all of the new ideas that I've been exposed to and try to reach some sort of conclusion by the time I pass Kennedy Airport. I hate walking into my house as if I didn't have a great weekend. My astute parents could pick up on that and began to question me when I returned. By the time I turn the nose of that 1968 Cougar into the driveway, I have put things in order. I'm going to do something with that *All white people are racists* idea. It's too delectable and beautiful to leave unattended. A smile comes on my face as I think of my world, my problems, and my week. It's going to take some doing, some effort and even a little bit of research, but I'm determined and evil.

Monday I'm back on campus and go to the library to get my hands on as many college catalogs that I can. They keep all of the old ones in a small separate room that is reserved for the archives of Queens College. Most of the material is on reserve. It doesn't matter. I really don't need to take anything out. Just need a look at the back of the bulletin where all of the professors are listed in alphabetical order. I flip vigorously since I want the tail end of the alphabet. S, yes, that's the letter I need and want. Right near the top of the Ss, SALLINGER. Yes sir, right where I thought you'd be, baby!

Sallinger, Hannah. BA, University of Maryland, 1955, Ed.D., Columbia

and the rest of the stuff is irrelevant. University of Maryland, 1955, that's what I wanted. That's the jackpot. There's the rub and every other great expression that connotes I have what my devilish mind has been searching and hoping for. This Friday, at 4 o'clock, she's in for a big surprise. This is going to be a session like we've never had before or maybe will ever have. For once, there will be no comeback answers, retorts, or questions. When I talk, there is going to be silence. She won't have anything to say.

Thursday came and even a series of good tutoring sessions could not assuage my pain and anger. I was single-minded and was going to see this plot through to its logical end. I walked into her office that Friday at four on the dot, swaggering, plopped myself down in the chair, folded my arms across my chest, and smiled. She could see that something was up, but she allowed me to unroll this fantasy in the same manner she had borne witness to my sexual intrigue. Therapy is truly the one relationship where one can talk about anything one desires and can start the conversation wherever one wishes. There is no need or requirement for transitions and segues. Overall, it's the complete opposite of reality where if you were talking to someone, a friend, relative, you would have to pay attention to the past, present, and future. You just don't blurt out things without remembering the context. Not in therapy. Therapy, you just jump right down the person's throat and they have to take it. There's nothing they can say about your failure to adhere to the regimen of social intercourse. This isn't social intercourse. This isn't a normal conversation. This is one crazy person talking to one sane person, so they give you a lot of freedom. She did.

I commenced my attack with that smile on my face. One deep breath and the prepared words came out, "Doctor Sallinger, I noticed that you never talk about your college days too much. As a matter of fact, I've never heard you talk about your days as an undergrad. What was it like? Were you a good student? What was your major? Did you meet a lot of black people then?" She shook her head and her black bangs danced over her forehead. They swept from left to right, right to left. I was distracted by the hair and searched her eyes and mouth for hints of consternation and pain. There was a pause and she said, "I get the feeling that you found out that I attended the University of Maryland, and yes, you're right. It was segregated. So obviously, I didn't have any black friends on campus. I could have had other black friends from other parts of my life, right?"

I was gleeful. I had more prepared remarks. I said, "No, not really, you know the way racists are. If you weren't racist, you wouldn't have attended a school like that. There were other colleges that you could have attended, even in the 1950s, that weren't segregated." I was really rolling on her. This was like Muhammad Ali against Frazier. I might not win, but I was going to give you the beating of your life. I was really starting to pound her, and there was nothing that she could do. My smile had become a smirk. I looked at her face and thought, you white racist; you're racist through and through and now you're quiet because I've exposed the truth. All you can do is just sit there. We were both silent.

I got scared when she swung her legs up onto the chair. Sometimes I thought she did this because she didn't want me to try and look up her dress, but there was nothing like that going on. I just wanted to kill her. Why would she swing her legs up on the chair and hold them at the ankles with one hand. That was always a sign that, that, . . . I wasn't sure what it meant but it dismayed me. She spoke in a way that I had never heard before.

"The University of Maryland was segregated then. You know that. I didn't like it. It always made me feel troubled and uncomfortable to know that. It was a bad time; from all of history you know, you could perhaps even explain it better to me than I can to myself. And I lived it. I doubt if this is a satisfactory answer, but what special meaning does all of this have for you? What does it mean that I attended a segregated college back in the 1950s?"

"You know what it means."

"Dexter, tell me. Tell me how this changes things."

I couldn't resist the moment and was as cagey and coy as I could be. "Doctor Sallinger, all these months you've been trying to help me and I'm starting to see how you could never help me, not in a million years. How could you ever understand, even for one second, what I am going through?"

In my mind there was a jumble of thoughts, false ideals, and most of all, rhetoric. It was the early 1970s. Black militancy prevailed on many American college campuses. At certain universities black rhetoric dominated any forum for debate; it was constructed around the premise that a moral victory could be achieved if white students (or anyone else for that matter) innocent of the petty intrigues that were being foisted upon them, were forced to bear the burden of guilt for America's racial injustice, past and present. From the landing of the first nineteen African slaves (actually indentured servants) to the lack of black students on campus, this was their fault. White people made it this way. I too was a victim of this distorted ideology. This perspective linked with preposterous notions of Elijah Muhammad's Black Muslims coupled with the aggressive language of the Black Panthers, all combined to paint a picture of black people as victims, white people as devils. It was difficult to avoid this sentiment. True, I didn't have to digest this cheap intellectual meal, but I had my own motivations for feasting, wining and dining on victimology. This ranting and raving possessed a delicious appeal when the alternative was hard work, honesty and a constant struggle to uphold one's integrity under trying circumstances. Therapy is like being in a room with a can of snakes in the corner. The can is covered and the snakes can't escape, but every now and then, the entire can shudders. In order for you to be healthy, you have to walk over to that can, on your own volition, take off the lid and start taking out those snakes, one by one. Grabbing them by the head, you have to wrestle and choke each one before they choke you forever. That's the only way back from the darkness that you dwell in. The reward? You can sleep the whole night through once that last snake is removed and killed. That afternoon I didn't have the courage to confront them. I chose the easy way out.

"So, Doctor Sallinger, to put it plainly and simply, you could never help me and we've been wasting a lot of time. A white person with your background can't . . ."

At this point she cut me off and it was the only time that I can remember that she lost her objectivity. She leaned forward, gave me a stern look and said, "I want you to know that my father spent his entire academic career at Howard University, teaching black students at an all-black school. Does that pass your test? Now, are you going to keep on wasting this hour or are we going to do some serious work today?"

"Howard University?"

"Yes, Howard University. Do you know whom it's named after?"

"Yeah, sure, a famous Civil War general of the Union Army . . . Howard University?"

"Good, Dexter. Now that we have that all straightened out, can we proceed?"

"Yes, Doctor Sallinger. Yeah, I was just," and my voice trailed off into some sort of mumble and she gratefully didn't pursue my meek apology.

From that day on, I kept on the beam with only some minor digressions. I suppose the most important revelation that Dr. Hannah Sallinger gave me was that I had to understand life from a human point of view first. And when it comes down to it, race is not human; it's an artificial categorization employed to justify what is inherently inhuman: weakness, fear, diffidence, and timidity. By concentrating on the human side—my family, my relationships with my father, mother, brother, and sister—I was able to make some substantial progress in consolidating an awareness of who I was, am, and might be.

Another trip to Princeton on a Friday afternoon. Alonzo and George were royally hilarious as I told them of what had occurred at the *You're a white racist* session. They laughed beyond control when I told them of her rejoinder, *Howard University*. The laughter, guffaws, "Dexter, she put a woof ticket on your black ass like you never knew existed," Alonzo said with glee. George, with tears of laughter, intermittently wiping his face, got out, "Dexter, why are you fuckin' with this person? We talked about this before. The woman is trying to help you and you just wanna go and fuck with her. Alonzo, Alonzo, give me five on him gettin' his ass righteously put down and under." They both slapped five like a thunderclap and I shook my head at my situation. They struck hands so hard that they winced in pain, but the laughter quickly relieved their momentary grimaces. The raucous laughter continued.

Alonzo said, "Dexter, tell me one thing. No fuck it. You ain't got nothing to tell me. But one thing I got to tell you." He paused and I prepared for some long-winded, involved, and convoluted linguistic ballet, but instead it was just a low and well-paced comment, "You are indeed a fool. That's all I have to say. You are a fool."

I looked at both of them and just mumbled, "Sometimes, sometimes."

Journal Entry
February 21, 1974

Been thinkin', been doin' a whole of lot of thinkin' lately. Man, what a fucked up world. People are crazy and me being ignorant doesn't make dealin' with the world any easier.

I mean, man, my roots are in the street, not Harlem, Bed-Stuy or Brownsville, but it's a black street near South Jamaica. And it's from that provincial street, with its one generation removed southern sharecroppers, that my world is colored. And my view of the outside world, which is mostly white, has its telescopic eye back there and no matter what you do to hide the street, it's there.

A few of my English professors saw it and it made them feel uncomfortable. I was an unknown quantity until I opened my mouth and then being known only made things worse.

It's there. It's there just in the fact that I don't know certain things and if I told Paris Blake, Calhoun, Speedy, Midnight, and Nigger Charley, the guys who hang out on the corner of Farmers Boulevard and 140th Avenue, some of the things I learned up at college, they would say, "Boy, you're lyin'."

And Higby—Higby, goddamn, Higby. You taught me everything I needed to know. I worked in that dry cleaning store for five years. You taught me about being young and black, running numbers, gypsy cabs, beer, mixin' Johnny Walker Red with milk because it goes down smooth. You fine-tuned things like turning a distributor cap just a little bit to the right or left to get that engine running exactly the way you wanted it to. Damn! Told me and explained the difference between cuttin' someone and stabbin' someone with a knife. The difference is that when you cut someone, you just slash them and give them stitches. No jabbing. No punctures.

And Higby, you told me. You swore you would tell me everything, things about sex, everything that I would ever need to know. Puttin' it in and takin it out and VD. But Higby, you never told me about homosexuals and lesbians.

Higby—I got to tell you something. Up at the college, Queens College, these people, one-third of them are fags, one-third of them are lesbians, and one-third of them are vegetarians.

Higby, that's a whole group of people who don't know what to fuck or eat!

And Higby, you might not believe this, but I swear, Higby, some black people, I swear, I ain't lyin', there are some black people, who are, I'm serious, who are, yeah, Higby, they're funny too.

Do you know what Higby would say to all that? "Nigger, all those white people and all that schoolin' has made you crazy."

And They're Off!

HOW MANY BLACK men are buried at Belmont Park Racetrack, Nassau County, New York? Not too many, for all I know, just him and maybe that's the way he wanted it. The only one. Just one. No one else. No other contenders. Just my old man gets his ashes spread at a racetrack; that definitely should have fulfilled the ultimate need to be special and unique. I know the feeling, and I know it's connected with being black. Sometimes you just want to be the only one and you are proud that you are that, and no one can take that away from you. He made it. He wanted to not only be the only one in so many different aspects of life in America, but he also longed to be in another set apart, as a math teacher would say, in a set that has no intersecting or overlapping sets. A set of one who was further removed from all others. He wanted to be a special Negro who was even then extraordinary for his singularity.

Somehow he achieved that every Saturday at Belmont Park, Aqueduct, sometimes at Pimlico, Monmouth, and Bowie down in Washington, D.C. Yes, he would drive that far on an early Saturday morning, New York to Washington, to be there for a race. If the odds were not in his favor, there would be no wagering. He then would drive the two hundred and fifty miles back to New York City. Some men and women time their vacations through the year so they're free late in November and early December for hunting season. They wait, prepare, and stave off all other desires for time during July and August, so they can have those three weeks of bow season, muzzle loader season, and finally, rifle. My father had the same compulsion. Sometimes he would arrange his vacations to follow the seasons of the horses. In those days, the early

1960s, there was no horse racing in the winter in the New York metropolitan area, so he was compelled to endure some sort of withdrawal during those cold months. One day an idea came to him like a bolt of something. Horses kept on racing and running throughout the year; they just weren't in New York. So go where they are. That is exactly what he did. He packed up, took his vacation days and his saved-up sick days and moved to Washington, D.C. for a week or two, so he could be near his beloved horses. Taking a room in a motel, bringing his charts and papers with him, he had his ideal vacation.

Driving hundreds of miles sometimes to bet one horse, compressing weekends into five- and six-hour drives (one way) so he could make the post time at Delaware Park or Laurel. The process began on Friday night when he would drive from Queens to Manhattan to get the *Morning Telegraph*, the early edition that was sold at one newsstand on Delancey Street. He would ask me if I wanted to go for a ride. My passion for riding and driving was fierce. Taking his keys I hustled to the garage where his 1967 Chrysler Newport was parked and warmed it up for him. It took about five minutes for a car like that to reach operating temperature. I watched the green light that flashed the word COLD finally flicker out. Waiting for it to twinkle itself away gave me time to turn on the radio, check the lights, low and high beams. His 8-track player with Charlie Parker and Miles Davis was ready. It was going to be a good run.

He'd get in as I slid from the driver's side to the passenger side. It was still dark in the garage. We were there together in the darkness. He would turn the lights on, press on the accelerator to give it one good rev, and knock down the automatic choke. There would be a pause. He would turn to me and say, "This is really a great car, a fine piece of machinery." I would return his salutation with a grin as if the compliment had been made toward me. With the car purring, it was time to reach into his jacket pocket for those Pall Malls. For some reason, he never used the cigarette lighter too much, preferring matches. The match is lit; there's that special sound. He cups his hands, and you see this little Promethean glow in that darkness as the match gives life to the cigarette; the interior of the car has enough radiant light that it's reflected by the windshield. One long drag and glow and that reflection shows his face. I'm still in the dark. The cigarette goes in the ashtray. Shift, reverse, he turns to his right with his right arm over the back of the seat, sometimes touching me, saying, "Excuse me, I couldn't see you there in the darkness," and we're slowly moving out of the garage and down the driveway.

It's another nice long drive to Manhattan, and there's not too much traffic in those days on a Friday night. The roads are literally clear. We roll. Sometimes we talk. Sometimes we don't. I know we're cruising when he rests his right hand on the shift. Even though the car has an automatic transmission and he hasn't had a standard in years, he still likes to keep his hand on the shift. Some sort of comfort. I sometimes question my importance on these drives, but he always reassures me that he wants me to come. I don't do anything. He replies, "It's nice to have some company." I feel weird when he says that since I don't talk too much. When we reach Manhattan, he makes it clear that I have a utilitarian function. "Here's a dollar; hop out and get the paper. That way I don't have to look for a parking place." I jump out of the car and hear the word "Careful!" yelled through the closing door. He's right. Delancey Street in lower Manhattan is jumping, even this late, and there are cars and trucks that have to be dodged. The newsstand guy now knows me and grins. "Evenin' buddy." My muted "Hi" comes out, and he continues, "*Morning Telegraph*, right?" I nod my head given the opportunity not to have to talk. That dollar goes into that cold and tough hand that swiftly returns to his newspaper dealer apron pouch. I back around the newsstand and head toward the car, paper carefully folded.

"Pop, fast enough?"

"Like *Bold Ruler* coming down the top of the stretch in 1957."

"Man, I wish I could've seen him. All those records."

"He was a great horse, a horse with class."

My old man talks about horses like they're human beings, and I'm surprised about how much passion he has for them and how little he shows for people. Anger, plenty of that, more than enough to go around three or four times. To him, my brother is not even human; he's a *geechie*, something my brother and I both have never heard before. Smiles and giddiness ran riot as we got under the covers of the top bunk of our bed. *Geechie* we would say imitating his low raspy voice. It sounded funny, so we had to laugh. *Geechie* sounded like it could be both good and bad but not totally bad. It was the *y* or *ie* sound at the end of the word. We didn't even know how to spell it. We inquired among our friends about the word *geechie*. No one, white, black, or brown ever heard of it. After years of inquiry, we're convinced that it's an Italian curse word that goes back to his days as a bookmaker for the mob. He got in deep, and according to my mom, it was another case of him being the only one, the only Negro the mob would let handle their bookmaking operations. He was a Negro, not a moolie, and they called him Stan. He picked the horses, and they bet on them. It was a tricky business. My brother and I were sure that *geechie* was one of those Italian curse words. *Geechie* this, *geechie* that, he never called me this, and I was happy. It was his last resort and retort. With a twist of anger and dismissive contempt on his face, it would come out, low and mean, like a radial saw blade that starts to bind up because the wood is damp. "You lowlife *geechie* piece of trash" or "You *geechie* bastard." Surveying a project that my brother was putting a great deal of time and effort into my father would assess it and not shake his head but would say, "You're a real *geechie*." *Geechie*.

My father's sense of race and racism was impenetrable, disquieting, and hinted at a tormented man. Born in Virginia, spending seven years there and then moving to Harlem during the Great Migration, he grows up a native of New York City and is only remotely conscious of his connections to the South since he refuses to visit his relatives in Front Royal. To board the train at Pennsylvania Station in 1934 and sit anywhere he chooses, but to then be informed in Baltimore, that he has to move to the "car for colored" is not even a possibility. He would rather drive or not go at all. He doesn't go at all and is able to shun that segregated world for many years. It's only when World War II begins and even then for a year or two, he doesn't comprehend that in America, one's future, despite his race's advancement and progress can still be undermined by dormant and regressive elements of history. My father thought he beat the South and its racism. Confident that he would never see a Jim Crow restaurant, hotel, or any other public facility, he basked in the relative freedom of movement obtainable to him in New York City. He was living an unreal existence with his membership in the Communist Party where whites and blacks valued him. He lived his unreal existence with his white wife whom he was married to in 1936 and will stay married to for the next forty-one years in relative social peace. Whatever privations he has endured in Harlem, Brooklyn, and Jamaica, Queens, there was just nothing that could have prepared him for the world of Georgia. However, Georgia is far away in 1941, very far away.

Initially overjoyed after Pearl Harbor because of the prospects of the United States joining the Allied effort against the Axis, he calls my mother from Washington, D.C. They were estranged during 1941, and my mother remained in New York City while my father went to Washington to find work in the Government Printing Office. Their expensive long-distance calls from Washington to New York are always short. However, on the evening of December 7, 1941, my father doesn't call collect and is prepared to drop quarter after quarter into the coin box. Despite all of their personal problems, racial animosity because they are an interracial couple, tensions between in-laws which are ameliorated once both families start to meet each other and become acquainted, they have weathered the Great Depression and five years of marriage. It's inevitable; there were breakups and separations. My father is confident that this Sunday night his testimony regarding this monumental and historic event that has occurred in a place he's never heard of, Pearl Harbor, will help reinitiate contact with my mother. They hadn't spoken for months at a time. Just, "How's work? Family? What do you think of that new tenor saxophonist for Duke, Ben Webster? Have you heard him blow yet? I'm learning to use printing machines that use inks, no more black-and-white offset. There was a girl just like you the other night at a demonstration, outside of the theater that keeps showing *Gone With the Wind*."

Tonight is different. Something magical has happened. A fantasy has come true that will dissipate five years of frustration and despair, and deem the five protracted years of enduring the fascist takeover in Spain worthwhile. Besides enduring the Great Depression and separations and racial slights at some restaurants, movie theaters where they're not permitted to sit together and have to compare notes at the end of each film, they also have had the stamina to withstand the great isolation. They have lived through the period during which the United States has been unequivocally unperceptive, not heeding any current event that might prick its conscience to take action against evil: the invasion of China in 1931, Mussolini's violation of Ethiopia in 1935, Franco's plundering of Spain in 1936 and the hulking nexus of fascism, Nazi Germany, which mutates geometrically, commencing in 1933. Demonstration after demonstration, rally after rally, from Manhattan to Brooklyn and then back to Union Square and 14th Street, they are tramping and giving out pamphlets for one reason. To wake America up before it's too late. The rise of right-wing dictatorships is not just an abstraction to them. They have personal friends who have joined the Abraham Lincoln Brigade and have gone to Madrid, Barcelona, and the Yampa Valley.

Harlem swings with jazz and rallies for the Communist Party; the C.P. has the best parties and dances and that's where they met, at a C.P. dance at a YMCA on Carlton Avenue in Brooklyn. Black Harlemites enlist, not in the American army, but in the Republican Forces, the Loyalists, set to do combat with Franco's Guernica-bombing brutes. Some are killed, and Harlem mourns these young black men who have traveled so far from Harlem, the crossroads of black America to die in Spain fighting for people and causes that seem disassociated and foreign to some residents of the "Main Drag of Many Tears," 125th Street, or others who labor and live on "Big Red With the Long Green Stem," Seventh Avenue. Not since the 369th Infantry Regiment's triumphant return to Harlem in 1919, Harlem's segregated National Guard unit that won so many medals and commendations for its heroic service in World War I, not since that day when they marched up Fifth Avenue to Harlem, has black America had any connection with the military establishment that generates a sense of self-esteem or celebration. The Army and the Navy (the Marine Corps refuses any black applicants peremptorily) during this time period are just overt symbols of how grotesque America is. America's ties with apartheid run deep, and at times seek to contaminate other nations and continents. When the 369th first landed in France in 1918, War Department officials quietly asked the French if they perhaps could accommodate us, our peculiar manners, and segregate their bars, restaurants, and trolley cars. The French don't even reply. Those are the insulting and humiliating memories for all the black New York City veterans that last long after 1919. However, when blacks join the Abraham Lincoln Brigade in 1936, there's a real sense of self-respect and pride as Harlemites read of the exploits of their neighbors in Richard Wright's columns for the *Daily Worker*.

There's a sense of shame too, at least for my mother and father. It's hard to be proud Americans knowing that the United States is committed to a stance of unparalleled neutrality; this neutrality injures the health and welfare of certain nations and their peoples, leaving others curiously unscathed. This is hard to fathom. Once World War II begins, my mother and father are positive that this *America First* attitude will vanish in days, weeks, and then months. When they watch London blitzed in 1940 and comprehend that the United States' platform of sentimental ignorance and isolation may result in one of the great nations of the world being pummeled, they are in true despair. That sense of impotence is deepened after June 22, 1941, since that's the day that the Nazis roll into their beloved Union of Soviet Socialist Republics. Their Communist Party meetings grow frantic and depressing. It's one thing to be a witness to England dying; England is the mother of colonialism and imperialism. But the USSR? Something has to be done. A second front has to be opened up to aid them in their struggle with the invading German armies. When my father hears that the Japanese have bombed Pearl Harbor, he can't bear the next few days waiting for the United States to declare war on the Axis powers. That's inevitable. He calls my mother wanting to celebrate. There will be a "Second Front." The United States will tap all of its power, material as well as human, the 13,000,000 unemployed; ships will be made and tanks will be coming off the automobile production lines instead of Chevrolets. This is the perfect opportunity for a rapprochement for an estranged husband and wife, two estranged comrades. My father makes the call:

Stan: Hello, Pops, it's me.

Marilyn: Yes, I can hear you. You needn't shout.

Stan: I'm not shouting because of that. I'm shouting because the most important thing in the world just happened.

Marilyn: I thought you called up to talk about us.

Stan: Pops, this is bigger than that. This is the most important event of our lives, the 1930s, I mean, 1940s, maybe the twentieth century.

Marilyn: The only important thing is what's not happening between us. What are we going to do about our relationship?

Stan: Pops, I'm talking about Pearl Harbor. The Japanese have just bombed Pearl Harbor. This is stupendous, the second front. Military aid to the Soviet Union. America's going to supply the Soviet Union with arms, weapons, food, everything.

Marilyn: I don't give a damn about any Pearl Harbor and don't call again until you're ready to discuss our relationship.

My mother hung up the phone, and my father had only so many quarters.

Geechie. For years it eludes us; decades go by, and I never hear any other human being utter it, not even a word that sounds remotely close to it. It fades away out of my consciousness until one evening I'm in a Manhattan movie theater. My wife and I had gone to see a film that I had wished I had seen when it was still a play on Broadway performed by the Negro Ensemble Company. Whenever I drove a cab past the marquee of the theater, I would say to myself, "Better see *A Soldier's Play* before it moves, flops or becomes a film." For whatever reason that didn't happen. When you're driving a cab at night and teaching as an adjunct professor in the day, a theater ticket is a bit of a luxury. That's why Eleanor and I were watching it after it had undergone its transformation into the Hollywood production, *A Solder's Story.* The film had a paralyzing effect on me as soon as I realized that my father, although dead for seven years, was alive, right there up on the screen with Adolph Caesar playing him. I shivered. I shuddered. My wife knew I was having a hard time because she searched in the darkness and found my hand a few times to comfort me. When we walked out of the theater, I'm so ill that Eleanor offers to drive, but first we must get a drink. I am sick. She's right. I had figured out what *geechie* meant. It's not an Italian curse word that they've held onto in their small environs of Mott and Mulberry. It's not a funny word because it ends in *y* or *ie. Geechie* is the same word that the vindictive sergeant used in the film whenever he wished to refer in a derogatory manner to the black soldiers from the South. And it has nothing to do with being a soldier.

The first time Adolph Caesar uses the word, it's to tell a soldier that he's less than human, that he's somehow a mutant throwback reminiscent of the missing link between civilized man and his primitive ancestors. Adolph Caesar as Sergeant Waters is unrelenting in his pursuit of C.J. Memphis, one particular southern soldier whose provincial rural background and "down-home Negroness" he perceives to be an offense to him and to all progressive black men who are battling white racism. My ears and head take a pounding as I hear the word repeated over and over again, so there is no ambivalence. I can't fool myself into thinking that I am hearing something and misconstruing it. *Geechie,* again and again: "low-class *geechie,*" "the day of the *geechie* is over," and "I got two *geechies* in Fort Campbell and three in Fort Huachuca." *Geechie:* it evokes some kind of primitive malignancy that should have been left behind on the shores of Africa or at least should have been lashed out of you during the Middle Passage. Your last opportunity to relinquish your uncivilized junglelike behavior was during slavery. If it did not succumb to the domesticating conditions of slavery, you were truly hopeless and should be vanquished.

Caesar's Sergeant Waters kills a southern soldier because, "You're a shame to the black race . . . we don't need white folks thinking we're all a bunch of fools because of you." As I hold Eleanor's warm hand and feel nauseous, I wish I wasn't there in the theater and wish I were somewhere else. I've never been sick in public but it's coming; these revelations are a dramatic avalanche that can't be stopped. It's indigestible, and as the credits of the film roll over a bedrock of patriotic music I'm wondering how will I ever be able to explain this to her, as I vomit part of my soul out, how will a white woman comprehend this? I'm wondering if I will be able to look my brother in the eye and see his pain. I had told him to see the film before I had viewed it based on the critics. How would he feel while he sits in the film and realizes that our father found him an offense to civilization. How will that be encountered? My brother has heard so many things, things designed to maim but not kill, but now I see the killing part was there.

"Paul," my father intoned with the most serious nuances, "You're never going to be anything. That's obvious. Because of that I have a suggestion, a very relevant one. Relevancy is the key here. You should go up to the train station, Locust Manor, you know, on the Long Island Railroad. It's easier than you think. Stay at the end where the train enters. Right when you see the train coming, just step in front of it and all of your troubles will be over. That's all you have to do. Your pain will be over in a second, you lowlife *geechie*." My father had recommended that with the same coolness that he offered someone advice about the advantages of a straight six motor versus a V-8. I laughed when he told him that, but I was scared since he had shown no emotion at the beginning, middle, or end of those words.

My brother had gotten into trouble. Maybe school, maybe the neighborhood, or just his own homespun version of crime. My father was fatigued with my brother's antics and was convinced that my brother was crazy. He told him that, "You're crazy, you know. There's really nothing that can be done for you. Your mother and I have done all we can possibly do." Offering him a long-drawn-out list of all the rational approaches that had been taken with him, my father was sanguine about

his psychological analysis. Maybe that's why my laughter was the classic anxiety-ridden type. He framed it in social and political terms and in
a way that was destined to make my brother madder than he ever could
have been. In that same rational and methodical manner, he spoke with
perverse buoyancy in his voice. The rhetoric of a sadist was there in,
"Paul, you see, you've got choices right in front of you. Be a constructive Negro or hang out with your spook friends. Look around you. Why
are you so determined to be a spook? This isn't 1910. You have opportunities that I never dreamed of. You can apply for jobs and colleges
that I only could have dreamed about. I was a Negro at the wrong time.
I couldn't even put in the applications. Yes, they wouldn't even give you
the application. It wasn't a question of them throwing it out later after
you left the office. They would look at you as soon as you walked in the
door; as soon as they knew that you weren't there to run the elevator or
wash or cook, they would say, 'No, thank you.' You know, I graduated
from Brooklyn Tech in 1931 and was never able to get a job based on
that training. You know how prestigious that school is? Even now you
know. I graduated from there an expert draftsman. I could have been a
designer, an architect. It's 1965 and they just passed a law about discrimination. Look at you. You're handsome, a good-looking Negro, and
yet you want to be a *geechie*. Why? Just tell me that because I want to
understand. Why would a Negro from a good home with good parents
in 1965 want to be a *geechie*? That's why I'm suggesting what I'm suggesting. Long Island Railroad, the station down on Farmers Boulevard,
just step out in front of it. Boom, your pain is over and our pain will be
over and you'll stop torturing your mother and me. Because that's what
it is, what you're doing to us, here in the house. You're trying to kill us."

All those years. My brother's a *geechie* and the thoroughbred race-
horses are . . . that's where the care and attention is. The horses. They
are his favorite sons. So of course, I'm conscious of anything he says
about them; my humanity antenna is up because I want to know and
understand if there is another side of him. There is. It's just not about
human beings. However, he talks about them all the time, "He's a young
horse; he's afraid of the fence. That's why he's nervous." A horse. Or,
"It's going to be tough on her; they added extra weight." A horse. Or,
"Shuvee is sensitive; she doesn't like to start on the outside post like
that." A horse. It was amazing. Whether they won or lost, I could see
this wasn't the reason he was there. The monetary rewards were normal

as with any other type of gambling. You won every now and then, lost most of the time but you had that fifty-dollar horse come in every now and then that left you with a sense of wonderment and triumph that you were reinitiated into another round of betting and losing. When we won like that, my father would buy two fried chicken dinners with french fries, and say, "We deserve this after all that hard work and anxiety." When we lost, Hershey Bars with almonds.

There was something distinctive and unique about him being at the track, and it had to do with being black. Took me a long time to figure this out. Just recently as a matter or fact. When I was younger and started accompanying him to Belmont Park, I just remarked to myself that he was involved in something rather esoteric. I have never been to any place like it since. The track. Big, open, angular, a mixture of modern-day architecture, coexisting with trees and grass from the 19th century. You're in a park, a beautiful bucolic park. That's the word: bucolic. You're well aware that you're participating or at least observing some rite of social intercourse from another era in history. The colors are immense, particularly in the fall. I get to know the pattern of colors because there is plenty of time to take in the place and study it. Between each race, which only lasts about a minute or two, there is a break of about a half hour. In autumn, oranges, reds, and yellows blaze from the ancient trees and the grass has that unparalleled green that one will only see at a track. The track has reddish brown dirt that looks so good that you could eat it. Like frosting on a cake. Things are groomed to immaculate perfection. Groundskeepers at Belmont Park make the guys who take care of Yankee stadium look strictly plebian.

When we go, my father dresses for his role. Suit or sports coat, always a tie, fedora hat and the crown jewel, a classic gray *Casablanca* raincoat, like Bogey wears when he says adieu to Ilsa at the airport with Claude Rains looking on. I didn't know that this was the official uniform of the fan or bettor until one time I got lost and even though he might have been the only black man there among twenty thousand people in that outfit, there were so many other possible candidates with the exact same outfit; I couldn't find him for about an hour. And now I think that is what he wanted. To divine one place in America where a black person could be and not be black or Negro. He wanted to be invisible but not in that Ralph Ellison way. He wanted to blend in. He wanted that public place where he could be Stanley Diaz.

My brother and I had suggested other public places that would have permitted us to enjoy ourselves and feel like we were participating in America. How many times did my brother and I ask him to take us to a baseball game and he peremptorily crushed this request: "No, I don't like baseball." At first we pressed him and decided to use the whining appeal of, "Can't we just go to one game, one game a year?" No, baseball was an unacceptable alternative. Painful. My brother and I would look at each other in complete bafflement. The Yankees had practically established a dynasty in the early 1960s. Roger Maris, Mickey Mantle, what could be painful about seeing gods worthy of the ancient Olympics. The Yanks were unbeatable. We two tag teamed him and tried to persuade him to go. My brother would start with, "Dad, how come we never go to a baseball game? Everyone else does." I would join in and continue the harangue, "Pop, we'll be good. We'll be good for the whole week and we'll be good at the game."

My father's expression wouldn't alter during these pleas. He just kept smoking or chewing a piece of Juicy Fruit gum. Out of left field came, "You guys don't understand. It's painful to watch baseball because a Negro doesn't have any opportunity." This had us perplexed when we were younger but by the 1960s my brother Paul was prepared with a historical update. Paul countered that with, "Dad, come on. Baseball's been integrated since 1947. Jackie Robinson, Roy Campanella, Larry Doby of the Cleveland Indians. Negroes are in both leagues." We weren't ready for my father's outburst that came as a rejoinder to this seemingly innocent and innocuous request. My brother knew his sports history, and we both prided ourselves on knowing the important role of Negroes in sports, especially the first, the first Negro to do this, the first Negro to do that. "Jackie Robinson, don't mention that Uncle Tom's name to me. Not in this house. Do you know how many picket lines your mother and I walked so that Uncle Tom Negro could play at Ebbets Field? What do you think; he did that all by himself? He had plenty of Negroes and whites and political people getting their heads split so he could sign that contract so he could play in 1947. Do you know how that Negro paid us back for all that pain and suffering? Nothing. Nada. No acknowledgment. He forgot about us. When he needed us out there at the demonstration, we're his friends. When it came time to do something for us, forgotten. When it comes time to be a man and go to Washington D.C. and not testify, that Uncle Tom gets his handkerchief out and is ready to sing *Mammy* if he had to. Jackie Robinson, that backstabbing sonofabitch. Baseball, I don't want to hear it; I don't care if another Negro plays for the major leagues for the rest of my life." We were silent. We had to be. This anger united with his history left us barren and empty. Take me out to the ball game became take me out to the racetrack and it just wasn't the same.

The history of baseball was racially ugly for him, and the history of the track, if there was such a thing in sociological terms, was neutral or positive. When he was there, there were no veils and shadows. Sometimes we were the only nonwhite people in an entire section of hundreds of people and in a mezzanine containing thousands of people. Within those thousands and within those hundreds my dad blended in and talked, conversed, and even held forth. He always demonstrated restraint since if one talked too much about his theories about winning and losing, he might reveal some very precious secrets. Men with raincoats and fedoras exchanged talk, gossip and analysis with other men in raincoats and fedoras. Because he was so sensitive to any racial slight, when I first started to accompany him to Belmont and Aqueduct, I thought we were doomed to a racial confrontation. My father knew how to make these things happen and in retrospect, I'm sure he played his own role in being an *agent provocateur.*

One of his lithography friends recalled an incident in a small bar in Brooklyn to me twenty years after it occurred. The story was told with respect and awe. Tolliver was one of the few black lithographers who had been through the glory days of organizing the local and the union and getting decent pay and wages. My father did not have a batch of friends from the war years. No buddies who came over once a year or every couple of years to recall their service overseas. For him the war had already been fought here, organizing the labor force during the 1930s. Tolliver was that type of comrade. Tall, black, with a slightly pockmarked face and a mustache, he was handsome and anytime he did visit he had his wife, a girlfriend the next time, his wife the next time, and then a girlfriend.

"Dex, are you kidding? You don't know Stan!" he exclaimed in reaction to my saying how quiet and reserved my father was. "Stan, you never told Dex the time we were fighting those Puerto Ricans in that bar?" My father shook his head and continued to sip his beer from those small glasses that are almost the size of your hand. He continued, "Dex, your father doesn't like Puerto Ricans; no, it's not that he doesn't like them. It's a . . . er . . . and he imitated my father's manner of speech, 'They don't have any culture.' " The story continued with that remark that just made me wonder more about just how convoluted my father could be when it came to race and racism. "So, Dex, your old man and I are in this Brooklyn bar, little dump, drinking a few beers and your father whispers to me 'Did you hear that?' I looked around the place, and there were a couple of Spanish people, and I just said, 'Nothing. What's up?' Dex, your father proceeds to tell me that the Puerto Ricans at the bar are talking in Spanish about us and calling us the equivalent of nigger. I look around at the people, and they don't even seem like they're interested in us. Couldn't care less. Next thing I know, your dad has punched a Puerto Rican who goes flying off his stool, down this little bar into the door. No big thing. The guy comes at us but now he's backed by a buddy or two who are pissed off. Your dad decks one of these guys, and we can't believe that when this guy hits the deck, a little gun comes flying out of his pocket. Goddamn, I go get it. Whole bar clears out. Everyone's gone except the bartender. I put my coat on, ready to hightail it out of there and your dad, you know what the hell he's doing?" I shook my head as Tolliver unraveled a battle story, and I wished I could drink a beer with both of them, my old man and Tolliver.

My father has been quiet during this retelling. There are no real expressions of emotion on his face. Tolliver stands up to bring the story to a close. He starts to reenact how he pleaded with my father to "Come on, let's get the hell out of the bar." The gun was given to the bartender for safekeeping. My old man won't budge, telling Tolliver that as an American citizen he has a right to drink this beer and even order another one if he wants to. Alarmed at the prospects for getting out of this little tavern unscathed, Tolliver starts to panic when the bartender tells him that's there's a crowd of Puerto Ricans outside. With a quick look through the red neon sign that flashes Schaeffer, Tolliver sees that there was a crowd of people who are yelling and milling around. The bartender is black, but Tolliver gets him to go outside with him and translate what is being yelled as a chant in Spanish. They open the door cautiously and a bottle comes crashing into it. With one hand waving and indicating that this is a peace entreaty, the owner of the place goes outside and the crowd quiets down. He walks over and says a few words. As he walks back with an occasional look over his shoulder for any more flying missiles, he goes back in the doorway. The closer he comes to the doorway, the louder the chant becomes.

When Tolliver comes back in, my father asks why the strange face and what are the Puerto Ricans chattering about. Tolliver doesn't laugh and says, "Stan, they're yelling, according to Joe, 'we want the old man.' " With a laugh, he keeps drinking his beer. He finally talks, "Tolliver, go out there and tell them they have to come in here and get me." Tolliver is completely animated now. "Dex, do you believe that? Twenty to thirty Puerto Ricans yelling for your father, he's cool as a cucumber, and he sends me outside." I was pretty excited and enthralled at this point and to rush the story, asked what happened? How the heck did you guys get out of this jam?

With it being 1975 and the incident occurring in 1965, he can now laugh and he does. Tolliver laughs as he says, "Well, I go outside. Tell the Puerto Ricans what they don't want to hear, that your old man isn't coming out. They start kicking the crap out of me. On my back, on my neck. I'm just flailing away and hoping that I hit something every time I take a swing. But they're getting the best of me, and I hit the ground. They really start giving it to me. Kicks, pointed Puerto Rican shoes, oh man, a guy gives me a shot right in the temple, you see that mark, yeah, that's it, right there, a Puerto Rican alligator shoe got me. I'm starting to think this is it. Punches, kicks, no letup, and now I'm just hugging a guy's legs and hoping that he sees that I'm finished and he'll say, hey, take it easy, this guy's finished. No. They keep on and I'm just feeling the thuds. Then the thuds slow down a bit. Instead of three per second, it's two per second, and then, I feel like there's a space clearing above me. I don't know what's going on. Then no thuds. I turn my head, I'm still on all fours, I look up, you know what I see? Jesus, there's your old man, throwin' bricks at these people like hand grenades. And he's hitting 'em, yeah, right in the head, each and every one. No misses. The Puerto Ricans can't believe it because within a few seconds, with three, four guys down, and two to three guys needed to carry each one away, there's almost nobody left. Yeah, Dexter, he's throwing these bricks, and they're hittin' these people in the head or the chest and they're just falling like flies. He runs over, scoops me up, puts me in the car and we take off."

I look at my father, the troublemaker and wonder and smile. He's finally laughing and smiling. The story is not over yet. Tolliver is laughing and almost spitting up his beer. Tears are coming into his eyes. After catching his breath, he takes a rest and sets the question in his mind. "Stan, seriously, I always wanted to ask you something, really, all these years, well, ten, more or less, it's been bothering me. Where, where the hell did you get all those bricks?" My father is prepared to reveal a secret, one of the few he's ever laid ownership to. He explains that when he ran to the back of the bar to look for a way out, he found that the place was under renovation and there was just a fresh pile of bricks back there. He had methodically brought them forward in a few trips to the front of the bar so he wouldn't run out of any ammunition.

"The horses are approaching the gate for the eighth race," were the words I heard more than once. Or the ninth race. My old man never went to the track for the first seven races since those were the ones that he felt were relegated for the suckers, the short odds, and the sure things. He wanted no part of that. There was no challenge to figuring out "Maiden Claiming Races" for two-year-old fillies. There was no challenge for any race involving juvenile horses. The real challenge occurred after the seventh race was over because there were now going to be the allowance races and claiming races. These contests were not so simple, and the odds were not as predictable, and plenty of horses came all the way from out of nowhere and ended up in that winner's circle, and that is where he wanted to be. The crowd had thinned out. Men and women with hardened faces thinking about their rent and their car payments had more to live, bet and suffer for. Desperate looks for desperate people. My old man, not a hint of fear or trepidation. His *Morning Telegraph* has come out of his inside suit pocket. Like a secret agent he's kept his double-breasted raincoat with belt closed all this time. It comes open with a flourish. He peers down at the totals board and asks me if I can give him the odds for the "Six horse." Sometimes he doesn't want to put on his glasses or he has forgotten them in the car. I rattle off with accuracy, "Five to one, Pop, seventeen to one, Pop, Pop, you're not going to believe this, that number six horse, thirty to one, I'm positive, thirty to one." The broadest grin is on his face. He takes out his yellow legal pad paper and makes some last minute calculations.

This is what he wants and desires. No one else but a few other scattered patrons in the crowd of twenty thousand knows what he knows. That horse that has come from California. The horse that doesn't like the mud but has won at shorter distances and this being a shorter distance, this is his day.

To make sure that I don't have the numbers incorrect, he asks for another reading of the odds but this time by name. I take out my program which makes me an official participant and conspirator and read as though I'm announcing the race myself, "Zarco, eight to one; Shelter Bay, three to one; Elephant Walk, ten to one; Irish Party, five to one; Hydronaut, six to one; Big Shot second, thirty to one; Minksy, five to one, Pop, he's by Northern Dancer, that's good breeding, right?" My father says nothing, as he doesn't like me to break the routine with commentary. I return to my duties and end with, "The Pruner, eight to one, and Wilkinson, fifteen to one." There is a chill in the air because it's late October and long shadows are cast at Belmont Park. The last ray of sunshine hits a horse's velvety red coat, and it shimmers in your eyes. The jockey reaches down and gives him a pat of confidence. My father, silent, as he watches the horses pass in review. Quiet. Silence. Pen scratching on paper. "Dex, who's riding Elephant Walk?" Without having to refer to the program because I've memorized all of the horses and their jockeys, I blurt, out, "Robyn C. Smith, Pop, the woman." He nods his head and says, "She has a good record. You're going to see more women jockeys." Quiet. Silence. The raincoat comes open; he reaches in his inside jacket pocket for his wallet. He looks at me, and it's too much to look into his eyes, so I just look to his lips as they say, "Dex, put twenty on the six horse to win." With as much gravity as I can muster at eighteen, I repeat, "Twenty on the six horse to win." That's it. He never bets on the horses to come in second or third, to place or to show. He claims that requires no brains.

Whenever I walked away, he had taught me to take one last look at him in case he changed his mind at the last second because of the ever-altering odds board. I would turn around, look at him up a few rows, and check. He would be talking by that time. His coat was buttoned back up and his fedora was deftly placed on his head. White men were talking with him and he was at peace. Irish, Italian, Jew, Wasp, even Puerto Rican, there they were, all dressed the same and talking from the book, the racehorse book. Maybe it was because they were horses? The horses were all the same. Up in those stands with row after row of green wooden seats, race disappeared, and the most consuming problems were which horse had the best shot, the best chance, or no chance. I never heard or felt the pain that wrenched his body in so many other places. Bars, restaurants, gas stations, baseball stadiums. Those places made him crane his neck and put his racial antenna way up, as Tolliver had proven to me in that long, sad, and funny narrative. My father heard things even when there was nothing to be heard. At the track, all he ever heard was that trumpet, that pure golden trumpet that the steward in white pants and red jacket blew with such urgency, announcing that the "Horses are on the track" and soon they would be off.

Duke's in Fargo, North Dakota

———⋙⊶((◉))⊷⋘———

DID YOU EVER hear Ben Webster take a tenor sax solo? It could be the one after Rex Stewart on their 1941 recording of *Linger Awhile*. There's another one where Ben rides beneath Ivie Anderson as she rocks through a rolling version of *St. Louis Blues*. When the recording was made, the band was on a road trip, way out there, in a place called Fargo, Fargo, North Dakota, 1940. White people from a long time ago. They really never did see another black person before. And yet the band played on. I sometimes wonder if that era of black people will receive the same accolades that a current news commentator has applied to white people from the same time period. Just for what they endured.

The Ellington band had come down from a previous night's playing in Winnipeg, Manitoba. They had taken a train down from Canada and were now in Fargo, at the Crystal Ballroom. The music had started at eight, and they were playing their last number, the grand finale. Ben backed Ivie up with some obbligato in the most wonderful way and then plowed through a most ferocious version of that W.C. Handy classic. Chorus after chorus, blasting, climbing, jumping and the whole time the vibrato from his reed makes you think that just prior to the show, he had taken a piece of plywood due to an emergency and with a single-edged razor blade, fashioned a reed. How else could you get that astonishing sound out of that tenor sax? During the course of three fiery solos you hear more black anger and solace than in any piece of jazz. The reed threatens to split; even finished wood has its limits. He honks a few times and when friends of mine listen to this, they mistake his blasting sound for another instrument. They'll say, "I never heard a trumpet like that before." Or "I didn't know that a trombone could sound that way." Or, "Did they invent some special kind of sax during that era?" No, Ben was just Ben and even when he held that tenor in his hands, he was so much a bear of a black man that it looked like an alto. Ben Webster, the man who would comb his mother's hair when she was an elderly woman. What does all that mean? There's the Ben who played with Jimmy Blanton as he strummed that bass in a revolutionary way. There's another Ben who gets into an altercation with Duke Ellington, so disquieting that Ellington will never appear in the same studio or on the same album with him again.

I met Ben about a year before he died. It was my first purchase, my first record. I never bought records when I was young. I wouldn't even buy a 45-rpm even though they were what made my generation sing and dance. My brother and sister took care of that and the house was filled with that music. The double album jumped out at me with big purple letters stating that it had chronicled *The Commodore Years: The Tenor Sax: Lester Young, Chu Berry & Ben Webster.*

This was the beginning of my active connection and excavation of jazz, black culture, and black life from a time that was quickly vanishing. This exploration became so intense and dramatic that I was pulled from my world of 1973 and lived in 1943, 1933, anything but 1973. There was no longer any reason to think about Sly and the Family Stone, Hendrix, the Beatles, Marvin Gaye, and Aretha. I had found Ben and when you find him, you go back to the roots, the essence. There was emphatically no longer any reason to listen, to study, to waste one more minute of one's time on anything that was a derivative or extension of the original concept. By the summer of 1973 I knew that rock and roll, was such a derivation. Jazz came first. I was mining the roots of black history and culture. What a quandary to be in! I was falling behind my peers by years, decades and soon scores. They were, in 1973, still depressed about the breakup of the Beatles. I was dwelling in late 1940 and was terribly upset about how Cootie Williams left Duke Ellington just when he had assembled what was to be the greatest jazz orchestra in jazz history. Every seat in the band had been filled with a genius. It was the equivalent of having Mozart, Hayden, Ludwig von, Stravinski, Bach, Ravel, and some other classical cats all in the same symphonic space. I mourned an event that I was born a dozen years after.

"Cootie to Leave Duke" the headlines had read. Why? Cootie, why would you leave? You're sitting next to Rex Stewart. You've got Johnny Hodges playing alto, Ben playing tenor, Lawrence Brown on trombone, and Barney Bigard on clarinet. And if that is not enough, you've got Sonny Greer on drums and of all things, of all occasions, you've got young Jimmy Blanton on bass, and he's only going to live a few more months, so Cootie, what the hell is wrong with you? Why leave Duke? Duke, the guy writes, *Ridin' on a Blue Note* just for you. You're so dear to him he pens another classic *Concerto for Cootie,* also known as *Do Nothin' Till You Hear From Me.* Brilliant black men working in tandem with other brilliant black men. Where else can you play in a jazz band where the genius of jazz composition, Maestro Ellington, creates individual pieces for each guy in each section of the orchestra? Jesus, Cootie. To leave Duke just like that. Damn.

Out of place again. I had known this feeling in terms of race, and now I was going to understand from a new perspective. The person who looks around and says to himself, *this is not my world,* is in constant angst. Nothing can remediate it. If you want it to be 1940 and it's now 1970, well, you're in a jam. The contrast is always there and you are sharply aware of it.

But the comfort in it—that was why I went there. And perhaps there was a racial impetus or motive to it. I wanted to be with black people that I could like and liked me. Luckily because of my acting abilities and my lack of commitment to any one regime I lived in my world without the rest of the universe detecting my treachery. Even the most complicated chord progression of rock and roll didn't compete with Ellington's *Mood Indigo,* or the score he had expressly written for Rex Stewart called *Boy Meets Horn.* It was rather easy to hum and have access to rock, Mick Jagger and Simon and Garfunkle and me still totally committed to Duke, Johnny, and Ben.

The world was complete because there was even a language, and I needed a way to express myself if I were to proceed on this journey to other worlds, leaving 1973 behind. Without a new language, I wouldn't be able to tell what I've seen on my odyssey. I commence to immerse myself like some monkish historian for days and weeks, not to be seen or heard from. Weekends blurred from Friday afternoons when I left Dr. Sallinger's office back into Monday with classes again. Whenever I returned my friends were positive that I'd been away since I greet them with, "What's the story, morning glory?" If they retort with the standard response like "What's happening" or the ever-exotic Que Pasa? I retort with something they've never heard before, and they have to smile when I say, "Solid, solid like a block of Vermont marble." They do ask questions, and I tell the truth. If you are going to understand this music, this black method of dealing with the world through melody and language, you have to think like these men and women which means you have to adopt their lingo, Daddy. At first they were humoring me, but once one of my friends hears my story, he starts calling me Gate, one of the many wondrous nicknames for Louis, and I'm Gate to this day. He was Irish and there was something Joycean about not only what I was doing, but also where I was going that reminded him of his own rich, complex, and frozen culture. When we're at an English department party and I tell him that it's time to "Rudolf Hess" this scene, he knows its time to leave inconspicuously. When I tell him "I'm scoffin' fish heads and scrambling for the gills," he's well aware that something bad has occurred in my personal life, and I'm in desperate straits. He's Irish, and he wants to listen and go back there too, and I'm shocked since I didn't see the connection then but do now.

Terry O'Connor, an Irishman from Jamaica, Queens, the same Queens, the same Jamaica, which was white, Italian, German, and black and was ultimately to be just black, had a new sort of soul. He alleviates me of all the pain in my life because he's Irish, a good writer, and when I confess to him as I was in the habit of confessing to all white and black people that I was half this and half that, he says, "Who gives a fuck?" I needed him, needed him bad. I just couldn't live on the charity of Dr. Sallinger. Therapy is like that though. It's easier than you think to just love them, have them become your friends and lovers.

My twisted method of approaching the white world reached its apex during college days. I crept around people so awkwardly that they sometimes asked around to find out what was really going on. When a man is not comfortable with what he's seeing in the mirror every morning, that feeling remains with him for the rest of the day. As the day goes on, he will see all the proof needed to confirm what he needs to hear over and over again, "I'm worthless; I'm a real piece of garbage, and I deserve to be treated accordingly." I'm so uncomfortable with myself that it's inevitable I make others around me feel the same way. The pattern was set by the time I was twenty. Run between both groups, making allegiances and alliances for anywhere from three to six months.

Hang out with whites until I was offended by some insensitivity, joke, or racial remark. It's only now that I realize that with my super-racial antenna I probably was the victim of my own devices on more than one occasion.

The retreat would begin in earnest; after deciding to abandon whites with a fury, I would actively look for black students, new black friends on the campus of Queens College and then discover that there were none. As an English major, I'll never forget that I was the only black student in every class that I ever took. I was desperate and befriended an African student from Senegal once. We found out we had nothing in common. He had contempt for me and who I was. I didn't take it personally but winced when he said, "Dexter, you nigger. Me, black man. You understand? You can never be like me or other African." His English was very poor, but he had assessed one particular aspect of the American racial panorama after being here for a few years and fashioned a reductive formula that informed me that we could never have a relationship. I defended myself quickly with my knowledge of black culture, history, and legacy. I suppose that Franz Fanon's *The Wretched of the Earth* had made an incredible impact on him for he replied, "I know, but still, you only be nigger here in America. Leave maybe, maybe you change? Stay here, nigger only."

I'm also happy in a frenetic way during these times of racial allegiance and betrayal and constant vacillation. I'm a madman that people around me have decided to humor due to the richness of the madness and can see that I have no other way of dealing with my complex racial situation. People are uneasy because I can explode and question in a passive-aggressive manner a gesture, a thought. After three or four tortuous hours of pulling someone through a psychological gothic tour de force, I end it with, "That's why I don't trust white people." An entire weekend can be spent with me welcomed into your life and arms and I'll conclude it with, "Black people don't want to change. All this opportunity and they just want to stay behind."

All that anger and energy had to be displaced, and this was the most constructive outlet that I ever discovered. I was fortunate though because what I mined and excavated was so rich, so extraordinary; I hit a mother lode so resplendent in aesthetic and historic value that I became valuable for the first time, for being me and making something accessible. At the time I was not cognizant that this trip back into the history of jazz and a lot of black people slowly transformed me into a museum curator, preserving something that was about to be forgotten. I make astute and cogent musical parallel lines between Eric Clapton and Jimmy Rushing, that great blues singer for Count Basie. My comrades are tickled with what I bring to them and learn to contradict me only at the beginning of the evening. At that point I'll smile and just pull out an old 78-rpm record and play it and say nothing. Deny me twice and I'll load up the record platter and lecture as each one concludes; I'll teach during that second gap before the next one drops down to make another point that proves, I am, "solid like a block of Vermont marble and I'm cooking with gas and I'm never off the cob."

I walk the walk and talk the talk, and my first published piece of writing is called *The Joint Was Really Jumpin'*. It's a piece written entirely in the jargon of a hipster from the 1940s. Was also one of the first pieces that I ever read aloud in front of an audience, even though it might have only been fellow tutors from the writing skills workshop but that's how we maintained our sanity and cameraderie. We were all English majors, all juniors and seniors, and some of us were participating in the team-teaching program. A very innovative professor had come up with the idea of pairing freshman composition teachers with promising and highly motivated tutors. It was another example of Queens College being at the cutting edge of educational thinking. Some of us did both, team-taught and tutored.

Both activities were demanding and stressful and one way we sought mutual relief was to read to each other. There would always be one cubicle that was empty or that we used to store supplies, which meant it was ours if we didn't mind sitting athwart grammar exercises on how to use the past tense and why a comma comes after the end of a dependent clause. They read and I listened and I liked it. Here were kids creating and exhibiting. I listened some more and knew that I couldn't be a creative writer because my life was far too messy, and I had too many secrets. However, I knew that if my connection to Lester Young, a light skinned black dude who suffered for his complexion, could be elucidated, I would be telling part of mine at the same time.

As soon as I read the liner notes of another double album about Lester's life, I understood that he and my father possessed many parallels, that they both suffered during World War II because they were sent south for training. It was the first key I unearthed that hinted at why my old man was unsettled and disturbed. Prez, as he was known by Billie Holiday and associates, could never adjust to army life. How could he? Can you imagine Yeats taking orders from some surly first sergeant who doesn't like him because he's Irish? That was what happened to Prez. One of the most important and influential jazz musicians of all times was drafted and sent south. He too has his own language; he's one of the original progenitors of jazz slang, be-bop talk, and jive. Lester possessed many words and expressions that had to do with how he felt the world was hurting him, *no eyes, big eyes,* and *bulging eyes;* these words all demonstrated how he felt that just by a look and a gesture one could perceive exactly what was going on. I think that generation of black men had to. It was definitely a requisite skill for survival.

Prez, that tenor saxophone player who held his sax up at a strange and awkward angle, almost like a flute, plays it like a flute. He enrages many jazz purists with his light and airy tone. The world must accept him on his terms and when it does not, he pays a high price. Court-martialed and given a dishonorable discharge, before he's released from the service, he spends almost six months in the stockade. Six months in an army jail. The original charges against him stemmed from a white sergeant who saw a photo of Lester Young's wife who happened to be white. Enraged, this racist soldier commenced a tirade of abuse in the hope of breaking this soft-spoken man who preferred to wear slippers to recording sessions. He broke him. Jazz musicians and critics said, in an evocative and haunting manner, "Prez never played the same after being discharged from the army." They could see that he wasn't the Prez anymore; he had been reduced. My father's image came right up as I read these liner notes. I know he had been sent south; he had been in hell. And he had a picture of his white wife in his footlocker.

Fort Benning, Georgia, is one of the largest army bases. It's a case of an institution being the center of the universe. Some tentacle of the army connects everyone for fifty square miles. Of course, the town, Albany, only thrives because of its symbiotic relationship to the base. My father's entrance into the war is delayed despite his commitment to the Communist Party which has been demanding a Second Front since June 22, 1941. He mouths the words *Open Up a Second Front* at plenty of demonstrations but doesn't embrace the thought behind the words. He wants to. He had thought about going to Spain back in 1937. It would have been too much literary irony, perhaps. A black man, a Negro, with the last name Diaz, whose stepfather is a Cuban from Havana, would have reversed the path of history. He wanted to join in what Churchill poignantly described in 1941 as "the struggle, until, in God's good time, the New World, with all its power and might, steps forth to the rescue and the liberation of the old." However, he cannot.

With the Germans at the gates of his surrogate political homeland, pounding away at Leningrad, and with Paul Robeson singing the most inspiring version of *Homeland* that you will ever hear, my father should have been at the recruiting station on December 8, 1941; 1941 passes, 1942, 1943, and if the judge had ruled in his favor, maybe he never would have been fitted for an olive drab uniform. Somewhere, in a file drawer, is a case, mimeographed copies, that state to the effect *U.S. vs. Stanley Diaz, docket number #723584.* The charges are evading the draft. My father wanted to fight and be on that second front, but his refusal to go was a matter of principle. He told me this a few times. Based on his reading of the Constitution, a "Jim Crow army violated the 13th, 14th, and 15th amendments and therefore I shouldn't have had to serve in the Armed Forces of the United States of America because of this gross infringement of my rights." Stanley Diaz is not a conscientious objector; he is not against war and believes that there is no other way to stop fascism but armed struggle. However, he will not make any contribution to a war effort that aids and abets racist and pernicious practices. The same legal organization that helped to defend the Scottsboro boys in the notorious rape case, the ILO, became his advocate and informed him that even if he lost the case, it was good publicity for the party. It would be a political triumph in any case since it made the federal government vulnerable to the allegations of the existence of racism in one of its most vulnerable institutions. There are hearings, delays, but there is impatience on the part of the authorities. They do not view this exercise in political melodrama entertaining or as a frivolous diversion. With one last appeal denied, he is told to report for active duty or go to prison.

It's bad but not as bad as it could have been. He's drafted into the Air Corps and of all the branches this one has the most liberal policy in regard to the treatment of "colored troops" There is almost an air of civility and compassion in the following excerpt from a chapter from *The Officer's Guide,* 1941:

America is a composite nation embracing many distinct elements. The great national melting pot has not yet made us one homogeneous people with easily distinguished national characteristics. This fact adds greatly to the difficulty of the American officer. It is a well-known fact that in our army that some officers who succeed admirably with white troops fail entirely when they come on duty with our negro soldiers. This is due to the fact that they do not understand the negro character, and success comes more frequently to an officer when he is managing men with whose characteristics he is entirely familiar . . . In our country all men are equal. . . .

My father's war stories emanate from this milieu, one where race is at the center.

These are my father's war stories, and they are my only connection to that event which that commentator is convinced produced the greatest generation. This is a distortion but it is his version of World War II. I like the honesty of the quote from the guidebook for American officers of the greatest generation. The segregated base, Fort Benning, Georgia, is reflective of the surrounding town where blacks must endure Jim Crow policies in every restaurant, bar, hotel, train station, or bus depot. My father writes letters to the Negro newspapers, to the *Daily Worker*, and other small left-wing publications. In his possession is the one seminal anecdote that removes any illusions that he is fighting to help make the world safe for Norman Rockwell's *Four Freedoms*. As his troop train heads north from Georgia, they do stop in Tennessee for a ten-minute break with calisthenics done right on the railway platform. Just when his infantry outfit is about to reboard the train, they watch as German prisoners of war are escorted from another train, for a similar break but they have one more advantage. They are permitted to get some doughnuts and coffee from the makeshift free coffee stand that is on the platform. When my father complains to the white officer in charge, he is told that a separate coffee and doughnut stand for colored soldiers will be built by the end of the month.

"Dexter, that's about the only story about the war that I have."

"Pop, you must have been in one battle. One fight, World II is big."

"No, Negroes were not allowed to fight. That was the rule. It was a law."

"So, you don't have any stories about the war?"

"Just one. I'll tell you my favorite World War II story."

We're in the basement and my father is talking over the hum of his ten-inch DeWalt radial saw. He's making some small wooden trestles for a model train table that he has constructed in the basement. It's gargantuan, taking up half the basement. American Flyer trains are arranged in lines and divisions, freight and passenger. He's built the table completely from wood. He tries to avoid plastic at all costs, saying it doesn't look natural. When the blade rips into a piece of wood, there is this screeching noise accompanied by the smell of fresh pine. If the blade hits a knot, the noise is louder and there is a burning in the air. If it's a big knot, the motor slows down and you hear the pitch drop down. As it eases through the knot, the rpms increase and there's a high whine that means the cut has been made. Sawdust, fine and clean, floats through the air; my mother's wash that is hanging in the basement gets a coating, and my old man shakes his head and murmurs, "shouldn't be there."

"Dad, you're gonna tell me that story, right?"

"Oh sure, let me just make this trestle. I want to finish that passenger line tonight." There's a pencil behind his ear and every now and then he glances at some drawings that he has done on graph paper. All the drawings are in perspective with draftsman's notations. The print looks like it comes from a typewriter. One more look. Lines up the soft pine. The cut is made.

"So, this story is about the end of World War II and the greatest thing that ever happened to me."

"Man, oh, man."

He reaches over for the switch and turns the saw off. It spins for a long time because he has told me about bearings and bearings are the most important thing in the world. It keeps on spinning, and he starts to talk, as the whine gets softer so he doesn't have to yell.

"Let's see, it's the end of the war, and I take a plane from Tinian to San Francisco. From San Francisco, we are put on a train that is going all the way from California to New York. It's crowded but everyone is pretty happy. We probably made a few stops but at one, which had to be east of Kansas City, I get a newspaper and read an article about this young alto sax player, Charles Parker. I had heard about him even on the island, yeah, way out there in the middle of the Pacific. Charles or Charlie

Parker can play better than anyone. I want to hear him. I just have to hear him. I've been away for years and haven't heard any good jazz in a long time."

"Pop, but this means that you're in the United States."

"Yes, you're not kiddin'."

"Oh."

The saw is still spinning and the dust is starting to settle in the basement. My job is to clean, and my father is pulling down the whisk broom off his tool board for me since I can't reach it. I accept it and keep listening.

"The closer we get to New York, the more papers I try to buy at the stations. Finally, I get one that says Charles Parker will be playing in Boston when I get home. I can't believe my luck. But I have to get there without any delay. The train has to stay on time. Therefore, you can say I was a little anxious. That mean's nervous."

I sweep the bench in the way he has taught so I won't "make the place any messier than necessary." Long calm strokes that make me look more like I'm painting the massive workbench that he has made from doubled up three-by-six beams, are watched out of his careful eye.

"Dex, good work. I'll finish the story because it's rather unbelievable. The train stays on schedule. It arrives in Pennsylvania Station, Eighth Avenue and 33rd Street, and it's great to be in the Big Apple again. Your mother meets me and tells me that she has a party planned. I tell her, no way, I'm heading up to Boston that afternoon so I can see Charles Parker play. I borrowed someone's car, drove straight there and listened to Charlie, Yardbird, Parker. Wasn't that good luck?"

I can see that he is truly happy and I nod my head that this is the greatest World War II story that I've ever heard. He holds the dustpan for me a long time so I can sweep very, very carefully.

Journal Entry
Mother's Day, 1975

What a day! I'm beat. I'm tired, physically and mentally fatigued. Drove from five-thirty in the morning to four-thirty in the afternoon. Booked sixty-five dollars and made fifteen in tips. It was

Mother's Day. A lot of people were on the move. Never drove so much in my life: one hundred ninety-one miles!

I noticed a couple of things. Rich people were angrier than usual. They usually treat me with a lot of hostility, but I couldn't figure out why they were turning the screws so hard today. Then I got it on Park Avenue. No doormen! All those dudes are on strike. Nobody to open the rich folks' doors. Nobody to salute, nobody to tip their hats, say *good morning, good afternoon, good this, good that.* Nobody to see and feel better than. Those doormen are in the rich folks' private army. They wear uniforms. They salute. They follow orders and give none.

These doormen are down at the bottom end of the social order, yet I've never had any sympathy for them. If anything, I possess a lot of antagonism for those guys. When I drive up to a big apartment house or hotel on Fifth Avenue, they look at me like I'm shit. They got their rich costume uniforms on, hats, braids over their shoulders and shiny shoes. I'm wearing my old army field jacket, dungarees, and imitation Earth Shoes. But damn! I don't know what these guys got against me. Well, I guess I know. They're just like any other person. They want to feel better than someone else. And I guess I'm the same because every now and then, I prove to that doorman that he ain't no match for a young taxi driver when it comes to hustling these rich folks.

Sometimes, I drive up to a hotel and before you know it, goddamn, I'm out my door, around to the other side, and I'm opening the door for the rich dude. Do you know what that means? That means that I get my regular tip, plus the doorman's tip. You should see that sucker's face when I drive away. But I think, sadly, this capitalist system got me and this poor doorman fighting for the scraps, just the crumbs of their big fuckin' pie. Well, got to keep on driving and think better thoughts.

Rarely, very rarely, I guess when I'm feeling down on myself, I put on my *Richard Wright-Ralph Ellison-Invisible Man-Malcolm X-Dexter Jeffries*-hustling the man act. It gets the money, but what a price. It goes something like this:

Setting: Fifth or Park Avenue. Wealthy person, preferably my age or over.

Good morning, sir,
Yes, I know where that is.
Do you want the express or the local?
The express, that means I drive real fast. The local means I just drive fast.
Yes, sir.
Nice day, isn't it, sir?
Yes, I hope to drive for a long time; maybe someday buy my own cab. That's my dream.
Thank you, sir. I really want to own my own cab.
Yes, sir.
No, sir.
I don't know about that, sir.
Do you want the east side of Lex, or the west side?
Far corner or near corner?
Thank you, sir.
Oh, thank, you, sir.
So long, motherfucker!

Well, getting back to Mother's Day. Went out to Kennedy Airport early in the morning. Got my mother a thing of flowers and went home. She was happy. Went straight back to the Big Apple and an incredible thing happened. I made every fucking light on Queens Boulevard, every one from Hillside Avenue to the 59th Street Bridge. I think it had to do with my speed, 33 mph, probably the perfect speed or some weird shit like that. I don't know but it did happen.

Quick review of the day. Saw Ruth Van der Keith, chairman of the Queens College English department coming out of a church on Madison Avenue in the seventies. Man, I'm scared if she's praying for her job. Some swells got in my cab. Man, they must have had a lot of bread. Talking about a meal for one person costing thirty bucks and me, I got my Big Mac, two for a dollar special coupon from the Q.C. student newspaper. Wealthy people can't communicate either. I listen real close and even though they're speaking English, I don't know what the hell they're saying.

And finally, in the early afternoon, the most beautiful woman that I've ever seen, got into my cab. I've seen so many women in Manhattan, thousands, temporarily falling in and out of love with them and hoping they notice me when I yell out of my cab, "Hey Cupcake!"

It's hard to describe her, as most beautiful things are difficult to narrow down and be specific about. She was old, at least seventy. She spoke with a heavy Yiddish accent, and she had this Old World quality about her. Her voice was so raspy that I could hardly make out what she was saying. I picked her up on Third Avenue and 76th Street, and she wanted to go to 183rd and Jerome Avenue in the Bronx. I tried to explain to her that I wasn't sure how to get there. She didn't understand. She just sat back in the cab with a bouquet of flowers, graciously, her head up in the air and looking all around. She was proud like an aristocrat, but she wasn't sullen or arrogant. And all the time she was smiling mysteriously. Even when I told her I couldn't get there, she smiled and said, "Take me, you're the driver. Take me."

I go to the FDR Drive and it's a mess and she's smiling. I get out and ask for directions. When I get back in, she's smiling more and says, "You're a good young man." Her smiling is strangely drawing me to her. Finally, I just have to turn around, open the glass partition and smile back at her. I squint my eyes because the sun is coming through the back window, and it's filling the cab up with this brilliantly clean light. I keep on driving, and all the time, while I'm going up the FDR Drive in this crowded traffic jam, in a brand new Checker cab that's being inundated with this clear white sunlight, there's me, and this old lady, and we're smiling.

I take the FDR Drive and go across the Willis Avenue Bridge to the Bronx, and I'm not scared. I'm usually a little scared when I don't know where I'm going. I just follow the natural course of Willis Avenue. After the bridge, about three lights later, I pull next to a car for more directions. The people looked Spanish:

Ou esta Third Avenue?
You're on it man!
Thanks a lot.

I turn around and told her that I knew where I was going. She smiled broadly and said, "You're a very good boy," and started to hum.

Jerome Avenue in the Bronx follows an elevated train. The sun flickers intermittently through the ties of the railroad tracks. The flashing light, and the old beautiful lady's smiling and humming is making me think. She's swaying her head from side to side to this melody which I know is from Russia or Poland, and I know that is where this lady is from. I'm thinking—thinking hard. This lady, with her glowing Slavic features and her graying hair is from there, from the plains of Russia, and she's humming a song that she knew as a child in some small village. That's it! I know it! She looks like my mother's cousins in Russia. The two sisters in the old photograph. The two sisters and the rest of the family that the Germans killed when they came to their village, killed them for nothing, just peasants working the land.

"That's the place young man, right there."
"Yes ma'am."
"You're a good driver."
"Thank you, ma'am."

She gives me the money, clutches her flowers and walks away. I don't pull away. I sit there for a minute thinking. I drive back to Manhattan slowly, going past two girls in shorts who flag me down. I drove real slowly under that El, thinking, thinking that I had someone real special in my cab today. She was old but walked erect. She was old but had grace and dignity. She was old but still remembered the music of a lifetime ago. She was old, but she wasn't old. She was old and beautiful and it made me sigh deeply and breathe hard when I thought, "Can you imagine what she looked like when she was young?" And as I drove down Second Avenue, listening to the thump-thump-thump of my tires on the temporary wooden ceiling of the new Second Avenue subway, I had this crazy idea of going back to 183rd and Jerome Avenue in the Bronx and looking for the old beautiful lady, finding her, and caring for her.

Othella

I KNEW IT would be difficult to be a black professor from the first time I met one, because from that first introduction, or confrontation, I could see that a black professor's job was immensely more complicated compared to that of his or her white colleagues. The job was so complex that you weren't even a black professor any longer. You were whoever they (the English department) wanted you to be.

There she was, and I had been anxiously waiting for her for years. I had waited four semesters. I had never seen one. I knew they might be there someplace and by choosing the course, Black American Literature Survey Part II, I was guaranteed a black professor.

Well, that's a lie, not on my part but a lie anyway. Because I had taken Black American Literature Survey Part I with a white professor I knew that these scenarios did exist. One could register for a course that said X but that particular course was not taught by a person from the X group, and they could be diligent. Once you got over the shock of a non-X person teaching that course, you settled down, listened, learned, changed. That had occurred during the summer of 1973.

Professor Tyne was brilliant, absolutely brilliant. She knew everything about black literature that a person could know. Besides her comprehensive and in-depth knowledge, there was a passion and fire that made the literature live and breathe for me. I'll never forget her presentation of W.E.B. DuBois' *The Souls of Black Folks*. At one point when she was discussing DuBois' capacity to capture the voice of southern black oratory and what it meant to be able to articulate this voice, she had tears in her eyes. I took a breath before she returned to the passage from Chapter I, *Of Our Spiritual Strivings:*

> It was the ideal of "book-learning"; the
> curiosity, born of compulsory ignorance,
> to know and test the power of the
> cabalistic letters of the white man, the
> longing to know. Here at last seemed to
> have been discovered the mountain path to
> Canaan; longer than the highway of
> Emancipation and law, steep and rugged,
> but straight, leading to heights high
> enough to overlook life.

I had tears; she had tears. We both caught ourselves, and I was not the only student looking to hold on to something. It was too much. Too much feeling. And she was white and she was feeling.

Professor Tracey was indeed black, or at least I thought she had all of the equipment to prove it. She had a small tightly cropped Afro, which perhaps made up for her very light-skinned complexion. She was thin, angular, wore suede miniskirts which were the order of the day. She had an aura of an Egyptian Nile queen about her and was fiercely nationalistic from that first of September to the last day of the semester.

I was intrigued.

So, Professor Tracey was my first black college teacher, and I had been waiting a long time for her. I wanted things to happen. I was excited. Even though there were no black students in the class, something which I had been accustomed to by then, that imposition made me feel all the more special since I thought she would latch onto me and vice versa, and we would discover some bonds of solidarity. I did not expect this to manifest itself in any demonstrable way. I would have been satisfied with a subtle shake or nod of the head. I would have been content with a sly smile at some point. A wink would have been the cause or stimulus of a rapturous moment.

We started. She seemed surprised that she was teaching the course. She was one against thirty. There were thirty white students, me—whatever she perceived me to be—and this unfortunately made everyone uncomfortable. Because of her Black Nationalism, she felt compelled and obligated to prove things. Her favorite expression, which I had never heard before, *Cultural Amnesia,* I found to be cute because she repeated it with such frequency as if it gave her some sort of stability or an anchor. That was it. That expression, *Cultural Amnesia,* became the basis of all her lectures and talks and responses to questions. We did not understand what it meant: "I want to tell you people something. I really want to tell you people something. There's this thing going around, you know, and it has a lot of power. And it's been going around for years. It's called *Cultural Amnesia.*" We stared and tried to understand. Our ignorant stares only pushed her a few octaves higher. With legs crossed, standing, leaning with her back to her desk, hands on hips or sometimes arms folded across her chest, she continued,

> I can tell from your faces that you don't know what I'm talking about . . . and that is what I'm talking about. Cultural Amnesia is working right now. As I speak. It's working. Right here in this classroom. Does anyone here know what I'm talking about? Do any one of you know that you have it, as I speak, right now? Yes, some of you are infected with it and you don't even know it. Right now.

Of course, we were baffled since she was telling relatively liberal and intelligent students that we had, with intention, been dismissive of another culture's legacy; she was hurling the accusation that we had consciously erased the contributions that black Americans had made to the cultural heritage which was America. She never told us what we were forgetting, but she was angry, and this became her rhetorical stance. The silence was long and silvery. You could hear the air vents blowing. No one was angry except her. We were a little scared not so much about what she said but what she was not able to express that seemed so important to her, as though she was attempting to explain why she was suffocating, and was bewildered at our inability to furnish her with an oxygen mask. We were clumsy in any of our attempts to give her the air she needed because on some level we were aware that it would be almost impossible for her to accept mouth-to-mouth resuscitation from us.

We plodded along. That was September, and we had four months left. We were to study Black Literature from the Harlem Renaissance to the present day. The class was still excited since the literature of the latter half of the semester was going to bring us to works of current and important thinkers and politicos: Eldridge Cleaver was alive. Langston

Hughes had only died in 1967. A writer named Maya Angelou was making her mark. Ralph Ellison was conducting his ritualistic readings of passages from his epic and unfinished novel. Black Literature was alive, current and the class, all twenty-nine white students and I, were waiting. We wanted to be taught.

Even with *cultural amnesia* as a starting point, it was inevitable that books, poems and stories would be read and discussed, and we entered a world that I knew, loved and had studied on my own. I wanted to hear what a black professor had to say. I wanted to hear the truth. Professor Tracey taught.

When she did teach, I was worried. The mistakes and misstatements poured forth two times a week. Misinformation, misquotes, wrong names, places, publications. I was a bit shocked and thought I could be of some service to her by presenting the corrected information in a non-threatening manner. I would slowly put my arm up, acting as innocuously as possible and prefaced every remark with, "I think" or "I'm not sure but . . ." and then tell her what Frederick Douglass had done, the influences on Phyllis Wheatley, Ralph Ellison's notion of race and identity and that 1940 was the year *Native Son* was published. She did not take these "corrections" the way I thought she would. She huffed and puffed and became irritated. I was informed that I was mistaken with my facts and what did facts matter anyway? We were here to study literature, not history. Her thin angular body blew up like a Macy's Thanksgiving Day Parade balloon. The folded arms made her a bit reminiscent of an emaciated Il Duce and with the suede boots up to her knees the picture seemed a bit complete. At first I was Mr. Jeffries to her. Then it became Mr. Jeff-er-ries and sometimes Mr. Jefferson. She was angry.

This was our routine, but I tired of it before she thought I would and that made her happy. Silence was rewarded with an occasional, "Mr. Jeffries, do you have any comment on that?" This was rewarded with, "No, I'd have to think about that first." When I saw how she handled the white students who were contributing to the class, I found out that there is nothing worse than to have an angry black person in charge of a group of white people. There is no analogy that is appropriate for this situation in our society. No question, there are tons of racist white people who are in charge of a corresponding group of black students, bureaucrats, factory production people, and service personnel. Yet the white person does not possess that sort of anger because they are not angry. They're irritated, harassed, but they are not bona fide angry at what they see before them. When you're that kind of racist, you are above or below your enemies. Vengeance is not in their hearts; that would mean that they had made themselves vulnerable to a black person's machinations and that situation is not psychologically impossible.

Professor Tracey had a difficult time because of this. Anything a white student said was subject to her scorn, and I felt sorry for both parties. It's a hard reality but a true one. When you read Ken Kesey's *One Flew Over the Cuckoo's Nest,* one is struck by his firm understanding of McMurphy's down-home American racism, that good ol' boy type; you're also conscious of his intimate understanding of how enraged the black personnel in the hospital are. Of all the jobs to be given to black people, taking care of old, white, crazy people has too many Sophoclean ironies to think about. "I hate these people and I got stuck taking care of them." This was Tracey's predicament. She readily forgot that even if she despised white people, her first job was to teach Black Literature to her class, whether it be black, Japanese, or purple. There's an entire generation of African Americans who benefited from the alterations in our society who had the good fortune of entering civil service jobs when that sector of the American economy finally opened its doors. Civil service was akin to serving in the United States Army. It was a place where a black person could be judged rather fairly and judiciously. Tests were competitive; job openings were listed publicly and if you filed your application on time, you took that exam in a rather anonymous fashion.

The second generation who came into civil service in the 1980s and perhaps followed in their father's or mother's footsteps was not so grateful, content, or happy about this achievement. The triumph that the previous generation lauded, modeled, and built middle-class lives eluded them. No, now civil service had come to be or appeared as a prerogative. Blacks began to envision civil service jobs with a sense of entitlement. Along with that entitlement came anger, resentment, and even racism. Tracey had her peers in every station in life. And just as their oppressive white counterparts could not disguise their hatred and loathing of blacks when they were asked to perform some routine tasks, neither could a black token clerk for the New York City transit system, a clerk for the Motor Vehicle Bureau, or a correction officer at Rikers Island. Rudeness, brusque retorts, glares, unresponsiveness are all qualities that have manifested themselves when this second generation of civil service administrator came into contact with the white community that he or she was paid to service.

It's an ugly thing to witness. How many times have I been on a line and listened to the surly comments from black civil service workers as they were asked to respond to rather routine and mundane questions from white people on their particular line. I cringed because I knew that it was inevitable that I would arrive at this person's desk and would be reduced to the status of a supplicant and hope for a waiver to be issued. The closer I got, the more I developed my projected model of behavior that would, at least, dilute the offensive remarks that would, be relegated my way. When I finally did arrive at that counter, desk, glass partition, all of the rage that had just been directed at the white patrons ahead of me was gone. Was the person gracious? No, but they were civil service pleasant and bore me no ill will. The questions were answered, the forms handed out, the applications stamped. I was not told by gesture or response that I was somehow a burden to this clerk. After this occurred with enough frequency, I could discern that I was receiving preferential treatment because I was not white, and I felt lucky, for a while. That sort of providence, however, always has to be followed by sadness.

Professor Tracey dished out her special brand of anger, and the class attempted to placate her. They had to. After all, these were intelligent people, English majors, specialists in communication arts and sciences. It was just natural that a committee was formed to aid and improve the diplomatic relations between Professor Tracey and her class. A few students formed this group after much discussion. Many different overtures were envisioned, debated, and even role-played. The white women in the class felt that she deserved second and third chances. There was a grand buildup of schemes and what platitudes should be sent her way, and we even pondered how to approach her, orally, or in writing. It was concluded that a letter could be taken the wrong way. A few students talked to her after class.

These students became a conspiratorial group whether they wanted to or not. Anytime you cannot conduct human affairs out in the open due to fear and tyranny, it's a natural consequence. Yet the white students had good intentions, and I wished them well. When I saw her face, a few seconds after she listened to their well-disposed entreaties, I could tell by the baffled expressions on theirs that they were going to be conquered and violated in a brutal fashion:

> Do you think you can even speak like that to me? We do not have that sort of relationship. I refuse to have to even contemplate having that sort of relationship with you. I have nothing to say to you, and you have nothing to say to me. We are not friends, and we are not going to be friendlier. That is not my purpose here in this classroom. I am not your friend. I do not wish to be your friend nor am I interested in improving what you call "our relationship." We do not have a relationship.

From that point on, we were in a stalemate situation. I stopped correcting; she kept talking about *Cultural Amnesia* and we half listened to whatever she knew or claimed to know. The tension was there, every Tuesday and Thursday at 3:00 P.M.

December. The semester was practically over and we had all weathered the coldness in the classroom. For Professor Tracey it was going to be a rough winter. She was going to make the headlines, and her recognition was not going to revolve around her latest appreciation of Alice Walker or her literary analysis of Lorraine Hansberry. No, Professor Tracey had landed herself on the second or third page of our local tabloids for being involved in a sordid love affair. This love affair had turned sour, and her boyfriend had decided to break a flower pot over her head in such a fashion that everyone on her block on the upper West Side of Manhattan could not help but hear about it. When we walked to the room on the following Tuesday at 3:00 P.M, there was a message on the door. Just the facts: "Professor's Tracey's class is canceled today. Contact the English Department if you have any questions."

We sat down in the room. A few of us were privy to her private humiliation, but no one brought it up, and there was no real cheering at her literal downfall. We just felt that this could only compound whatever anger she had toward the world only more. We were not sure whether we would ever see her again since it was late in the semester and if it was just the question of administering a final exam, another professor, any sort, could have done that. But we were to meet her again, and it was in a very intimate setting: her house. We were shocked. She sent a letter to each one of us, to our homes, and requested that we meet her at her house for a double period that would make up for the missed class time due to her misadventure.

She lived on the upper West Side of Manhattan, and we were duly impressed. We conjured up many scenes of her apartment and since we were from Queens, the lost satellite of New York City, feelings of excitement and anticipation filled us. We were going to Professor Tracey's house, the professor who did not like us, and she was going to teach us at home. And even if she did not instruct us in anything educationally sound about Black Literature, we would get to see the angry professor's home. What would it be like?

It was a cold day, and we took buses and subways from Queens to Manhattan with the mutual goal of getting up to West 93rd Street between Central Park West and Columbus Avenue. I made it. As soon as we entered the parlor floor of her brownstone, the aroma of a long-cooking stew filled our nostrils. We were in a trance already. On a long black coffee table were crackers, cheese, and jugs of white and red wine, and plastic glasses. There were rugs and drapes that exhibited a sense of taste and intelligence. It was a dark Victorian parlor, and I guessed that is the way they should be. A piano was sequestered in the rear with a small lamp turned on over some music books which were propped against the wood rack. And further back, in the kitchen was Professor Tracey wearing regular blue jeans, and a black turtleneck sweater that made her appear more intelligent or cosmopolitan. She was standing armed with a large wooden spoon, leaning over a stew pot and stirring its ingredients. Because the bandages were on only one side of her face and head, it appeared as though nothing was wrong. It was only when she turned to say *hello* that you were alerted to how severe her physical confrontation had been. She slowly moved her mouth to say *hello* like a stroke victim who works very diligently to pronounce or make the few remaining sounds they still retain in their possessions. A black eye, busted nose, and the bandages deflated whatever exhilaration we had, but she was resilient. She had made all of these preparations. The wine and cheese was presented as it should be, and the stew certainly smelled great.

We all found chairs, a couch, loveseats, places on the rug, even leaning against a wall. I looked at her face and wondered what her bandaged eye was doing while her good one was surveying us. White people in her house. More white people than she ever had or wanted. I felt triumphant to be in her house like that, but the victory was small and petty since she had really been disarmed. We took out our notebooks and started to record what she was saying. She spoke slowly and deliberately, chewing some of the words twice that she found difficult to swallow. Baldwin became "Balwin" and Lorraine Hansberry became "Lourwain Hansburry."

We ate sporadically as she encouraged us to, but no one really desired to make that sort of noise, chewing, or crunching crackers. Wine drinking was the one alternative that did not create some nuisance, so the bottles of red and white Rhine wines were drained during this session. I took small sips since I never drank in those days and watched her. Her fierceness was gone and without the sullenness and arrogance she took on a new appearance.

The semester ended in her living room on a peaceful note since we all had signed a mutual peace treaty not to be anything but neutral or friendly because of Professor Tracey's condition. People started to help clean up and the white girls who had originally sent her their entreaties months ago were talking about domestic things with her, the house, her cooking. I looked at the entire situation from a distance. I grabbed a garbage bag and unceremoniously put myself in charge of collecting cups and paper plates. When I went into the kitchen looking for where the trash was to go, Professor Tracey made contact with me and half smiled. I asked her where to place the trash and she pointed toward an old dumbwaiter door. As I walked to the dumbwaiter, she asked if I could stay and help with the cleanup. Without looking or turning around, I just said sure.

After second helpings of her stew, the class started to file out. Winter coats were put on and thank-yous were offered. I managed to keep collecting and cleaning as if that were my job, and I always did this. Finally the door slammed and it was just she and me. I enjoyed the moment. It was just she and me. I heard her sigh and looked at her. It was a simple sigh of relief and fatigue.

"After you finish, I would like to talk to you," she said.

I nodded and muttered No problem, as I sized up the rest of the cleaning and straightening that had to be done. She slowly moved out of the kitchen into the living room, taking slow and focused steps; each one was painful and probably jarred her head. In about ten more minutes I was finished. I walked out to the living room, the same one that had been filled with about twenty students. It was quiet, and I heard the floorboards squeak under my feet as I came into the large but still darkened room. She had leaned forward in her chair when I came out. She sat back in a large chair, grabbing the armrests thoughtfully as she methodically sat back, reclining inch by inch so as not to cause any more pain than necessary. Because she was thin, she was able to nestle her body into one corner of the chair. This nestling of her body relieved some of the pain that she was in. She sighed when everything was just right. I sat on the edge of my chair.

"You're a smart young man," she said without moving; whispering allowed her to speak without that much distortion.

I didn't know how to react and just said a neutral, "Oh, thanks."

There was silence because I never could carry on a conversation, and she was in pain and probably did not want to waste any words or sentences. She started again:

"You're smart and know a lot about Afro-American literature."

"I like to read."

"Yes, you certainly know a great deal."

"I'm also interested in history."

"Mr. Jeffries, you were right."

"Sorry, I didn't hear what you said."

When she gripped the armrests, this gave her the extra strength that she needed to repeat her words with more force.

"Mr. Jeffries, you were right, all those times, all those facts, ideas, things, about the books. You were right every time. I looked the things up later and you were right."

"Oh, thanks."

She nestled back into the corner in the chair and looked at me. Since it was dark and half of her face was covered with white tape and bandages, I was prepared to listen to whatever she wanted to tell me.

"I'm not a black professor."

Because I was listening now and that was because of her mummy-like face, I didn't have to ask her to repeat herself. I heard what she said, but I quickly understood that I didn't understand. Her one good eye discerned my confusion.

"It's true; I'm not a black professor and that's what you were right about all of those times when you raised your hand. From the first time to the last. You were right, and I was wrong."

I leaned a little farther on the very edge of the chair. "But you're black, right?" I said with an intimation that angered her.

"Of course, I'm black. Look at me. I mean, I am not a black professor. I don't know a great deal about black literature."

My ignorance was apparent with my next remark, and I could see that I was trying her patience and putting her in more pain, a different type of pain.

"Professor Tracey, I thought that to be a professor, you had to know a lot about whatever your topic was."

"You do, you do, for every other subject, have to possess a comprehensive range of knowledge of your field; you have to study, write articles, and a dissertation, and even books. But not for this."

"Why?"

"They don't care."

"Who doesn't care?"

"Them."

"What do you mean, *them*?"

"Mr. Jeffries, they don't care. I'm proof of that. Do you know what my subject area is?"

"No, I thought . . ."

"Yes, you assumed that I knew black literature, when in reality, my area of specialization is Shakespeare."

I tried to sound intelligent and said, "William Shakespeare?"

"Yes, Shakespeare, William Shakespeare, *Hamlet, Macbeth, King Lear, Troilus and Cressidye;* I'm writing my dissertation about *Hamlet.*"

"Oh, good."

There was silence, and this allowed her to rest and determine how much more pain she could take, her own physical pain, the pain of her confession, and the pain of my rambling and insipid questions.

"You see, Mr. Jeffries," she continued, "they needed a black professor. They needed a black professor for a black literature class. I told them I knew nothing about it. I told them what I just told you. I know about Shakespeare. They didn't care. They wanted a black face and that's how I was selected. That's how they do things."

I sat back and was quiet. What she was telling me sounded so strange that I had no compartment to conveniently sort out what she said.

However, I was starting to smile inside and say, *I was right. I knew I was right. All those times I was right, right, right.*

"So, Mr. Jeffries, I just wanted you to know this. You knew more than I. This wasn't my topic and I had no time to prepare. I was hired at the last second. There were white professors that knew more; you could have taught the class," and for the first time she laughed a little bit. "No, you really could."

"Oh no, I don't know about that. I just like history."

"Well, that's what I wanted to tell you. Do you want any food to take home?"

I told her that I was all right and asked if there were any last minute details that needed to be done. She shook her head slowly. I walked into her bedroom where all our coats were flung, and mine was right there on her bed, the only one left. I came back out, and she was still sitting down, half shrouded by light and bandages.

"Everything all right, Mr. Jeffries?"

"Yes, ma'am."

"Have a good Christmas."

"Yes ma'am."

"You're polite."

"Yes ma'am."

"Take care of yourself," and with that I walked down her long hall-way thinking and wondering about how a black professor wasn't a black professor, and I tried to make one of those jokes to myself, a pun or rid-dle, something I was never good at, something like "When is a black professor not black? When she is a Shakespearean!" It didn't come out right or sound right, but it was right.

Do You Do Dreams?

"Do you do dreams?

"Yes, I think I know what you mean, but tell me what you mean, just to make sure."

I looked at Dr. Hannah Sallinger and said a little prayer, a prayer about having the courage to bring up the idea and then another prayer about whether I would have the guts to tell her the specifics of the details, the dream itself.

"I just wanted to know if you could do dreams. Just by coincidence we never did them. I don't want to waste your time if you don't do them. I know you said that you were an eclectic, and I know what that means, but you still might not do dreams."

I spoke in the most reserved and temperate manner now that I was in love with Dr. Sallinger. I loved her and thought about her and only wanted to do good things for her. So the last thing that I sought to do was offend her in any manner, shape or form. I looked at her beautiful face and jet-black hair. We had talked about love and me loving her a year before so she knew I loved her and that I wanted to sleep with her. I told her that a long time ago so why should I hesitate about telling her about the dreams.

I got my last look at her legs because I knew from previous sessions that she felt most comfortable when she pulled her legs up to her chair like a kid and leaned on the armrest with one hand. She held her legs up right about at her ankles. Then when she switched to the other armrest you could still see the mark of the imprint between her calf and her ankle. Sometimes when I walked in I noticed that she wore pants, and she would ask me, "What's wrong?" I lied and said that something physical was bothering me. The few times I wasn't prepared with a quick response, I said, "Oh, I was just thinking of something," but it definitely didn't have to do with therapy. I would spit out, "Doctor Sallinger, I was just thinking and that's why I made that face. No more, no less. Honest."

"Dexter, you're asking me whether or not I can interpret dreams, correct?"

"Yeah, I don't mean that you have to do it exactly as Freud would. I don't want to lie down on a couch. Do I have to lie down on a couch?"

"No, you can sit right there." She pulled her legs up onto the chair and that was my last look at them. However, I was lucky because she forgot to turn on the little fan that created ambient noise that helped or encouraged the patient to talk more; she had to unfold her legs, stand up, and walk over to the table. There she kept the tools of the trade: a big box of tissues and the little fan. The tissues, whenever I grabbed them were always in clumps, bunches, because when you're really crying you can't even see the box. You just reach out and blindly grab for it, hit it as another spasm of crying catches you, and then you just search and out comes seven tissues all crumpled together. You push this messy batch of Scotties or whatever the hell they are toward your face and breathe easier. Just when you think that you're all right, you can't believe that it has come to this and you start to cry even harder and, finally, you just let it go and that's what I'm afraid of happening with this dream. If I go there, who the hell knows what's going to happen? A dream, and she's not even a dream person. She says she does them the way a mechanic says he can do engines and on occasion, a transmission. The only problem is when she puts me on her psychological automotive lift, will she take her light out, give a look, take her rag out of the back pocket, and shake her head? She sat back down, and I didn't look at her legs because in a way she gave the answer that I didn't want to hear; she does do dreams, or at least she'll give it a go. That means I have to keep talking. This is a game of put up or shut up.

"Well, this isn't really a dream. It's a nightmare." She laughs and makes me laugh as I hear how ridiculous I sound.

"Does it reoccur?"

"Yeah, I have it on a regular basis. At least once a month. Sometimes more, but at least once a month."

"Do you wake up?"

"No."

"And in the morning, how do you feel? I mean, how do you know that you've had it? Is it right there when you first wake up?"

I started to think and felt good that she was giving me some easy questions. Keep it concrete and I can run with this for an hour. But I knew by then that she wouldn't do that. She's going to start pushing the treadmill to a faster pace, and I have to keep up or get off.

"I know I've had it when I wake up. It's pretty vivid and 'cause I've had it before, I'm sorta used to it. Can you imagine that? I've gotten used to being in this nightmare and it's pretty bad. It's pretty fuckin' bad."

"Well, tell me about it. I don't want you to have this dream if there is something that we can do about it. It's not pleasant to have something like that ruining your sleep on a regular basis."

I looked at her and said to myself, *"Man, it's so nice to have someone who is always looking out for you. Always. Always thinking about whether I'm wounded or hurt and how bad."* I was silent for a second or two since I really didn't know where to start. I was innocent.

"Doctor Sallinger, just one thing. Where do I start? I really don't know what to say."

"Start from whatever point you can remember the dream, or nightmare. Even if it is at the end."

Now I was relaxed since I knew I was going to tell a story, and I was always proud of myself for remembering details, especially from my dreams. Since I had this dream several times, maybe a dozen, the details would fall right into place.

"Well, I'm on this bridge."

"Which bridge is it?

"What do you mean?"

"Which bridge is it? You're not just on any old bridge?"

"But in the dream, I'm on the bridge already."

"Tell me how you got on the bridge."

"But you're asking questions that don't make any sense. I'm on the bridge already, and you want me to go back to the beginning, like there is some entrance ramp in my dream, and it just starts on one side and ends on the other. This dream, it's always the same; it starts, I'm in the middle of it, and I'm already on the bridge."

I had already gotten things to a point that I favored: logical argument and incontrovertible details, the kind of stuff that wastes thousands of hours of therapy but hints at something in its own way. The therapist discovers how you wrestle with the world on a daily basis because whatever you do in her office for sixty minutes, you do with the rest of your entourage when you're out there with the real folks. You're never that quite removed from who you really are. And by picking up on certain patterns and trends they can even start to lay out how you dealt with the world when you were a kid or at least when you commenced to place things within a certain paradigm. It's always helpful to see how a person lies to himself. It's always insightful to see how people lie just in general. Therapists are pretty smart.

"Do you think black people go to therapy more than white people?"

"Dexter, where are you going? What happened to the bridge?"

"Yeah, the bridge. Well, to be honest I never thought about what bridge it is. I'm not lying."

"I believe you. What does it look like? Try, try hard to give me some details."

"Yeah, I know what you mean." I shut my eyes and saw that this bridge was very intricate, layer upon layer of steel girders intertwined with latticework and a maze of crisscrossed steel beams making a labyrinth of a superstructure. I didn't know whether I was looking up at the bridge of a battleship or some ornate structure that actually straddled a body of water. It was gray and very broad. There were extra railings and passageways encased in a net of steel. Places to walk were adjacent to roadways for cars and those roadways were next to railroad tracks. It was a hodgepodge of a mess.

"Dr. Sallinger, do you know the Williamsburg Bridge?"

"Yes, it lets you out in lower Manhattan."

"Well, this bridge is either the Manhattan Bridge or the Williamsburg. I definitely narrowed it down to those two. It's not the 59th Street Bridge, and it's not the Triborough. Definitely not the Brooklyn Bridge. That one always stands out in your mind."

"That's good. You see, when you thought about it and concentrated, you discovered you could pinpoint some things, even a more specific place. As long as you do that, we can work and perhaps even figure out the specific bridge and what specific time and what you're doing on it."

I was impressed again with her power, and it was reconfirmed that my nickname for her, *The Big S* was more than appropriate. I had told Alonzo and George how she "had the power" and could make the crippled walk and the blind see and the hurt heal. In my case, the damned became the saved. They looked at me and saw a passion similar to the one that they had already experienced with me when I was spreading the word about Louis Armstrong like an apostle. I was in the same mode again. Familiar with my moodiness and reveries, they were ambiguous in their response to my new religion, my new goddess. I spoke about Dr. Sallinger incessantly and with reverence. I added drama to the re-creations of certain apocryphal sessions that we had already mutually experienced by talking about them until three o'clock in the morning. We gave them names and nicknames, creating metaphors for events that were akin to a series of great militaristic or sporting contests: The Battle of Being Black; The Battle of Being White; The Two Session Battle of Being Black and White. The time she made me understand my brother, my relationship to him. The Friday she got me to see how I felt about my parents. The Two-Hour Friday where I cried for the first time. Finally, the time she did the Bridge Dream.

After hearing my stories and accountings, Alonzo had decided that he had been in the presence of one who had been touched, saved. Because of his personal devout religious experience in the black church, where people felt the spirit, were moved, jumped and shook, he felt a new kinship with me. Even though I was still a resolute atheist, he could see that I had a spiritual side to me. It was just manifesting itself in a new manner, in response to a different balm. It was he who gave her the name *The Big S*. It was Alonzo Smith who talked about her power. One time he said it in his own special way, "Big S got the power. She is the power. She's powerful." I agreed and felt proud of my special friend.

"Doctor Sallinger, uh, well, I'm positive now, now that ya made me think about it, it's definitely the Williamsburg Bridge. I got it. I see it. It's the Williamsburg Bridge."

"Very good, you worked that out. We're getting near the end of the session, I just wanted you to know that we should stop in about five minutes." This was her cue; I never wore a watch in those days but now I can see why she kept that little electric clock out on the desk. It's so easy to be swept up and away when someone is being saved, rolling on the threshing floor, praying, crying, and sweating.

"Sure, yeah, almost five o'clock. Well, we made some progress. Right?"

"What do you think?"

"Yeah, sure, I never thought of it as being any specific bridge. I feel better just knowing that. That's a breakthrough. Also, I got to tell you about some new things, the dreams. We never did that before. That's a lot of action for a Friday afternoon." She shook her head positively as the tissues were moved and the little fan was shut off.

"Good, how do you feel?"

"You know, I feel better. Even though we didn't do the other stuff, am I black, am I white, am I Jewish, is that why I'm crazy, the usual stuff, I still feel better."

"Good, very good. I just want you to do one thing between now and next Friday. Try to think about the bridge and when you've been on it. OK? Also, try to think and remember if that bridge has taken you to any place specific, other than just lower Manhattan. OK? Oh, I forgot, maybe it's just connecting you to some place that comes long after it. That's a possibility we have to take into consideration."

"Sure, that's easy. I'll give that ol' Williamsburg Bridge a good workin' over."

I got up and shook her hand. Sometimes I shook her hand; most of the time I wanted to hug her, but I was always afraid that a quick appearing and raging erection would ruin our parting. There were days when I would look at her legs a little too much and would rearrange my posture in my seat or look at some of the posters in her room as a distraction. I never hugged. Shaking hands was the extent of our physical contact.

I started to look out the window. We were on the first floor of a building so it was easy to see students walking by, going to classes, meeting with each other, or just sitting on the grass of the courtyard. I really became anxious at this moment and went through my ritual of slowly opening the door, looking up and down the hallway, going back to the window, timing things just perfectly, so I wouldn't run into anyone who knew me or who even vaguely could identify me. Even after a year, I still had to hide from the world, hide the fact that I was seeing a therapist. My father had shamed me so much into thinking that anyone who consulted a psychotherapist, psychiatrist, or counselor was sick and crazy. He coerced me into thinking that I had to hide, at any cost, my crazy sickness from the world. I was successful in this deception, but it caused me to proceed through some rather ridiculous and silly conniptions.

"You didn't check the other window yet."

"Oh, yeah, thanks, yeah, hate to bump into somebody coming out of the Dome." With a genuine smile that exhibited pity and concern, Dr. Sallinger watched me go through my painful formal procedure every Friday at 5:00 P.M. Sometimes it took only a few seconds; other times, minutes. One time a group of friends was camped right outside of the building, and I asked her if it was OK to hide. She said OK, but just this one time. I hid for about ten minutes as she read something. While she put on her coat and scribbled my name and "4:00 P.M." in her red day book, I constantly looked out the window, paced up and down before the window, apologized for hiding but explained that under no circumstances could anyone ever find out about my weakness, my illness, my fault. And getting out of the office wasn't the end of this ceremony. Just the beginning. Walking out of the building on Friday afternoon at 5:00 P.M. raised so many questions and the kind that couldn't easily be answered. As I walked obliquely toward the parking lot for students, I kept my head down, sometimes reversing direction, posing like I dropped something so I could slink around a car or two. I looked and sweated, even in the wintertime. Because I wasn't such a good liar in those days, I had to prepare and practice stories and explanations for the random possibility of finally meeting someone who just naturally wanted to know what was going on, what's happening, why are you here so late on a Friday?

"Had to do some extra work in the registrar's office, Jefferson Hall."

"Was in the library doing some research for that term project."

"Went to the gym to go swimming." (I had already made sure that the pool was indeed open and open to students on Friday afternoons.)

"Met this dynamite girl in the student union and we just got to talking" (my most inauthentic and disingenuous lie since I never met any girls who talked, let alone talked to me).

"Did some tutoring; student had a tight schedule and could only meet me on Friday afternoon. Bummer, right?"

I never was caught. Two years' worth of Fridays and never caught. That was great because I really didn't need that. I had so many problems with being black and white and being crazy, and going to therapy because I was crazy, that to have the general public be privy to my secret hell would have been more than I could have borne.

Only Alonzo and George, George and Alonzo, my loyal friends from P.S. 156 days. There they were, twelve years later. Sometimes they were home for the weekend from Princeton. We would meet, gather, commune at George's house because his mother worked at night. That meant that the house was ours and we could indulge in our orgiastic activities, getting a pizza, eating a pizza, and listening to Louis on the stereo as loud and long as we wished. They liked a band named Chicago and they turned me on to some of their music. They were the only ones I could talk to about her, Dr. Hannah Sallinger, The Big S.

The Big S, that's what she became to me, Alonzo, and George. Alonzo started calling her that instead of the professional nomenclature of Dr. Sallinger. We invoked the name with a reverence. Three black guys or two-and-a-half black guys sitting on a terrace in Rochdale Village; Rochdale Village was the big social experiment in housing, bigger than Co-op City in the Bronx with its own power plant. During the 1965 blackout it's the only place in New York City that has power. We hung out on the terrace of his apartment; we surveyed the endless buildings of this beautifully doomed test in the mixing of the races, Jewish and black folks living together. Jamaica Racetrack had outlived its usefulness. All of that fallow land was eyed by some visionaries who thought a racially integrated cooperative would be a good replacement for the clubhouse. Sometimes as we looked out from the terrace with blurry memories, we could still see horses, the grandstand, and the special trucks that carried the thoroughbreds, and black guys from the South leaning on open bay doors, keeping the horses calm because the trucks made them nervous.

We reminisced about the racetrack, high school buddies, but mostly we discussed my sessions and what she did. We prayed to her, and she dwelled in our imaginations. We quoted her. She was refashioned in an exploitative manner and that configuration was used to give order to our disordered lives. "Big S wouldn't say that" became our most robust refrain. She was drawn into our conversations like a real living third party that groups use to frame discussions and sometimes we even felt competent enough to talk for her. All three of us dissected her. I told them that she could do anything. Alonzo used the name *Big S* so much that I adopted it and started referring to her in the same way. I told them triumphantly,

"If you tell her something, she will remember it. Weeks, months, or years later. I'm serious. She sees through what you say and even knows when you are lying."

I lay it on thick telling them that when you are in pain at four o'clock, you will not be in pain at five. And when you cry and if it is the first time, she will be ready. She knew you were due for a fall and she is there to pick you up at six, that's right. Six. The first time I started to weep, cry, break down, I stayed in her office from four to six, just holding on. She got me through that first time. Alonzo said, "That's not power; that's not magic. That's healing. Big S is a miracle worker." He was right; the Big S was a miracle worker. You went there feeling terrible and you left feeling great, and the feeling was concrete. When you came in, your chest did hurt. Your throat was tight. When you walked out the door, your chest felt better. That pain in the throat was gone. The tears were gone and if there were any new ones, they were out of joy, and gratitude.

The Big S lived with us, everywhere we went, sojourned. I took her with me on what was to become one of my favorite ways to spend a weekend during my college days, a trip to Princeton. Leaving Queens College on a Friday afternoon and journeying to that Ivy League campus was one of the most gratifying events of my undergraduate days. Going to Princeton, driving from Queens to Brooklyn, over to Staten Island, and then down that long commercial strip, Route 1, was a magical trip. I was already in an eye-opening mood. To leave therapy, climb in my 1968 Cougar, exit the campus and head for such a pastoral setting was a journey of transformation. Alonzo and George were at Princeton. When I told my other Queens College buddies where I was going for the weekend, this was almost always met with surprised looks and the name Princeton being repeated, "Princeton?" My answer was always the same, "Yeah, these guys are real smart." I was so proud of them. Black guys at Princeton. My father held them up as being the finest examples of "Negro youth" of that period, the late 1960s and the early 1970s. Returning on Sunday afternoons, going back over all those bridges, yeah, all those bridges, and waiting for another week to go by before I saw the Big S. Monday, Tuesday, Wednesday, Thursday, and . . .

"I've been thinking about that bridge but can't get that much out of it. I just wanted you to know that I did try." Dr. Sallinger smiles that I've remembered and trusts that I did think about it and just didn't let this important clue lie dormant. I don't know what else to say and feel a little silly not knowing the answer. She smiles because she has a plan and tells me, "So many other people won't even try to remember or work on something during the week. You always do. That's why I enjoy working with you." My heart leaps at that and I know I'm special to her even when I can't figure things out.

"Dexter, where does that bridge lead to? If you take it, where does it go?"

"Williamsburg Bridge, let's see, takes ya to Delancey, lower Manhattan but above Canal Street."

"Does that part of Manhattan have any special meaning for you? Maybe not now, but in the past?"

"Damn, I just can't think of anything. Shoot, wish I knew. Hey, wait a second; I go over that bridge almost every Friday night. Is that important?"

She perked up at the word *every* and looks right in my eyes, black against black. I'm not going to drift.

"You go there every Friday?"

"Sure, or almost. Every Friday night my old man needs the *Morning Telegraph* as early as possible. He wants to start figuring the horses' charts as early as possible. The *Morning Telegraph* isn't at every newsstand in the city. Just a few places. One of 'em is right on Delancey at the foot of the bridge."

There's a way a therapist has of communicating to someone when you're not giving her the right answer. Very subtle because they just can't say, "No, that's not going to help you. That's not the answer; that's going to take us to a new place or even an old place. That answer takes us no place." I know from being a professor now that the hardest thing is to tell students they're wrong without telling them that they're wrong. The Big S must have had several thousand occasions like this with me although she led me to believe that I was a decent client. One time she asked if she could tape me. My curiosity shot up and so did my client self-esteem. I immediately conjured up the idea that I must be so psychologically problematic that she needed to study my case at home, in her off hours.

I was let down when she said, "No." Again, she didn't say, "No, you're wrong again." She turned it around and said that I could be of help to her. I perked up a bit but it wasn't the same as being a complex case that needed special study and attention. She was teaching a class at Columbia and wanted her students to hear what goes on during a session. "Guinea pig," I thought to myself. I had to ask her one thing though. "Doctor Sallinger, I just have one question before I give ya the go-ahead. This class that you're teaching. You want to use me as an example of a good client, not a crazy one." Her reply was disappointing. As she looked through her appointment schedule, she said, "It really isn't about the type of client. It's about the nature of the session. I'm teaching them about the rhythm, like jazz, the beat of a session. Sessions have beats and this can be taught or at least exemplified. You and I have rhythm, and I want the students in the seminar to hear it. Is that OK?"

I shook my head that I understood and was agreeable. So I knew that even when I gave her wrong answers like this one about the newsstand, she still learned something from me, something about how a human being thinks and feels. That is another facet of psychotherapy and teaching that you can't fathom when you're in it, whether you're a student or client. The professor or the therapist is always learning. Even if it's for the ten thousandth time, there's some small nuance or twist that has never made itself present in all their years of teaching and listening. I've seen it many times. A student looks at a line of poetry or a quotation from a play and they react, respond, and even though you've heard the same basic analysis before in regard to William Carlos Williams's the "red wheelbarrow" or Arthur Miller's haunting line, ". . . when he died—and by the way he died the death of a salesman in his green velvet slippers in the smoker of the New York, New Haven, and Hartford going into Boston—" you still hear something different. I know this process is somehow replicated during a therapy session. It would just be a lot easier if they could tell you where you were supposed to go. Yet they can't.

I thought and rubbed my forehead and tried to think about that stupid Williamsburg Bridge. Nothing. She interrupts with, "Do you know anyone who lives near there?" I shake my head in the negative and am a bit surprised that she doesn't know I only have about two good friends and they're currently at Princeton. Then I'm moved.

I explode, "Doctor Sallinger, I do know someone. Holy shit, I never thought about this. My sister lives there, not exactly at the bridge, but only a few blocks away, up on East 6th Street, East Village. That's it. That's the only other reason I would ever drive over that bridge. I, uh, I, uh, I . . ." The words came to an abrupt halt. My body, which had just expressed victory over bad memory, repression and denial, fell back into a slump. This wasn't going to be fun. I mumbled something about my sister being a hippie and how she's been away for years in Europe. Dr. Sallinger asked me what else was going on and I said, "Forget, it, just some more stupid shit."

I became quiet and just sat there. By now the Big S knew my routine. I would talk, but I had to think about it because telling the story correctly was still more than getting to the meaning of it. I am into details, chronology, and design. In a whisper, the words finally came out, "My father put the ban on her."

Her legs have come down and she leans forward to hear my faltering soft whispers "What is the ban?" she asks. Anytime I'm asked a question that I don't like, I attempt to render the questioner a nuisance by implying that she's ignorant. "Doctor Sallinger, the ban, you know what a fuckin' ban is. The ban." I'm sitting up now because I'm mad. She smiles and says, "Dexter, I honestly don't know what this means. This is the first time I've ever heard you use this expression." Now I'm really mad because the Big S is the one person you can't say, "oh, you're lying, you've heard me say this hundreds of times because she'll frown a bit and that black hair is going to fall down and you're going to say to yourself, *"This fuckin' person never forgets anything you say; it's like talking to a tape recorder. You never used the word ban and she's going to prove it to you in about three seconds so why not just drop it while you're ahead."*

I start to explain. One of the most complex issues that I ever tried to get her to understand was how a black person, my father, could despise black people. It probably had to do with the absurdity of it, the illogic of it. If you're black, you should hate and loathe white people. And if you're white, you should hate and loathe black people. These types of thoughts were in my head like geometry axioms that hold true not eighty percent of the time, not ninety-five percent of the time, but all the time. I never wanted to talk about things where I had to admit to the contradictions and paradoxes myself. This was a grand one. I hated being a minister of misinformation. To tell her something on one Friday with Euclidean confidence and then for another Friday to roll around and to have to explain that this axiom was flawed and the final proof was not really exact, was one position I detested. That was another reason I avoided so many topics. My father reviled Negroes but his loathing was so complex since he liked some and it would have been better for me, my brother, and sister if he just found them despicable all the time. But to then tell us about the Negro's contribution to art, jazz, history, and literature, always placed us in a precarious position. That's what he had done with my sister.

One evening my sister Vivian brought her boyfriend over for Sunday dinner. Olin was a photographer who did freelance and wanted to document varying aspects of the black experience that Gordon Parks had started to explore. His photos were piercing black-and-white portraits of New York City during a time of decline. If you were in the East Village during the days of the Fillmore, the chaotic and energized street scene was misleading; everyone mistook that to mean that people from that neighborhood had power and authority over their lives. Maybe for the white kids it was that way. Things were charged up on Second Avenue and 9th Street where the greatest rock musicians in history held forth. However, if you moved a few blocks farther east toward Alphabet City, you knew that these hardworking black and Hispanic people were doomed. With heroin pouring in on Avenue A, junkies and dealers make Tompkins Square Park a scary place, day and night. The projects were transformed into anguished isolated enclaves, reminiscent of firebases in Vietnam. There, American soldiers carved out small fortresses in enemy controlled areas, but every GI knew that *Charlie* was out there, omniscient and omnipresent. Your fate was really in his hands, not your own. Olin's photographs of the East Village caught that tension, that fear and trembling. He was an artist.

Olin was black, and I'm still not sure what offended my father more, that, or the fact that he and my sister were living together in that apartment on East 6th Street, above a restaurant called The Cauldron. Sitting together on that Sunday night, all of us at the dinner table, we all knew that this wouldn't work out. Before the bread was passed and buttered, my father made sure that he insulted Vivian and Olin in a gross way so that they had to leave. As they exited the door, my father flung their coats at them. That's fast. The splendid dinner that my mom had prepared was starting to age and I saw a spiced ham sandwich with American cheese on the horizon, once things had been thrown away and cleaned.

Before the sandwich my father issued an edict, one of the many. My sister was banned. My brother and I weren't supposed to see or talk to her. She was forbidden from coming to Westgate Street, back home. That was the ban. He couldn't monitor the phone calls so that aspect of it was relegated to be ineffectual. But our visits, he could create some surveillance system that kept track of our movement. Just at the time when I wanted to see my sister the most, she was removed and excommunicated. When you're in Queens and the excommunicated is in Manhattan, that's going to work. A moat that can't be crossed works.

The Big S had listened during this five- or six-minute explanation. I looked up and waited. Because I was a bit wasted from getting all of that out and thinking about the possible ramifications of this iceberg, I only half heard what she was saying. I heard the words, *complex and painful*. When I looked up, she was smiling though. I asked her what was the occasion. She replied that, "There is one good thing that we're going to get out of this." I thought about the madness and the ban and heard nothing else that she had said, except for, *complex and painful*. I was exhausted and didn't even feel like playing the first inning of this game, so I could only lash out at my anger with, "What fuckin' good thing can you pull out of this, this fuckin' mess, a black guy who hates blacks but not all of them, the ban on my sister, and me not going to the Fillmore anymore with her and Olin?"

Black eyes met mine and I heard an emphatic, "Dexter, you're not going to have that dream anymore."

"What?"

"Dexter, you're never going to have that dream again."

I was already looking at her, but I had to look even closer. I sprang up to my highest level of attention and said, "Sorry, I wasn't listening to everything you just said. You said, I'm not going to have that dream anymore, the nightmare anymore?"

Her hands were confidently clasped together like a Supreme Court judge who has just rendered a decision in which the vote was nine to zero. Her voice came back on, and this time I heard her when she said,

"Dexter, you're not going to have that dream again because you just solved it. It took some time. It was tough. As always, but you worked it out. You went from not even knowing what bridge it was to guiding me and yourself to a street where your sister lives. I know it was tough. But you did it. Some things take longer than others and in no way are we through with your father and what he means to you and I know, I'm overwhelmed by what you've told me sometimes too. It's incredible what you've gotten through. But I want to stay focused. You're not going to have that nightmare again because you've figured out what's on the other side of the bridge. That's what's important."

She was wrong, a little. I did have that dream but only one more time. Within a week or two I had the same dream. I was back on the Williamsburg Bridge. It was as dilapidated as ever. Yet this time, I was able to navigate around the loose beams and girders. I shifted plywood to cover the chasms that were too wide and the plywood was secure. When I got to the middle, as always, it became very dark, but I kept on walking and finally started to run, but not with fear. I could actually see some sunlight coming through the superstructure of the bridge. The closer I got to the other side, the more the light was coming through. As I finally hit Delancey Street, there were crowds of people cheering me the way they do when a marathon runner comes across that finish line. Spanish people, white people, black people, they were all cheering for me. I had made it.

I told Dr. Sallinger about this dream and she smiled, black eyes with a little bit of wetness in them. When I told Alonzo and George about the three-segment session that had started with no hope and ended with a small victory, we all became quiet. I told them how I had had that last dream and had stopped having the nightmare. I hadn't had the dream in months. Alonzo looked at me and mouthed the word, "Damn!" George said, "These people really know what they're doing." There was a gap of quiet. "That's therapy, that's therapy in action," I said as I nodded in the affirmative. But Alonzo shook his head in the negative. He took off his glasses, rubbed those spots where glasses people always get those marks, and put them back on. With glasses adjusted just right, he said, "Shit, that ain't therapy; that ain't healing. That's voodoo. Goddamned voodoo."

Journal Entry
April 9, 1975

It's Sunday, and I'm drivin' my cab. As usual, Sunday is always quiet, and this affords me the one pleasure of driving a taxi, taking in New York.

New York is a true visual experience. The whole atmosphere of the city mainly has to do with the architecture. That is dominated by the big skyscrapers. No matter where you look or what you're doing, you always find yourself looking up. Your eyes are in a constant battle to stay on the road and not focus on the buildings. For me, one of the hardest stretches is between Broadway and 63rd to about Broadway and 57th. First, you've got the Gulf & Western building on your left (goin' south). Then you've got 10 Columbus Circle on your right, and then back on your left, a distraction of a different nature, you have Columbus Circle with the statue of

> Mr. Christopher Columbus,
> He sailed the seas without a compass
> When the man started to rumpus
> Up spoke Christopher Columbus
> There's land somewhere,
> Just wait until we get there
> We'll be safe and soundo,
> As long as we stay rhythm boundo,
> Everybody was makin' merry
> Mary got up to go home . . .

Good ol' Fats Waller, he knew how to pen a tune. Like I said, getting around Columbus Circle can be hard.

Sunday is the worst day for hacking; sometimes you can drive for forty minutes without one ride. You try everything that you know. Go to your favorite streets, drive slow, drive fast, and sometimes just stop at a corner and wait.

Well, it's one of those Sundays, and I've tried all my tricks and none of them have worked. I did my pattern: up Broadway, down West End, up Amsterdam, down Columbus, up Central Park West.

I don't ever mess with the East Side. Those people are depressing and make me sick.

Yeah, all that and nothing worked. What do you do? You've got forty miles on the cab, only got six bucks in your pocket when you should have about sixteen. Shit, only one thing to do. Go home. Back to my roots. Back to where I know the joint will be jumpin' and I'll be welcome. Hell, you know where I'm goin'. Yeah man, that's right, Harlem, good old Harlem.

I turn the nose of my cab north and head up Broadway to the main drag of many tears, 125th Street. You can always make money in Harlem. There are never enough cabs. Most drivers are reluctant to go there and the gypsies are not numerous enough for the demand. Harlem is always jumpin'. Sunday morning, people are either comin' home from some late night partying or others are headin' out for church. Harlem dresses up on Sunday. Little kids with their clean suits and dresses, old men with their hats and canes and finally old black women with furs and necklaces, things they have held onto all their lives, they're all goin' to services on Seventh Avenue. They also can be seen at 125th and Madison.

I spot one. She's an old black grandmother. Probably lived in Harlem all her life, raising her family, and struggling to keep things together. She's elegantly dressed with a large hat that almost makes her look younger than she is. A gypsy cab tries to rip me off, but the old lady waves him away. I like her already. I hate those East Siders who frantically flag you down. You do your best to pick them up safely, and then they take another cab that just made a reckless maneuver and got there first.

I pull over to the curb. She gets in very slowly, majestically, as if I'm drivin' a Cadillac limousine. She speaks with reserve when she requests, "Saint Luke's Church, One-Fortieth and Convent."

"Yes, ma'am."

"It's a beautiful morning for services. Which church do you attend?"

"Well, ma'am, I have to work, as you can see, but as soon as I get time, I'll go."

The interrogation continues, and I think about turning on the radio to disrupt this conversation.

"Driver, what denomination?"

"Ma'am, oh, I have change for any size bill you might have."

"Young man, I'm asking you which denomination are you."

"Oh, well, a, a, Protestant?"

"You're probably a Baptist."

"Yes, ma'am."

I'm uptight. This old lady is givin' me the heebie-jeebies askin' me all these questions. I don't like talkin' to people in the cab. I ain't got too much to say in the first place.

"Do you drive in Harlem often?"

I decide to tell this lady the way it is. With a surliness to my words, I bark at her with, "No, only on Sunday mornings. OK?" She's silent, and I'm afraid I scared her. Finally after a long wait, long enough for me to regret raising my voice, she responds with a little guffaw, "Hell, that's the only time it's safe up here."

I laugh hard and so does she. I laugh out loud and to myself. That's the common bond between us. Not that we're black or live in the same area or even come from the same class. It's something else, a little more abstract. It's a feeling for humor. Not minstrelsy, self-ridiculing, and debasing humor. It's laughter, a rich hearty laughter that has developed out of our pain and sacrifice and lost aspirations. It's a smile, an arm around the shoulder or the gesture that symbolizes our most sacred of bonds, the giving of some skin: *Gimme five! You're on my side!*

It's a gesture that represents a brotherhood of man; the extended hand that waits to be slapped is like an open soul that warms to a reciprocal caress. It's the constant reaffirmation of a contract, an agreement that will hold as long as there are black Americans living and struggling for their rightful place in this country. That extended hand that waits to be slapped will always, as sure as the sun will rise, slap another hand in return, due to that understanding. The return *giving of some skin* is always commensurate in strength with the love and affection that was inherent in the first one.

It's a serious and important gesture. This is evident in the reaction when a response to the gesture, the first offering of *five*, is not given. Hostility, anger, and contempt are the feelings present. It's an effrontery in interpersonal relationships when the gesture is not returned, is missed, or is done without a sense of robustness: so white people, when you see me with my hand stuck out, slap it, slap it hard, like you mean it. Give me some of your life in return. Show me that there can be something substantial between me and you.

Take a chance. Stick your neck out and goddamn it, when I say, "Give me five!" show me you are on my side.

German Ghosts

THE AMERICAN MILITARY barracks in West Germany are old Nazi army bases and one always feels a little haunted by the setting. If you're Jewish, your spine shivers and quakes every now and then, especially if you find some relic of that grotesque past. When I was stationed in Frankfurt for a few weeks, I was stationed in a Wehrmacht barracks from World War II. Anytime the words *Take five* were yelled by some old sergeant I would take a walk around the building. It was the I.G. Farben building, corporate headquarters of the makers of Cyclon G gas. When I made this discovery, I went pale. I didn't know whether it was the Jewish side of me that was ill, the American, or the human. At the end of the war, the American army, looking for suitable housing for its own troops and administrative staff, chose this building because it hadn't been damaged that much from the air raids on Germany. It was a monstrously big place, like a medieval castle that an architect had re-structured so as to house a 20th-century bureaucracy. And whether it was designed for an entrepreneurial nature or a military one, it did its job.

On one of my *Take five* breaks I had wandered down to the court-yard. I surveyed the four walls and noticed that all of the bricks were deeply pockmarked. I stepped back and figured it out quickly. They were pocked from the height of four feet to about six and a half. "Goddamn motherfuckin' Nazis," I yelled to myself, had shot who knows how many people right here, right in this place. This got to me. I wasn't lifted out of my daymare until the words *Break's over, troop* were shouted down at me from a second-floor window. I looked up at the sergeant and waved my hand to acknowledge the request. I was glad. This was not supposed to happen but it did. I was glad that some mandatory army detail was being cast on me and no matter how troublesome that burden may have been, anything was better than thinking about them, what they did, and how they did it.

Of course, being lodged in the home of the laboratory that made the actual gas that was used to kill 6,000,000 Jews didn't make things any easier. This gas, originally developed for the elimination of rodents was perfected for use as an antidote to human beings that the Germans deemed unfit for life. They had tried many things along the way, shooting, hanging, injection, but something about the gas and its cleanliness appealed to their sense of order and stability. I had read Kafka in college, so I knew that he too was aware, thirty years before the insane deeds of the Nazis, that this was a group of people who admired structure and record keeping. Man, did I really hate those bastards that day. If I could have crunched them all up into my fist, I would have squeezed them like a batch of oranges going into the Tropicana vat, the one with the pulp.

When you first get to your outfit overseas, Vietnam, West Germany, South Korea, you name it, there's a lot of confusion and extra pain and suffering. It's bad enough that you don't know what's going on, but the army preys upon this condition, exacerbating it, making you suffer all the more. It's something that they've been perfecting since the days of the Roman legions and Achilles waiting outside Troy. The unknown. They have figured it out over a few thousand years that a soldier will be all the more obedient, complacent, and easy to handle, when you have him confused and confounded. The goal is to wrest all control and autonomy from him, reduce him to infancy, make him suffer a missed meal or two, and deprive him of sleep for a few days. You then throw on people yelling at you things like "I want every swinging dick whose last name ends in a G to go down to the mess hall and report to Mess Sergeant Evans for duty. The rest of you guys will be issued orders later. That's all."

It's the "rest of you guys will be issued orders later" part that gets to you. The guys who are down in mess hall hell are lucky; at least they are doing something, and they know that they are suffering, but there is a reason. Their pain is simple: will I be an outside man who takes care of returning army food containers? Will I be a server? Will I peel potatoes in this big machine that makes a lot of noise? Will I be a pots and pan man which means you will live in a sink that has no bottom and the grease will leave a ring a little bit above your elbow? No matter, they're lucky. The enemy is in sight, and it is a shift of KP. The guys, who are back in their racks, those are the ones who are suffering. "That's all" just left them in limbo for another few hours and that's true misery.

So after about five days in the 21st Replacement Company in Frankfurt, I'm ready to go anywhere, even back to the States, back to the world. Everyone has a theory about where we're going. Everyone has a rumor about a scenario that is going to improve the lot of one or two lucky sonofabitches. Everyone is wrong. You're going to wait, and it's going to strike when you least expect it; you may be a pots and pans man at 3:30 A.M. Then some loud army voice, combination of the South and John Wayne's version of Texas, will yell, "Jeffries, 126-12-1108. Get your shit. Fast. Now! Move it, what do you think this is, some Western Union telegram? Yeah, you, put the pan down. Put the pan down. Drop the goddamn sonofabitching pan, right now. Yes, that's it. Get your shit; your orders just came through. Report down front in three minutes. Well, don't just stand there. Get your goat-smelling ass in gear. All right, I want everyone whose Social Security number ends in an odd number below five to come with me. We've got a little detail to take care of."

There's a comfort in that, having that old sergeant come a-yelling for you. You don't want to admit it, but as the tears come to your eyes you own up to the fact that you thought they forgot about you, and you were going to stay there forever, trapped in 21st Replacement Company hell. You really believed that you were lost and were never going to be found again. Somehow, and you are astonished by this, there is a system in place; they did keep track of you and somehow that sergeant knew that you were way in the back of the kitchen, scrubbing trays that are as big as a piece of plywood, with a greasy ring around your biceps. He found you and you're happy for the first time in days.

When I went out front, there was an army ambulance with both back doors wide open and a few other troops with their duffel bags, smiles all around. I climbed in and someone shut the doors with a bang. The driver was pretty thoughtful because it was dark for about three seconds, and then he turned on the interior lights. We smiled again. It was a bumpy ride, and we didn't know where we were going, but we didn't care. The ambulance driver knew where he was going, and in about five minutes we came to a halt that was more official than a red light. When we heard his door slam, we knew it was only a matter of seconds before real light would come hurtling through the opening of the two doors. That's exactly what happened. He was a corporal with a clipboard and a batch of papers and carbon copies in his hand. We got out and found that we were in front of the Frankfurt Bahnhof, the main train station for all of Frankfurt. "Garcia, you're going to Stuttgart; here. Black, you're going to Hanau; Towers, you're going to Kaiserslautern, lucky sonofabitch, that's good duty; Jeffries, you're going to Darmstadt, not bad, halfway between Heidelberg and Frankfurt. OK, listen up. These tickets are only good for one way, so don't fuck up and get lost. *Auf Wiedersehen,* troopers."

Our five-minute acquaintance ends, and it's funny how this happens over and over again in the army. You meet a guy, for two minutes, half an hour; you pull some detail with a guy from Chicago who keeps you entertained with stories about being a pool hustler and you never see or hear from him again. Or another guy tells you how he worked at a Lays potato chip factory, night shift, in charge of the salter. Just guys, generally nice, the bad ones you forget. But it's definitely weird to meet so many men in a short amount of time and most of them you will never see again.

We get our duffel bags and swing them with authority up onto our shoulders and head into the train station. It's big, cavernous, like the old Pennsylvania Station I knew as a kid when my Cuban step-grandfather worked there as a redcap, before they tore it down. Announcements are being made in German, but because I'm from New York, I get the lay of the land pretty quick. *Ankunft* means arrival and *Abfahrt* means departure. Therefore, I'm looking for the side of the station with *Abfahrt*. I stand in front of a large schedule board and see Darmstadt, departure: 3:35; arrival: 4:07. *Gleis* number 6. *Gleis* has to be track. I'm feeling pretty good, as I've already picked up some functional German. I walk over to track six and there she is. I had a few minutes, but wanted to get on early and find a comfortable place. I walked up front like a little kid, wanting to be right behind the engine. I settled down in the first car and threw my duffel bag up on the baggage racks, which were mostly empty.

At 3:35, not 3:34, not 3:37, not 3:40, all the doors slam, a whistle is blown and a conductor waves a flag; the train starts to move. I'm heading to my new home and I'll be there pretty soon. The German people, really the first ones I've seen up close, don't pay any attention to me. Good enough. I fold my arms, fold my army green raincoat on my lap and enjoy the ride.

At 4:07, not 4:11, not 4:09 not 4:08, the train comes to a halt and all of the doors fly open. I pull down my duffel bag and put on my raincoat. I step off the train and lead the crowd even though I don't exactly know where I am going. There's a logic to the station, and I just walk up a flight of stairs to the main waiting room. The information booth is dead ahead, and I'm happy. With a gesture, I point myself to the front of the station where there must be some army vehicle waiting for me. There is, a jeep with a beat-up looking soldier in the driver's seat. His fatigues have actually faded a shade or two from constant washing and starching, but there is no starch in his clothing today. His hair is incredibly long, and he needs a shave. He's friendly and just says, "Six-Seventeenth?" I hadn't taken one look at my orders all this time and for all I know I'm in the 406th or the 99th. From the baffled look on my face, he knows to grab my personnel jacket with my orders out of my hand, looks, and shakes his head, "Yep, Six-Seventeenth. This is it. Hey, try to sit only on the right side of the seat or else you'll get your dress greens dirty." I thank him for being so polite and concerned about my uniform and sit on the right half of the worn-out cushion.

With my duffel bag in the backseat I get prepared for another ride. He said that it wasn't too far from the train station, so I'm not worried that it's an open jeep; there's a roof but no sides. Being October, a ride for more than a few minutes wouldn't be pleasant. Because I'm really not acquainted with army talk I say clumsy things like "nice day" or "the train was fast." Nothing gets a response until I ask about the army:

Me: How's the outfit?

Sergeant (He yells back with one hand cupped because the wind is really whipping through the jeep): What?

Me: How's the outfit, the Six-Seventeenth?

Sergeant: Whatta ya mean?

Me: Is it a good base? Is it a good outfit?

Sergeant: No, no, it's totally fucked.

Me: Oh, what do you mean?

Sergeant: It's just fucked up.

Me: Drugs? Racial problems? What do you mean?
Sergeant: Yeah, yeah, those things. It's a mess.

The Jeep keeps moving, and I can see that the traffic lights in Germany are set to regulate the speed of the vehicles. It seems like every car knows it's supposed to go thirty-five miles per hour. I'm disturbed. The two affirmatives from this sergeant in the beat-up fatigues were not the answers that I was looking for.

Me: Tell me one good thing about the outfit.
Sergeant: Speak the fuck up. Can't hear ya 'cause of the wind.
Me: Tell me one good thing about the Six-Seventeenth. Just one good thing.

He paused after acknowledging that my yelling was loud enough for him to understand. He kept his eyes on the traffic and pointed to the traffic light. That was the sign to let me know that he would talk when we stopped at the red light. We rolled to a halt, and I looked down and noticed that I had slid a little bit into the dirty area of the seat that he had warned me about. He pulled his cap down a bit and took a cigarette out of his right field jacket pocket. Before he lit the cigarette, he just shook his head and said, "I can't. I really can't."

We made a right turn into an entrance that was a replica of a castle, arches and turrets, and we were silent. He smiled and said, "Don't worry; you'll get used to it. I been here three years. Just imagine that you're in opposite land and you'll be all right." I started to laugh and felt better but wondered about that expression *opposite land*. Through my laughter and smile I asked him about *opposite land*. He had given up on lighting his cigarette because there was just too much wind slashing through the Jeep. The Jeep slowed to a crawl as it circled the quadrangle. The low base speed limit was demanded by these giant bumps that rose out of the asphalt every thirty yards.

We were going the perfect speed for a conversation, and I finally was able to get a look at his name tag over his right pocket. He had a cool name: August. As we pulled over to the curb in front of my barracks, more words came from August's mouth with exhaustion, as if he were describing something that had robbed him of a trust he had had for the world, "Look, about one-third of the outfit is made up of guys from 'Nam. They're in charge. In opposite land you have to forget everything. Here, everything that your parents ever taught you that was wrong, is right, and everything your mom and dad ever taught you that was right, is wrong. Got it?" I looked at August's face which had become serious and didn't look so young anymore. I wish I smoked cigarettes at the time so I could share something else with him instead of this haunting talk. He had offered me one, but I had turned it down. I didn't have anything. Reaching back into the rear of the jeep for my duffel bag, he had it up as I protested that I could handle it. "Jeffries, carry your orders; I got the bag. No sweat. Let's go meet Top."

That night after meeting a lot of soldiers, people with just last names, mostly friendly, I settled into my room for four men, but there was only one other bunk in use, and he wasn't there. My missing roommate was from Louisiana. Brinkley was on leave and wouldn't be back for two weeks, so I had the room to myself. I had been told by some old-timers that it was a rite of passage for new troops to be initiated into the company with a hazing that ran the gamut of having a bucket of water poured over you to being bound in a blanket and being beaten by anyone who felt like it. My squad leader mumbled that I was "Too old for that horseshit" and that in all probability nothing would occur. I didn't even think about it. I lay on my bunk and thought about how I would spruce up the room a bit, if it met with army regulations. At about midnight I heard a loud howl outside the window; since I was on the third floor of the barracks, I knew that I was in no imminent danger. If that howl had been outside my door, I would have prepared myself for a physical confrontation. The voice, human, went from howling incomprehensible sounds to words. "You nigger loving bitches; you goddamn nigger loving bitches. We're gonna kill you all someday."

I jumped up and threw on my fatigue pants, T-shirt, and some shower shoes. I walked to the windows, which swung out, and opened both of them. Others joined the one howl, and the sounds of bottles being broken made whatever was happening more ominous. "You fuckin' traitor bitches; if your boyfriends knew you were sucking black cock, they'd kill you and they would . . ." This voice was interrupted by one that overrode the screams and the shattered Budweisers. "We're gonna kill you for them; we're doing them a favor, sucking that nigger cock, no-good cunts." I ran over to the door and opened it cautiously. I remembered at the last second that I might be due for a hazing, and those individuals responsible for it might be lying in wait right outside. However, no one was in the hallway. It was pretty quiet and empty. I took a chance and knocked on the door across from me. A muffled, "Yo, who is it?" came through the solid door. I called out, "The new guy." A young guy with blond hair who was dressed exactly like me opened the door.

"Hi, I'm Jeffries, new guy in the third platoon. You hear that racket?"

"Yeah, Daniels, that's me. Second platoon. Yeah, just some guys fuckin' with the WACs."

"Oh, I didn't know there were any women on the base."

"Yeah, right across from us. WAC detachment, clerks, admin people."

The voices kept coming through his window which was open. When I heard a window break, he turned to see what had happened and invited me in since the mayhem could be better viewed from his side of the barracks than mine.

"Jefferson, sorry, I mean, Jeffries. Yeah, definitely, those are our guys fuckin' with the WACs who sleep with the black guys. They're really pissed."

He closed the windows and said, "Don't worry. CQ has probably called the MPs already and someone's going to get arrested. The army protects the WACs. You fuck with them and you end up in Mannheim; that's the stockade for all GI prisoners."

I walked to the door and wondered how Daniels rated his own individual room. He shared it with no one but himself. There was another bunk, but there was no mattress. He had placed a piece of plywood on it and used it to lay out all of his TA-50 field equipment. Because of the look on my face, he felt obligated to answer some question I had and decided it was the racial one.

"Look, Jeff, alright if I call you that? It's just some white boys who can't get laid. They get mad at the German *Schatzies*, too. They hate seeing that salt and pepper stuff. That's all that's to it."

October becomes November and November becomes December. I quickly digest the world of the army and in terms of race relations it is an anomaly. When you examine the internal machinations that are in full force for improving race relations, you're impressed that they have trained personnel whose sole purpose is to monitor racial acrimony and keep simmering tensions simmering. Once a month the whole company is shoved into a room with two or three counselors who perform their version of psychological therapy. During these confrontational sessions one witnesses and feels the same intensity that would be evinced in a therapeutic drug community. Officers are assigned to companies, battalions, and divisions who aggressively search for hints of racial friction. Films, role-playing, pamphlets, a plethora of materials is present at all times. Of all the American institutions that I've been a part of, I feel that this one was honestly going above and beyond the call of duty to work out the age-old plague. Sometimes it works. Sometimes it doesn't but for a half white and half black Jew from New York City, I feel pretty secure. For the first time in my life, at age twenty-four, I feel like someone is on my side.

Besides the army, I have another life outside of the barracks. We're paid once a month and this means a trip to the brothels of Frankfurt which are elaborate, Victorian, and prodigious. I choose the same girl every time and the others all think that is cute. Prostitution is legal in West Germany and the girls keep track of our pay schedule. When the financial officers at the Pentagon decide to switch to twice a month, the Frankfurt girls rejoice, since that means we're certain to return in thirteen days, instead of twenty-eight or twenty-nine. Maria, from Milan, with black hair and skin like Sophia Loren is happy too.

Every now and then when I'm in a local bar, a native of Darmstadt, a town which is right between Frankfurt and Heidelberg, asks if I desire his unofficial history of the 7th Army in West Germany. My ears perk up just like an old hound that knows a story when he hears one. I sip my beer and listen. "Yes, I must tell you of this time, once, a time, not too long, just before you arrive. Big *kampf*, big, no, little *krieg* over at the *kaserne* (the base). Yes, I speak truly. Black soldiers fight white soldiers. White soldiers fight black soldiers. Base closed, maybe, one day, maybe one day and one night. Yes. Big fight. White and black. Oh, very bad. Good, not, good for you, not present at that time."

I lean over my beer to get closer to this German storyteller. His blond hair is combed straight back from his narrow forehead and he's athletic looking. Around the bar are pictures of the local soccer teams and he's already pointed to a team photo of himself. Yet, he doesn't wish to talk about sports. Karlheinze is really convinced that there was a war on the base one time, just a year or two before I disembarked. I am sitting on the edge of my brown bench. I really want to hear what this gentleman has to say. German bars (*gastehaus*) are small; this guarantees the *gemütlichische* effect. There are really no separate tables. When you first walk in and if you're an American soldier or tourist, you are one hundred percent positive that there are no seats. A waiter in black pants and white shirt will point to what he considers the available *platz* or space. There are waitresses who will lead you to a table where there are people already seated, and you swear that she's made some mistake. She looks just like that Saint Pauli girl, buxom and Wagnerian, and you imagine what it would be like if she were on top, so when she suggests that you sit with perfect strangers, you do. The German inn, bar or *gastehaus* is antithetical to what an American wishes for or desires. You must sit next to someone whether you like it or not. Because space is at a premium, you must share and Americans hate sharing. Sometimes you walk out and hope that if you go to the next bar, there just might be a vacant seat. However, even if there is a vacant seat and table, it won't last for long. If new people come in, they will notice that half or more of your table is unoccupied and you must share. Americans don't like to share.

I have no problem sharing. I'm from New York City where "no space, my space, or any space" is a psychological state of mind, and I want to hear what these people are saying. If this middle-aged German man who happens to speak pretty good English, wants to tell me a story or two over a cold Darmstadter, well, that's OK with me. I think I know what this Karlheinze is talking about or referring to. There was that tension on the base the first or second night that I got there. I was lucky. The battalion was out on maneuvers up near Czechoslovakia or East Germany. The base was empty and there was no chance that they were going to send a raw recruit up into the line during the winter. Karlheinze's grammatical mistakes pulled me away from thinking about that first night, which was months ago, and I listened. "Yes, a fight so big, that another army people has to come and try to make peace. It is *unmöglich*. Impossible, you must know this word. I write it on the beer card. Very important word, Mr. Dexter. Very important word. *Unmöglich*. Impossible."

This story is later confirmed over and over again by other Germans whom I befriend. There was a race riot at the base of a magnitude that required troops from other bases to be called in to quell it. A hesitant peace dominates the base. I'm never sure if it is in reaction to all of the race relations classes that we're forced to attend or if losing the Vietnam War has drained us temporarily of all our energy. One has the energy to pursue age-old wars that preceded our excursion to Southeast Asia. White and black soldiers get along except as Daniels said, "when it's the salt and pepper stuff." We work, soldier, and get high together.

Every now and then in the mess hall there is an atavistic display of black solidarity that eases the tension. A group of black combat engineers will all stand around a large round table. They'll extend their fists into the middle of the table with black gloves which are regulation. Ten to twelve black hands in black gloves make a nexus of the sugar shaker and clenched fists, Huey Newton-style, touch each other. After a second, the words *Power Check* are yelled in unison so the whole mess hall can hear it. Some soldiers laugh and others just have quizzical expressions on their faces. *Power check on the Man* is another one that is often heard. Last, black GIs engage in a fascinating display of dexterity that can sometimes take a minute or two to perform. Two soldiers will walk up to each other and start "dittying." Elaborate and intricate movements with the fists, fingers, forearms, intertwined, and locked and unlocked, exude an intimacy that gives this community its own special recognition codes. I watch and because I'm deemed somewhere in between white, black, and Puerto Rican, I'm dittying with the black GIs when I want to. I talk to the tough low-riding Chicano guys from LA and Chicago. Walking across the parade file for chow with a bunch of white soldiers is a daily routine for me. I walk the line between white and black and Hispanic and no questions are asked. This is the way I like it.

When it comes to race and ethnicity, I haven't thought about being Jewish since the sixth grade. Before going overseas, those memories were distant and like a mirage. I didn't feel Jewish that much, but once I'm in West Germany, I started to become acquainted with my roots whether I desired it or not. I had my own reasons for repressing contact with that side of myself. My father had a normal streak of American anti-Semitism running through his veins. It was uncanny, just like the U.S. Army being in the I.G. Farben building and not having too many recriminations about it. Then again, America always had an odd relationship with the Nazis after the war. If it came down to trying a Nazi for war crimes or exploiting his rocket-making genius for our own needs, that Nazi got a job at NASA, no questions asked. Maybe that's why Jewish people are a little uneasy being in America sometimes.

My father possessed that routine loathing of Jews that comes with being an American. Black, turquoise, or purple, this is one hatred that almost every American comes into contact with. Yet he had married a Jewish woman. He saw Jews in classic terms of the scheming business-man, the cheater, and the unfair tradesman. He knew this wasn't true. He had saved Solomon Cohen. But that's the thing about America. You take action based on the details of a situation, but late at night when you're thinking by yourself, other thoughts take over and dominate the better half of your soul. You're not concerned or perturbed about the contradiction. You live with it. You squash the whole paradox by say-ing, "Well, some of them are OK." Perhaps my mother made this para-dox easier to live with or even more confusing for him since she did not openly embrace her Judaism. She was Jewish, had been raised in a Jewish household, but rejected what it had to offer. Therefore, she was Jewish but not Jewish, the way I had a Puerto Rican last name but wasn't Puerto Rican.

Things were all screwed up when I was a kid. I'll never forget the day that my mother, at the last second, as she was going to her secretary job in the city poked her head in our bedroom. It was a wondrous moment. She told us that it was a holiday and that we didn't have to go to school. My brother and I were shocked, shocked into happiness. We asked her if she was certain since no one had mentioned this to us, and not one other kid had even talked about it as a rumor. No, she said. She was sure that we didn't have to go to school. We lay there after she left thinking of every fantasy that was going to be played and lived out that day. It was only seven-thirty so we had more than enough time to go back to sleep, wake up later, and start our adventures.

It was a day with a shadow since our father would be home because he worked at nights and slept until about ten in the morning. We always prayed that he would sleep longer and perhaps never wake up. We felt it was unfair that he had been working all night, sometimes until six in the morning. He would get home at seven and sleep until ten. Quiet and re-strained, we got up in a little while and started tramping around the house. As quiet as we were, we could hear those two feet hit the bed-room floor and walk over to the bathroom. We continued our activities with hope. There was always the chance that during the course of the day my father would have some errand to run, and this would take him out of the house, and the television would come on, without a picture of course, but this was better than nothing. Listening to TV programs without a picture had become a high art form for us, and we relished that opportunity. Daytime sound. Yeah!

My old man came downstairs to heat up the coffee that my mother had left on the stove. He saw us and just from our attire knew that something was wrong; we had our play clothes on, old corduroys, old sweatshirts, and sneakers. Passing back into the kitchen to get a second look at the clock above the doorway, he was certain that something was amiss, and he hadn't just slept for only an hour and was up by eight by mistake. "What the heck is going on? You're both sick?" This jolted us out of our play. My brother took the lead with confidence, and I have to admit I backed him up because our mom had spoken with some authority. This was an official holiday, and we just didn't know about it. "Dad, today is a holiday."

Still confused and not sure what was going on, my old man walked over to the bulletin board where he posted our daily chores. He drew his finger across the third week of September. On this American calendar there was no mention of a holiday. Before he could speak, I talked and was more assured but less aggressive.

"Pop, it's a Hebrew holiday for Jewish people. It's a holiday."

"Who told you this cock and bull?"

My brother and I were surprised at his reaction. Two reasonable answers from us had resulted in irrational anger and I was already getting scared. My brother didn't give up, and I felt an allegiance to him and my mother not to back down. "Pop, Dex is right; this is a holiday for the Jewish people." Before my father could react, I cut in with, "Pop, there are Catholic people, Protestant people, and non-Catholic and non-Protestant people. This is their holiday. We're positive." I had learned how to use the word *non* and got to use it twice in one sentence. I had also started to use *positive* and *negative* and felt incredibly confident about my ability to converse.

"Both of you, get your butts upstairs and put on your school clothes. Ties, shirts, and shined shoes. Cut the crap. Move."

We ran upstairs. Since he only had on his bathrobe, he was naked and without his dreaded belt that he pulled through the loops of his pants like a slithering snake. That sound always meant move quickly.

Upstairs I started to cry. "What the hell are you crying about? He didn't even hit us," my brother said as he pulled the sweatshirt up over his head. I sobbed that we were going to be late, and I was never late, and I was going to have to walk into the room after everyone was already seated. Paul shook his head and said, "Damn, we weren't even watching TV, I mean, listening to the sound. Don't cry. I'll make up a story for you. Mrs. George won't do anything to you." My father shouted as we theorized, "Get your butts down here. Stop talking."

In unison, we yelled back, "We're coming Pop." We ran down the stairs with our ties askew. I got in front of my father, and his anger assuaged a bit when he saw that my tie needed straightening, and I was silently asking for help. As he was tying mine, he looked at my brother, said, "You look sharp, Paul. Very good." As my father did my tie, my brother launched our last ditch effort at not going to school and celebrating a Hebrew holiday for non-Catholic and non-Protestant people. "Pop, you're wrong about this. Mom told us this morning. She didn't make anything up." My father was just tightening the knot and made sure it didn't chafe and spoke slowly and deliberately.

"First, we don't celebrate Jewish holidays or any other sort of holiday."

He was close enough to me because of the tie-making process that I could feel his breath, cigarette and coffee breath. I didn't have to yell either.

"Pop, but we do have a Christmas tree. That's sort of a holiday."

My father was now straightening my collar my mother had ironed the night before. He raised his voice a bit not because he was angry, but he just wanted to make a point and end this back and forth that was digesting valuable time, as far as he was concerned.

"Look goddamn it. Christmas is not a holiday. Christmas is the biggest celebration that the capitalists have, on earth, in history. They are celebrating capitalism. There is nothing religious about it. We get a tree because we're helping them to celebrate even though we don't have to. That's the beautiful thing about America. All holidays are voluntary and let's cut the crap and get in the car. Paul, here are the keys. Start the car. First, put it in neutral; leave the brake on. Pull the choke out, you know how and just warm it up. I'm going to get my clothes on and take you guys to school."

My brother was already happy with his chore, and I started to put on my light jacket with the silver zipper that had the little letters on it, ILGWU. As my brother hit the pantry door, my father said, "One more thing; the other reason that you can't miss school is that you're going to miss work. You need that. You can't miss a whole day of school just like that and expect to be smart." Yelling out the door, he said, "Paul, are you the smartest kid in your class?" My brother yelled back, "No." He looked down at me and repeated the same question, "Dexter, are you the smartest kid in your class?" "No, I think it's William Buchanan. He gets one hundred in everything, spelling, math, and everything." With a sigh of relief pouring through his body that he had reached us with Marxist and Aristotelian logic, he said, "There, you understand. That's why you have to go to school. So you can be the smartest kid in the class. No more Jewish holidays. That's it. Forget about those things."

Those are some of my faint memories of thinking about being Jewish. Just being in West Germany, the home of the worst holocaust ever devised by man, makes you wonder about them, the people in the bars, restaurants, trolley cars, and parks. It is so apparent; the accessibility is the problem. In 1976 the Germans make you think things because they won't talk about them. I establish a methodology that when assessing a group of German citizens, I instantly know what are the historical possibilities. I figure out that the average age of soldiers in the Wehrmacht was twenty to twenty-five during World War II. That means, in 1976, they're about fifty to fifty-five. Therefore, when I walk into a bar with some middle-aged gentlemen, there is a very good chance that some of them are Nazis. Subtracting the number of them who tell me that they were students, leaves a pretty large portion. It took me some time to figure out that if all of them who told me they were students, were students, there would have been nobody to march east to Poland and the Soviet Union, or west to France and Belgium. That's the only variable in my formula of what these men who are buying me a beer were doing from 1939 to 1945. I'm tempted to tell them that I'm Jewish sometimes. Just to see their reaction. It's childish but it's in the back of my mind on many an evening at the Black Cat, The Crown, or Tilly's.

Thirty years is not a long time, but by the time I get to Germany, the official rehabilitation is over. West Germany is an important partner in the Atlantic Alliance and the American army is now worried about offending them. For us, for soldiers of the 617th Combat Engineer Battalion, offense takes on one particular connotation. If we are driving our

heavily armored vehicles through the bucolic German countryside, especially between Warzburg and Nuremberg, we are supposed to pay careful attention to German property. When I say property, I mean literally
the earth. Anytime we are on maneuvers, there are specially assigned officers who are monitoring every piece of German soil that we soil. If
someone drives an M-60 tank through a farmer's field, that farmer will
be lavishly compensated for the violation. If a large truck with an accompanying trailer makes a turn too tight and brushes into a house on a
corner of some small German village, the owner of the building can possibly look forward to retiring, courtesy of the U.S. Army and the taxpayers back home. This awareness, that we are paying them to protect
them makes us a little more reckless and some GIs just don't like the
'rads (short for *comrades*) or *Krauts*. It seems like we're motivated to
make sharper turns than can ever be negotiated, and we possess more
incentive to plow not just one tank path, but a whole batch of them
through farmer Johan's asparagus field. We're the army that has just lost
the Vietnam War, so our anger has to be displaced somewhere, and it's
usually on the heads of innocent Germans.

My time in the *gastehauses* is spent well as I try to learn everything I
can about the historical Germany. I suppose I'm looking for some revelatory moment that will dilute the tension. I want to hear a confession. I
think the Jewish side demands it. I listen and am motivated to learn
German because I wish to know when they are telling the truth. I drink
beer after beer and eat wurst after wurst, but I am plagued with their innocence. There are some people, however, who will talk about World
War II and you are impressed by their genuine need to apologize and explain. They do it profusely. I meet plenty of Germans who are my generation, between twenty-five and thirty-five. We find each other as though
a homing device has been set up in my inner ear. Since my days at
Springfield Gardens High School, wherever progressive, left-wing, or
artistic people dwell, I'm able to pick up their signal. When I was at
Queens College, even the professors I befriended were fierce, politically
active, fired up, and they weren't going to take it anymore.

It's no different in Germany. By the winter of 1976, not only do I
make contact with a large community of Germans with whom I social-
ize often, many of them are all members of radical artist groups, com-
munists, socialists, and independents. On becoming acquainted with
these people, I see that there is a ritual involved, a very somber and sad

one. First, they apologize for World War II and what the Germans did. Then there is silence. "I feel guilt for what my father did in the Soviet Union. It was a terrible thing." Silence. Silence. "He never came back from Russland." Silence.

Because of one Saturday walk from the barracks to an acquaintance's house, my life was going to be turned again, for the better. It all happened on a Saturday that I will never forget. On this day I met the second love of my life. She never loved me but that didn't matter. I had already learned that men can love many things, other men, women, ideas, institutions, and those things don't have to necessarily reciprocate. Gisela took me into her heart and life and always offered more than love. When I was to have my deepest and darkest moments, overseas, five thousand miles from home, there she was, presenting me with charity and benefaction. She's always here, right now, a quarter of a century later. And all it takes is a gray morning in New York with impenetrable clouds and I see her face, flaming red hair that's parted in the middle, and she lives again and I live again.

Soldiers stumble out of the barracks late on Saturday mornings in West Germany; most miss breakfast. Between the heroin and the hash, which we all ingest except for the few who drink cases of Schmucker or Licher beer, unconsciousness reigns supreme. An occasional O.D. rattles us for a few weeks and the junkies clean up their acts, muttering, "You have to take it easy with that shit; it can kick your ass sometimes." The heroin is so potent that a slew of overdoses occur simultaneously or the junkies become ill as if they were programmed by a lab experiment.

One day while walking down the company street with Sergeant Nichols, the windows of the barracks started to fly open like cuckoo clocks. A second after the window was flung open, out popped a black or white head with a soldier propping himself up on the sills. First floor, second, third, and even from the rec room way up at the top. As each one held himself up, they all seemed to vomit on cue. Long gushes of green and yellow liquid came pouring out simultaneously. I looked with amazement and disgust but more amazement. I said, "What the fuck is that all about?" Sergeant Nichols kept on walking without breaking his stride and said, "Big shipment of smack came in from Turkey yesterday. Too rich. They're not cutting it enough." The cuckoo clock windows closed and sleeves and handkerchiefs were used for the cleanup, and I thought about my brother and was thankful in a way that he and Dutch had prepared me for scenes like this. I was still impressed with what I saw in the army in West Germany, but I was never really shocked.

This was an ordinary Saturday in the sense that no one had died; we were all alive, at least physically. By midday I find two of my best buddies dressed in civvies, Danny Riverton and Steve Johnson. I'm lucky because there is nothing worse than staying on the base. Even though we didn't make a plan to hook up with each other, they see me also and wave me over to them. I'm known around the base as "Shakespeare" because I graduated from college. I'm interesting to them and they're interesting to me. I quickly discover that if a GI plays chess, there's a good chance he can read and write. In addition, there's an excellent chance we might be able to exchange a few words beyond "Fuck you, motherfucker" or "That's some stupid shit" or "Fuck the pigs" or "Fuck this motherfuckin' army."

They look good. Sporting German clothes, they don't have that cheap PX clothing issue look. Danny's brown boots are gloriously shined; he's put more work into these than his combat boots. They have been in the land of the square doorknobs for a few years and understand German. They understand both, the country and the army. They've mastered a world unfamiliar to me. I'm hoping that under their guardianship they are going to pass on skills and tricks to their most willing disciple. With wavy black hair and a stocky build, Danny speaks fluent German and has married a German girl, Renate. They're walking to her house and Johnson, who is slightly balding and lean asks me if I want to tag along. I hesitate for a second but already know that one has to avoid the deceptive appeal of the base. With its bowling alley, gym, movie theater, bar and restaurant, the army has replicated small-town 7-Eleven America, and plenty of guys are satisfied with that. As long as they have the heroin. As long as they have the hashish laced with opium, and cases of German beer, everything works out.

Germany is cold and gray in the Rhine River Valley. Where I was stationed the oppressive clouds hang low and stay longer, taking up permanent residence in November. Day after day, week after week, until finally that battleship gray atmosphere makes your eyes adjust a bit to this perpetual opaqueness. And if and when the sun does come out, you would think you were witnessing some ancient ritual. Soldiers come running out of the barracks, pointing and howling. Some don't even put their boots on. The guys from California suffer more than the rest of us since they're not used to this type of weather. Danny is from New Hampshire and Johnson is from Colorado so we walk through German streets undaunted. Danny's house is only about five blocks from the barracks, and I'm in awe of his whole setup. Renate is there with a pot of hot coffee. She speaks perfect English and within an hour we're discussing Malcolm X, Camus, and Lester Young. It's beautiful.

At about three o'clock, after almost three hours of nonstop talking, with Danny and Johnson playing chess and the hash bowl being passed around, Renate jumps up so quickly that the bangs over her forehead bounce for a second or two. "Danny, Danny, why didn't we think of this before? Danny, why didn't you think of this?" In the middle of a knight taking a rook Danny barely looked up and said, *langsam. Langsam.* This means slow. "Renate, Johnson and I are playing; you don't have to yell." *Entschuldigung* (excuse me) comes out with a sincere tone of apology and Renate continues, "Danny, I just thought and remarked to myself that Dexter has to meet Gisela. She would love him. Don't you think so, that I am correct?" Danny, with his hands clasped in that contemplative chess mode of thought nods his head a few times as he prepares for Johnson's counterpunch. With deliberate affectation he speaks and says, "Yes, Gisela would certainly like Dexter. They would be perfect. Johnson, after this game is over, let's swing by Gisela's." Johnson can't be distracted too much either, since he's hoping to make a tactical feint that will leave Danny in jeopardy.

All I can think of is Renate and Gisela and how duty in Germany is not necessarily a series of hellish maneuvers or enduring sordid conditions in the barracks. The most difficult lesson for me overseas is how to leave New York behind. As long as I can't sever those ties, all of my Germany experiences are diluted. I have to force myself to terminate my continuous compare and contrast mode of existence. *That person reminds me of so and so. This place is just like a neighborhood in the Bronx. This rolling countryside is a bit like Long Island on the North Shore.* I ruin many experiences and go through so many bouts of utter depression. I'm not there. That's the problem. At first I tried to blame everything on the army and the soldiers but after six months, I realize it's me, pure and simple. I'm immature and childish and whine to myself. I put up a good front but inside I pout day after day. I'm not as old as I think. I'm not a man. The chessboard is put away with delicacy, because Danny has purchased these handcrafted figures down in Turkey on one of his furloughs. We bundle up warmly for the walk to Gisela's and I'm happy. I'm there in the cold on a gray Saturday afternoon in Darmstadt, West Germany.

It's 1976 and in Europe I am getting a chance to live through a time that I missed. I was so consumed with jazz and Charlie Yardbird Parker that in terms of popular culture, the sixties went around me. I heard the songs and the groups but the words, I hardly ever listened to the words, except for a refrain every now and then: *Good bye, Ruby Tuesday, Break on Through to the Other Side, Hello, Good bye, hello good bye, hello good bye, Baby Love,* and *Positively 4th Street.* God is good. Europe is ten years behind America in terms of our popular culture. Time has stopped and it's really about 1965. Clothing, fashion, music, fads, they are ten to twelve years behind us; one gets a chance to do everything twice.

As we near Gisela's house, I see shades of Haight-Ashbury and the trip I took cross-country to California with a college buddy named Wayto. Multicolored, bright flashy colors and designs, stars, moons, faces, and words, and I'm wondering who and what Gisela is because I am supposedly, as least according to Danny, Johnson, and Renate, a perfect companion for her. It's a large white house, square with a peaked, tiled roof and stucco exterior walls. Since the basic background is white, the exotic colors are really highlighted. The colors are too much. Renate sees my face and says, "Hippie house, *richtig?*" I nod my head because I know that *richtig* means right, as in correct.

We walk up a path to the side door and Renate reaches up for a door-knocker that is not there. At first I figure this is something European, as in their doorknobs. For the GI there are certain symbols that reflect the cardinal differences between us and them and their square door handles are one of them. When a GI talks about going home, getting short, getting close to ETSing, getting out of this motherfuckin' army, he's been known to yell, "Short, going back to the land of the round doorknobs." Searching the door I can see that Renate is looking for neither. No bell. No doorknocker. Her hand starts to turn a small little handle and I'm thinking, *In New York, you would* . . . but I catch myself, and I am proud that I'm not killing the moment. I had read in a textbook for psychology 101 that some people don't live in the moment. Even though they are next to you, in their head they're in September. You and the rest of the world are in May but this person is thinking far, far ahead. You look at them and wonder why they're not in sync in the moment. You don't even notice it because it's the kind of emotional withdrawal that can be covered up with day-to-day social intercourse and mindless vernacular. I was guilty of something similar. I watched Renate's hand turn a small handle and I started to hear music. She cranked it and a tune came from a small music box. The tune was familiar, and I was glad that she played it twice for my sake. Turning around to check my reaction, she smiled at me and said, "Do you know this tune? This is an exam for you? Hardly American soldiers know this." Danny interjects quickly, "Hardly any, Renate." Renate paused and continued, "Hardly any, yes, I can say, no, I will say, that only one man got it correct and Gisela said this was a long time ago." "*Bitte,*" I blurted, another frequently used German word from my early vocabulary days. "*Bitte,* play it one more time. Please, I know the tune; I just haven't heard it in a while."

Once more she turned the handle. The tune was played, and I yelled, "The Internationale. The Communist Party anthem." As Renate was clapping, the door opened and there stood a woman in a long nightshirt. It went from her broad shoulders down to her feet. Her hair was red and she wore glasses. Her skin was very white and the contrast between her skin and her hair was brilliant. I knew I was going to love her right then and there. Johnson, who had known Gisela for years, said over Renate's applause, "Gisela, this is a cool guy from New York, Dexter. Gisela, New York City, not the country. Not upstate." Gisela smiled. When she stuck her hand out, I took it and smiled as we shook hands. "Dexter, Dexter Gordon, like the jazz musician," asked Gisela, and my heart melted as I knew we were already connected.

Renate started to tell Gisela that I knew the tune, but I interrupted her with a practical question that showed another side of myself. "Gisela, how does it work? How does a small music box work as your doorbell?" Gisela swung the door halfway open so we could see the other side and she turned toward us. I saw her profile. This is what I'll always remember, Gisela opening the door to explain how her doorbell worked and how that side view, that stance was to make a lasting imprint on my consciousness. The darkness from the house defined her body more; *darkness*, that white nightshirt and her white skin and the gray light all combined to create a 19th-century portrait of her. "Sure, I'll show you." Gisela spoke perfect English too, and had an American accent. Many Europeans learn British English, and it marks them in a funny and peculiar way. Gisela's *sure, I'll show you* sounded like she was from Tulsa, Oklahoma, or Dallas, Texas. "You see, this door is so strong and solid, oak, that it picks up the vibrations from the little music box and acts like an amplifier; you can hear this way up on the top floor, no problem, or *keine problem*."

We walked up the stairs single file. All the furnishings in the rooms were from another time, and I was happy. On each floor I kept meeting new people and by the time we reached the top floor, I had met ten people, five adults and four kids. Gisela lived on the top, and she noticed that I had noted that she had the best apartment in the house. "You're an American; you'll understand. I work, the others, they work but not as hard as I do." I responded, "Got ya covered, you're right. You're top dog in this operation. You work the hardest, you deserve the most." Danny mimicked a textbook voice and said, "As Sir Walter Raleigh said, if you work, you eat. No work and you'll starve." Johnson became thoughtful and said, "I think that was John Smith, when they were building Jamestown." Gisela doused this possible argument about who and what with, "That's the trouble with you Americans. You take everything to an extreme. I work but I don't live to work. I work to live."

We were chastened and quiet. Renate steered another course when she reminded Gisela that I had known the song from the music box. Eyes wide and with a big smile, she started to speak German to Renate. They were very excited about something. "Dexter, you must be from the left, the American left, the real left. To know that song. Not everyone knows that song. She came over to me and gave me a big hug. *Eine kleine rot*. This is wonderful. Renate, you have brought him to the right house. Yes, you have done a good thing, Renate."

That was the first time I was to see Gisela. We were to become the best of friends during the next three years. I discovered that she and the other ten people were living in a commune and were experimenting with a "social living situation." Six adults: Frieda, Ingrid, Lise, Franz, Robert, and Gisela. There were four kids: Hedwig, Valdi, Lillith, and

Thomas. They all warmed my heart. This commune was to become my second home. The children did their best to teach me a few words of German. Often I would drop by when they were the only ones there and no matter what question I said to them, they would reply, "*Vielleicht.*" Out would come that yellow-and-blue dictionary and in that small print on page 316 would be "*Vielleicht, Vielleicht*" means maybe. Of course, it all made sense. There I was asking them where was Gisela, what time was she coming home and was she at the market or work? There were the twins, Hedwig and Lillith, Gisela's son Thomas, and another girl named Valdi. "*Maybe*" was the best answer since they didn't know enough English to give me a more detailed answer.

I would sit and wait. Gisela would always come home. In she would come with packages of food. It seemed like she did do everything for this commune. I never saw anyone else take care of the daily necessities of life besides her. Not only would she buy the groceries, I also saw her doing the cooking. When I inquired as to the seeming inequity of this domestic situation, I remembered the first thing she had told, me: "I do all the work around here." Now I understood why she had the largest room with the most amenities.

I loved to hear Gisela speak and talk English. I could listen to her all night and sometimes I do. Her boyfriend Robert did not mind me too much since he was consumed in his academic work for a local college. They had a relationship that offered both of them a great deal of time and space. All three, four, five, six, and more of us go out to movies, the cabaret, picnics, parties, and bars. There are many meals and I make my contribution. From the PX, I can bring great amounts of food at very cheap prices. I become a hero to Hedwig, Valdi, Lillith, and Thomas because I can bring them unlimited jars of peanut butter. The supreme treat is for me to take all four of them, who are all about nine years old, to the barracks on a Saturday for milk shakes. They never speak that much to me but when the guy at the counter asks them what they want, they have no problem blurting out "chocolate, strawberry, or vanilla."

The commune becomes a refuge for me. Whenever the base, which was nicknamed the Kelley Zoo because we American soldiers were more than capable of proving how beastly we could be by robbing German taxi drivers and assaulting them in bars, squeezes my head to the point of cracking, I discover that I can drop by the commune without notice.

When I was on the verge of being court-martialed once, I called Gisela and asked her if I could stay at the house for a couple of days. She said, "Sure, you must come. Immediately." I rode my ten-speed bike from the barracks to Knauss Brothers Street in ten minutes. I cranked the *Internationale* and heard Gisela say that she would get it. I had a little knapsack on the back of my bike. By the time I untied it, Gisela opened the door, with the red hair and white skin that always took my breath away.

"Hi Gisela, it's me."

"Dexter, I know. I must ask you something."

"Gisela, what's up, you look upset."

"I am. I am very upset with you."

I threw my knapsack over my shoulder and made a face. I thought about whether I forgot to bring something, a food item, or a carton of cigarettes. I was confounded. With genuine consternation and concern in my voice, I said, "Gisela, I don't know what I did to upset you, so I can guess, or you can tell me." She took my shoulders and spoke in a low voice, "I spoke to Renate and she says that you were in trouble for some time, some days." I started to feel relieved that it was not anything personal. "Yeah, you can definitely say I've been in some trouble with the army. For a few weeks, that's for sure. Mad Bob, that crazy colonel, he's wants a piece of my ass." She leaned forward and took me by the shoulders. "That's why I'm mad. You've been in trouble for days or weeks. Why weren't you here? I would have hided you." It was the word *hided* that made me choke up and almost cry. As perfect as her English was, she still made a mistake here and there.

"Gisela, is that true? You would have *hided* me."

"Dexter, of course. I would have hided you from that Mad Bob person. I don't give a goddamn about him. I love you."

I waited for the tightness in my throat to abate so I could get a word out without crying. "Gisela, life is long and it's made up of many days, so many days, and I hope that I can always remember this one and what happened at about four o'clock in the afternoon, right here, in the little alley next to the commune. What you just did for me in the last minute . . . I have to stop talking." I took off her glasses and kissed her on the cheek. "Gisela, one more thing, I have to tell you, sort of a confession. It's only because you're getting kinda close to me."

She crossed her arms and started to pull me into the house, but I held fast.

"Dexter, goddamn you, you haven't had a decent meal in days. Come. Confess upstairs with the children around."

I then looked at her and said, "Gisela, I have to tell you that I'm not white. I'm not black either, one hundred percent. I can see that you've let me into your life and I don't want you to get mad later."

Standing with her arms folded across her white blouse, red hair amplified by brown glasses, she stared at me. She then leaned forward and eyed me very closely. At one point she took a whiff of me. Mocking a doctor's examination, I relaxed but she kept a serious face. She then backed away.

"Dexter, well, you're right."

"Right about what?"

"I looked at you closely. You're right. You're not white. You're not black. You're a little crazy. I know that. You are a little crazy."

Between *hided you* and *you're a little crazy,* I started to cry. The starched fatigue shirtsleeve felt rough on my face. The material cut across my face and instead of acting like a handkerchief, the tears just rolled down my cheeks. Gisela was wearing one of her great hippie dresses that went all the way to the ground. "Here," she said, "Take this," and she pulled her dress up so I could wipe the tears. The material felt so much better than the starched cotton. I rolled my face in her soft dress.

"Dexter, we must look funny to the people walking by."

"Yeah, but when you're nuts like me, you get used to it."

She laughed and said, "Come on, I have more hippie dresses upstairs." We went upstairs and I heard kids yelling, running, and chasing after each other. They didn't stop when they saw it was me, and that was good.

Journal Entry
September 7, 1977

Free writing, that's what I'll do. It's what I want to do. Journal writing has amazingly lost its freedom, flexibility, and openness. It's not fresh. But free writing, ah, that's something else. It's always open, no doors, walls or ceilings, nothing to close in and suffocate me.

Free writing launches a lot of ships, takes me back to Queens College, back to classrooms with people, smart people, the quad, grass, trees, September colors, long lines at the book store, registration, new classes, new professors, new assignments, new books, deadlines; new, everything's new in September on a college campus.

Man, I've been feeling pretty good lately; even though my old man passed away just one month ago, I feel good. I feel good knowing that the army doesn't last forever, something I just realized when I figured out that I only had twenty months left in sixty more days (have to stop counting the days). In sixty more days I'll be at the halfway point—eighteen months in, eighteen months to go. Oh yeah, this is what writing is supposed to be like. It's beautiful. It's beautiful again, the way my journal writing used to be when I first started writing. Free writing—I'm so glad I found you again. Man, it's like old buddies coming together after a stretch of not seeing each other and lighting each other's cigarettes and they bend close to each other to get the light and their hands touch. I haven't seen you in a long time, and it's good to see you again. That journal got so oppressive in the last three months. Now I'm back on track; I'm writing what I want to write.

Feel good, damn, so goddamn good. I feel alive. Could really dig hearing some Charlie Parker. When? Right now, you motherfuckin' army. I don't care that I have twenty-four hours of duty on September 7, 1977. I want to hear Charlie Parker right now. I demand it. I demand that Bird records be played all over the post, all through Kelley Barracks, all through the Seventh Army. Fuck it—I want Charlie Parker played on every radio station in Germany. They gave three days of air time for Elvis because he kicked off, so I want a week of Charlie Parker, twenty-four hours a day for seven days. I want to hear Charlie Parker with Dizzy Gillespie, Miles Davis, with Strings, with his All-Stars, and by himself. I want to hear Bird play his jazz right now, right now. I want to hear him get on that alto sax and just play and play and play and play and play and then, just then, right about then, he'd be warmed up enough to really start playing.

Charlie Parker, Yardbird, Bird, a black dude from Kansas City. Bird, a man with a new idea, a new way of playing, sounding, thinking, and finally a new way of being. An alto man who died when he was only thirty-four, thirty-four, man, that's so young. Charlie Parker dying young just like Jimmy Blanton and Charlie Christian, young black jazz musicians changing the scene completely and then disappearing forever before the full impact of their genius had even blossomed. Young black dudes doing things that no one else could do. Damn.

Damn, Charlie, why did you have to die so young? I would have loved you, worshipped you. The feelings I possess for you now are just a mere pittance of what they would have been if the New York *Daily News* had never had to announce in a headline back in 1955: Bop King Dies in Heiress' Flat. Charlie Parker, master musician, master technician, a real artist: *My Old Flame, Embraceable You, K.C. Blues, Funky Blues, Dizzy Atmosphere, Hot House, Air Conditioning, Lady Be Good,* and *Dewey Square.* That's all he wrote.

It's an all-right day even though I got guard duty. Whitfield just walked by, a lifer sergeant if there ever was one. Probably thinks that because he's black he can't be a bastard, a pig of a man. That's a myth, a legend, a lie. The day my old man died, all he could tell me was, "Jeffries, you need a haircut. If you don't get one by seventeen hundred, I'll burn your ass." White people don't know this, but when a black goes after another black, especially in situations like the army, shit, I'd rather have Local Chapter 65 of the Po-Hunk Ku Klux Klan after me. Black on black, a story as old as the hills. A tale that goes back to the days of the plantation.

But it's still a nice day, and I'm groovin' high on my writing. I feel high and a couple of guys have already inquired what kind of hash I've been smoking in my bowl. Ain't hash man, ain't dope, heroin, and it ain't liquor. I just feel good even though I'm in the army, six thousand miles away from home and my old man passed away.

Man, this is the way Thoreau must have felt when he was sittin' at his pond, just gettin' off on his own nature-connected meditative trip. Thoreau, definitely cool, laid back. Just sittin' at the pond checking things out.

Can't stop writing since I've made the mistake of writing on a window ledge, and I'm watching the entire universe and what's going on. The base is starting to jump. Where the hell are all those "deuce and a halfs" going? Five-ton dump trucks, cats slicking their hair down so they won't catch any flak from Top, the first sergeant. Yeah, everyone is running some kind of game to keep his hair as long as possible. Have to stop writing because there are some things that stop even the most dedicated writers like myself and that's a sergeant yelling at me about some detail. But I still feel good even though I'm in the army, six thousand miles away, and my old man just passed away.

Big Jim

———)(0)(———

I'M SITTING NEXT to Big Jim in the NCO Club at the base. The NCO Club is more euphemism now; I think during World War II it really had a meaning; there were some class distinctions maintained among enlisted men. A sergeant meant something and a corporal meant something, and that's why Officers' Club stood for one class of soldier and a noncommissioned officer was another species. Since the end of the Vietnam War, a war that obviously blurred everything, the American army became a mob, a bunch of rebellious men who decided that wars were never going to be fought again in the same way; Big Jim is a product of that chaos, all 350 pounds of him.

Big Jim is a full-blooded Cherokee Indian from Oklahoma. His weight precedes him though. Before you notice that he's an Indian, you notice his girth. This 350-pounds cannot fit into his web belt, which has his sloppily slung flashlight, his Buck knife used for cutting and laying wire, canteen, and other things that we have to carry on field maneuvers. Never buckling the web belt always gives him a disheveled appearance no matter how clean and well kept his equipment may be. His first-aid pouch and ammo pouches ride so high on his body that he would have to remove the entire harness if he ever wanted something in a hurry and by that time he would be dead. He sweats and breathes heavily during any physical exertion and has a dream-come-true medical profile that excuses him from all physical exercise. I used to wonder about the contradiction because I'm the type of guy who will ask that incredulous question, "If a guy can't do any physical exercise, how does he stay in the army? If there is a war, wouldn't he . . . ?" I've learned after a few years that type of thinking only leads down a frustrating path. You just accept that fact that this 350-pound man can't tie his shoes, not because he can't reach them, but because the swollen ankles and feet that lie at the end of his stubby legs won't allow it. That's how fat he is. He's grotesque, but I love his voice. American Indians sometimes have the most sonorous voices. He resonates whenever he speaks in the most brilliant and vibrant colors. I wish I could talk like him. We're having our classic conversation and I think it's intriguing that he says the same thing every time that I talk to him. Reaching for the small Budweiser that I've bought him for fifty cents he shakes his head.

"Jeffries, I just want to ask you something." This comes out with Shakespearean hues and tints. Because he's drunk, he repeats it, "Jeffries, I just want to ask you something." The second time it's sweeter because he's added some vocal assonance. "Jeffries, you're smart; I just want to ask you something."

"Yes, Big Jim," I say, pronouncing every word and saying yes instead of yeah because I'm ashamed of how I sound around him.

"You're smart. I just want to ask you a question. Who's worse? The niggers or the spics?"

The first time he said this to me I was shocked. It was incredible. It was the incongruity of it. Here was a man who possessed such vocal charm and appealing expressions; it should be impossible for him to utter such crude and ugly sentiments. Second, he's an American Indian and if there is one man that should be capable of understanding what the consequences of racism are, it's him; therefore, he should view with absolute contempt any aspect of racial hatred or animosity. Big Jim set me straight a long time ago about Indians and my noble vision of my red brothers. I had idealized them based on movies and books and didn't know they were like any other group of Americans. They were infected with the cancer too. It was just harder to accept that from them because of their history. That history was rich in desolation, despair and pain, all revolving around what America had inflicted upon them.

"Well, what do you think? The niggers or the spics? One of them has to be better. right?"

"I don't know, Big Jim."

"College boy doesn't know."

"Big Jim, weren't there some segregated units with good battle records?"

"Hell no, who told you that?"

"Big Jim, haven't you ever heard of the Ninth and Tenth Cavalry, all black regiments, out West on the frontier? They had good battle records."

Big Jim explodes and I'm taken aback when I see the spittle on his lips. He leans forward and yells, "Goddamn buffalo soldiers killing my people! How am I supposed to feel?"

I look at him and try to smile that stupid smile that connotes how dumb can I be to mention the buffalo soldiers to an Indian. A couple of people turned when they heard him yell, but there's nothing more.

It's time to squelch this discussion so I say, "It's a complicated question."

"Jeffries, it's not that complicated. Not if you study it, like I have." The *have* reminds me of the Caedmon Recording Company in England. They have famous British actors and actresses read drama, poetry, and prose. Big Will could have been one of their voices. I would give anything to talk like him.

His big hand sweeps back all the jet-black hair that has fallen over his forehead and for a second he looks like a cute kid. Indians don't shave that much because they rarely have facial hair. Without whiskers and with the full shock of black hair being swept back again, I see how handsome he was at one time. I can't help but idealize him even now. I hear the ugly racism spewing out of his mouth, and yet I see him as a young boy on an Indian reservation in Oklahoma, and I see a little boy running around through beat-up houses and trailers in the late 1940s and early 1950s. Because of the despair of the reservation and its always-present death's head of whiskey and suicide, the army doesn't seem like such a bad idea back in 1955. It gets a Cherokee Indian out of the empty, dusty streets where jobs are nonexistent and the only thing that one is really sure of is *they've won; they got us where they want us and there is nothing we can do about it.*

I study him and soon he fills the silence with his didactic explanation, saying, "I think the niggers are worse; they're so goddamn lazy. Jesus, you ask them to lay a field telephone from a forward observation post back to the C.P., and you find them sleeping with the wire wheel in a foxhole somewhere. Damn spics, talk some mumbo-jumbo language. Catholic. Spics are worse. That's for sure."

"Big Jim, you just said that the blacks were worse than the Puerto

Rican guys! Now you're saying that the Puerto Ricans are worse than the blacks!"

"I said that?"

"Yeah, I mean, yes. You said that."

"Jeffries, oh, buy me another beer. I'll buy, you fly. I just have a hard time getting up."

"Are you sure?"

"Sure, I'm sure. Go get a nice Miller High Life, the Champagne of Bottled Beer."

In the darkened NCO Club I amble over to the bar. They've turned the lights down low because there is going to be some live entertainment. I'm a little too drunk to care if it's a local German rock band or an American group that's being sponsored by the USO. I'm always a little ashamed if it's the latter since we're so damn rowdy and violent that we shock the Americans who come to entertain us. If there is a lead female singer, which there usually is, I know she's in for a shock. Nothing back in the States can prepare her for a bunch of sex-deprived GIs yelling, "Suck my cock baby; I wanna jam this down your throat. I'm going to split you wide open baby with this ten inches." I hide on those nights. I almost got into a fight once when there were some American actors doing famous scenes from Shakespeare's plays. The usual catcalls started, "Juliet, you beautiful bitch, suck on my dong." I shoved Sergeant Anderson, and he was so surprised that it was me and mumbled something about, "What the fuck is wrong with you? There's enough room for everybody."

"That person is an actor, a real actor. She knows about literature and poetry."

"What kind of feather you got up your ass tonight, Jeffries?"

"Don't fuckin' curse at her anymore, you sorry lowlife mother-fucker."

"Jesus fuckin' Christ, what's eating you?"

Luckily nothing happened. Even though we were off duty, getting in some fracas with a sergeant wasn't going to do my record any good so I just leave it at that. The bar is a little makeshift operation. It has wheels and can be pushed out of the way like a piece of stage scenery.

"Jeffries, what's up? Hanging out with Big Chief tonight, huh?"

"Yeah, Big Jim is an interesting guy. Gimme two Millers."

"Big Chief is a good guy to know. He knows a lot of shit. Killed plenty of gooks overseas. He knows what he's doing."

"I guess so," and I try to imagine if Big Jim ever went to scalping any Vietnamese and laugh at the image of him carrying around a few scalps on his web belt like trophies. I walk back to our table and hear the band starting to test mikes and amplifiers. It's Country Western night, and all the shit kickers are wearing their cowboy hats. These hats cost seventy to a hundred bucks, and their boots go for two-fifty. That's a real investment. I thread my way through Stetsons and rawhide. Big Jim is right where I left him. Nothing has changed.

"Jeffries, you know that Miller High Life is the Champagne of Bottled Beer?"

I start to hum the commercial tune, and he smiles. "Sure, Big Jim, I know about Miller High Life. When I was a kid, that was one of the biggest commercials on TV."

"When you were a kid? What are you now?" These words come out with a fatherly tone of concern that expressed I don't know who I am and I don't know where I'm going. This is true, but it just sounds strange coming out of his mouth.

"Jeffries, heard you got in some trouble up at headquarters. You must have fucked up pretty bad. You were in S-2, intelligence, right?"

"Yeah, had it dicked. Office, warm in the winter, custodian of maps and documents. It was a good job."

He speaks as he shifts his mass in his seat, "So what the hell happened? You made corporal in four months, got a college degree. You would have made sergeant in two years."

I'm uncomfortable and feel guilty that this reference to my personal troubles in the battalion has caused more trepidation than his sordid racism which can come out at any time. No question, I got in trouble but I didn't know the rest of the outfit knew about it. Rumors and truth spread pretty fast on an army base.

"Look, I fucked up. I messed with the colonel . . ."

"You messed with Mad Bob?"

Sipping my Miller I nod my head, and he leans back in his chair and shakes his. He puts his hand on his forehand and slowly swivels it from side to side.

"Testing, one, two, three; testing, one, two three; gimme a little bass on that left one, will ya buddy?"

Big Jim looks up and snorts a grunt of disgust. "C&W tonight; the shit kickers must be pretty happy."

I turn around to look at the musicians with denim pants and shirts, red handkerchiefs and genuine string ties. I'm glad the music is about to start since I want this conversation about my troubles to end, one way or another. Just to show that I'm an adult, I decide to bring the conversation back to the charges and allegations that are going all around the base.

"Like I said, I fucked with the colonel . . ."

"What a kid thing to do."

". . . and they sent me to a line rat company to be a line rat because . . ."

"What did you do?"

"During the AGI, I complained that Mad Bob was wearing a British tankers sweater when we had to wear standard GI issue. That's all."

This has made Big Jim perk up. His Miller is almost all gone, and I'm only down a third. He puts the beer down and because of the heat in the NCO Club starts to roll up his sleeves. When he does this, GIs at a few other tables start to look with consternation on their faces. I know why they're worried, but I'm not, because Big Jim is with me and that still means something, notwithstanding my confession.

"So I complained to the inspector general. He was a nice guy, took my side, said he understood the nature of my complaint and you know what he said? He said, 'Jeffries, I want you to know one thing; Colonel Harris will not be wearing that sweater this afternoon.'" Big Jim coughs into his hand a mighty cough and speaks through the cup formed by those five meaty fingers. While gasping a bit he finishes the conversation with, "And Colonel Harris wasn't wearing that sweater that afternoon and you were with us line rats the next day. Man, what a kid thing to do. Just goes to show you that you can have a college degree and that doesn't necessarily mean you're intelligent."

I wince and look at him because this has come out so rationally, so methodically. He comforts me with a smile. He says, "Look, every man fucks up one job, one relationship, and himself, one time. That's it. You won't do anything like that again." I start to spin the bottle of Miller beer, so I'm looking at it from the back side. I notice that on the inside of the front label, from the back, you can read *Miller High Life The Champagne of Bottled Beer*.

"I wanna thank ya'll for coming. We're the Green River Boys from

Steamboat Springs, Col-rado. Wanna give a big hello to all you guys of the 617th Engineer Battalion and a special hello to all the folks who came out to hear some good ol' C&W. One, two three . . ."

Because of the steady flow of Budweisers and Millers, Big Jim is starting to metamorphose into a walrus right in front of me. He blows air out of his lips with a blustering sound, and I'm ready for him to keel over from the chair to the floor. But Big Jim has proven on so many previous occasions that no amount of alcohol can bring him down. He's legendary in the battalion for drinking cases of beer at night and staggering to the first formation at six the next morning, reporting for duty. I saw him get into a fight once; it wasn't a fight. It was a barroom brawl with guys from another outfit. Chairs and tables were flying. Bottles were catching people in their heads and not breaking the way they do in movies. They hurt, but they don't break. At one point, while someone was choking me, I saw that Big Jim had picked up two soldiers, one in each hand, like some kind of giant and rammed them together once, twice, then dropped them to the floor. He had actually lifted each guy off the floor with one arm and had held him for about five or six seconds. It was something.

In addition to his fighting prowess, another claim to fame that made the other GIs swivel their heads in curiosity before when he rolled up his sleeves, is his ability to smolder cigarettes in the flesh of his arms. I don't know when this began. Maybe Vietnam. Maybe a tour in France before de Gaulle kicked NATO forces out in the sixties. Maybe Japan. Some of these lifers who've done twenty to thirty years have been everywhere. It's a terrible and beastly thing and he has contests with other soldiers to see who can put out the most cigarettes in their forearms. The skin on his forearms is really not skin; it's just one continuous pus-running scab that he never bandages. He can take it. His arms are constantly infected, and the medic at the aid station gave up on warning him about the dire consequences of a prolonged infection. His pride comes first.

Both arms are pockmarked with holes because once he starts to bet, there's no telling how long the contests will go on. So many guys in the outfit think they can challenge Big Jim and put out more butts in their arms than he can, but he's never been beaten. No one can beat him. His normally fleshy skin is green and gray from the infections. The filmy scabs on his arms have caused some guys to joke that it's not fair since the ooze is a liquid and that gives him an unfair advantage when smothering lit cigarettes. Big Jim just obliges them by picking some other unadulterated piece of flesh on his arm, hard as that is, and starts the process all over again. I peruse his beefy arms and drink my beer. With the Green River Boys in the background I inform Big Jim that I'm heading back to the barracks.

"Hey, wait a second, you never answered my question."

"I told you. I fucked with the colonel and Top Blackstone, and this is what happens when you're a corporal fucking with a colonel."

With exasperation in his voice and this walrus blustering he says, "No, you didn't tell me who was better. The niggers or the spics." I stand up, drain my Champagne of Bottled Beer and place the empty on the table. "Gotta go, Big Jim. Gotta go." The last thing I heard as I walked out, even over the hootin' and a-hollerin' of the good old boys as they urged the Green River Boys on, was Big Jim's perfectly enunciated voice, "Jeffries, what about Top's little babies? Do you think that's fair? What about Top's little babies? Do you think that's fair to the whites and the Indians? Top's little babies are treated differently and you know it. What about Top's little babies? . . ."

A few months later I'm in the orderly room clerking for Topkick Baker the first sergeant. He knows I got kicked out of headquarters company but doesn't hold it against me. He believes *Every man deserves a fair chance*. After giving me my one fair chance, I've proven to him that I can cut the mustard as company clerk and jeep driver, and I'm a pretty good combat engineer. I want to serve because since my old man died I have really gone out of my way to make Top my father. He knows it on some level and doesn't mind. He has a son in the States that he hasn't seen in years, and I comfort him with my longing, and he comforts me with his missing. Topkick Baker is black, a well-spoken gentle man, and a gentle soul. Quiet, low-key and restrained, he reminds me of Stanley Diaz. One day when he was conducting an impromptu drug inspection of the barracks, he pulled a book off my shelf. I laughed as I thought of my brother and how nothing would come pouring out of this book, no matter how hard you shook it. Instead of shaking it, he looked at the title, said, "*Lessons in Racism*, huh? I could add a few chapters to this book."

At six feet four, Top cuts a lean figure, and with his trimmed mustache he carries a lot of dignity with him; he's been in since World War II and has over thirty years of service. When he first joined, the army was segregated and he got in some trouble on Okinawa with a white officer that "insulted him." He grabbed that good old entrenching tool, the handy dandy shovel that folds in half, and slammed this second lieutenant and got in big trouble, court-martial, the whole nine yards. He worked himself back up and proved that he could soldier with any man; now he's first sergeant of Charlie Company of the 617th Engineer Battalion.

But that's not what makes him special, at least not to me. When your father dies, you get all these new feelings. I did not think there was anything fortuitous in my almost getting court-martialed for insubordination; they were thinking about shipping me home and had already scheduled my out-processing medical examination. I hitched a ride to the local base hospital to take the physical. I was in a quandary about getting kicked out for not wanting to follow an order here and there, especially a stupid order. It was that damn Sergeant Brenner. He had pushed things to an edge, threatening me, and forcing me into a corner:

Brenner: Remember one thing, Jeffries. If I ever give you an order, you have to follow it.

Me: Look, I'll do anything you say, as long as it's by the book.

Brenner: And if it's not by the book?

Me: I ain't doing it.

Brenner: Just for the record, you're stating that you won't follow an order and you're stating this in front of witnesses. Hughes, you heard what he said, right?

Me: Hughes can go fuck himself. I don't need no witnesses. I'm just telling you how it's gonna be.

Brenner: What if I tell you, check that, what if I order him to kill some dink kids?

Me: I'd kill you first before I kill a bunch of gook kids.

With that response, Sergeant Brenner took off and went straight to the first sergeant's office. In about thirty seconds I heard my name being yelled by the company clerk that Top Blackstone wanted to see me, immediately. I knew the script from movies and books. All I had to do was listen and act out my part. It went by the numbers. Sergeant Blackstone informed me that I had threatened a noncommissioned officer. That this was a court-martial offence. Sergeant Brenner had witnesses. I was restricted to the barracks until further notice. I calmly walked out of the office and went to my bunk.

Everything had gone exactly as I knew it would. And I knew that within a day or two I would be taken with an escort of one sergeant over to the JAG office to see my lawyer. But from that point on, those old army lifers didn't know that a new movie and a new script never produced before was going to be unveiled and a lot of their predictions would go awry. The American army that men like Brenner, Blackstone, and Big Jim had joined was conjured up in the 1950s. This was 1975 and the war—Vietnam—not World War II, was over, and things could never be the same. As soon as I walked into the JAG office which was made up of college graduates who had gone on to law school and had made some deal for a student loan in exchange for a few years as an army lawyer, I felt at home. Blackstone, Brenner, and every other soldier from the old army didn't comprehend for a second that if you were a lawyer in 1975, there was an excellent chance that you were a college student in the 1960s and that made all the difference in the world. Just as the American army would never be the same after the war, American colleges weren't the same institutions during or after Vietnam.

Walking into the office of the army lawyers was like walking into a college union building where students routinely hung out, rapped, smoked dope, and girlfriends met boyfriends. Whatever little fears that were still remaining with me dissolved when I heard a captain, with the longest hair possible say, "Jeffries, what's happening?" I was home and it felt good. Captain Welch held up his clenched fist in the "power to the people" sign and I did the same. He never spoke professionally or *armily* once during my interview:

"Dexter, yeah, Queens College, New York City, home of Simon and Garfunkle, good college, yeah." I noticed that he had my personnel folder on his desk and that was where all of the information was coming from. Captain Welch informed me that we were on a first name basis from this point on. A few other lawyers came over to the desk and started asking me about Queens College, its good reputation. One was obsessed with the fact that Queens had a first-rate women's basketball team, and he even cited some statistics. "That's so right on, to have a women's basketball team, one of the best in the eastern division. I mean, that's really right on. I mean, how many colleges have a women's team? Plus, didn't Jane Fonda make a speech there, like a really right on speech?"

"I saw her that day."

"What?"

"Yeah, I saw her."

"You goddamn saw Jane Fonda?"

"Yeah, she's little. She had big shades on."

"Hey, Jack, Jeffries here saw Jane Fonda at Queens College."

"Way to go, Jeffries."

"I remember it as clear as day. It was right behind Jefferson Hall, the registrar's office. On the Quad. I think we had turned the flag upside down."

"Holy shit!"

"Yeah, and she's little and beautiful and she was too small for the mike, so they had to lower it for her."

"Keep going!"

"Well, it was fall, I think, and she had this little white shirt on, like I said, shades, and no bra."

"You gotta be shittin' me."

"No, I swear. No bra. But she had little titties so you really couldn't see anything."

It was beautiful. I had been sent there with the expressed purpose of finding out what my rights were and the possibilities of being prosecuted, found guilty for insubordination, and being sent to the dreaded stockade down in Mannheim which was known as "Little Leavenworth." Instead, it was like old home week. At one point, just to bring everyone back to reality, I asked them about the case. Fumbling around and remembering why I was there, Captain Welch, I mean, Jack of Boston College, flipped through some papers and mumbled to himself "Army regs state that an order given from a noncommissioned officer to . . ." and then showed my folder to another JAG officer. They smiled and asked me about the order. "Did Brenner tell you that you had to kill some gook kids?" I replied that's how the whole thing got started. Big smiles came across their faces.

Jack: Look, ever since that My Lai incident, Calley, the massacre, the army's taking a hard line on the killing of civilians.

Captain Collister: Noncombatants.

Jack: Yeah, noncombatants, so this asshole is lucky we don't bring him up on some charges himself, Brenner, right? We'll squash this thing ASAP. Strictly a bullshit case. You can go back to your outfit if you have transportation arranged or you can hang out with us. English major, right. Me too, most lawyers are either poly sci or English. I had this great Victorian lit course, Robert Browning, beautiful.

I hung out with my buddies seeing that I was to have a day off from the army and it was only 0900 so why rush back to the Kelley Zoo when I could rap with my new friends. A few hours later, I asked to use the phone so I could call up the company driver to be picked up. I found out that his blurring of the lines between officers and enlisted men occurred frequently and if you were a college graduate, as I was, most of the officers longed to have someone to talk to. We basically dropped all protocol, and the only rule to remember was not to call them by their first name in front of some other higher authority. That was easy to remember.

I got back to the base and looked solemn. Top Blackstone triumphantly asked me what happened, and I told him that I wasn't supposed to talk about it. He reminded himself that he wasn't supposed to ask me about things, now that there were legal concerns, and left me alone. A few days later I was summoned again into his office. He had official interoffice army mail on his desk. He rubbed his chin and shook his head. He was flustered. I could see written on an envelope was "Copy for Sp4 Jeffries, Dexter." He coughed and started to read his copy. He coughed again and said, "Jeffries, I don't know how the fuck this happened, but all charges are dropped against you, and they want to see Sergeant Brenner about taking 'a course on the articles of war with an emphasis on the role of soldiers and noncombatants.' In addition, he's supposed to retake a course on race relations for abusing you with racial epithets." I looked and tried not to smile and knew if I stayed focused on some object in the room that I would get through this little comedic scene where the world has been turned upside down. I coughed too, and said, "Top, I think you're supposed to give me that copy. That's the disposition of the case. Need it for my file."

First Sergeant Blackstone examined me up and down and said, "Sure, this is your copy." Even though the charges were dropped, I was disciplined for my attitude and found myself transferred to a company of line rats. The army has steps that it must follow and despite the fact that I was not going to be prosecuted for anything, the bureaucracy had started to roll. I was instructed to take an out-processing physical in case I was prematurely discharged. The last thing Top Blackstone said was, "Jeffries, I'm gettin' you out of this outfit if I have to go to Mad Bob myself." That's how I met Topkick Baker, black Top.

Top Blackstone was right. He got me out of headquarters company and transferred me to Charlie. I moved all of my things in a duffel bag and on a dolly from my old barracks to my new one. Hurt that I couldn't stay with my friends of a year, I was depressed as I walked from one part of the base to another. Ray Gary helped carry my field equipment to my new barracks and mentioned that it wouldn't be so bad, that we'd still see each other in the mess hall three times a day, and I conceded that worse things could have happened. I reported to black Top to find out what platoon I would be assigned to and what my job and fate would be for two years. I stood in front of his desk at attention as he sifted through my personnel file. He took off his black-rimmed glasses and said, "To tell you the truth, I don't put much credence in rumors and hearsay. Every man deserves a fair chance. Looking through your record, I can see that you are pretty qualified to do a few things. I need a driver and a clerk; headquarters platoon also needs one rifleman to man the .50-caliber machine gun. You can do all three, so that's where I'm going to put you until further notice."

I looked at him and felt warm from head to toe, the good warm. All I could get out was, "Appreciate it, Top. I'm a good trooper." He closed my folder and told me that the CO wanted to see me and interview me about the incident with the colonel and Sergeant Brenner. Captain Parker was in his office, and I was to report to him immediately. I walked into his office and gave the perfunctory, "Sp4 Jeffries, reporting to the company commander as ordered." Parker was not a West Pointer; I could see that immediately. He had come up through ROTC at some midwestern college campus that still thought we could win the war in Vietnam. Even though the war was over, he still believed. A thoughtful man, he informed me in clear terms that my record was shaky and that just in case I needed some motivation, he wanted me to take that out-processing physical as soon as possible, so as to expedite any other transfers or discharges. I kept my remarks brief and said "Yes, sir." He saluted and dismissed me. I reported back to Top and told him about the request for the physical, and he nodded.

Two weeks later I report to the base hospital for my physical. I tell the medic who I am and why. He looks through all of his papers, files, personnel jackets. Nothing. With a shake of the head he lets me know that no physicals can be given without the appropriate papers authorizing one. "Jeffries, check with Top; somebody fucked up. Nothing here." On the way back to the barracks I figure out why my paperwork is missing and smile. Black Top is a good guy.

I started to work for black Top within an hour of setting up my bunk, receiving my new M-16 from the armorer, and a gas mask from the sergeant in charge of germ warfare. The jeep needed a new rear end, and he asked me if I could handle that. I smiled and told him that I was a pretty good mechanic and could take care of it. I got under that jeep the next morning at about seven and crawled out at about five. For the entire day I was under the jeep, droplight in hand, sometimes hanging from a brake line, wrenches and ratchets all over the place. It felt good to work on the jeep. The rear end was on order from the States, and it was being routed through Bremerhaven by ship. The jeep stayed up on a jack, and Top put me to work typing and filing. He could see that I was quick and efficient. I liked Charlie Company. I had found a new home and an intelligent black man who could do the *New York Times* crossword puzzle in less than twenty minutes. That was our only problem. I was of no help to him when it came to doing the puzzle.

Baffled at my inability to do the puzzle he inquired as to how I could be an English major and not be able to do it. I explained that I was puzzled by that myself and how I wasn't good at Scrabble either. He shook his head. He had wanted to have a contest. About once a week we would get a two-week-old copy of the *Times*, and he savored it for the crossword puzzle. He thought I was going to keep him sharp. Sadly disappointed he was at least able to get a laugh out of the whole thing. Once he gave me the clue, *Catfish's Milieu*. I actually thought I knew the answer and said *river*. "Jeffries, wait until I tell you how many letters. It's a word with seven letters." I became thoughtful and concentrated and quickly said *old river*. Top began to shake his head and laugh. He took his glasses off so he could wipe the tears that had come into his eyes. He brought his sleeve up to his face. I started to laugh because I was making him laugh so much. "Jeffries, the answer is *stadium* as in Yankee Stadium. Catfish, Catfish Hunter, don't you get it?" I start to laugh a little more at my lack of imagination and he repeats *old river* a few times. We get along well on many a day with me correctly answering a few crossword questions on occasion. I'm good for jazz, history, and some poetry.

Our bond becomes an alliance, and we start to work as a team. We confront Captain Parker on issues where a little common sense could make all the difference in the world in terms of pure physical suffering. For instance, we were on a winter maneuver once, snowstorms, freezing conditions, and no hot food for days. The whole time we're eating cold C-rations or nothing at all, the mess sergeant and his truck which was capable of preparing many hot meals, stood idle. Top stepped into Captain Parker's tent one night exasperated at the grumbling of the men. Their morale was low, and this wasn't necessary, at least in his opinion.

Top: Sir, pardon my language, but this is a bunch of bullshit. We could be giving the men hot chow in this freezing weather.

Captain: Top, no question, no question at all, but this is a good field training exercise. The men should know what it is, deprivation, not having things their way.

Top: Sir, how is that teaching them anything positive during this FTX?

Captain: The deprivation. I just pointed that out. Do you think it's going to be a sunny day with hot chow when the Russians come?

Top: Sir, don't give me that bullshit, pardon my language. We had hot chow flown in on choppers so many times I can't remember. Yes, right after fighting Charlie in a hot l-z.

There was silence, and I heard the flap of a canvas tent being opened and closed brusquely. Crunching snow and the sound of galoshes approaching told me that Top was headed back toward our tent, but because of the snow I couldn't tell from his footsteps whether this had been a victory or a defeat. In any other season, I would have known from his footfalls that he had succeeded or failed in his request. Snow slows everything down to one speed. One doesn't know what's going to happen.

When his footsteps come right up to the tent, I hear them stop. The flap doesn't come hurling open. Top is standing outside brushing the snow off the flaps, so it doesn't come flying in. It's a little detail, but it shows how careful he is and how much he knows about deprivation. The flap comes open, and he bends a bit to enter. As he brushes the snow off his winter parka, he says, "Jeffries, get your stuff on. Go over to the mess truck. Tell Sergeant Matthews I want a hot meal for the men within an hour. Soup, main meal and a dessert. You got that?" I unzip my sleeping bag and smile. Hot chow sounds good to me. I have all my clothes on except for boots and galoshes. While I put them on, Top remembers one more thing: "Jeffries, tell Sergeant Matthews I want a pot of coffee in fifteen minutes." I tell him "Sure" and walk out of the tent, and I'm proud that he's done this for the company, the men. He makes sense. He always makes sense.

Back at the base, months later, Top gave me another order. I was typing some forms, and he was checking the readiness chart that instantly informed him how many trucks worked, how many were waiting for parts, and how many would never be prepared or at least not while he was first sergeant of Charlie Company. His grease pencil was scribbling little letters next to each vehicle. I noticed that he smiled when he looked at the code of his Jeep and realized again that I had fixed it. I had put that rear end in the Jeep the first week I reported for duty. While he looked at the board, he turned slightly toward my desk and said, "Jeffries, you know Sergeant Kenny?" I kept on typing since the answer required no thought. I murmured, "You mean, Big Jim?" Top sounded frustrated, and he replied, "Yeah, Big Jim, Big Chief, whatever. You scoot over to the Commo section ASAP and tell him I want to see him immediately. Got that?"

I jumped up because his voice had frustration and urgency in it. I didn't have to acknowledge with words. I put my field jacket on, pulled on my black gloves, and put on my hat. I half walked and half ran over to the Commo section. Big Jim was at his workbench, testing batteries when I walked in. I told him that Top wanted to see him ASAP. He kept reading a meter with needles and dials and just nodded. I waited and my presence forced him to end his tests. He struggled with his field jacket and hat, and we started to walk back to the barracks together. However, Big Jim walked so slowly that I told him I had to "keep on trucking." I quickly left him behind and got to the office five minutes ahead of him.

Top looked behind me when I opened the door, and he could see instantly that Big Jim was not with me. He waited a few seconds before saying anything. "Jeffries, when you were walking back with Big Jim, could you tell whether he was deliberately walking slow or was he walking with a purpose?" I was at the coat stand when he asked me that and didn't turn to answer. I thought about the question, though. I said, "No, Top. Big Jim is pretty fat; he was walking as fast as he could." There was no reply, just quiet.

Now we can hear his huffing and puffing. He's arrived. When he walks in the door, he's covered with sweat, and I feel a little sympathy for him and understand why he's prohibited from physical training. Top's at his desk and takes off his glasses. He pauses for a second before saying, "Sergeant Kenny, I've been meaning to talk to you about something. Big Jim looks toward the chair that is usually drawn up to the side of the desk. Top shakes his head and stops his outreached hand with, "Keep standing. No one told you to sit down." Sergeant Kenny is surprised but not hurt. There's a knowing smirk on his countenance. There's no time to waste and Top starts right in with, "Kenny, there's already enough racial animosity in the company without you adding to it." The huffing and puffing continues, and Big Jim draws his air easier and easier which means he's catching his breath. "I know that you've been sowing racial discontent in the company," Top continues. Top's voice is sharp and penetrating. Big Jim is finally breathing easier, but he wants to sit down as though this will alleviate the seriousness and tension of the situation. Top won't have it. He keeps looking at Big Jim and just to make sure that things can be as clear as they can be, he removes his black-rimmed reading glasses, holds them and says, "Do you understand, Staff Sergeant Kenny?"

"Top, I'm just telling the truth. I'm just telling people about you and your little babies. I'm just . . ." and before he can finish, Top throws his glasses on the desk and shouts, "What the hell does that mean, mister?" As if he's been waiting for this opportunity to clear or vindicate himself, Big Jim appears relaxed. The raised voice has done nothing to his facial or body expression. No remorse, no regret. With something between a smirk and smile on his face, he responds, "Top, everyone knows, all the whites and the Indians know that you are promoting the niggers over them. You're putting them first." I say the word *shit* to myself, the awed and scared *shit*. Top's swivel chair on wheels goes hurtling back from his desk across the room as though jerked by some catapult. It crashes into the metal radiator covers and then bounces and rolls back toward him. When the chair hit the radiator cover with a boom, Top was already around the desk, and he had grabbed Big Jim. My heart is thumping as they start to grab at each other. I'm scared and get up and Top yells, "Stay right there, Jeff!"

They're both big men, and they were in a stalemate. Big Jim is stronger but his weight has him hamstrung. Top is lean and mean and is just able to pin him against the wall. It's a real fight. It's quick, and there's not too much punching, just holding and struggling. With his one hand that is still free Big Jim moves it down to his belt, in search of that Buck knife. Every Commo sergeant has one for cutting and laying wire. I start to move toward them, and Top has enough presence, strength, and courage to look at me and shake his head *no*. When Big Jim's hand gets to the Buck knife cover so he can unbuckle it, Top drops his left hand on top of his. I see what he's doing. He put his hand over Big Jim's and latches on to his belt, so he has something to hold on to. Every time Big Jim tries to unbuckle the case, Top's strong black hand holds on to that belt. With his other hand, he starts to choke Big Jim. He rams his head into the wall as he chokes him, and Big Jim's hair moves like a set hairpiece. One, two, three rams into the wall and between the rams and the choking Big Jim is really turning red. No punches have been landed, no Hollywood fight, just a great deal of pain and emotion. "OK," comes out of Big Jim. Top keeps choking him and his next "OK" is clearly heard and Top relents a bit. Even though he lessens his choke-hold on him, Big Jim still announces a third "OK." I'm only two or three feet away, haven't done anything since Top shook his head at me, but I'm perspiring. All you can hear is the breathing.

As he lets go of Big Jim's throat, he shoves Big Jim's knife hand away like it's broken and swiftly unbuckles the cover. He takes the knife out and throws it on the floor. "Pick it up, Jeff" comes out at me. I walk over and follow it as it keeps spinning on our newly waxed floor. I lean down but keep looking in their direction. A Buck knife is a solid knife, and I feel its weight and threat when I pick it up. "Kenny, get the hell out of this office; I'm going to keep that knife for a while." This long sentence reveals that Top is completely out of breath also because he paused after the word *office*. Big Jim is still leaning against the wall, laboriously breathing. He's red as an apple. He nods his head and winces in pain as the sore part of his head comes back into contact with the wall. He turns, using the wall for support and starts to slide and half walk toward the door. At the door, he looks at me and says, "Negro lover." I look at him. I've been called many things in my life, all having to do with race, but never that. He keeps on walking and rests for a second, using the square door handle for support. He leaves the door open as he walks out.

"Top, you OK?" are the first words out of my mouth. He nods his head and leans against the desk. He's breathing hard, not as hard as Big Jim, but hard. I can talk. "Top, you want me to get you some water?" He wipes the sweat off his forehead and says, "Yeah, I just got some new Dixie cups from the PX; get me some water." I go out to the water cooler in the hallway and return with a cup of water. He drinks the water in one gulp, and I knew to bring two cups so there is one in reserve. After the downing of the second cup, he says, "Bet you've never been called that before." I quickly respond, with, "Yeah, I thought he was going to say 'nig . . ' " Top cuts me short with a "Me too." As he walks to retrieve his chair, he wipes the sweat from his brow. After he returns the chair to his desk, I hand him the Buck knife. He takes it and walks over to a filing cabinet. He drops it in the top drawer, and it lands with a thud. The thud echoes in my head for the rest of the day.

Journal Entry
June 14, 1978

Some funny things have been happening lately. Three guys from Charlie Company went to France this weekend without any passports or border passes. You need at least one of these items to cross the border legally. Anyway, they tried to hide in the bathroom of the train when it crossed over on the return trip to Germany. The custom officials who usually search the trains pretty thoroughly, looking for drugs, contraband, illegal immigrants, found our boys. These guys are in trouble. We had to send a truck all the way to the

French border to pick them up. I don't know why they didn't have some border passes, which happen to be one of the easiest passes to obtain. They were young and dumb; I'm starting to use that expression as I hit 25 and realize there is a difference between being 18 and 25. To join the army at 23 instead of 18, yeah, I definitely have something on these guys. Have to admit though I've fouled up a few things despite the age. Back to these guys, young and dumb, particularly Donald Johnston. What a dope! I've known him since basic training at Fort Leonard Wood, Missouri. In two years he hasn't made too much progress. Jerky, prankster-playing asshole. He and his buddies got all the way to Paris and were on their way back when they were apprehended, almost made it all the way. Too bad.

Last night I had a very unique, interesting, and touching experience. I'll try to describe it as best I can. I feel at a loss for words not because they're unwieldy or awkward but because the experience itself was so strange and bizarre. Not the experience, but my reaction. Jesus, can't write when I want to. Can't find the things to let me convey the thing I'm feeling. Jesus, that's literate. No wonder I can't do the *Times* crossword puzzle. Gonna ramble on and maybe some searching will do some justice to the special incident that occurred.

It was about 8 o'clock in the evening. I was riding my 10-speed around Darmstadt on the way back from Gisela's house. I know Darmstadt pretty well (it's about as big as Flushing) mainly because I've never owned a car all these years that I've been overseas and have always traveled by foot or bike. I used to think it was a terrible tragedy that for a guy who had his first car when he was 18, not to have one when he was in Germany at 23. Just the opposite. I've seen a lot more this way. I was going to take the usual route home to Mauer Strasse, but for some reason, I still don't know why, I just saw a street that I had never been up before. One reason I never checked it out was just for the plain and simple fact that it's off the main drag, and it was a one-way street. Germany is probably the only place in the world, because the goddamned people obey all the rules, that you feel guilty about riding a bike up a one-way street. You actually look behind you to make sure you're not going to get a ticket from a traffic officer.

Fuck it; I went up the one-way street the wrong way because I just wanted to see what was at the other end. It was about twilight which is a weird time of day no matter where you are. Things tend to seem different at that time of day. Well, not different but things are always slightly amiss in an odd sort of way. I was pedaling up this street which became narrower and narrower, darker and darker. It started to wind and twist like a paved cow path out in the country. It took me into another neighborhood.

This neighborhood was totally out of place for Darmstadt. It was strictly residential, private homes with large yards, and there were large fences surrounding them. There were no streetlights, however, and instead of being warm and cordial, at least on the surface, everything was cold and eerie. It was the atmosphere that dismayed me. I never feel at home in Germany even though I have many German friends. Too much history and memory, even if it's not mine. But I kept on plowing along. By now this road was only about as wide as a living room or less. Really spooky. All of a sudden it took a sharp bend and on my right, there was a strange archway with writing above it. This archway was the center of a large concrete wall, about eighteen feet high and one hundred feet long. There was a large metal gate that framed the archway that appeared locked. I was about to go right on past this wall when I noticed this strange lettering directly above the iron gate. I usually bypass all German monuments and statues because everything is in German, and this only frustrates me. Yet this lettering was different, and I could see it wasn't the standard German type, high Gothic printing. Even though it was dark I was positive it wasn't German. I rode right up to the archway and looked straight up. The lettering, which was engraved about two inches deep, was Hebrew. Hebrew, man, I hadn't seen any Hebrew writing in Germany in the two years that I have been stationed there. I don't read Hebrew and couldn't figure out too much, but I was determined to figure out what was behind that archway.

I looked at the rest of the façade and saw that there were also some engravings in German. I was at a loss for their meaning also. Everything was like a puzzle: Hebrew writing, in a country which once vowed to exterminate European Jews and practically did for all intents and purposes. In Germany today, which once had a thriving Jewish population, there are only 30,000 Jews and that is out of a total population of 60,000,000. Another reason I was feeling weird had to do with the fact that I just finished reading *The Rise and Fall of the Third Reich* by William Shirer and started to read *Spandau* by Albert Speer. Both books reveal a good deal of information about the Holocaust and the feelings and times that brought about such a catastrophe. I don't know. Just being in Germany gives me the creeps sometimes. Back in 1977, goddamn people blew up the television transmitter when they first attempted to broadcast the series *Holocaust*. I wrote to Doris about this once back at Queens College. You have a feeling every now and then that there are dark undercurrents in the air around you. Strange and cold, strange and cold. A Nazi war criminal, Hans Frank, who was the military governor of Poland during its occupation, summed it up in a journal that he kept of the atrocities,

"My dear Comrades! . . . I could not eliminate all lice and Jews in only one year. But in the course of time, and if you help me, this end will be attained."

All the time I was checking out this place, I kept on thinking and wondering, why was it so well hidden, whatever this place was? Was it an estate, a park, a private area? Why was it in the back of Darmstadt, completely isolated from the rest of the town? That's what added another unsettling dimension to this whole search, finding something in this out of the way area of Darmstadt, a city I thought I knew so well. I started to give up because it was becoming dark, a little cold, and I'll admit it, a little scary. I got on my bike, and it was at that time I remembered something. In the red saddlebags on the back of my bike, there was a German-English dictionary which I had picked up at my friend's house. The old Langenscheidt dictionary. It wouldn't help with the Hebrew, but it would definitely clear up the labyrinth of German. I started to look and translate as fast as I could since the sun was going down and it was the only source of light. *Den Opfern Judisch Gemeinde, Darmstadt, 1933–1945.* It took time: *Den Opfern Judisch*

Gemeinde Stadt, 1933–1945. I had to look up each word: *Den, Opfern, Judisch, Gemeinde, Darmstadt, 1933–1945. To the Jewish victims of the Darmstadt Community, 1933–1945.*

I was shocked, silently shocked. I shivered. I was quiet and cold. I read the inscription over and over again. It was not such a puzzle now, not even the German. In the word *Opfern* I could see the word *offering,* which in Germany could also mean *sacrifice.* The word *Gemeinde,* yeah, I remember the word *Gemeinschaft* from sociology class, Queens College, Max Weber. Sure, it means community. The word *Judisch* was obvious enough. I put the dictionary on top of the bike rack.

I was moved. I quickly climbed the metal gate in the archway, so I could finally see what was on the other side. I got on top of the archway and peered into the darkening twilight. It was a Jewish cemetery. It was so well kept, immaculate. The tombstones were neatly lined up with greenery abounding over each grave and stone. The headstones were of all variety, and there was something odd about the differences between them. Some were old. Some were newer than others, and some had been damaged. The damaged ones look repaired. Cracks had been sealed with small traces of cement. Where pieces of stone had been chipped, holes had been filled. They were of all different styles, shapes, and sizes. The dates on the tombstones and the construction of the archway that I was perched just didn't jibe. This cemetery was of recent construction, not very recent, but definitely post-1945.

It was at that point that a couple of things from those books that I had been reading helped me solve the last part of the puzzle. During those years, 1933–1945, many Jewish cemeteries had been vandalized and damaged beyond repair and recognition. All of these tombstones had been collected and repaired by someone and placed in this cemetery where they would be safeguarded forever. This was to be their last resting place. I imagined also that there were a few general monuments inside which were dedicated to people who were killed during those terrible years of persecution. Damn, someday in the daytime, I'm going to have to go there and stand in silence for a few seconds and pay homage to all my Jewish brothers and sisters that the Nazis killed. That's one thing I promise to do before I leave Germany. Return to the Jewish cemetery.

I crept down from my perch, very tired, drained. I think the sight of all the tombstones sapped a lot of my energy because I slipped and fell most of the way down. I wasn't hurt or anything, just a little dusty. I limped for a second, hopped for another, and then walked a few practice steps. I was alright. I walked to the bike and put the dictionary back in the saddlebags. I got on my bike and started riding slowly home. I rode and thought for a long time. I kept on thinking as I started to move from strange streets to familiar ones. Never had I had such an emotional experience like that in my life. I probably never will have another one like it. For some reason, and I think I know why, I was a little reassured about something. Maybe even happy. I was happy that I could still be moved and that after two full years in the army, I'm not apathetic, indifferent, dead. I'm still capable of being moved. The army and all of the callous things that one has to witness tend to deaden one's emotions. There have been a lot of crazy things over here which I haven't written about too much. Maybe someday I will. There are just these things that happen which should be left alone. Despite them, I'm still here, alive and well. Man, it's so good to know that. It is so good to know that.

Journal Entry
November 1986

Funny, I could have sworn this started back on Eighth Avenue and 126th Street, Harlem. Then I moved it back to Amsterdam and 118th, right around Columbia, and then finally, I figured it goes all the way back to the morning hours. I had been driving the cab since six Sunday morning, and that's when this thing really got started; it was First Avenue and 16th Street. I was kind of angry because I had just missed a ride. Then my anger was heightened as I saw another fare about two blocks away, tantalizingly close, but with all those cabs flying by—Dodges, Impalas, and Checkers—I knew that I didn't stand a chance of reaching her in time. Sometimes, I'm always surprised at how upset I become when I miss a fare, especially if it's by only one other cab. For hours I'll hurt, thinking to myself, if I had only been faster, if I had only looked on that side of the street, or why did he have to come from that block when the light was red for me and green for him? With her two blocks away, I felt the pain coming on again because this was going to be two in a row. To miss two fares in a row on a Sunday morning when you don't have any money, damn!

I jammed my foot down on the accelerator with a sense of impotence and listened to the transmission as it moved from first to second, grinding under the strain of having over two hundred thousand miles on it. I looked up to see that she was still standing there even though a few cabs had gotten to her before me. And that's how it got started. She was black, and all of those drivers had flown past her, turning down her offer, her money, her green money. I smashed down on the accelerator just to make sure she did not become the third lost fare in a row. This has occurred too. Then I can't stop myself from debating all the logistics of a certain situation. Will I make it? What about the other cabs? Will the person still be there? I moved through this neurotic process and discovered that she's still signaling up ahead.

The cab took off, and I coasted to her, a young woman, about twenty-five, tan cashmere coat with a belt tied neatly around it. Her hair was pulled back in a bun.

"South Ferry and please take the FDR Drive."

"Yes ma'am."

I drove, made a turn to get on Second Avenue, headed south on that, hit 14th Street and made the last left so I would be heading east toward the Drive. I felt kind of foolish for literally driving in a circle, but the one-way streets dictate such a maneuver. I put the visor down since I was heading into the sun. I waited for her to say something about being passed by, but she was pretty quiet. I finally said, "All those guys passed you by because you're black." There was enough of a questioning intonation in my voice that it did not sound like a statement of fact. She said, with a little laugh, "That's right." She said nothing for the rest of the trip, except, "Let me pay you right now 'cause the ferry's in; I don't want to miss it." That was the end of the ride, something about not wanting to miss a ferry because it was at the pier.

Hours passed, fares, bumps, fumes, sunlight blinding me, back and forth, up and down; a lot of people going a lot of places but nothing really special. Afternoon came along as only those sunny Sunday fall afternoons in the Apple can, bright blue sky, orange sun setting across the Hudson and the air chilling a bit.

I hadn't thought about the incident with the woman all day, forgetting just the way she forgot about it. It's easier than you think. I was cruising up on the West Side, and that's where 118th and Amsterdam comes in. I picked up a black couple, middle-aged, middle class or at least aspiring to become members. They wanted to go to Eighth Avenue and 145th Street, Harlem. I said "OK" and kept the nose of the cab pointed north. I started to think about the young black woman for the first time since that morning, I suppose, because these were the first black people in the cab since her. I kept mulling over the incident in my mind, and a host of other thoughts were triggered in my mind.

I remembered the taxi orientations that old and new drivers are required to attend. The cab company was a big one, large fleet, right next to the 59th Street Bridge in Long Island City. This haggard looking fellow briefed us on all the possible hazards that we would encounter on the streets. Since I had already driven before, tens of thousands of miles before, I wasn't really listening too carefully.

Then he moved to a new aspect of the orientation: crime. He said, "Don't pick them up. You know who I'm talking about. The blacks. Look, play it safe, especially with the young ones. Why take a chance?" Perhaps it was because there were a few black guys in the room, the dispatcher felt compelled to add: "OK, well, look, pick up the old ones, old black people. Old black people are all right. Other than that, you're taking a chance; let me tell you something. They're just as scared of their own as we are." I repeated that phrase to myself, *just as scared of their own as we are.* I said it a few more times. Nobody said anything and, again, I forgot about it quickly.

I went to 125th Street and made a right, in a daze but still aware of their destination, Eighth Avenue and 145th Street. As I headed east on 125th, I felt kind of foolish since I couldn't remember what was the new name given to Eighth Avenue. Many of the main streets of Harlem had their names changed during the late 1960s and 1970s because of certain political demands. Seventh Avenue became Adam Clayton Powell Jr. Boulevard, and Eighth Avenue was transformed into Frederick Douglass. The problem was that I couldn't remember which was which, and there were plenty of other named streets whizzing by were also possible candidates for Eighth Avenue. My solution to the problem was to put my left turn signal on as each block approached and slowly prepare to turn. And of course, each time I commenced that movement, the couple, surprised, would correct me. I hate to ask for directions and feel like I don't know where I'm going. Maybe I'm scared to ask. I'm still not sure after all these years. I guess I don't want to admit that I'm lost.

After a few more cases of trial and error, all error, we got to our destination, and I made the correct left. I let them off at 145th Street. I surveyed the area. Black people, tons of black people and most of them were not old. Here was the enemy. I felt in a quandary. Should I be like all the other cab drivers, turn on my OFF DUTY light and blaze back to what is supposedly safe territory, anything below 110th Street? Hell, I know some drivers who refuse to even go above 86th. What if something does happen? What if some young black guy flags me down? Won't I feel like a dope? I made a compromise. I left the light on, stayed on duty, but drove as fast as possible down Eighth Avenue and just took a chance.

I pressed the gas pedal to the floor and cursed the transmission for taking so long in catching up to the engine's rpm. I made it to fifty and hoped that I could remain with the synchronized light pattern all the way down to 110th Street. I had to make it. Right at 126th Street, an old man waved at me with his metal cane. If I had been five blocks away, I wouldn't have missed him, not with that oddly shaped metal cane. I pulled over. He was happy, and I was mad. He moved to the cab slowly, smiling, almost grinning, with the aid of his cane, leaning heavily on it, practically pivoting and swaying on it.

It took him a long time to get into the back of the cab, and I was furious. The engineer who designed Checker cabs had no sympathy for kids or old people. The cab was just too high for him. To get over that first step, he tossed his cane into the cab, placed both hands on the seat, and with a violent thrust hurled himself into the backseat. He breathed heavily and fell back onto the cushion. He had a beard, silver, just like a Brillo pad, a blue knit watch cap and a gray winter jacket, the kind with zippers all over it.

He caught his breath and then proceeded to make a new effort at reaching and closing the door. This was almost as difficult as getting into the cab, and he gasped for air. I was incredibly angry at his slowness, ineptness, oldness, and the fact that many black Harlemites were looking at us, the cab, the old black man and me. With a thud, the door finally shut.

"I sure am lucky to find you. I sure do appreciate you picking me up."

"No problem, man. What do you want?"

"I want you to take me to One Twenty-fifth and Seventh."

I gasped. Damn, that's only two blocks. I thought to myself that this old man must really be hurt if he couldn't make that on a sunny day. How much money could he have? His jacket was all ripped up; the rest of his clothes were worn out. I pulled off and got to the next red light. Just as the light changed, he threw something into the small metal cup in the middle of the glass partition.

"That's all I got, babe. I swear."

I didn't turn around to look because of traffic. The meter was automatically at a dollar as soon as I pressed the button. I looked into the rearview mirror, and he was slumped down so far into the seat that he was out of sight. I go to Seventh Avenue and asked him if this was "OK" with him.

"Babe, could you make it the far corner? Seventh is a big street."

"Yeah, I know what you mean. Soon as the light changes."

The light was a long one, and it gave me the time to think, too much in a way. I reached into the cup to see what was there. It was a neatly folded dollar bill. I unfolded it and ran my fingers along the smooth creases. I was about to say that the fare was a dollar sixty but cut myself short. I started thinking about Dante, the

Divine Comedy, The Inferno, Milton's *Paradise Lost,* and some other dudes who write. Faith without action means nothing.

"Here, man, take this dollar. You might need it for something real important, more important than this taxi ride."

"Thanks, oh, goddamn, God bless you son. You sure you don't need it?"

"No, Pop. You keep it. Plenty of people downtown, beaucoup people coming out of Bloomingdales right now, and they're only going a few blocks too. You understand?"

"Yeah, well, God bless you. Take care of yourself."

"OK, you too, Pop. Take care."

He got out of the cab and hiked himself onto the sidewalk with a move that he must have practiced often. He gave a big hello to someone who was walking by and started to point at the cab, relating what happened, I suppose. I heard the person say, "That's all right, Pop!"

I pulled off. I rolled toward Lenox Avenue. On the corner there were about eight young guys standing around a fifty-five-gallon drum, sticks in their hands, trying to keep their fire going. One of them brandished a knife and pointed it at me. I looked at him, them. They looked at me. I slowly went through the red light, a "solid red" as the police would say, looking at them and headed south.

Jacqueline's Roots

"BEFORE I PULL my pants down I have to tell you one thing." I was already exasperated about the slowness of this expedition but kept my cool and said, "Yes, are you a little nervous?" Jacqueline replied, "No." I felt better and said, "Oh then, what's wrong? Is it the AIDS thing? I'm nervous about that too. I know you don't have it, and I don't have it. But it's definitely normal to be nervous about it. I'm nervous about it, as we speak."

Jacqueline was black, sturdy, and about forty-five. I had courted her for a few months and after all this time I was going to see her body and maybe even get on top of it. She clamped her lips tighter. She continued, "Well, I know that you've been with white women." I cut her off with a sigh and said, "What does that have to do with anything?" She had crossed her arms, and this was a sign of resolve. I would have to hear her out or give up on being on top, bottom, or behind. "No, you're right," I said. I followed with, "Keep on talking." With my last breath out came, "You have a right to talk about your feelings."

Jacqueline continued with, "Well, I just wanna axe you somethin'." I had to stop her again. "Look, I can take 'they was' but I can't take 'axe.' We talked about this before and you promised." There's always a whine to my voice anytime I used the expression *you promised*. She was not irritated with this reminder and shook her head to indicate, "I know; I'm sorry." She took another try at it. "I wanna ass-ke you somethin'. You have been with a lot of white women, and I have to tell you that black women are not like white women." I looked at her with my perplexed but patient look. "Yeah, sure," I responded. She became thoughtful.

385

"Don't think that I'm pickin' on you because you're half white and half black. I tell this to black men too. I know that you're black, but to me you're white, but I still have to tell you. Even if I was with a Chinese, I would tell him this." To maintain my interest and not to reveal my angst I just said, "Yeah, continue; I'm listening to everything you're saying." Jacqueline uncrossed her arms as though she finally needed them for something else than defending her position. "You see, I'm an African woman and African women, it's in their genes to have large rear ends. There is nothing that we can do about it. It's hereditary. Really."

This was hard to take. This was the third or fourth time that she had told me I was white. I had found out by the 1990s that I belonged to a larger and ever-increasing number of black men who were being labeled white; we were identified as being white not so much for our physical complexion but for mannerisms, speech, vocabulary, or even our thought. Jacqueline had once said, "You even think like a white man," and her favorite expression was "For all intents and purposes you are a white man." When I asked her to clarify what that meant, she gave me a vague and obtuse description of some middle-class habit that I had, nothing more, nothing less. She was taking a middle-class trait and using it as incontrovertible evidence that this is what made me different from her; my response was that purple, green, and turquoise middle-class people do this and that on a regular basis. It doesn't have anything to do with their color. She was not convinced.

This was funny in a twisted way. That was all it took to be a white man in the 1990s. I thought about what any *other* person had to do to exert his whiteness one hundred years ago, fifty years ago, thirty and down to twenty. A century ago one would have to adopt a disguise involving clothing, alterations in speech, habits, and even keeping their black skin hidden somehow. In the 1960s I had suffered with my fellow black brothers and sisters because I was just too light. In the 1950s I was the perfect black man with my great and straight hair. By the late 1960s and by the time of the Afro, the 1970s with Julius Irving and little Mikey Jackson proudly sporting their resplendent Afros, I was finished, kaput. However, something radically different occurred in the 1980s. Somehow new concepts of what it meant to be white, black, and other racial labels had infiltrated the community, and the emphasis on obvious physical defects or assets had been modified. Never before had so much accentuation been placed on how one sounded. This new notion of defining blackness by how one sounded first reared its ugly head in my college classroom while discussing *Go Tell It on the Mountain,* by James Baldwin.

The class had viewed a first-rate documentary on his life, and I had asked for comments that would somehow amplify an understanding of the importance of one's biographical experience. Keith raised his hand and noted that the documentary was great. It was good to see the film footage of Harlem in the 1930s, and Baldwin's Paris of the late 1940s. He threw in a *however* and I waited for the objection. "Professor Jeffries, I just want to know why did the poet who knew him, Angelou, why did she speak in such an affected manner? Same for Baldwin. Was this a generational thing, trying to sound white?" This remark came from this intellectual-looking black student. As always, my emotions almost eroded my calm, my center. After teaching for almost twenty years, I had learned a few tricks, desperate ploys you might call them, to keep myself contained. I reached down to the desk, grabbed with both hands and held on.

"I'm not quite sure what you mean," I said slowly and methodically. I continued. "They didn't sound one way or another to me." Keith looked to a few of his black compatriots for confirmation. Their silence was not deafening and neither Keith nor I could be sure of what they were affirming or denying. I came up with one of my favorite clichés, "Well, let's not confuse the messenger with the message." I induced Keith to respond that he admired Baldwin and Angelou and what they had to say about black life and literature.

Still the wound hurt as I heard this very intelligent man inform me that he was alienated from some of our greatest writers and thinkers by the way they sounded. I was struck that twenty years ago this stigma of sounding and therefore acting white was not so pointed. A hyper state of consciousness regarding what basic qualities made someone black, had obligated the community to redraw certain concepts. These new lines seemed to exclude a growing number of people. People who would have been welcomed into the big tent throughout the years now discovered themselves sitting in the bleachers, maybe even standing in the back. Keith was telling me that Malcolm X sounded white, and Jacqueline was telling me that her awareness of her African heritage can be reduced to some esoteric information regarding the formation of her gluteus maximus. And I was being officially notified.

"Jacqueline, look, it doesn't matter and to tell you the truth I don't care. I'm glad black people are discovering Africa for the fifth or sixth time. This has occurred before and it will happen again. Only problem is that in terms of years, the last time anyone was there, keeps on getting further and further away. Some of these things, I hope they are true. I hope that African women have large rear ends." I tried to make a joke with, "Let's see. There's only one way to test this theory out. Right?"

When I saw her start to button her blouse back up, I regretted saying those words but I was too angry to have sex anyway. I had spent so many years hiding and then confirming and then apologizing, that I figured when I got into my forties I wasn't going to explain anymore, to anyone. She asked, "So you mean, we want to die because we're sad? I can see that a little with the drugs. I mean, those things take you away from your tears a little bit. But you have to come back." There was a touch of Billie Holiday's blues when she sings *All of Me* in her voice.

I shook my head. "Jacqueline, what are you talking about?"

She smoothed a twist in the cuff of her pants. I couldn't see her head and she spoke while she tightened the lace of her shoe. Her voice bounced off the floor. It had softened, "About two weeks ago you said that American black people are committing suicide. Slow suicide. I remember that expression, slow suicide."

I felt sad too and started to apologize but not for the traditional psychological reasons. "Oh, I was just talking out of my ass. I don't even remember that evening. Look, let's not talk about this anymore. Every time we do, I get horribly depressed and then we just eat. We're eating to get rid of the 'tears' like you said. Eating instead of doing drugs."

Jacqueline turned on the light that I had dimmed next to the couch. It was bright enough that I could see all the features on her face. Her lips were mildly thick and almost always chapped. With color a shade or two darker than a manila envelope, I found her quite attractive. "Dexter, I suppose I'm mad at you. We talk about so many things. I start off happy. Then I'm sad. I don't mind about you telling me the truth, or telling me different things about the black community, but you never offer any solutions. You just point about what's wrong and how bad it is and how things are gettin' worse than ever. But you never say what to do."

I got up and walked over to my box of Macanudo cigars that a good friend had given me for Christmas. A whole box of Robustos—they were so good that you could practically eat them. I was rationing myself to less than one a day because I wanted them to last and last. I lit one and took a long drag to help me relax. I wanted to feel my chest heave, sag, and then sag some more. A sagging chest for me was a sign that I was starting to come away from an anxious place. "Jacqueline, look, I don't know what to do. A lot of this stuff is just spinning around in my head. It's complicated enough that I'm just overwhelmed. As far as not having any answers, I'm sorry. You're right. A person, especially a teacher, shouldn't just point out the problems. You're obligated to come up with a few solutions. I'm not. I don't. I suppose I just leave some people empty." With the clipper in my hand I cut off the cigar with the cellophane still on it. I walked over to the stove since I didn't know where my matches were and turned on the front burner. Covering my chin with my hand so my beard wouldn't accidentally become a Brillo fire, I lit the cigar. I took some deep puffs.

Jacqueline got up from the couch and walked over to the kitchen. The electric igniter on the stove was ticking away. I just let it go. She came up behind me and hugged me. She hugged me very tight and spoke through my shirt, "I still want to make love. I just wanted to axe, ask, you some things." It felt funny and arousing. Her mouth had made a wet spot on my back where she had talked. I turned around, put the cigar in my right hand, and hugged her back. I was an inch or so taller than she and now she talked into my chest. "It's just that you're so sad. Are you always this sad? A person shouldn't be this sad."

I held her back so I could look into her pretty brown eyes. I studied every feature. "Jacqueline, I'm not sad. Things are just getting to me. That's all. Maybe it's because I'm getting older. I don't know." Without me noticing she quietly slipped off her shoes using her feet in tandem. She stepped on my feet to kiss me, and we were now almost equal height. We kissed and I rubbed her back, missing the place where the hinges of the bra came together.

"Put the cigar down. Let's not eat, like you said. Just, just don't say anything when I pull my pants down."

"Jacqueline, your wish is my command."

White Wife, White Husband, Black Husband

MY WIFE WAS white and I was me, and I don't think we ever thought about any colors, races, or religions until we started to get divorced. It was very strange and still unsettling to think about my marriage in that way. I'm positive that we were either beneath or beyond any racial categorization because we had little or no contact with official bureaucratic organizations. We were married in 1987, downtown Brooklyn, by a pleasant black woman judge. That was probably our last contact with an institution that regulates one's life. I always thought it was ironic that when I was an attorney, defending myself in court, I was only one block from the same building where I was married. That's the way all those court buildings are situated in Brooklyn. One building is for felons; one is for the married and another for the divorced. All within three hundred yards of each other.

Eleanor never made any discernible statement to me or anyone else about who I was or wasn't until she started to contemplate the divorce. I'm not sure whether it strengthened her resolve, weakened, made her think twice or do double takes. Definitely made her think because she wrote a letter to an old friend from her Canadian days that she hadn't seen in perhaps twenty years. Anytime you start conducting retrospectives that take you to places and people from two decades or more, there is something desperate afoot. You're sad. You're wounded. You're searching for a Medivac back to Saigon and will hop on board that chopper as quickly as you can. I read the letter and started to think about how much we loved each other and what did it all mean that race was finally having some bearing on how she remembered and loved me:

Dear Barbara,

Good to hear from you again. Well I guess there's a lot to catch up on. I don't know how you met your husband or how you got to Halifax, but I'm glad to hear you're in a good place with people you feel close to. I think I understand what you are saying about your relationship with Clark. It's tough when you don't feel equal to someone. As for wanting someone to take care of you, I'm very familiar with that . . . I also understand what you mean about being thrown off by the attraction. It's something I struggle with all the time . . . separating that from outer feelings, that is. Does Clark live in Halifax? Is he Canadian? What does he do? Does he have a good relationship with your boys?

I admire you for having the clarity to know that you need to feel grounded, centered, whatever, and that you feel strong with a man. I feel I'm something of a baby in this area and am trying to deal with it in therapy. For the last fifteen years I've been married—first to Matthew's father (I think I told you a little bit about him long ago) then to Dex. I'm finding it difficult to think of myself as "I"! I've known Dex since the seventies because we taught together at Queens College. When I left Spencer (first husband), Dexter kind of rescued me. I think I needed him a lot at the time; among other things, I think I was terrified of being alone, being a single parent, not being strong . . . Anyway, we have been together almost nine years now and we both agree that on the whole it's been good—we've been close and we both love Matthew, and we have done many, many things together, including building our own little cabin ourselves in upstate New York. Then, we have a lot in common; he teaches at another division of CUNY. All this probably sounds good, but in other ways we are so different. Dex doesn't talk about his feelings; he just sort of withdraws when things aren't going well. What's coming out now is just how many things he was unhappy about that he never told me. Then—just to make matters truly complicated and crazy—Dexter is half black and half Jewish. He published an article a few years ago about how hard it was to grow up and try to pretend to be one thing and then another and always to feel that your identity was being tampered with in deep ways . . .

The words *crazy* rang true but hurt so much. Was that the way a person of mixed race is viewed, that somehow they are subject to special psychological problems that no one else will have to endure? In her eyes, was that how she always looked at me, late at night when I was sleeping? Playing with her son up at our cabin in the woods of Petersburg, New York, did she trust me or was that all a mirage? As I went through my own thoughts about what was wrong with her and how she was crazy because her father was gay, I sometimes wondered if this wasn't a case of two people who had loved each other too strongly and were going mad as they witnessed the destruction of the most important relationship that they had ever had in their lives. I heard a radio show on National Public Radio once about how divorcing couples go through a madness and irrationality when all they can concentrate on is destroying each other. There is a sort of madness that leaves one making choices that under any other circumstances, would never be pondered. I had lost my mind one fine spring day. I remember it like yesterday.

I was wrong. Not wrong for deeply falling in love with someone but wrong for not thinking how this would affect others, my wife, my son. This relationship with someone other than my wife concluded. After that, Eleanor started to date a professor. I was guilty as charged and said nothing. I told her that it was OK and that this was what I deserved, within reason. I thought that this was the appropriate punishment for a man who had violated someone's love, trust, and loyalty. I sat quietly each Wednesday night as she would go from therapy to his apartment and thought about how effective therapy could be under those circumstances. You talk to your therapist about the problems with your husband at 7:30, and then you meet your adulterous lover at 9:00 for dinner and then you're back in bed with me at 1:00, sometimes 2:00, sometimes 3:00. It was the sometimes 3:00 that made me mad.

I started thinking about this English professor character that had presented her with his special present, a book that he had written about the birth of popular culture. To me, this already said enough about the guy as a human being. Anyone who applies deconstructive methods to Ben Johnson, Maid Marian, and Robin Hood is desperate for a promotion, or tenure. The day after Eleanor came home after spending half the night with him I looked at the book he had given to her and the inscription: *To Eleanor, at the start of a beautiful friendship.* I flipped through the small book with a gray paper cover. A drawing of Robin Hood, my boyhood hero played by Errol Flynn on Channel Five on Sunday afternoons who fought against the evil Sir Guy of Gisbourne played by the equally evil Basil Rathbone, was on the cover. I wondered what this scholar had to say about one of the great swashbucklers of all time. I found a few lines:

> Like Robin Hood, the slain deer represents both the vitality—the phallic function—and the vulnerability of folk culture . . . likewise, the phallic function Robin Hood represents is threatened in both the decaying aristocracy and the rising middle classes by what is perceived to be the castrating woman.

Jesus, I thought, *no wonder this guy is sleeping with my wife. He's definitely got one thing on his literary consciousness and it ain't being literary.* It was that, and not having the dignity to write a real book of literary criticism, and the fact that he would see another man's wife in such a blatant fashion that pushed me beyond reason.

I decided to pay him a visit in his class and discuss dating my wife. Before I commenced this action, I spoke to Eleanor one more time, just to make sure that there would be no mitigating circumstance in his defense. I asked her three key questions over coffee:

1. Does this guy know that you are married?

2. Does he know that we're having trouble in our relationship?

3. Is he aware that we are going to three therapists, one apiece and a mutual one in order to make our marriage work?

Her answer was an emphatic *yes* to all three questions. I brooded throughout the day and by early afternoon knew what I had to do. I proceeded to visit his class and found out that I wasn't an English professor like him; I was just some Hispanic janitor who had stumbled into the wrong class. That hurt more than the kids ganging up on me. That hurt more than only getting a few punches in here and there. That hurt more than seeing him stand off to the side while his students did his fighting for him, standing there with that Norton anthology tightly clutched at his chest.

I walked in and knew it was him. He was a victim of trying to be young when he was old and the punk rock thing must have caught his attention. Black turtleneck sweater, black jacket, black shoes, black pants. He was sitting on the desk pretty comfortable, talking in that passive-aggressive manner that English professors are known to hold forth in. I looked at him and shook my head in disgust. I thought I was going to talk but I couldn't. I couldn't waste my time, not even a second or two. I picked the desk up and flipped it over. He was pretty surprised. So was the class. That class had never been so electrified. Unhurt, he stood up. Before he could say anything, I told him not to see my wife anymore. At that point he asked rather feebly, "What are you talking about?" For one second I was terrified that this wasn't the right guy since I had never seen him, but then I kept pushing him, and I could tell there was nothing righteous about this man. I looked at him quickly and remembered one of John Milton's lines, *For now I see Peace to corrupt no less than war to waste.*

It felt good to fight. Even though I wasn't fighting him, it was good to tussle with his kids as he looked at this Battle Royal scene in horror. His kids were giving me a good going over, and I was doing OK. At one point I was fighting with about four of them and even though one had jumped on my back, I was able to, just by spinning and whirling, to keep the other three at bay. Then *boom,* a big bruiser of a kid straight out of Bay Ridge or Bensonhurst, gave me a serious shot to the head and I was stunned. A shrieking voice brought me out of the daze and gave me some last-minute encouragement. "Stop it, stop it. Oh my God. Stop it. He's Professor Jeffries. That's my professor. Stop hitting him." I looked around and couldn't believe it. Even though I was at another branch of the City University of New York, one of my former students who had transferred there, became my Thetis, my Pallas Athena. She was hysterical. "You're hurting him. You're hurting him. He's my professor." I came out of the blur and started to wrestle some more. I was feeling strong, but they finally managed to drag me to the door and toss me out. As they pitched me out, I heard my old nemesis; one of the kids muttered something about *crazy Puerto Rican.* I looked at the Asian kid who said it and just barely refrained from saying, "Sorry gook motherfucker," but didn't. I didn't want to end up like Big Jim.

"Who do you think you are, coming off the street like this into the college?"

Instead of answering I got past these students and went right back into the room. The left side of my head started to throb a bit, and I figured out that I was a little more hurt than I thought. When they were dragging me around, they were actually helping me to stay in an upright position. Now that no one was holding me, I felt a little woozy. As I felt their hands grab me from behind, I resisted little and was almost glad that they would accompany me back into the hallway, where at least I could rest for a second.

Out in the hallway I heard the commotion in the class continue after the door had closed, but the only thing that echoed in my head was *crazy Puerto Rican*. Damn, after all those years of being an English professor, all those kids saw was some guy who should be serving them coffee or making them a sandwich or sweeping their hallways. This was to be the theme of my divorce. When a dark-skinned person is involved with a white-skinned person and there is some conflict, altercation, even an Asian kid from Saigon will take the white person's side. As Richard Pryor said, when an immigrant first comes to the United States and takes his first English as a second language class, the initial lesson is the pronunciation of the word *nigger*. Once they've mastered that lesson they'll understand more about American history and culture than they'll ever need to know.

Before going home I left a note on the punk rock professor's door that told him not to call or see my wife again. By the time I got back to Brooklyn, I was almost late for work myself and had to wash up, get my books together and go teach at Manhattan Community College. I took some aspirin, one Johnny Walker, went to Manhattan, and taught rather well considering the conditions. I had planned to tell my wife what had occurred when I returned from my evening class. I knew that he would never call the house again, but I forgot that she could call him anytime I wasn't around with impunity. Eleanor and I had a long battling argument when I got back. I had no explanation. I loved her. That was all.

Eleanor had other concerns, practical, and pragmatic. She was a teacher at the City University of New York. I got her the job and was always proud of that. It was one of my major life accomplishments. I was connected enough to ensure that her résumé would be pulled out of the three hundred that came in for that job. It was one of the few adult victories of my life. Maybe she was worried about publicity.

"Dex, aren't you worried that he might call the police?"

"Huh! No, I mean, not really. I mean, I'm not thinkin' about those kinds of things."

"God, he could call the police. They could arrest you."

"Eleanor, the way those kids were beating the hell out of me, I think maybe I should call somebody. My head feels like a grapefruit. And I still taught my evening remedial class. That's dedication. Good class too, sentence combining and different types of paragraphs. Damn, my head hurts, only the left side, though."

There was a pause. But I would rather have had a steady blast than what followed.

"Dex, have you lost your fucking mind? You hit my, my . . ."

"Eleanor, come on, get it out. Start off with the first letters in the alphabet. A, B, . . ."

"You're mad. Really mad. You're crazy."

"Cupcake, listen, you were about to say *boyfriend.*"

"Friend."

I stared and sighed.

"Boyfriend."

"Dex, he's not my boyfriend. He's just a good friend."

"Man, how the world is giving to lying. We could use Falstaff for a second. Why don't we all just head out to the tavern in Eastcheap and trade lies over a few pints of Guinness?" She turned and started to walk out of the dining room while were exchanging love and anger.

I couldn't raise my voice too much because I hated for my son to ever hear any anger, any fights, any pain. I caught up with her so I could almost keep a normal tone. However, it was hard, even when I got right next to her and had to maintain myself. I ranted and didn't wait for answers.

"What do you think is gonna happen? He's gonna walk into a police station and tell the story. The police are regular guys, not the most brilliant, but they know their job and they know about life. They're gonna ask him why would another English professor walk into your room and turn over your table? What were you guys arguing 'bout, Shakespeare or somethin'?" Eleanor started to laugh and smile for a second, but it became thin and disappeared. I kept up my monologue.

"They're gonna look at him and see him and as they imagine me, instead of seeing a Puerto Rican, they're gonna see the *Paper Chase* guy. Right? They're gonna keep asking him, why would John Houseman, come into your room and right in front of your students . . . come on Professor, tell us what's going on between you and this guy. Another

English professor just doesn't walk into your room and start poundin' you for nothing. As we say in the trade, there's always a motive." Eleanor didn't like this crude version of the narrative but I liked it. Any time I get to go from regular CUNY English professor, to Puerto Rican janitor, then back to a guy doin' commercials for Smith Barney, I'm pretty goddamn happy. It only happens a few times in one's life and after all the beatings and insults and racial injustice that I witnessed or suffered, I figured there was a little justice in the world. By this time I was yelling.

"So, they're gonna ask him what was goin' on between us that got me so mad that I went into his class and started wrestling with five or six accounting majors. Your boyfriend, sorry, I mean friend, is gonna start sweating and they're gonna offer him a cup of coffee, glass of water, you know, good cop, bad cop. They're gonna lean on your boy, and he's gonna start sweating. They'll give him a chair. He'll sit down, just the way he was in the classroom this afternoon, except he won't be so fuckin' passive-aggressive, just the former. He's gonna look around and realize that not even the best Foucault bullshit in the world is gonna explain what's happening to him. Even that Nazi deconstruction professor can't help him, right? They'll talk soft to him. They'll start to whisper and I know this guy might be smart and I know he's smarter than me, but finally, after they talk to him in those soft, sorta comforting voices, one of them is gonna say,

> Look, I went to John Jay College of Criminal Justice. I know you professor guys. What did you do to get this guy so mad, that he walks into your room, an English professor no less, who knows all this stuff about poetry and books? You must have done somethin' to get him that mad. Right, come on. Tell us. It won't go any further than this room. Right, fellas?

Eleanor had folded her arms. She wore a white sweater that made her look warmer than she was. I was on the verge of finishing my soliloquy. "So, your boy is gonna look around in this sheepish way. He'll have the shakes a bit but he's gonna feel better because he's about to purge himself as Aristotle would say and there's nothin' like a good cleansing, Eleanor, right, your boy goes to therapy I'm sure. He's gonna look around and make sure they're not all listening and whisper, 'I'm seeing his wife.' " Eleanor was looking at me a bit puzzled and horrified at the same time. I was almost finished. "Eleanor, you get the picture? Now, one of the cops is going to turn to his buddy and say, 'Get the professor another cup of water. He's feeling better already.' Then after they give your boy that second cup of water, one of the old cops is gonna get real close to him and whisper, with a bit of sympathy and say, 'You know pal, how would you feel if this same guy was seeing your wife? You'd be pretty pissed, right? Seein' someone's wife is a risky business, even for an English professor.' "

We never really talked that much after that night. Once you get the lawyers involved, there's no more human interaction. Those guys will take you to a place that you never thought or imagined. It's more like a third grade fight where you've waited for three o'clock to come around but you forgot about it after lunch. However, some of your best friends remind you that you're supposed to fight Little Ricky and you become a bit nauseous. No one is rational. No one is human. No one loves.

My mom never scared me in my adult life. Once I got back from being overseas in West Germany, we had a most splendid relationship. I think it mainly had to do with my being exposed to political ideas in action as opposed to theory. In addition, I had finally made a pilgrimage to the motherland while being over there for three years. On one of my generous leaves signed by black Top, I ventured to the Soviet Union. I spent a few weeks in the socialist state, her dream, traveling to Moscow and Leningrad. I was impressed. She knew that she had won me over. We were friendly adults. Yet, there was this one day while getting divorced that she scared me into feeling like a kid again.

I had run out of money for my attorney. My lawyer was competent, generous, and I'll always remember those qualities. He was working his way up and I never felt bad about his fees. His office was his apartment and I could relate to that. He remembered his roots and we exchanged stories about being overseas. Robert Tomkins was there for me but never gave me any illusions. I felt bad the day I called him to say that the next time I saw him would be the last time. His wife was his receptionist, and she always had a mug of coffee waiting for me. I always liked the contrast; she wore her hair in a ponytail and wore faded blue jeans. I would carefully carry the mug, taking a sip first, so there would be less to spill. Bob's office was just the other side of the apartment, and I thought this was quaint and human.

"Bob, I can't use your services anymore. Damn, I'm sorry. I didn't know how . . ."

"Yeah, sure, take it easy. Yeah, it's pretty expensive and things add up rather quickly."

I took another sip and felt calmer.

"So Bob, I can't go beyond the five thousand I gave you. I'm just a regular guy, you know. No big money. I just don't have any more left. Jesus Christ. Five Gs just like that. Plus, I owe half of that. Man, oh man."

"Dexter, don't worry about it. I understand. Don't worry about the half either. I know you're good for it. The question is, what are you going to do?"

"I don't know. What do you do when you run out of money in these things? Surrender at some sort of official ceremony."

He laughed and took a white handkerchief out of his pocket and waved it.

"No, Dex, you don't do that."

"Maybe I should. I'm tired. This thing really kicks your ass. I'm never getting divorced again."

A laugh from the little kitchen traveled out across the floor and it was Jane. I spoke up a bit, "I mean, if I ever get divorced this time, I'm not getting divorced again."

We all laughed for a few seconds. Bob came back to the topic as he placed the handkerchief back in his breast pocket.

"Dex, normally, I don't recommend this but you're not the average client. Did you ever think about going pro se?"

"Oh, to tell you the truth, I don't even know what that means."

"You can defend yourself. The reason I don't recommend this is obvious. However, you're pretty smart and you're accustomed to doing research."

The word research did set off something familiar in my head. The coffee mug was still warm, and my hands felt good.

"Bob, Mr. Tomkins. What are you saying? A regular guy can defend himself in court? Is that legal?"

"Sure it's legal. Look, you're an English professor. Who do you think is smarter? An English professor or a lawyer?"

I started to chuckle. I took him seriously though. "But Bob, a lawyer really has to know a lot of things, I mean, look at those books behind you. An English professor, you know, you master a few areas of material and . . ."

"Dexter, look, I know you can do it. You're working on your Ph.D., right? It's the same process. You go to the library and look at books, and cases. These forms you can pick up from any good copy shop. You're downtown, Chambers, hey; you're right next to New York Law School. In between classes, you amble over and go to the library. They'll let you in—just show them your CUNY ID. What do you think?" I looked at him and Jane walked by and just nodded her head affirmatively. Before I could reply, Bob, said, "Jane, right, you're going right now. You've heard us talk. Don't you think Mr. Jeffries could handle this?" Jane nodded and smiled. "Yes, I don't mean to butt in, but you could. Look, I'm going to law school now. Most of the people can't write. Write, that's all you do. You teach it; you do it. You could handle it. You could fight this, this . . ." Now it was her turn to pause. This was serious, and I tended to react to every subtle nuance and suggestion. I asked Bob what was up.

"There's just one thing. I hate to say this but your wife's attorney is really ugly. I'm lodging a complaint against her with the New York State Bar Association. Have to get the forms. You have to be prepared for her mouth. Every other word is *fuck* and *shit*. I wasn't ready for it myself but she's just a vulgar person."

I thought about my one encounter with Ms. Greene and that hadn't been pretty either. It was ugly, one of the ugliest days in my life. Before any court action, there are days of preliminary hearings, short encounters, sometimes only lasting less than a minute. You walk in, hear your docket number called, two attorneys whisper in front of the judge for a brief moment and then they turn around, walk to their respective clients and out you go. I wish I had had one of the abbreviated hearings. No, my first hearing with Ms. Greene brought me face to face with my old foe, racism, and it was in the most despicable manner. Because of the high fees that she charged my wife, Ms. Greene was obligated to do something rather dramatic. There was a hearing about her request for a Restraining Order. Tomkins filled me in on what the particulars were and was confident that it would be temporary. But the chances of it becoming permanent so I couldn't see my stepson who I had raised since age three, were not feasible. Yet Ms. Greene did her best and she knew her American history the same way George Bush knew his when he invoked the image of Willie Horton during the campaign for president. There is one word that a defendant of a certain color never wants to hear uttered in conjunction with a white woman.

"Your honor, I would like to point out that the defendant raped his wife on the night of March 1, 1992."

The judge was a kindly gentleman, black-rimmed glasses at the end of his nose and a pile of papers in front of him. Before my attorney could jump up, the judge said, "Excuse me counselor, I don't see any mention of this in any of the paperwork before me. No reference to this by either counsel, the commission of a felony or a misdemeanor. My attorney sat down and said, "Good, this guy has some sense."

The word *rape* spun around and around in my head. The court fluttered and tittered. Ms. Greene continued, "Your honor, there was a case before the New York Supreme Court in which a learned attorney argued that a husband can rape his wife and both parties can continue to then have consensual relations with each other, after said rape."

"Counselor, you're tossing around a very serious charge in front of this court with absolutely no claim other than the plaintiff's affidavit in exhibit B."

In a short gray suit that stopped a little above the knees, Ms. Greene flipped through the papers. After a pause, she said, "Your Honor, this concept has been put forth by a feminist legal scholar, who . . ."

"Put it in your brief."

". . . in a paper before the New York State Bar Association . . ."

"I'll read it in your brief."

". . . in 1985, posited that a husband, legally married, under New York State . . ."

"Counselor, put it in your brief. We're in Brooklyn, not Manhattan."

The court laughed. I didn't. I had my head down. Rape. If there is one thing that a black man does not ever wish to hear in his life, I don't care if he is half black, one-fourth, one iota, his worst nightmare is to hear the word rape, connecting him with a white woman. Even though Bob Tomkins had whispered, "We got her; he didn't go for it," I was ill. So this is how Bigger Thomas felt. I had taught *Native Son* so many times but never quite comprehended what accusatorial injustice felt like, until then. Bigger Thomas, looking around that ominous courtroom. Spectators referring to him as an ape and gorilla. I looked around the court. Goddamn, she had to pull out the last ugly piece of America that I had forgotten about. It just existed in books until that moment. Eleanor and her attorney could have conjured up so many other magic potions; I could have been a drunk, a wife beater, drug addict, no, they took their best shot and came up with the line, "Dexter Jeffries, a man with a long history of physical violence, including the rape of his wife." I put my head down in both my hands and got a little sick. I rolled my head from side to side and just heard brief murmurs of the rest of the proceeding.

Someone tapped me on the shoulder. It was Harvey Zweig. He had his trademark yarmulke, and I knew him from all my days of attending divorce hearings and trials. Handling the most difficult cases, he specialized in Hassidic interpretations of the Old Testament. When he invoked the law, it was always with a sense of history and literature. His clients always wore black hats and the women wore scarves. We had talked about the Bible on many occasions. I could see he was a true scholar who applied what he knew on the behalf of his Hassidic clients who found themselves entangled with modern-day problems of marriage and divorce within the realm of laws and traditions that stretched back five thousand years. I turned to my right with my head still bowed. He spoke first, "My friend, my friend, don't cry. Don't cry, my friend. Look up. Hold your head up. I've seen this before, this Feminazi thing. My God. They don't care. It's nothing. Just be grateful, thank God, she didn't say you raped the kid. I've seen that too. Right counselor?" His last words were directed toward Bob Tomkins, and he responded, "No question, they throw that in sometimes just to make it a complete three-ring circus."

That was the first admonition. The second one came from my mother and that one left me more frightened than this one. I took Tomkins' advice and discovered that with some diligence and common sense, a person could master a very small aspect of the law on his own. I have to admit there were a few evenings when I was in the New York Law library that I felt like *Abe Lincoln in Illinois*. Since all of the texts were reference copies, I had to accomplish my research on the spot. Bob was right. There was something familiar about a few legal pads on top of books, pencils scattered at angles, little note cards and dog-eared pages on a desk with a lamp casting its glow. All the legal papers that were sent to me in large envelopes from my wife's law firm, were no longer intimidating. I started to welcome them since it was like being assigned a new topic, a new question. Occasionally, there were questions that I couldn't fathom either due to protocol or just inexperience. This is when I made a mistake. I called my wife's attorney.

"Good morning, Ms. Greene. This is Dexter Jeffries."

"Mr. Jeffries, are you going to discuss coming in here?"

"Oh no, I just called about that last batch of paperwork you sent me."

"Mr. Jeffries, I want you to come in . . ."

"Ms Greene. I just wanted to ask you about this term *discovery*."

"Look, this isn't fuckin' law school. If you want a fuckin' law degree, start going to school."

I was quiet and said, "You shouldn't curse at people." She left me with "See you in court, Mr. Jeffries," in singsong fashion.

It was always a bit stupefying and I was still too naïve to understand what was occurring. A few days later I received a letter from Ms. Greene that amicably requested that I show up in her office. The cursing baleful woman was gone; her alter ego was on the phone and she was pleasant. I felt that maybe I had caught her on a bad day when she had cursed at me. Her telephone number was right at the top of the page and I prepared to call her. I had visions of meeting her and discussing this in a more humane manner, as I had done with Bob Tomkins. I was hesitant. There weren't too many people to turn to so I decided to call my mom. I told her that this lawyer wanted me to come in and talk with her.

"Dexter, whatever you do, under no circumstances go to her office."

"Mom, what's up, you sound so ominous. I sorta know what I'm doing." When she didn't laugh at my small comedic aside, I knew that she was serious and this wasn't the time for jokes. I quickly changed my tone.

"Mom, I was just kidding. Joke. Really."

"Dexter, I worked as an executive secretary for almost twenty-five years for some big law firms. I know one thing. I remember this from listening to the attorneys. This was their own admonition that they lived by. A defendant should never appear at the plaintiff's lawyer's office without counsel. If they said it once, they said it a thousand times. A defendant in the law office of the plaintiff's attorney is the most vulnerable person in the world. Anything can happen. You could end up signing papers that you would regret for the rest of your life."

"But Mom, maybe she wants to tell me something good."

"Then let Ms. Greene tell you that in a restaurant, a public place, a library. If she's willing to meet you in a place outside of her office, and I still have reservations about that, think about it."

My mom was right. She scared me, but I needed to be scared. I was so close to walking into this woman's chess game in which I would always be in checkmate. The only time I was to see Ms. Greene was in a courthouse and under the supervision of a judge and a court clerk. I was going to represent myself after a year of filing papers, motions, cross, motions, and answering every piece of correspondence that Ms. Greene sent to me. I tried to be as professional as possible.

The date of the divorce proceedings was April 1st, April Fool's Day, and I wondered as I walked to the courthouse early that morning if I was being a fool. There I was, amateur lawyer at best, walking with his brief and all other important papers, perhaps walking to his doom. I stopped off for some breakfast. Court commences at nine-thirty. That's *first call*. I knew from attending court many times that you don't have to appear for that first call. You can come as late as eleven and make the *second* call and your case will be heard. I ate slowly and tried not to lose my confidence. I had grits instead of home fries. Don't ask why. Maybe I wanted to get in touch with my black side that fateful morning. I left the restaurant and my half-eaten grits at about ten-thirty and headed for the courthouse. As I walked up the steps, I started to feel my heart really thumping in my chest. At the doors I thought to myself, *What the hell are you doing? Have you lost your mind? You're entering the halls of justice and you don't have a lawyer, just a bunch of notes taken from some law books. You must be out of your mind.* Of all things to come back to me, I thought about the time I was in trouble in the army and how I had gone one-on-one with the colonel and everything came clear. If I can take on a colonel of the U.S. Army, I can handle some shyster lawyer who has a foul mouth.

I knew the routine. When I walked into the elevator, I started to relax. I had been there before. I had come in to observe many cases, in all different divisions. I had taken notes, watched the lawyers, listened to what they said and even eavesdropped on them in the men's room. Any scrap of information that I could pick up, I picked up. Up, up, up, up to the nineteenth floor and there I was. I saw my wife and her attorney sitting on the right side. I came in from the back so I could size up the situation. I got in the row behind them and leaned forward and said, "Good morning, counselor." Ms. Greene had only met me once and that was six months before. Eleanor smiled and said "Hi." We had to wait for second call. When it came, Ms. Greene and I went forward. The court clerk called the case. Just as he finished and before Ms. Greene could say anything, I crossed my arms and said, "Your honor, I suggest we conference this case in room 1913 with Mr. Rothwax, court clerk. That seems the most expedient thing to do in this matter." Greene and Eleanor were shocked. That was the first one. As we accompanied the court clerk to the conference room, I walked next to him and made some small bantering remarks about the weather and spring training.

Room 1913 was really a storage closet that had been converted to a "conference room." Because I had seen it dozens of times, I was not dismayed or alarmed at the exposed pipes, the dusty boxes, the bare lightbulbs or any other missing amenities. I could see that Ms. Greene wasn't prepared for this at all. "This is it?" she said to the clerk. Without turning around, he just said, "Yes, Room 1913." I let Ms. Greene enter first and then as Eleanor tried to follow Mr. Rothwax, said, "Sorry, conferencing is only for attorneys." Eleanor looked hurt. He explained. "Only attorneys can conference cases under litigation," he said. Just from her eyes and the look on her face as she viewed me, he could see that a further explanation was obligatory. "Your husband is defending himself. He's pro se. For all practical purposes, he's an attorney, at least for today, so to speak, so that's why he can go in and you have to remain outside until the conference is concluded."

Nothing really good comes from being in front of the law. I had felt my blackness at times in front of it. That day, even though I won on every point, I still left feeling dissembled. I thought back to the letter Eleanor had written to her best friend. I had become a thing to her. Being black, white, and Jewish was somehow an explanation of all my motivations, fears, and weaknesses. She slowly used this to finally undermine me about the past, about important and loving people. She knew I was vulnerable about certain issues. For instance, because of my homophobia, I had a very difficult time dealing with her father who was gay and living with his partner of many years. It was problematic to think about him, and my loathing of homosexuals.

I never understood the hatred behind racism until I was forced to contemplate why I hated my homosexual father-in-law so easily and freely. All those years had gone by, at least twenty. Consumed with race and racism, I had designated myself an expert on this illness the way an internist trains for his biological specialty having to do with the heart or lungs. I was the expert on race relations, pain, discrimination, and bias crime, and never thought about my own illness, my own weakness. Too blind to see anything but my own private hurt, I glossed over my contempt as if it were a minor contradiction in my own personal philosophy. I was really pushed to the limits when I had to confront the fact that my father-in-law was gay. The kid from Queens who routinely made fun of homosexuals, wanted to beat them up, condoned harassing them through college, was physically and spiritually offended by them. That person, me, had to rethink, retool himself, and awaken some dormant memories and feelings. Why? Because there was my father-in-law sitting on my couch, with his lover and there was no way to get around it. Tough situation.

No connection, no overlap, no thoughtful reflection penetrated my consciousness until I looked at him one day and figured out that I hated him the way white and black people and sometimes Spanish people had hated me. I was just like the rest of them who wouldn't take the time to understand, listen, and think. Maybe that was the problem. There are thoughtful ruminations. If I had been capable of that, at least in regard to this particular problem, I would not have arrived at this ugliness in the first place. I would not have dwelt with this excrement in my life so easily. But that's the way things are sometimes.

I thought it was normal to dislike or hate homosexuals because when I was a kid in the 1950s, this was the practice. You ridiculed and made fun of any boy in class, woodshop, gym, who had the slightest proclivity for being awkward, clumsy, and shy. Sissy, fairy, and fag flew out of my mouth and the mouths of others and sometimes these labels were worn by those tagged for an entire year. After all those years of me asking why people discriminated against me, my most revelatory insights dawned on me when I figured out why I was engaging in the same sordid behavior. Tall, with graying blond hair, intelligent, lover and patron of the arts, he had accepted me into this family with open arms as his son-in-law. There I was. Dark, surly, rough-hewn, and spiteful.

How did I change? Slowly, very slowly. Seeing him in the evening after work, or at work in his office, eating and cooking, reading the Sunday *Times* and cutting out every possible article he could, for me, regarding black literature, jazz, movies, and how to build cabins. The language of the transformation was simple and pure. I did look in the mirror one day after receiving a clipping from Lewis, germane to me. I went into the bathroom, grabbed both sides of the sink, leaned as close to the mirror as I possibly could and said, "You've got some nerve. Talk about hypocrite. Jesus, you are one sorry individual. I'll say it again, Dexter Jeffries, you are one sorry individual."

It took years of reflection, nausea, and more reflection to learn to love the man and learn more about why people can't love. It was my greatest course in human relations, not race relations. Because we lived in a duplex apartment with my father-in-law on the top two floors, and Eleanor and I and our son on the first two, we saw each other frequently. Lewis and his partner Joe were very happy together. I could see that. I was still a little uptight when I was around them and pushed myself to the limits to see why. However, I must confess, there was still an undercurrent of tension. I never could trace it but something unsettling was in the atmosphere of the house. After my father-in-law's funeral, I asked Eleanor why she had prevented me from making some remarks at the memorial service. Eleanor said, "I was worried that you might make some untoward remark. I could see that you were never at peace with his homosexuality." I stuttered for a second and then blurted out, "You're right, in a way, but I would never do anything like that." Even to the end of his life I tried. I really tried to change the way a sexist guy tries, or an anti-anything person tries to change. It's the habit, the laziness of it, the ease in which one falls back into what he is familiar with.

However, I was haunted by my perception that there was "something in the air." I thought about why I never felt completely comfortable in the home of my father-in-law and his lover, in the house, kitchen, or living room of Lewis and Joe. One day, about six months after the funeral, I wrote Joe a letter asking him if I was wrong or right about my perceptions that "something was in the air." I apologized ahead of time, but it was worth taking the risk of alienating someone whom I was very fond of. Joe was one of the best men I ever knew. He wrote one of the most honest letters that I have ever received in my life.

Dear Dexter,

Speaking as a therapist—if you were ever uncomfortable around us, you should know the following three things:

1. Lewis and I thought you were amazingly handsome—and we did discuss this;

2. Lewis and I had both had affairs with men who were very much like you, physically;

3. and you would have to be a block of stone not to sense those vibrations from us and feel, very understandably, uncomfortable. This is not homophobia.

This letter was emancipatory. I read it and have kept it in a safe place no matter where I have moved. I always keep it close by. The guilty weights that hung around my neck dropped off, and I was able to raise my head above water and breathe again. I had lived with this terrible guilt. Depleted and war torn by the divorce, this guilt just compounded my sense that I was not a good husband, father, son-in-law, and, ultimately, human being. I felt liberated. I felt free. I had fought against prejudice and won. It wasn't a question of being white, black, and Jewish. The question is, can you just be human? If you are, that's more than enough. That's more than enough.

Sylvia

SHE WAS GOING to be special and different, and I felt undermined by her upper-class mannerisms, her pursuit of the ballet, and her weekends in the Hamptons. This was a world that I had known about only from my brother whose affectations extended to that world. What he saw in it, I'll never know. The black bourgeoisie never possessed any appeal for me, and under my parents' tutelage, I was convinced that these people were just as responsible for black suffering as those who were members of the Ku Klux Klan. It always surprised me that he would have anything to do with people from that class or that they would have anything to do with him. He was a hustler, small-time and petty thief, who knew the streets and felt at home there. Sylvia Anderson was home there, too. Where was the connection? I don't know but we had some intriguing conversations.

Out of her smooth and loving voice would come, "I think you've been angry since that time I asked you about your income."

"Yeah, you can say that I was ... a ... something; I don't know if I was mad. Just a funny question to ask someone on the first date. Or any date for that matter."

We had an apocryphal dinner one evening in the West Village. It was our first official date. The other meetings had been literally for a cup of coffee. She had a soft face, long dancer legs. Intelligent and insightful, we were having a *New York Times* Weekend Section relationship. Everything was right but nothing was human. The suggestions for activities were from this section or that one, and I went along because in my new world of never dating professors again she still seemed a better choice. She had problems. I could see that she was nuts. Just couldn't pinpoint it. I figured it was the upper-class upbringing in Philadelphia that had incurred the damage. Or maybe a *Mistuh*-type father. Who knows? These days you can't tell what you are going to run into. I adored her way of speaking and her clichés. They rolled off her tongue all throughout a conversation at the most appropriate moments. "Cat got your tongue, Mister Jeffries?" or "Put that in your pipe and smoke it!" Many remarks were prefaced with "My father says" or "My roommate thinks." Her center had been dislodged a long time ago, and all I had in my hands were the crumbling pieces of the periphery of a life. I think she was aware of this though, and my being with her was a confirmation of something long and distant from her past.

"My dad thinks that all professors are egotistical. He says that they are the most narcissistical people in the world. That's a quote, a verbatim quote, word for word. What do you think of that?"

My words rolled out also. "Your dad's a jerk. No, let me rephrase that; your dad's an asshole. That's about the best I can do when I hear something like that."

Sylvia looked at me, smiled, and reminded me not to say things like that because I probably didn't mean them.

We walked down Canal Street, which is a tired commercial strip in lower Manhattan that should have had the dignity to die years ago. It has gone through a few revivals, but none of them ever brought back what I wanted and needed to see. When I drove a cab, one of my favorite stops for lunch or dinner was Dave's Luncheonette. This was a place where you could get "two with everything" and a genuine egg cream. Sylvia walked past Dave's and I revived this memory. It fell on deaf ears and a puzzled smile as I failed to remember, don't try New York City nostalgia with people who are from Philadelphia. The night breeze from the Hudson River made her pull down her Yankee cap, and I noticed how she had threaded her hair through the opening in the back: "That's how girls wear baseball caps?"

"Is this the way you go home every night?" came from her sweet lips.

"Yeah, I take the A train," and stopped myself before giving a lecture about Duke Ellington, Billy Strayhorn, and how the train routes itself from Brooklyn to Harlem and what this meant for a generation of

African American people. "The A train is a good train; it's the quickest way."

I thought about the expression *quickest way* and wished there was a word to capture the notion of doing something in the most expedient, but not necessarily the most pleasurable manner. There should be a word for *quickest but not pleasurable,* but I couldn't think of it. Sylvia mentioned that she had taken the train only to get to the Port Authority, and that was to connect to a bus that took her to New Jersey on a daily basis. We walked down the steps and got our tokens. Going through the turnstile I could hear the distant but close rumbling of the train and motioned that we should hurry. With her sneakers and baseball cap she really looked fine as she skidded down the steps.

The A train rolled in with a crashing thunder, and we hopped on. Nothing ever quite prepares you for the A train. This is not the Ellington A train. It's definitely not the A train as imagined by the New York City Transit Authority either. You can see it by the faces of the people and the characters that play regular roles. The train has an ebb and flow that is strictly coordinated with the neighborhoods. I've watched it for years. It used to be that the farther and deeper you entered into the environs of Brooklyn, the darker the train became. The whites always started to file out as soon as the train hit High Street Brooklyn Bridge. That's Brooklyn Heights, a very fashionable neighborhood and some were headed for DUMBO. When Jay Street came, the mass exodus occurred; these whites were transferring to the F for whiter parts of Brooklyn, Park Slope, Cobble Hill, and Carroll Gardens. My use of the A train as a barometer for sociological patterns, change, and the impending alteration of Brooklyn life was pretty accurate. Now a flurry of newcomers, Asians, whites, Indians remain well after Brooklyn Heights and get off at stops like Lafayette Avenue and Clinton-Washington Avenues.

A few years ago, though, those passengers who stayed on the train after a crazy station named Hoyt-Schermerhorn were easily reduced to a few common denominators: hiphop street thugs who had no desire for the task of earning a living with a traditional job; hardworking black people, those making up the civil service force of New York City, and black businessmen and women. There was a smattering of Russian janitorial women, night workers. They spoke behind closed hands in Russian as if they were still apprehensive about being under surveillance. I wondered if my Russian relatives from Odessa looked like these women, the ones the Nazis killed in 1941. That was not the time to be a Russian Jew once the Germans and Ukrainians start to do their work. Even the Nazis were impressed and at one point asked the Ukrainians for a little restraint, a little. Sylvia saw me inspecting the scene and detected a habit of mine. I couldn't tell which one. But she spoke about it. She commented behind her hand, "These people aren't winners." I nodded my head and said, "Life is tough."

I look around some more, breaking every rule of an old friend who used to be scared of the subway: never look up, never look down, never make eye contact. Secretly he wanted to die and be killed on the subway, but I knew that that wish was never going to be granted. No such luck. You buy that Westport nightmare and you're stuck with it. He's been doing it for twenty years, and it got exhausting after ten. He wanted to be mugged and murdered so he wouldn't have to go back to his law office at his corporate job and support some suburban madness that never stops. From Metro North in the morning to Metro North at night and Home Depot on the weekend. Kafka couldn't have thought of a better, short story, or novel. I did it once for a year, up and down, one year on the commuter train, and it took something out of me. I drove to the station at Beacon for a 6:45 train. Pitch black and cold even in September. Noticed that people were standing in bunches and wondered why would people stand in preplanned bunches like that. Every thirty feet there was a batch of people. Then there would be a gap. Then another batch of people. Of course, I avoided these batches and stood between two of them. The train rolls in heading down from Poughkeepsie and when it stops, the doors of every car open up at exactly where the clumps of people are standing. Man, did I feel foolish because I had to run to one batch or another. There I was in the middle. You would think somebody would have mentioned that I was going to be screwed but not these people. With their heads buried in a paper, the darkness of the station, and their lives, they barely had enough strength to take care of themselves. This was truly a case of every man for himself. They figured that a newcomer to the station crowd would learn, would be initiated, would be hurt like they were, and would take it.

I look around my car and gladly see that there is no graffiti. Sylvia and I have one moment together when we say that it's good that the graffiti is gone. Now the kids scratch the windows like a primitive beast working on the inside of a cave hoping to make contact, hoping to be noticed. Hoping to be remembered.

The other people are noble. Most of them are black and Puerto Rican, Dominican, Caribbean, Haitian, and they work at those jobs that no one ever talks about or wants to know about. There will never be a TV show about some city worker who drives the bookmobile. Or the woman who maintains it. No shows about real black people, just comedy blasts that keep you laughing so you don't cry. I rarely watch television. I never watch it as a matter of fact. Once, no twice, a year I attempt to watch it because I'm a teacher. I should make myself available to "pop culture." I try. I really do. I start at 6:30 with the news. My plan is to watch it straight through until about 11:00 P.M. I usually start to get nauseous at 6:33 when the first commercial comes on. Something about old people who don't want to die and how they should have the right to urinate on themselves in private. I guess that's a right. Then I watch a few more minutes and start to become physically ill at the news and the commercials. I've never made it to 7:00. There's nothing on. I get up and turn the knob to OFF.

An hour later I'm better because the need to vomit is gone, and I turn the knob to ON. I flip the channel. I see black people, and I'm interested. I sit down and listen. Within a few seconds, I realize that I'm watching puppet people who are not real. I'm amazed at the genuine effort not to be genuine. Whoever is writing this stuff is brilliant, inhuman but brilliant. All of the black people are young, attractive, and funny. They laugh a lot on these shows. Every language moment is turned into a joke and every response is turned into a laughing retort. The call and response pattern of my ancestors used to posssesses something unique. In the fields, in the South, and in Africa, those field hollers, those call and response patterns formed the core of an African's existence. If you were a slave in the Americas, it was most important. There was a leader of the group whether it be one hundred slaves chopping cotton, picking tobacco, or using pickaxes while constructing a railroad, this special type of singing rallied your beaten spirits and pushed you through the misery of your job. Whatever drudgery you were performing, that field boss yelling something and you and another hundred men and women yelling back in unison, that was community. That was strength. That is what pushed you on to survive another day with the "white man boss." Now this source of succor and consolation is employed to make fun of each other, with the eyes enlarged in that minstrel exaggerated manner with the character saying, "Oh, you must like her a lot. You pushed her shopping cart all the way home; I know you really like her," or "I don't believe your hair—what happened? Was you struck by lightning?" The pause, the eyes get bigger than Al Jolson's, then the response, and the nausea.

"Hey, where are you? Come back. Come back, come back, from wherever you are." Sylvia is talking. My station is next, and we get our backpacks up from the floor. I look around and silently sigh. I am not going to add to these people's discomfort. The train stops and the station is announced. "Lafayette Avenue, Clinton-Washington is next on this local." I turn to Sylvia and say, "I'm here; I'm sorry. I'm here. Just thinking about things." We walk out of the station, and there's a skip in my step when I remember that sex may be involved this evening.

I live on the third floor of a quaint three-floor frame house built in the 1850s. The house possessed a special comfort that helped me get through my divorce. Funny, houses can do that. This house had been there in Brooklyn for 145 years. If it could make it through that century and a half, I could get through my divorce. That was my simplistic inspiration. We walked in the wooden door that was never square with the floor, and I let Sylvia explore the place. That took about thirty seconds and the "It's cute" came from Sylvia. I took out two wineglasses and offered her some chardonnay. She sipped it just the right way and asked me for a napkin. "Whatta ya need a napkin for," I said. She swiveled her dancer hips at my question and said, "Oh, just a habit." I went to the cupboard and got her a napkin and said, "Whatta ya need a napkin for?" She coughed her mouthful of chardonnay at my second request. "You're not going to make a big thing of this, are you," Sylvia said. I stood my ground and said, "Look, you got the napkin so you won that. I just want to know why you need a napkin for a drink, no more, no less." There was a pause. Sylvia was more relaxed and said, "You have a nice table; I don't want to leave a circle on it with my glass." I replied, also more relaxed, "Oh. Good."

"Dexter, are you interested in Africa? I noticed the little statue."

"A little bit. You know I teach those courses so I know a little bit about it."

"Well, this is the kind of thing that you would never learn in a textbook or the library. Something that I learned on my own."

"Yeah, I know one thing, Sylvia. I know what Africa means now."

She started to laugh and said, "What do you mean now?"

"I mean that. I know what Africa means, now."

"Please, just speak plainly. What do you wish to say?"

"The Latin word for Africa is *aprica*. This means *sunny*."

"Are you serious?"

"Yes, man, as serious as a black man can be."

"What else?"

"In Greek, the word *Aprike*, that means *without cold*."

"So you're saying that the original word Africa is not even an African word."

"You got it, baby. That place has been named and renamed more than any other continent on the planet. Yeah, think about it. The Greeks start heading south over the seas, the Aegean, the big one, Mare Nostrum, guys like Ulysses and Agamemnon, and they find a place and the first thing they say, is, 'Hey, it's not cold here like downtown Athens, so it's a place without cold, *Aprike*. And then a few thousand years later, Aeneas and his boys started heading southeast from Rome, and they hit a place after sailing over the cold and wet Mediterranean, it's sunny all the time and there you have it. So much for sunny Italy, right? When they hit North Africa, they never had it so good. Why do you think they wanted to kick those people out of Carthage?"

"Are you making this up?"

"Baby, no one could make this up. This is history. Real history as opposed to Kwanzaa or some other ersatz bullshit like that. People have been using Africa for a long time, from Homer to Haley. Hey, I like that. Homer to Haley. Haley to Homer. Only problem with Haley is that he called it history. Homer had enough sense to call it a poem, a myth, a legend. That's what inspires, right?"

"You mentioned that Haley made things, up, that's Alex Haley, right?"

"Yeah, did you ever read that big article about Haley ripping off other writers to write his book *Roots*? Ripoff is ugly; plagiarized would be the more appropriate term."

Sylvia was genuinely engrossed now and said, "I'm really interested in this."

"Couple of years ago, there was this legal case against him. I think a couple of writers were suing him. Black writers. Things became apparent to the judge and Haley admitted that he had borrowed and fabricated some parts of the book. But one thing, and I respect him for this, he had a good explanation. Well, he had an explanation. It was intriguing. He said that black people, like any other group, need a myth, a legend, a legacy. I could understand where the dude was coming from. We need something, maybe a myth; maybe we have too many myths."

She looked at me and stared. I knew that I had gone on for a bit and remembered that it was she who had initiated this discussion about Africa. "Sylvia," I said with a hint of guilt in my voice, "What did you want to tell me about Africa? Sorry for going on like that. But you wanted to tell me something about Africa."

With a smile that let me know she wasn't angry or upset at me taking her time or space, she leaned forward to take another Triscuit from the batch I had set on the table. She managed to break a small square of cheese which I had also put on the table into even smaller squares. "Well, it's nothing like that; I just wanted to know if you know anything about African women."

"A little."

"Well, being that I'm African, I have some interesting things to tell you."

"Sylvia, you're throwing that word *African* around like you were born and raised on the continent, like you hail from Nigeria or something. Your boat got here a long time ago, and you're talking like it was yesterday."

She moved on the couch preparing herself for another assault.

"Well, if you feel that way, maybe I shouldn't tell you what I was going to say."

"Look Sylvia, it's not the way I feel. I'm just trying to make a point. Here you are; you've been here for four hundred years, almost as long as any other group of people living in America. Do you know what white people call themselves if they've been here for four hundred years? Think about it. You've been to the Hamptons. How many times on that stupid Hamptons Jitney bus with those people and their sunglasses propped on their foreheads reading the *New York Times* or they got the

New York Post stuck inside it. They're bringing special white people out from the city; even the white people out on Long Island don't like them."

Her smile told that my re-creation of that bus with a bunch of ignorant yuppies on it was accurate and poignant. She started to laugh, and I had to laugh too. I decided to keep it up since it was relaxing us. "Yeah, fuckin' people wearing Dockers shorts, Dockers shoes and Dockers white boy shoes without any socks. Right." With this she burst out laughing and raised her fist to her mouth like the Russian women back on the A train. I laughed. "Goddamn white people with stiff backs and necks, riding on a damn bus. No pride. I wouldn't go out there unless I had a car or could at least rent one." I had her going and the napkin reserved for the coffee table wineglass ring was brought up to her face. I could have kept the Richard Pryor monologue going but wanted to get back to those serious points.

"Sylvia, before we get carried away, one more thing, one more question."

Tears and a muffled "What?" comes from behind her hand.

"What do you call a person who's been here for four hundred years?"

"What do you mean?"

"Just what I said. What do you call someone who has been on these shores for three to four hundred years? There are white people who have been here that long, right?"

"Dexter, what do we call them? We call them Americans."

"That's it, baby. You got it. That's the answer. If a white person has been here since the beginning, you call them an American. But for some strange and perverted reason, if it's a black person, you call them . . . what do you call them?"

We both became quiet. It was that silence that comes at one o'clock in the morning when things are serious and turning even more serious. I got up and walked over to my stereo to put on a cassette with some Charlie Parker on it. My back was to her as I toyed with the stereo.

"Black!"

I was still fiddling with the buttons but turned and said, "What?"

"Black, or African."

I pushed the PLAY button and waited for Bird and Miles to come on. They were going to help do some healing. When they made those cuts back in 1947, they were healing each other. Bird was out of the hospital, feeling better after his breakdown and Miles was out of Juilliard learning from the master. That first solo of Bird's on *Embraceable You* started the process.

"Yeah, that's what I'm talking about. Any other group, they put in four centuries and they don't call themselves English or Irish. Have you ever met one of these people who would introduce themselves as English? After four hundred years you don't say, 'Hi, I'm William O'Neil, Irishman.' No, that guy says I'm an American. Black people should be doing the same thing. Take a hint from the people we've been working next to or under for all this time. They call themselves American. Now, how does it sound? We've been here all that time, and we say we're black, and now we're saying we're African. Gimme a break. You spent that much time away from home in a new place and you're a new thing. Right? Right?"

It was quiet, and all I could hear was Miles with his mute taking a nice eight-bar break. Very lyrical, very poetic young Miles. I needed both him and Bird that night. Duke Jordan had already taken his piano solo and J.J. Johnson had put up his trombone. Just that nice young sound of Miles before *the birth of the cool.*

"That's nice; what's playing? That's very nice. Who is it?"

"Bird and Miles. Charlie Parker and Miles Davis playing a long time ago."

"I've heard of them. Miles doesn't play like that now."

"No, he went crazy a long time ago. The important thing is that he did play like this one time, a long time ago. Listen to him hit that note on *My Old Flame.* What do you think?"

Leaning closer to the stereo Sylvia nodded her head. It was time to get back to her. I had let her and her ideas and feelings alone for almost twenty minutes. I stumbled with an apology about hogging the time and the evening, and she said it was all right. She still wanted to tell me about African women, and my silence let her know that I was not going to interfere.

"You might not know this, but African women have large buttocks. There's nothing that we can do about this."

I looked at her, smiled a stupid smile, and said, "No, I never heard that before. Sylvia, what about the gym? Don't you go to the gym twice a day, six in the morning and six at night? Right?"

"I know. I know," she said with a whine in her voice. "It has something to do with genetics. African women have large rear ends, and there is nothing we can do about that condition. And you know how much I exercise. God, twice a day, early and then late. All those machines and it's expensive being a member of Equinox." I looked at her and gave her a comforting look. That worked because she kept on confessing.

"I know you've been with white women so you're accustomed to a smaller figure."

"Sylvia, you're smart, attractive, have a dancer's body and there is nothing that you have to do. I can't stop you from feeling that way. I can just tell you what I'm thinking. It just doesn't matter."

Bird and Miles kept on playing; it was a nice forty-five-minute tape that I had put together, and I let Sylvia sleep in my bedroom, and I stayed on the couch.

Heritage

———————————

EVERY FAMILY HAS some way of hiding or conveying legacy, information, lies and truths. Photographs, diaries, letters, and of course, tens of thousands of stories that are told and untold. Even before man could talk, he still felt the need to tell a story through a dramatic re-creation of an event that had occurred earlier in the day. That night, around the fire, without words, maybe taking hold of a spear, shield, flower, rock, or bear's head, she jumps, leaps, and without any recognizable sound, has the clan thinking, wondering, and learning. In a time when there was no language, no records, no graves, she is offering a tangible method of passing on knowledge, skills, and, most important, memory. Without memory, there is no past, present, or future. My parents possessed a few family artifacts. But we were never really permitted to have access to them. Maybe they were there but my mother and father were perceptive and cognizant that the same items that offer liberation and guidance can become obdurate blocks of oppression. There are families that literally drag such memorabilia out and drown their pathetic longings and offspring in it. Once you are aware of it, your *heritage*, you're obligated to do something—either live by it, for it, or die by it. You can reject that birthright but never forget it.

My mother always kept personal items to a minimum and if she were to disappear without some forewarning, I would have had practically no connecting links, or items that would have revealed who she was, and how she became that way. A black book, rather thin but with a hard cover was kept in her nightstand for years. I was on one of my legacy tours, searching and rooting around the house like a mole. I had mastered the art of putting things back exactly the way I had found them. That wasn't a problem. When I found the black book, thin with a hard cover, it was in decent shape. I was starting to be satisfied with who I was by the time I was in my late twenties.

Senior Echoes, what did that mean? I opened the book and there, folded neatly in 1980, as it was when it was placed there in 1936, was a document. It was very fine parchment. Yellow, not yellow with age, just plain strong yellow. I unfolded it and it read, in Greek lettering, API-ETA,

This Certifies
That on account of Loyalty, Efficiency,
Helpfulness, Service and Scholarship
Mary Kravitz
Has been elected as an Active member
In the Franklin K. Lane High School
League of The Arista

Arista, I thought, man, that's something that I was never able to get into. Alonzo, George, and many of my friends were in it. I always felt jealous since I was in the high school senior band and orchestra and played the moving music that accompanied their ceremonies. My eighty-three average just wasn't good enough. I was up on the stage and watched them as they entered the darkened auditorium with their candles. Now I was finding out that one more person had membership in that elite organization, my mom. So, that's the first secret. My mother was not just a good student; she was an outstanding student and this fact had been officially recognized in November 1935. I found out that a yearbook in 1936 was very much like those put together in 1971, the year I graduated from Springfield Gardens High School. There's always the ubiquitous message from the principal attempting to inspire those who are about to embark on their greatest adventures. The deepest year of the Great Depression 1936. How do you inspire when one-fourth of the labor force is out of work? There was also an index indicating where one perusing the pages would be able to find the students who wrote fiction, essays, and poetry. It was also noted who are the celebrities and what pages they can be found on. *Knocks* was the strange and enigmatic title for a section of a yearbook where all of the photographs of the seniors were. I skipped everything and went straight to page sixteen.

When you leaf through a yearbook, depending on the mystery person's last name, you receive a preview of them by the messages that are left by their friends, teachers, and even antagonists. Since my mom's last name was Kravitz, I was going to proceed through almost half the graduating class, before I met her. Strange way to meet someone whom you thought you have known all your life. You know your father and mother and yet when you see them in the distant past, you too are embarking on a journey. They are going forward, leaving high school to take their chance with the world. To see what interests will pan out. To see what loves will enthrall them. To see other worlds that will capture their souls and imaginations. To see defeat. To see that sometimes things, people, and ideas don't work out. I was reversing that process. I was going back to 1936 and had only half of the alphabet to prepare me for my mother's birth, her reincarnation.

I started to flip the pages. Even though the photographs were all black and white, because of the passage of forty-four years, there was a gray sheen to all the pictures. No matter what the person was wearing the day they posed for that professional cameraman, it had become gray. Gray dresses, suits, ties, jackets, and blouses. There were many notes to my mother, last-minute reminders and messages. All of them offered encouragement regarding their hopes and dreams. A few voiced a slight trace of disappointment, as if aware that they weren't going to see my mother again and this was a tragedy in itself. All of them started to form a composite picture or at least a pretty detailed sketch of who that person was. You could tell by the tone of the notes, the catchy nicknames and the style of the writing that my mother was a special person, not a character in that classic American high school moronic way.

"Best Wishes for a successful Radical"

"Fellow Comrade"

"To the best Orator I ever knew"

"Don't get excited when you talk about Communism; it's nothing to get excited about because we know you're right."

"I must give you credit for trying so hard to make a Red out of me."

"Mutiny on the Bounty=Kravitz"

"Lane's Ambitious Communist"

There was her photo, finally. I saw a young woman with the sweetest smile. What struck me about the picture was the sincerity; the mouth expressed it all. There was something so genuine about the eyes, so intelligent, and incredibly sensitive. That was it. That was what made me well up. To be that sensitive in a time when there was so much horror. The 1930s, The Great Depression, the Japanese are raping China, the Germans are crushing everything human in the name of the Fuhrer. Spain, Picasso is not going to paint *Guernica* for nothing. I look at the epigram that is next to her name and realize that of all those read so far, hers is serious and sober. The other epigrams next to the graduates of Franklin K. Lane hint at some sort of joviality.

As useful as a refrigerator to the Eskimo.

He majors in minors.

If her humor were prosperity, we would never get out of the depression.

There was a frightening one for Richard Heinz of 212 Ralph Avenue, Brooklyn, *Me'n Hitler.* Yet, of all the rest, still nothing as solemn and stirring as what was written below Mary Kravitz of 1933 Park Place,

The personality behind the Communist Party in Lane.

I reread the line. I couldn't stop there on page twenty-seven. I had to have my theory confirmed now that there was an inkling as to how special my mother must have been. I started to plow through the thin pages, closely examining every message left to her from people long ago. I found more and there was a theme.

"Stop Talking and Sit Down."

"May you be the leader of the Communist Party someday"

"Good Luck from one Communist to another"

"So Long, Comrade"

"Here's hoping you head the Communist Party someday"

"Best wishes for a Soviet U.S.A."

"Good Luck, Comrade"

What did all this mean? I knew my mother had been involved in politics in some minor way. But memories from the recent past started to fall into some logical order. The PTA meetings, the Girl Scout leader meetings, meetings of the Tri-Community Council that oversaw three neighborhoods, Springfield Gardens, Laurelton, and Rosedale and probably other congregations and assemblies that I had forgotten. Papers, re-xographed, mimeographed, always staplers being punched down hard and always me, Paul, or Vivian being enlisted to collate some documents, some fliers.

Based on the yearbook and all the quotations and messages, I could see that my initial connection with political activism, born in me during those two summers at Camp Calumet, ran parallel with my mother's experience during the 1930s. Singing those songs and discussing social issues in an obtuse but genuine manner cultivated a soul in me that to this day still wants to fight and resist all the forces that seek to negate man's best side. I now knew that my mother had these experiences decades before me. My generation was inspired in the late 1950s and the early 1960s. Her coming of age moments, her songs, her music went back to the 1930s, a far more difficult time in American history. It was a time of severity, when no one could escape the history of their times, when people would be tried to the breaking point. Answers to questions that had gone unanswered were going to be explored and answered for the first time in years.

Those questions had always been there. My sister Vivian and I had the same question for my mother, but the way it manifested itself and the manner revealed so much about our dissimilar experience when developing and maturing as human beings. My sister, absorbed in her own personal bitterness and resentment, used to ask, "I just want to know; why did you marry Dad back in 1936? What made you do such a thing?" Her query implied that they had committed some wrong. With wonderment and adoration in my voice, a few words altered here and there, I made the same inquiry but with no regret and acrimony, "How were you guys able to get together back in 1936? How was it possible?

How did you tolerate the racism, the discrimination? The hate? The hatred of what you represented to so many people at the time?" When your father is black and your mother is the daughter of Russian immigrant Jews from Odessa, and it is 1936, you're in awe of this fifty years later, even in 1990. I was and still am.

1936: This is America in 1936, the pre-Civil Rights America, pre-Montgomery Boycott, pre-A. Philip Randolph's threat to have the first March on Washington, pre-Martin Luther King Jr., pre-Jackie Robinson, pre-anti lynching legislation that Congress never passes, pre-every major social and political movement that permanently altered the country and how it thought and viewed race relationships. It's a time when the pact that my mother and father entered into is illegal in every state of the Confederacy. That's the world they were up against.

My mom's answer grew less cryptic as the years went on. Despite the fact that my sister and I were asking completely different questions and seeking completely different answers, she was consistent. Oblique when she had to be, and perhaps this was a skill that she had picked up from being "the best orator" during her high school days, she diffused both our questions, even if she thought it would be far more fruitful to answer mine.

"Love, when you love someone dearly you can do anything. That is how we got through those terrible times. We loved each other very much." As we became older and the questions remained the same, she was aware that her intriguing romantic response was not as satisfying since we were no longer naïve about ways of the world. Now because we were living through the successes and failures of our generation's attempts at changing the world and making it a better place, Vivian and I needed some serious instruction and inspiration. Given this opportunity to stake her political and social claim on our souls, my mother would say, "No matter what happened to us personally or what was occurring around the world, especially in Europe, we had the Party. We always had the Party." Even then I knew that the word *party* was spelled with an uppercase letter. It was Party, not party. I could just tell from the way she pronounced the word. Now that I was looking at the photograph in her yearbook and read the small notes of remembrance, that was why Party was written with a capital letter.

A riddle that has plagued me for a long time was why was there a lack of personal fulfillment in my life? This had eluded me for so many years. I wondered why their lives were so different, so much more successful, particularly in the area of personal relationships. I reflected upon the possibility that their center core of stability and security came from being a member of those political organizations. In my mother's *Senior Echoes* some of her fellow seniors had proudly signed next to their name, N.S.L., which stood for National Socialist League. A dozen years after discovering this yearbook I knew what they had and what was missing from my life. I had figured out that what they had was this sense of a mission, this sense of building worlds, taking things under their control. Not only were they capable of having authority over one's personal affairs, house, and job, they had envisioned themselves playing an integral part in shaping and benefiting the community, city, state, and nation. They did not accept the world that was handed to them in 1936. Even at the depths of the Great Depression their world was rich because they always felt "now I have the opportunity to change and improve people's lives." The Great Depression was an ideal repository for all their talent, intelligence, and capacity. My mother was so deeply imbued, that for better or worse, her ideas and values drove me to take up other missions; thirty years after her promise that the forces of good would triumph over Franco and Hitler, and other evil, I made my commitments to groups and causes. From a radical group in the Bronx called White Lightning, to a Brooklyn group called CISPES, I walked and marched with and for people who never had the chance to talk for themselves or upon losing that, had no one to intervene on their behalf.

This is one way I look at my teaching. That's my way of upholding my mother's tradition of committing oneself to a cause higher than one's own personal needs and desires. Teaching people literacy, insights into literature, that has been my journey and though not as regulated as being a member of the Party, I definitely have a sense of mission. I would have to acknowledge that it is easier than what my mother and father were trying to achieve back in 1939 or 1946. Sometimes I think it is more difficult since history is not stagnant. And whether I choose to be American, which is my final choice when it comes down to who I am, I would be fooling myself to think I have complete autonomy over my existence, who I am, who I want to be.

In retrospect I never could have been even faintly aware of how complex a black teacher's role could be, and that is including my experience with Professor Tracey. In a quarter of a century, Professor Tracey's dilemma and her battle cry of *cultural amnesia* now seems quaint, as though she had constructed a manner of being able to exchange appropriate pleasantries. I was sharing an office with a black English professor at Hunter College. I respected her a great deal. She was intelligent, genuine, what the kids would call *for real*. Yet, she was depressed after returning from a class. Quiet and reserved, I decided not to invade her privacy until I felt that I could not bear to stand on the sidelines. I butted in while she was grading some freshman composition essays. I wanted to make it easy so I said, "Are these white kids getting to you?" She replied, "Something like that." I looked around at the office, the walls with pictures of favorite authors, quotes, and a poster advertising a seminal conference. The searching of the walls concluded with this exchange:

Professor Abrams: I've been meaning to ask you something; it's kind of an odd question.

Professor Jeffries: Great, are you going to confess that you don't know how to pronounce a word or is it a metaphor you were never quite sure of?

Professor Abrams: No, I wish. I wish it were that.

Professor Jeffries: Oh well, go ahead. We both have a break between classes.

Professor Abrams: Do you ever wonder why black students don't respect us?

I spoke very slowly and methodically, positive that I had heard her correctly.

Professor Jeffries: I don't think it's that they don't respect us. I think they don't like or understand what we represent.

Professor Abrams: What's the difference?

Professor Jeffries: I don't know, I guess.

Professor Abrams: Did you ever consider that it was the subject matter? That if we taught something else, we would have a different sort of contact or discourse? That if we taught, for instance, French, chemistry, mathematics?

Professor Jeffries: Maybe, go ahead, run with that.

Professor Abrams: I think they expect us to do certain emotional things for them.

Professor Jeffries: What do you mean?

Professor Abrams: Just this, they want us to do things either in the class or through the actual structure of it or through the material being discussed, to heal, soothe, or help them.

Professor Jeffries: So, your thesis is that because we are presenting black literature in the same manner that we would teach Shakespeare or Tennyson, they are disappointed.

Professor Abrams: More than disappointed. They're angry. They want to rap about the literature and we desire to have a literary discussion. We call on the white students, and our brothers and sisters can determine by our response, they can discern that their rapping is not appropriate. Or not valued.

Professor Jeffries: But that's it! They want to rap. Don't you see that inherently degrades the literature and the rest of the class; it doesn't matter who's sitting in the room. Because a few white students are addressing the literature in the manner which we feel creates a proper forum and . . .

Professor Abrams: And they're left out; they become truculent.

We continued to move and readjust ourselves in our comfortable swivel chairs but felt very uneasy. A few anecdotes were exchanged that verified our perceptions. My colleague was correct. Many memories of teaching black students who fell into this general grouping came back to me. They were in pain, and I always felt that I had failed them in some basic way. One time I asked them if they wanted me to lie to them. I was discussing the intramural warfare that existed between W.E.B. DuBois and Marcus Garvey during the early years of the 20th century. I had mentioned two notorious quotes from both of them. DuBois had stated,

> Is he a lunatic or traitor? Garvey is the most dangerous threat to the Negro race.

In response to DuBois' allegations, Garvey had responded in kind with,

Dubois is speculating as to whether Garvey is a lunatic or a traitor. Garvey has no such speculation as to whether Garvey is a lunatic or a traitor. Garvey has no such speculation about DuBois.
He is positive that he is a traitor. People like the 'cross-breed,
Dutch-French Negro editor' should be given a good sound horse-
whipping.

The black students became uncomfortable as if I had left on a Walk-
man at an annoying volume, where you hear it but can't find it because
it's beneath a seat cushion. They inquired whether or not I had made a
mistake in my research. This degenerated into what books I had read
and perhaps I had been duped by my professors when I was in graduate
school and a series of clichés about how white people can't be trusted. I
became dejected and as a last resort, asked them point blank, "Do you
want me to lie to you so you can feel better tonight or do you want me
to tell you the truth that will liberate you from history being a cure-all?"
Silence. They didn't answer *yes* or *no*. Finally, a student raised her hand
slowly and said, "I think, and maybe I don't have the right to speak for
the rest, we want you to lie, just a little."

I thought about that alternative and what my mother would have
done in 1937. I decided to tell them the truth.

Tamika

I HAD TO fall in love with her, and it was love at seventeenth sight because she wore something that took me back to 1958 and from that point on, I was hers. I was twenty years older than she. I was me and she was black, but it was the sweater. The sweater started my odyssey with her and if a man ever had to be tested by feats of strength and courage, it was me. Tamika took me to a place that I did not know existed and every American should know about this place. I assume that the same rock that struck me also hit Warren Beatty. He made the movie *Bulworth* because he had seen something. He had seen something so terrible that he had to let the world know it. I did the same.

The sweater showed that she sported a kinship with the *retro* look: brown, but a 1950s brown, reindeer, of all things, pranced their way across her bosom on this sweater. I was taken right back to Girl Scout meetings that my mother used to run every Friday afternoon in the basement of a church. I had to tag along since it wasn't worth the babysitter, and my brother was probably too young to take care of me. The basement of a church, thirty girls, all Girl Scouts, one assistant troop leader (I wonder if my mother ever tried to convert any of these girls to the Party) and there I was. Out of control. They wanted me to sit still and watch them as they stood in a circle and practiced Christmas songs. They were singing rather well, and I can still hear the echoes of the lyrics. Basements are good for that. All the girls were dressed in those green Girl Scout uniforms, but had sweaters on because it was cold downstairs. I started to run along the perimeter of the circle. It was fun.

I slapped the bottoms of every one of those girls. They got one girl, really tough, to take me into the bathroom and distract me with the water cooler. There were little Dixie cups for drinking; I became duly fascinated with them and the slapping of the bottoms of the girls, all thirty of them, as they stood in that singing circle, lost my interest.

But the brown sweaters didn't, so when I first saw her, with that one, I was taken back to that forty-year-old memory, and I was in a trance. While in that trance, Tamika took me on a descent to the underside of America that broke me, broke me on several occasions. I had never witnessed so much pain in such a short amount of time as what happened to me during that winter.

It started as I waited in line at the local video place. She had already said hello to me sixteen times because you have to at Blockbuster. I was on the line, but I had looked at her and the sweater; I let her know that I loved and would love her if she would talk to me. Lanky, sighing with attitude as she took care of one customer after another, she sighed at me even though I always sported what I thought was my interesting and intriguing customer look. I had let it be known that I was renting these films not just for personal use. I was a teacher. I was a professor who needed the films for his history of cinema class. When she was detailed to stock movies on the shelves, I always knew her, even from behind because of the truculently crossed arms on top of a short torso, which was atop a long pair of legs. I never understood those arms crossed with the look of truculence. I equated crossed arms with being smart or knowing something and she wasn't smart, although she was smarter than I. She was high most of the time. She would smoke pot before her shift and said that it helped her get through having to say, "Good evening. Welcome to Blockbuster."

One day something happened. Her hair had been in rows, braids, half dreads, furrows; I hadn't kept up with the nomenclature that accompanied black hair since conking went out in the late 1960s. I just knew one thing. It all took an inordinately long time, time that could be spent on other activities. This time could never be gotten back, so I saw hair-braiding as a useless expense of valuable time and figured that black people were the last ones who should ever waste time. Then one day I walked in the store and saw her in the back, in the *Action* section. Her hair was just as straight as Julia Roberts or Glenn Close. I did a double take as I searched for a few films because it was not her. It couldn't be her. Her hair was not straight on Tuesday. It had been in nappy little rows, and now it was Thursday, forty-eight hours later, and her hair was straight. Velasquez, my favorite Blockbuster employee because he always knew where everything was, noticed that I was staring at her. I felt ignorant that I was aware of another trend or fad that was going to have some cultural and historical significance. I was going to have to contemplate it, think, and wonder and fit it into another block of post-1960s history that no longer made any sense. I had understood everything up until the mid-1970s. After that, the courses and trends of black people defied any of my logic, and I had little or no grasp of what was occurring and how their souls were changing.

Maybe it goes back further than that. I was already losing connection in the late sixties. I remember going on a college interview for New Paltz, a decent college of the SUNY system. I had met the coordinators, deans, and professors. Now I was talking to student representatives of a certain program for minority applicants. I certainly fit into that category at the time. The representative asked me what type of *dorm situation* did I prefer. I wasn't sure what he meant, and he stated that black students had a right to their own dorm. "We have to build our own house before living in another," this righteous man had said to me. As I was filling out the form on a clipboard, he pointed at the dorm request to reiterate that I should live with him in his house. I knew that my admission to the college pivoted on being agreeable and stated in a very innocuous manner that, "I'll be OK in any dorm; an integrated one is OK with me. That's what we've been fighting for, right?" I wasn't admitted to New Paltz and later figured out that I had given the wrong answer. I was supposed to support resegregation, not integration. Of course, no one had the courage or audacity to use that word or something close to it, but that is essentially what was occurring on many campuses.

American black people were entering their first stage of withdrawal, a new game plan, and a new madness. A nation fosters, in a whimsical manner, the imposition of the following artificial classifications: Colored, Negro, Afro-American, Black, People of Color, and African American, and then expects that those who have entered this labyrinth of an absurd drama worthy of Beckett or Genet, to be normal just like them. African American people or their latest reincarnation are supposed to be like them, happy white people who want and covet everything that they see after the phony news at seven o'clock. No other group of people in the history of mankind has been forced to endure six identification changes within such an abbreviated period of history. Six, if you are born colored in 1910 and are still alive in 2002, and you're ninety and that is possible, you made six changes in one lifetime. White people, they're still the same. They're lucky. I had to be confused.

When Kwame Smith of the New Paltz Black Student Union, who was already suspicious of me because I was so light, queried me as to my dorm choice, there was a fifty-fifty chance that I was going to give him the wrong answer. I had already endured the usual questions of, "If you're black, how come you have a Spanish last name?" When Kwame called Alejandro over to see if I should really be a member of the Puerto Rican Student Union of New Paltz, Alejandro Martine wanted to know, "If you're Puerto Rican, how come you can't speak Spanish?" All of these questions were to eventually make me mad. They were to haunt every crevice of my life, and they were to be repeated as though I were some sort of designated steel ball in a pinball machine that never gets a chance to drop down into the hole at the bottom of the machine. People just kept banging away at me with their rational and irrational questions and as long as they jolted and rocked the machine from time to time, they never had to worry about me dropping out of the way of their flippers and bongs and bings and slaps.

This was alien to me. I was to be alienated many more times by political and social landmarking monuments such as this. Nothing worse than being informed that I was a "house nigger" and during slavery times I had an easier life than my darker companions did on the plantation. According to the theory, I was light and therefore had escaped the most ignominious and degrading aspects of slavery because I was a servant or butler in the big house. From Malcolm X to any well-read or rhetoricalized Black Panther, it was enunciated that black was good, black was superior, and black was perfect. A fantasy but a badly needed one. The blacker the better. The kinkier the hair, the better. The lighter you were now meant that you were a living reminder of the hierarchy of the Old South, and there should be some sort of apology forthcoming. I laughed and cried. Black people from Harlem in 1968 talked about the big house and house niggers and field niggers like they had just come off the levee after unloading a steamboat, and I knew that the closest thing to the Mississippi that they had ever seen was the lake in Central Park or the Hudson River. Some black people became gratuitous and aped the ways of the whites: "It's OK that you're light; there's nothing you can do about it." This was straight out of the liberal handbook of how to be liberal, which recycled itself in the classic line, "Some of my best friends are Negroes, really!"

My response was to read and keep current and perhaps be a little more prepared. I never wanted to be caught flat-footed like that again. But that was impossible. There were too many scenarios, too many ways to be wrong and only a few prospects of being right. No matter how I prepared myself, trained, practiced, rehearsed, I never knew that when struck the best thing to do was to fall to the canvas. I should have just listened as the referee of historical relics counted me out with, "Seven, eight, nine, ten, and the winner is irrationality." When I looked at Tamika's straight hair that evening, way in the back, I was ready for any and all possible explanations. I didn't know that black women still straightened their hair. I stared and stared. Why would a black woman in the year 1997 put a hot comb or any other type of comb to her hair? I started to talk to Jesus in another aisle of the store, gathering my broken ideas, my dismantled head. However, within a few seconds I was looking at her again. Thankfully, there was no reciprocal eye contact, so I could study her in private.

I thought about talking to her, requesting help in finding some classic film, just to make contact. That's how desperate I was. But with Jesus right next to me, that would be too obvious. He would have thought, "He's either really losing it or he's got something for her." He was right. Every time I walked out of the store, I carried her away with me. She was black. At one point I tried to convince myself that she wasn't. One afternoon before an evening class, I pulled Jesus aside and said, "There are some funny people in this store." He agreed and laughed a little. "Mr. Jeffries, you mean that crazy guy, Luis; the guy's retarded." he said. I laughed too and took my shot. "What about Tamika?" came quickly because I was nervous.

Jesus: Adams, you mean Miss Attitude, right?
Me: Yeah, long legs, mad all the time.
Jesus: Yeah, I don't know what's with her. She doesn't like anybody.

That rebuff sent me reeling, but I plowed on and without any hesitation said, "How did she straighten her hair like that? It's almost perfect." Jesus' laughter was loud and the shake of the head made me stand taller because I knew some insult was coming. I braced myself. Jesus responded, still shaking his head, "Professor, you think she straightened her hair? Are you serious? In one day? That perfect?" I thought it was time to bring this little chat back to my turf and quietly said, "Women have a lot of little secrets about their bodies we don't know about." This came out in such a grave manner that he stopped laughing but kept on smiling. "Mr. Jeffries, Adams, man, that's a wig. A wig. She didn't get her hair straightened. It would be impossible to be that perfect. A wig." Shattered again and not able to regroup, I was in Jesus' hands from then on. He informed me that young girls wore wigs, and they did that all the time and it didn't mean anything. It didn't mean that they wanted to be white, brown, or purple. Nothing was wrong with them. It was just part of their style.

That was the last time that I fantasized about her being a very dark light-skinned person with good hair. A wig; why would a young girl in her twenties wear a wig? If she were proud of her hair like she was supposed to . . . this got complicated so quickly I let it drop. From then on, I decided to study her and keep track of her *style* and any possible reconfigurations. Because the film class met four times a week and I was obliged to rent at least one a day, I could see what occurred over the weekend and then assess other developments during the week. I soon became familiar with all of her fashions and resolved that dressing was an obsession for her. The time devoted to this pastime was exorbitant. It slowly came to me. She was redefining herself with fashion, wigs, pink hair, green contact lenses, and clothes from the 1960s and 1950s. Tamika was presenting different versions of herself on a weekly basis. Sometimes she was satisfied with herself on Thursday and still content the following Tuesday. Nothing had occurred during the intervening four days to require a change. Other times, she was Tamika Adams A-1 on Tuesday and Tamika Adams A-2 on Thursday. Marvelous. Nothing to get bored with at all. It took longer for me to get to know her because of the constant metamorphosis. Yet I knew that beneath all of those masks there was something sweet and endearing. I still felt the need to find out things about her, about black life, new black life, what I had missed, what I knew, and what I didn't know. I thought it would be a smooth journey because I had dwelled in my own black world for years, even if it was just in my head. I was wrong, and it wasn't her fault.

First, I had to devise a way to talk. Nothing. There was no scenario that I could take from real life, literary or cinematic, that would make this happen. She didn't like me and had no reason to ever talk to me. The semester had ended in December, which meant one month off. I graded all the papers, final exams, and revised essays. Handing in the grades and placing the last C+ next to a student's name always made me feel a little melancholy. That meant that a relationship with a class had terminated. I was sad thinking that a penciled-in dot on a computer grade roster represented the end of a community that had been bound together for over four months. Christmas came and blurred into New Year's with me thinking, *Christmas Eve and New Year's Eve are always one week apart.* It was during a phase of my life where even noteworthy items like this one couldn't exhaust all of the extra time that I had on my hands. The Internet seemed like the logical alternative to thoughts like *Christmas Eve and New Year's Eve are always one week apart.* I was bored.

The routine was mechanical. Check ski conditions in upstate New York. Then check Mature British Women.com. Move along to Barnes & Noble, Amazon, search for books about Richard Wright, World War II. Go to favorites and hit Classmates.com and see whom I might remember from the graduating class of Springfield Gardens High School, 1971. Finally, switch over to Eudora and check in-box E-mail. All the addresses were instantly recognizable, and I planned my answers out depending on whether they were professional or friendly requests. "Tamikaypoo." Who the hell is Tamikaypoo?

Dear Mr. Jeffries—I wuz just wondering if u wuz still teaching and needed any classic films. Merry Xmas!!!
    PS Spelled the words wrong on purpose (Smile)

I studied the short message an inordinate amount of time and wondered why she had sent it. I sent an E-mail back to her:

Dear Tamika (I think), The college is closed for a month but I appreciate you remembering. Merry Christmas. Prof. Jeffries

Because I always spend about a month at my upstate cabin in a little town called Petersburg, about twenty miles from Bennington, Vermont, I had no occasion to see or talk to her for about a few weeks. It was good that there was a delay since I was not prepared for her and the world that she was going to uncover and reveal to me.

When I returned to New York late in January, I decided to send her an E-mail and with an offer to go to dinner. Her image had remained with me for a month and that meant something. In the E-mail I asked her how did she get my address and what made her E-mail me, out of the blue. Within a day there was a response,

Jesus said you liked me and we had your address because of the video rentals for the college (smile).

I thought about the distance between us, and it was immense, but I wanted to make that leap. Tamika accepted and I met her at the end of her shift at Blockbuster. It was hard. We went out to dinner in Manhattan. Taking one taste of the dinner was enough. She didn't like it. For the rest of the evening, she picked at the edges of the meal. Since we had met at Panchito's on Bleecker Street, I was prepared to drive her back to Brooklyn. I figured that she lived in Fort Greene, or Bedford-Stuyvesant. "No no, no, no, no. I don't live in no damn Brooklyn. You're taking me to Quisqeya Heights." I had just closed the car door and thought that that had distorted her answer. "What?" I said. With the doors closed and the quiet of Houston Street shut out and muffled, she said again, "Quisqeya Heights, Washington Heights. You ever hear of it?"

"Tamika, sure, I mean yeah, I know Washington Heights, just never heard that nickname. I thought you lived in Brooklyn because of the job."

"No, please. Livin' there with my moms on the weekdays but it's home to Quisqeya Heights where things are definitely poppin' on the weekend. Brooklyn, oh my Lord, Brooklyn niggers are so dirty. Don't know how they mothers let them out of the house. Niggers need some serious big ass jars of Vaseline for they knees, elbows, and faces. You ever see them in the A or G train? You know what I'm sayin'?"

I looked at her and laughed. I said, "I don't know. You know what I'm sayin'? Don't think I ever noticed this ashy condition you're talking about but I'll take your word for it."

We started to drive up Sixth Avenue. She knew her way around the city and insisted on the West Side Highway. During the drive she became very quiet. When I asked her how come she wasn't talking, she explained that it had to do with my job, teaching at the college. Most of her replies that evening had been *yes* and *no*, except for the outburst regarding Brooklyn versus Manhattan.

I was honest but naïve. "Tamika, say anything you want. Really." As we got closer to her home, the first time I heard her say, "I think that's they house" I figured that she had slipped because she was coughing. During her speech about "they knees and they elbows" I just thought I had not heard everything clearly. It was my hearing. Then I heard her say it again. "Jack, that was they neighborhood; it's the Dominicans now." I corrected her; you mean *their* and Tamika said, "I didn't say *they*. I said *their*.

Our relationship was quickly reduced to teacher–student with me correcting her to the point that she wouldn't talk and would make this sucking sound with her mouth. I made an effort to cut down on the corrections if she would make a commensurate one to eliminate just one of her offensive grammatical mistakes. We agreed. There would be no more *They was. They were* would be used one hundred percent of the time. My half of the bargain was to be quiet in the presence of all other mistakes. Whether we were in the car or on the subway, we sometimes traveled in complete silence and just exacted little painful smiles out of each other. The clichés came out. They were my only explanation as to why she should try to improve her English. Idle sentences about going on a job interview someday, answering the phone, meeting someone new whom you wished to impress. I sounded ridiculous and went back to something more basic: "I love you. Do it for me."

Tamika knew that I was in shock or numb as we drove to and from her house or visited her friends. It was more than my promised silence. It was the look on my face. It was as though a war had occurred against the black community, and I hadn't even been aware of it. At times I felt like I was driving through Berlin or Hamburg after the war and was witnessing the devastation wrought by our air force for the first time. I couldn't explain it to myself. The human wreckage that I saw for the first time caused a mournful despondency to come over me. My desolation finally had to be listened to. I asked, "What the fuck happened?"

"Damn, Jack, I ain't never heard you curse before. Damn."

"Sorry, I shouldn't curse, but what the hell happened?" Tamika was pleased and told me, "Don't apologize; sounded good. About time you let up on your tight ass. This is the shit that we live in." I flinched at this being the mutual point of connection between us, and she apologized too.

Tamika decided that she was going to be conscious of what I was experiencing. We talked about it after seeing the movie *Amistad* together. She didn't like it because it was a distressing past that she would rather avoid. I made the parallel. With a trembling in my voice because I had come up with a perfect analogy, I said, "But you see? That's like me not wanting to see this black hell up here and what's happened. I don't want to see it, but I'm forcing myself so I can live and learn and be a better . . . a better something. When you watch that film or read a book about the past, you have to force yourself to do the same thing. Maybe if you read and watch a little more, you and I will be able to make sense of this, this fucking Dante's *Inferno* on earth, right here on 145th Street." Tamika did respond and tried to soften my reentry. Anytime I waxed nostalgic about Harlem of the 1960s and the 1970s and getting my masters degree in English City College, she would say, "Oh man, that was a long time ago," or "Black people were different then; you're talking like my moms." "Don't get sad; there's nothing you can do for these niggers. Niggers ain't got no enz for nothin' but turkey with stuffing. Shit, they lettin' the Dominicans take over and ain't even puttin' up a fight."

My throat became the barometer of my pain; it recorded how much I saw and how much I couldn't digest. It would tighten and tears would wet my eyes as I witnessed something that was never meant to be witnessed. I toughened myself up and contemplated becoming a missionary returning to a neighborhood, Harlem, a place that I loved and knew. I thought about helping the natives. I became too sentimental or just plain soppy. Tamika would brace me with rap music or some one-liner that was brutally painful. "Don't show me any more tonight; I've seen enough. Harlem, this is not my Harlem. Those crackheads, those junkies, they don't fit in my vision, into my vision of, of . . ." Tamika would turn to me whiplash style and hit me with a line that stung because of its veracity, "What you suspect?" You finished your BA, MA or somethin' at City College but that was fifteen years ago. They kicked my ass out, dismissed me for having below a two point zero. And you started the thing back in the 1970s. So that means a long time has been poppin' by and you're wondering why things are different. You don't care about these black people. You care about those black people, the ones in your head, the ones from your backgroundpast. Can I say that? *Backgroundpast?*"

I never was as silent as I was when I was with Tamika, especially in the car. If it wasn't the dilapidated landscape and the police chasing kids around corners, and vans of cops pouring into a building and people coming out on Amsterdam and St. Nicholas Avenue, linked together in that modern-day chain gang of plastic cord holding them together, it was her asking me to help her out. The first time she felt secure enough to make a request I was moved. I wanted to help her. I wanted to be on her side and prove that I had some value, some connection to my brothers and sisters. We were in the car driving away with a take-out breakfast on the front seat.

"You said you wanted to help me right?"

"Tamika, anything, you name it, I'll do it. I want to, to, I want to . . ." and before I could use the word *intervene* which would make her uptight and me look foolish, she said, "Can you give me some money?"

"What?"

"Jack, I just wanted to axe you if you could give me some enz, money."

"Tamika, look, we have to make a new rule. I know I promised no more rules. But *axe* for *ask*, I can't take that. That's killing me. I'll take any rap song you want me to hear and listen to one after another, put it on repeat, anything. Biggy, Smally, the guy with the clock on his chest, but no more *axe*. That's too painful. Just say it, *ask, ask*. I want to *ask* you a question. What would you do at the end of an interview? Say, Oh, I want to *axe* you one question about the salary?"

"Later for all that bullshit; you're gonna have me talking like you're talking and then when you leave, people be here gonna be calling me white and stuck up black bitch and you're goin' to be whatever the hell you're doin'."

I looked at her as hard as I could but that never had an effect and then she pointed between her legs and said, "Anyway you don't care how I talk. You just want that nice tuna. The way you was lappin' at it the other night, I thought you was goin' to make me a four-course meal. Come on, laugh. That was funny. That's it."

I sighed and returned to the matter at hand. I started to search my pockets for a cigar and smiled at her sexual remarks.

"Yeah, I know. Tamika, yeah, but I thought you wanted me to help you out in a different way."

"Jack, this is help. This is a lot of help."

"Oh."

She knew this was going wrong, and I felt the morning souring and the uneaten half of a scrambled egg on a roll with bacon started to look disgusting. In the past few years before I met Tamika, I had become good with props and not talking. I wrapped the sandwich up in that thin aluminum foil and smiled at the same time. The coffee was still there and that would save me. I took a sip and saw that there was plenty of it left.

"Well, Jack, are you going to help me out?"

"Huh?"

"You see, were you, was you, are you even listening? Is you even listening anymore?" I turned to her and kept the car going straight.

"Sure, I'm listening. You were right. It's *were*. You want to borrow some money."

"Jack, I asked you if you could give me some money."

Because I had made her repeat the request, I had just enough time and a delay. I now had a viable strategy.

"Tamika, tell me what you need. I'll buy it. Isn't that just as easy?"

"Shit, you can't buy this for me. Just give me the money or forget it."

"Come on, Tamika, what is it that you want that I can't buy?"

"Chiba."

"Say again."

"Weed, Jack, weed."

I looked at her and paused. Before I could pose my Hollywood reaction of being aghast, she cut that short with, "Don't start this bullshit that you thought I didn't smoke pot. All old people think it's OK to drink and 'cause young people smoke pot, you always down on us."

"I'm not down on you. I'm just thinking."

"Well, don't think too long. All I want is three dollars."

Now I was interested and alert. I said, "Tamika" with genuine concern, "Where can you get pot for three dollars?"

Her medium sigh that expressed tedium and time is of the essence came out between her teeth. "Jack, listen, you can't get pot anywhere for three dollars. Me, Tosha, Aneshia, we're all chipping in to get ten dollars together, and we're gonna get puffed out. I just wanted to put in my share no more, no less." I was happy when she said that because she was starting to use some of my cliches.

I didn't know what to say. First, how could I not lend or give someone three dollars. The sum was meaningless. But at the same time, what did this mean that three people had to assemble all of their resources so that there would be ten dollars. And one source of the mutual funding, Tamika, didn't even have her share of it. Last, I didn't want to give her money for pot. I wanted her to ask me for money for books, art, books.

"Look Tamika, the money is not the issue . . ."

"Jack, start calling me Tammie; I like that better and that's what my girlfriends call me."

"Tammie, sure, the money is not the problem. I just feel funny giving you money for pot."

"Why?"

"I don't know. Just feel funny about it."

"What about if I ask you for money for food?"

"Sure, of course, I would give you money for food"

"Then give me twenty dollars for food for Tosha's baby. Baby's father won't give her any money; nigger won't even buy food. Ain't that something? I'm talking about a serious babymammadrama goin' on."

I started to feel the linguistic weight of Tammie's world coming down on my head. "Baby's mother, baby's father" Anytime I asked her what were the names behind these words Tammie just said, "Doesn't matter; they never gonna be together." The more I listened, the more depressed I grew since I could see that by not giving names and faces to the fathers and mothers, it was as though the reality of the situation could be denied, as least temporarily. Entire conversations with high drama were related to me time after time without the utterance of one proper pronoun.

"The baby's father came over with his new baby's mother to talk to his old baby's mother about how the Pampers could be divided up."

"That baby's father treats the new baby's mother better than the old baby's mother."

I wanted to navigate this world with a little more skill and I was meeting more and more of her acquaintances. To reduce the awkwardness, I just wanted to be able to put names to faces. It was a difficult task.

"Tamika, look, don't take this the wrong way. I'll buy as much food as you want or Pampers or whatever; I just feel funny giving you the money."

"You don't trust me?"

"No, I don't. I don't. This is another world. You guys can't keep yourselves in check. There are some big forces out there that I don't expect you to fight. Look, I'll buy all the things you need."

Tamika presented this plan to her friends over the phone. It was OK with Tosha and Aneshia. We picked them up, and they got into the car. They all wore stylish clothes. There was a range in their health based on their physical appearance. Some were old before their times. The ones with kids were no longer innocent and young. They reminded me of the women in the novel *Cane* by Jean Toomer. They had been on an accelerated aging plan that had made them old before anyone's time. The wounds were discernible. Some had long welts on their necks where they had been cut, as Higby and Lucky would have pointed out. The emergency room doctors had sewn them up and put them back in the fray. The cokeheads had their shiny and hard-spun eyeballs. Meth heads, you could always tell them because their mouths were caving in due to all the calcium loss in their bodies. Jaws decayed and teeth came out and even though some of them were thirty, they looked like they were ready for the home.

We got in the car and started to drive a few blocks. "Jack, stop the car and back up. I just saw my slave." I looked around and pulled over to the curb next to a fire hydrant.

"I thought I said back up, back up, please."

"Tamika, I'm not backing up. Whoever it is, you can get out and walk a few feet."

The seat belt unbuckled, the sigh came, and the door opened. In my rearview mirror, I watched Tamika as she approached a person who looked like a crackhead. The girl's white ski jacket had turned gray from street life. There was a piece of duct tape wrapped around one of the sleeves.

"What did she mean, slave?"

"Jack, that's Fudgy; she's our slave."

"What do you mean, that's why I'm asking. Tosha, slave means someone on a plantation, 1855, the South . . . !"

I looked up into the rearview mirror and they were still talking, Tamika and Fudgy. I could see that by their gestures some sort of plan was being made. As I looked, I spoke.

"Tosha, remember, I just axed you somethin'."

"Jack, I thought you said not to say that."

"Oh, it's OK. I just felt like fitting in completely for a few seconds."

Aneshia never liked me, strictly for classic reasons. I was taking Tamika away from her. Whenever she was high, she would speak to me with a slight slur. She sounded like she had a bad cold and would repeat things very, very slowly. Aneshia grabbed the back of my seat so she could pull herself forward and talk to me.

"Fudgy is a fucked up crackhead. For real. That's the dillio." Tosha, sensing that this version of the story would take too long, cut her off.

"Jack, Fudgy is a crackhead. She'll do anything for a dollar, two dollars. We just use her to do our laundry. We'll give her a few dollars to do our laundry." I sighed, nodded my head, and didn't have to look into the mirror anymore because Tamika was walking quickly toward the car. The door opened.

"Sorry, Jack, just wanted to get something together with Fudgy. Crackhead that will do a whole bag of laundry for a dollar. Or a whiting sandwich. That's better 'cause a fried whiting sandwich is only ninety-nine cents."

"OK, just tell me where to drive you guys."

There was a chorus of Mickey D's. I knew where it was and just headed toward Broadway and 181st Street. I parked at another fire hydrant since it was pretty crowded near this hub of subway and bus connections. I shifted into PARK and wondered why they were waiting to head into the place. Tamika spoke up.

"Jack, remember, the money."

"Sorry."

I reached into my wallet and pulled out a twenty-dollar bill. They all cheered and clapped their hands and even Aneshia smiled. They got out and ran across Broadway. In the middle of the street, Tosha, stopped, dodged a car or two and came running back to the car.

"Jack, Tamika told me to axe you what you wanted."

"Thanks for axing Tosha. Cup of coffee, milk, no sugar."

"That's all you old guys ever want, coffee."

"Yeah, I know."

With a sly smile as she turned she said, "And a little tuna." I grinned but it was forced. In about ten minutes they all returned with a shopping bag of goodies. They remembered the coffee and gave it to me first. I was grateful and gave it a few perfunctory shakes. They oohed and ahhed and I asked them what was the next stop. Aneshia spoke because she was the only one who didn't have a bunch of fries sticking out of her mouth. She was eating them one at a time, and she ate as slowly as she spoke about the food.

"Home, right, Tammie?"

Tamika nodded her head vigorously in the affirmative.

"I thought you guys wanted to get the baby some food."

Aneshia was still the only one who had a french fry in her mouth.

"We got the baby some food."

"Oh, I didn't even see you go to another store."

Tamika took a breath from her Big Mac, fries, and chocolate shake. She put her finger on the top of the straw so she could draw some of it neatly into her mouth. She swallowed and said, "We got the baby some french fries." I was driving and felt like putting the accelerator through the floor.

"You can't give a little baby french fries."

"We're gonna mash 'em up. We're not just giving them like this."

"Tamika, you can't fuckin' give an infant mashed up french fries," I yelled. "This is fucked up. Everything. The baby's father, baby's mother bullshit. You've got a slave to wash your clothes for a fish sandwich, and now you're gonna tell me that you're gonna fuckin' give an infant mashed up french fries. What kinda fuckin' fucked up heart of darkness bullshit is this. This ain't fuckin' civilized." There was dead silence. I was gripping the thin steering wheel of my old Ford Fairmont so tightly that the little ridges made indentations into my hand. I was heading south on Fort Washington Avenue and breathing hard. There was nothing to say.

From previous trips and drives with them I knew the order of dispersal: Tosha first, Aneshia and Tamika last. I made a left onto Tosha's block, and pulled next to a car so I could double park. One look in the rearview mirror made me think.

"I'm sorry for saying that. I shouldn't have cursed. I just lost my head for a second. I'm really sorry for cursing at you guys. Ask Tamika, I never curse, right?"

She didn't say anything. She looked scared and sad. After another second of delay, she just nodded her head, ever so slightly. Aneshia, who hadn't taken one fry since my outburst, murmured something. I asked her to repeat it and she did.

"I said, what about the white people?"

I breathed instead of talked. I looked at the center of the steering wheel and noticed that the Ford coat of arms was turned ten degrees to the left. Tamika said, "Jack, Aneshia's right. What about the white people?"

I turned around and pushed myself into the door so I could look at all of them simultaneously.

"Well, Jack?"

With my mouth barely opening, I muttered, "They should be shot. The white sonsabitches who are responsible for all of this, they should be fuckin' shot." Tosha got out. We drove a few more blocks and let Aneshia out next to a bricked-up brownstone that had a little jerry-rigged slot for the crack to come out and for the money to come in. I looked at it as the door slammed. We pulled off for the last stop, and I smiled a nasty smile, as we got closer to Tamika's house. I always questioned the sense of humor the person must have had who hung the official red sign above her door that read,

NO LOITERING.

NO DRUG DEALING.

NO SITTING ON THE STOOP.

NO YELLING UP TO THE WINDOWS.

VIOLATORS WILL BE PROSECUTED TO THE FULL EXTENT OF THE LAW.

"Jack, guess you still got some black in you."

"I don't know. Maybe. This ain't about white and black. It's about . . . I don't know what the fuck it's about. Sorry for cursing."

She leaned over and kissed me.

High Hopes and Prayers

A COLLEGE PROFESSOR hopes that sometime during the course of a lecture, hands will go up, bodies will lean forward, with eager faces connoting question, question, question. I've had this experience hundreds of times and have thrived in reaction to the possibilities, the notion of going someplace new, taking a mind to some novel alcove, and bringing him or her out of it. What greater satisfaction!

In my case most of the questions that commenced about twenty years ago did not lead to those intellectual alcoves. Let me correct that. They led to places, but not to the fruitful, aesthetically revelatory explosions I thought lay at the core of them. No, when hands go up in my English class, especially at the end of the semester, I've long discovered that they have nothing to do with Camus, expository writing, the forthcoming research project, or the rhyme scheme of a Shakespeare sonnet. My students, my City University of New York students, inevitably have their hands up for more personal and insidious reasons. They want real information. They desire real answers having to do with them; therefore, my vast knowledge of 19th-century American literature and the Harlem Renaissance has no use or function for them. My public university students, the children of immigrants, the sons and daughters of hardworking Puerto Rican, Haitian, Polish, Dominican, and Irish parents want to ask me the most important and pressing question of their age.

"What are you?"

Yes, that is how it comes out. Of course, it's more polished since many students have formed small cabals and have put some time and effort in constructing their questions. Many times the question is a compi-

447

lation of three or four students who have thought long and hard about what would be the best way to confront someone about who they are.

"Professor, I (*we*, sometimes it is a voice of democracy question) just wanted to ask you something very important:

a. What is your racial makeup?
b. Are you mixed?
c. We think you're Puerto Rican, but we're not sure.
d. You're white, but there's something else there.
e. Greek, we're positive you're Greek or maybe Italian.
f. I'm positive that you're Spanish but you don't speak Spanish. Why?
g. We thought you were Middle Eastern until you read those poems.
h. You're black but very light-skinned.
i. You're white but very dark-skinned.

Even the E-mail letters I receive revolve around the same question:

Dear Professor Jeffries,

I am sorry if I offended you by asking you what nationality or race you were. I didn't mean it to be an insult. I love to know about people's racial mixtures. I am an annoying Puerto Rican Jew. I thought that you were a Puerto Rican from the Bronx. Well, at least you look like one and that is not an insult either. I wanted to tell you something about the assignment . . . To tell you the truth, I read this book in the 8th grade and didn't think much of it . . . I am the darkest one of my mother's daughters. The other two have white skin, straight hair, and fine European features. I, on the other hand, don't have these traits my mother loved so much. I came out looking too much like her and not like my father. But I'll tell you something Professor Jeffries, I am going to write the best damn paper I have ever written about this book that I care nothing about, just to prove to you that I am a determined and dedicated student. Oh and by the way, though I really enjoy all of my classes and professors, your class is my favorite and I am not just telling you that . . . I really mean it. I love writing and expressing my feelings on paper. Well, that's enough of my excessive babbling. Have a good night. From your annoying student,

Frances R.

Yes, those are my questions. Nothing about Edgar Allan Poe's theory of the short story. Nothing concerning Richard Wright and how he constructed his most famous protagonist, Bigger Thomas. Nothing, not one question about Virginia's Woolf's notion of a *moment of being.* No, these students are asking questions that I truly can't answer. The literature and literary questions, even if I can't answer, I can answer. I can fake with the best of them a literary sounding response that goes, "Oh, that's interesting, did anyone else notice that Yeats used swans in that manner (*damn, swans, something to do with a myth but I forgot which one, Greek myth, or Celtic, should check that out tonight*)?

In retrospect, there were times I would rather have had those questions that really exposed my ignorance of books than the questions that exposed my ignorance of myself. The latter are so much more painful. To question me about the significance of Daedalus because we're reading that famous Auden poem about how the old masters knew everything about suffering and for me to mumble something about, *"Well, he (Daedalus) must be pretty important since James Joyce used him too"* is a diversion. It is a feasible distraction. There are so many ways to mislead, dupe, and lead astray where no one is really hurt, and there is always the chance that I can read a book that night and find out the correct answer and integrate that accurate answer in the next lecture. I can dust off that book by Edith Hamilton about myths, look up Daedalus, recall the construction of the labyrinth, Crete, his imprisonment, and slyly remind the class, *Oh, yesterday, I mean, the last class, didn't someone ask me about Icarus or was it Daedalus?*

But me, to ask about me, and who I am, and how I got here, there is no book, never was a book, and probably will never be a book that I can quickly pull off the shelf with confidence that will give me the answer that I can convey to that student or that group of students who form a sizable portion of my class. Asking me about who and what I am causes pain because it is a real question. The literary questions are cute and fun and keep you informed. Asking me about who I am means you are really asking me about who you are, and my reply will inherently play a cardinal moment in your life. Asking me to confirm or deny a dream, that is what makes it so painful to respond and to respond with the wrong answer is worse than misinforming you about iambic pentameter. Asking me "who I am" requires a great deal of thought and introspection because I can hurt you. I've come to realize that so much more rests on my perfect answer. You could have asked me many questions, many different queries, but you decided on this one, this all-important and central theme of your life. You want to know who I am in relation to you. And once you know who I am, in relation to you, we then can have a relationship. Of course, if I give the wrong reply, we will not have a relationship and will be torn asunder after getting so close, so inexorably close. You took a chance. You had to know whether you would love me or hate me, trust me, or be afraid of me, and all this bobbed up and down on one axis, all pivoting on one fulcrum that could easily tilt one way or another.

When students ask who I am, what I am, they truly want to know once and for all whether or not they can confide in me and rely upon this stranger, this alien who defies definition. I have entered their lives and disrupted something so basic and fundamental that I cannot help but be conscious of the uneasiness in the class. It starts as a small murmur, a low-level rumbling of sorts on that first day in September or that first day in late January. It broods. It simmers. It boils. I am making people uncomfortable, just as I did in P.S. 37. I am back at The Mountain with my sleigh with my brother prepared to fight. I have made many people uncomfortable, and I don't even have to lift a finger. All I have to do is be me, the indefinable man, and that's enough to ruin a college student's day. Well, ruin is a strong word since the very fact that I am causing you to think, that can't be all that bad. Thinking is painful, no question. And if you are in pain, that's a good sign because you are attempting to figure out something new; that activity has some credence in it. You're sweating about what I am, and I'm thinking about whether the bookstore has taken care of my order, will the Xerox machine hold out for a few more hours or which kids I'm going to kick out because they won't do the work. I suppose it's an even swap. Both activities have a lot going for them. People have hopes. We're just hoping for different things.

But you, you want me to be Black, Spanish, White, and Iranian because if I am, so many truths will inevitably be confirmed or denied, and that is essential. You want me to be your hero, your model. Puerto Rican janitors for years in all the colleges I have taught at, as they're emptying the trash baskets late at night, mopping the hallways, lean toward me and whisper, *You know Jose, Luis and me are really proud of you. Really proud. You're the only one. The only one we've got. Keep on teaching proffe. You're number one with us.* I have taught throughout the City University of New York and the refrain has been the same with black maintenance personnel also. I've heard it at Queens College, Eugenio de Maria Hostos Community College, New York City Technical, Manhattan Community College, and Hunter and an art school called Pratt Institute: *Every time I come in here to wash this board at night, and I see you gathering up your things, I feel pretty good that one of us is an English professor. You don't see too many of us doing this, right? It gives me a good feeling. Keep on teaching, Professor Jeffries.*

That's all I can do sometimes. Keep on teaching.